The
Tangled
Lands

The Tangled Lands
Glenda Larke

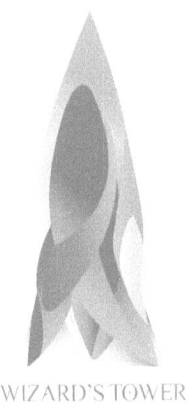

WIZARD'S TOWER

Wizard's Tower Press
Rhydaman, Sir Gaerfyrddin,
Cymru

The Tangled Lands

First edition, published in the UK January 2023
by Wizard's Tower Press

Paperback ISBN: 978-1-913892-48-7

Cover illustration and design by
Laine Phillips & Abby Ross

Design by Cheryl Morgan

https://wizardstowerpress.com/
https://glendalarke.com/

Contents

For the next generation of readers:
Eli and Molly

and for all those who asked
for another book

Praise for Glenda Larke

"The common link in Larke's novels is her ability to craft worlds that are vibrant and vivid, immersing us in a world that has depth and substance in a way that few writers can match without bogging down in 'info dump.'" – *Nexus* Magazine from Galaxy Bookshop

"She has the best world building of any fantasy writer I've ever read and it only seems to get stronger with each book ... it blows my mind ... if you are a fan of high fantasy and have not yet read any of Larke's books, you are sorely missing out!" – The Obsessive Bookseller

"Witty, gritty, and enthralling." – Trudi Canavan

"For those jaded with genre fantasy, Larke provides fare that is fresh, strange and intriguing." – Lucy Sussex

"Glenda Larke writes stories of real consequence." – Russell Kirkpatrick

From early reviews of The Tangled Lands

"*The Tangled Lands* is stylish, thought-provoking and feminist, set in a society that is delightfully un-heteronormative. The story moves from protagonist to protagonist, always revealing new layers and secrets as we go along, and building to a big, satisfying showdown." – Tansy Rayner Roberts

GLENDA LARKE

"Larke plays with the narrative form in delightful ways." –
The Middle Shelf

"Superb epic fantasy with twists that surprise and satisfy in
equal measure. Engaging leads and vivid characters right
down to bit players. Plotted and written with sublime unobtrusive skill." – Juliet E McKenna

PART 1

MONGRAVE'S WEAVING

1

Jordir Banlock, landlord of *The Twill and the Rose*, was the first to hear the tolling of the bell on the King's Keep. He tilted his head to listen, despair warring with a fragile sliver of hope. At twenty-eight he wasn't ready to die, so he welcomed a sound that heralded the possibility he'd live through the night instead. At least the waiting would be over.

He glanced to the centre of the taproom, where Lore-Adept Mongrave had missed the first strokes of the bell altogether while dozing in a cane-bottomed chair close to the warmth of the central hearth. Damn the man, he was about to destroy Jordir's life without a second thought.

His gaze moved on to the only other occupants of the room — a woman sitting on the far side of the fire with a fretting infant in her arms. She'd been his guest for five days, but he still did not know her name. He expected to see grief in those dark, calf-like eyes of hers, but although she'd swung her head up to listen to the bell, they were blank.

He swallowed a sigh. Four people linked forever by the horror of the crime they were about to commit: one of the most powerful loremasters still living; a stoic, nameless peasant lass; a babe about to be the centre pivot in a despicable crime ... and himself, Jordir Banlock, a man with a false name living a lie. He turned his attention to the Lore-Adept and stepped over to grip the man's shoulder. Mongrave groaned, wakened, and cocked an ear to the sound.

'That's the fourth stroke, Master,' Jordir told him.

Five ...

Six...

Thanks to the Lore-Adept, they were the only people in the establishment. The wretched fellow had tied a yellow rag of warning to the outer door handle of the dosshouse, so folk would think fever lurked within. Not true, of course, and Jordir simmered at his loss of coin. Three days without a single pallet upstairs rented to a wayfarer, nor yet an ale paid for!

Seven ...

Eight ...

But what could he say? Mongrave, born with the potential of redweaving conjury in his fingertips, had been trained to the highest level of redweaver lore, and no wise man thwarted a trained.

Curse the fellow, nonetheless. His arrival in Templebridge could well signal the end of Jordir, landlord. But at least it would be pleasant to be himself again, wouldn't it?

Nine ...

He held his breath. If the tolling ceased at ten, it would mark the birth of a stillborn child and all their preparations would have been in vain. Their plan depended on a prince. The King needed a male heir, and he'd pay a high price for a healthy son. Should the peals cease at fifteen, then the babe was a girl.

They needed to hear twenty, twenty for a living prince.

Ten ...

Eleven ...

'Alive, then,' Mongrave said. He scooped up his tankard from the floor and heaved himself to his feet, downing the last of the ale. Tension fissured deep into the pockets of his cheeks and dragged at the corners of his mouth. Candlelight highlighted the silver streaks in his grey hair and the liver spots on the backs of his hands. Age had not been kind to Mongrave. Only ten years older than Jordir, but he looked more like a man of fifty. Worry did that to a fellow, even an adept possessing the red conjury.

Twelve...

Thirteen...

Folk in the city that skirted the walls of the Palace Precinct where the keep was located must surely have woken to the sound, and doubtless waited, breath bated, as they counted. Perhaps they'd even beseeched one of the ten godheads of the Decasian Pantheon for the birth of a boy. A male heir held the promise of future stability, tempting citizens into believing there could be a definitive end to the squabbling of the powerful family dynasties of the eight duchies of the Kingdom of Talodiac.

Fourteen...

Well, seven powerful ones and one other: tiny Temar, where the Queen's father, the Duke of Temar, ruled the impuissant butt-end of the kingdom. King Edwild's great-great-grandfather had formed alliances and fought a war to unite them all so that he could plump his ducal buttocks on a new kingdom's throne. That had been more than a hundred years past, and now Edwild had ruled for ten and ignored Temar, for all that the Duke was his father-in law.

Fifteen...

Jordir flicked his gaze to the woman as the tolling continued, expecting to see something writ there: resignation, at the very least; grief, more probably — but nothing changed.

He bit his lip, waiting. Mongrave had thumped his empty tankard on the table and was now poised, motionless, not even breathing.

The sixteenth stroke reverberated and out in the street the cheering began as the bell continued to ring. The woman was the first to move. She held out the child towards Mongrave, saying, 'Chill air on his bottom'll wake this brat. When my Lore-Adept matches him up to yon princeling, do it *before* you unwind his swaddling. That way he'll sleep through the weaving. Be real quick with your unwrappin' of him after, else he'll fight your conjury and bawl fit to wake the palace, right down to the kitchen spit-dog.'

She gave the babe one last look, but there was no tender touch, no kiss, no tears. Mongrave nodded and plucked the child from her arms. Without another word, he lifted the bar to the outer door, handed it to Jordir, and disappeared into the smoke-smudged blackness of the city just as the twentieth stroke faded into the night air.

Unsettled, Jordir barred the door once more and turned to the woman, his head cocked in query. 'Not fretting, lass? You can't know they'll coddle your child as well as we'll care for theirs, 'specially once they know 'tis a changeling!'

She remained silent, expressionless.

'They will be told, y'know,' he said, troubled by her lack of concern. 'On the morrow probably, soon as Lore-Adept Mongrave is safe. They'll receive our demands in a letter and they'll have their arch-clergy look at your babe. Men or women with the ability to see conjury.'

'Think I don't know it?' She gave a disdainful snort. 'What's one babe to me? Me ma always said 'twas daft to feel aught for one's get till it's in its fifth year. Can't hope it'll live till then. Can't be sure any'll live on in Kanter, can we, if it come to that. Not nowadays, what with the warring.' She tilted her head, mocking his stance. 'Though, s'pose you don't much know 'bout that, do yer? Can y'even unnerstand me Kanter brogue after all them years here?'

She waited for an answer, and when there was none, she pushed back the greasy hair flopping over her brow before continuing, 'Let me tell you this. Since y'been gone, death dances daily in Kanter, snacking like wild curs at an unguarded flock, while you got a life here safe behind yon barred inn doors, fillin' your face with fine vittles.'

He didn't know what to say to that. She was right. He didn't know what had happened in Kanter in the years he'd been banished, not really.

'Don't judge me, boy,' she snapped.

'I wasn't—'

'Look at yourself! Staying 'ere for what? Ten year?'

'Six.' It rankled that she had called him boy. She couldn't have been more than three or four years older than him, if that.

'Cut off from all yer folk 'cause the Lore-Adept asked you to guard that redwoven gate that's hid in yon cellar? And you his bannerman with redweave in your blood, for all that its threads be weakling? Selling ale to Talodians and speakin' their strangled cant while we Kanterines bleed!' She spat on the floor.

'I serve my land. I left my hearthstone and our people for that.' Ash and brimstone, how he missed Kanter! But then, from what he'd heard from the redweavers who'd come this way in secret, Kanter was not the land of grace and beauty he'd known. Not anymore.

'Aye,' she said, 'y'all noble intentions, no doubt. Me, I was just a washerwoman, about to birth a babe I didn't want. But soon I'll wet-nurse a prince and have coins in me fob! Me, Arien from Brickletown, born of a drudge and a besom-maker. I'll not want for aught again. Them said they'll move me some safe place.' She paused and her shoulders slumped a little. 'Least, if there be any place safe from the esklet.'

'Have you no interest in what will happen to your own babe?'

Her bark of laughter, humourless and bitter, grated on him. 'His new ma be a queen,' she said, 'with servants waddling after her like a gaggle of geese after the goose girl's slop bucket. That brat of mine'll set his backside on satin cushions.'

'Could be they'll slit his throat,' he pointed out, the truth of that a sourness in his mouth. Sweet weaving, two babes swapped like they were no more than mewling kittens. Come next moon, odds were Arien's babe would be dead.

She shrugged. ''Tis blackmail you're planning, for all the high-falutin' words you give it. They'll keep my babe safe 'cause that'll keep their princely brat alive. They're just like you. You want to save your lore folk. They want to save themselves and their cushions for their fat arses. Us poor? All us care about is where the next loaf comes from. That's as far as our future sees — whether there be enough crumbs on the board tomorrow morn. And now I know that I'll have them, 'cause Kanter's Lore Council wants this puling prince the Lore-Adept's gone to steal, and it's my tits he'll suckle.'

He stared at her. In the five days since she and Mongrave had slipped into his inn cellar through the woven gate, she'd not said more than a word or two, but now the anger was ripping out of her, bitter as gall-wood.

And something more, too.

Smugness. Oh, she tried to conceal it, but he knew it was there. A coal of snide triumph gleamed in her eyes. She sat down again by the hearth, warming her grimy hands to the dying fire. He poured them both an ale from the cask and handed her a mug. Politeness he could grant her, but never trust. Had Mongrave not been able to find a better class of woman for this task?

He sighed inwardly. A decent woman would never have agreed, of course. It could not have been easy for even a lore councillor to find a mother so careless of her own babe that she would agree for her son to become a changeling.

'So,' she said, 'you know this queen?'

He snorted. 'I'm the landlord of a wayfarer's dosshouse, not a courtier. Did see her once, though, passing by in the street, the day she arrived in Templebridge.'

A seventeen-year-old bride, the daughter of the poorest of Talodiac's eight dukes, riding to meet the king she scarcely knew but was about to marry, and him a childless, widowed king twice her age. Poor Lady Thalia of Temar, smiling and waving to the cheering crowd lining the streets in welcome. Narrow-shouldered and slightly built, she was dwarfed by the guards around her. Although her smile was charming, there was nothing girlish about the determined tilt of her chin. He'd noted the way her unruly reddish-brown hair strayed from under her headdress and wondered idly at her choice of a mount and that riding habit. No noblewoman of Templebridge would ride a gelded taldeer stag, let alone wear a split skirt, and Lady Thalia had chosen to do both. The crowd had smiled and waved, but Jordir knew the court ladies would scarify her with their barbs. He even heard it in the gossip of the street.

A woman who doesn't know enough to ride sidesaddle on a doe!

Country bumpkin, eh?

Count their wealth in fish, where she comes from...

What he remembered best was not that smile, but her white-knuckled grip on the reins. A gift demanded by a monarch, fated to become a political pawn, her sole task to bring heirs into the world. There had been other women King Edwild could have chosen, more suited to the intrigues of court life, but he had wanted a wife who owed no loyalties to any of the powerful ducal families. Especially not to the ambitious Duke Vandaoc, ruler of Personata Duchy and heir to the King, who had been pushing his twenty-five-year-old widowed daughter. No, King Edwild had preferred a pretty lass, fathered by a disregarded duke who ruled a tiny sliver of coast squeezed between windswept mountains and a wild sea.

And she, poor lass, was about to lose her firstborn son.

Pity sucked at his guts and churned his stomach. *Oh, tangled threads, what have we loremasters become?*

'What sort of woman is she, this Queen Thalia?' Arien asked.

'Satisfactory,' he said, cynicism breaking through his calm. 'She's just done what was required of her and birthed a male heir.'

'Ah. Men demand such of wives, don't they?' Scorn-drenched words. 'Are not all women trampled 'neath the needs of menfolk, be they Talodian or Kanterine?' When he didn't reply, she added, 'Look at yer. When the loreman and me came through the woven gate into yon cellar, you scraped all humble before your master, that you did, but ne'er bothered to ask me my name!'

'You do me an injustice. I thought, as 'twas not mentioned, you didn't want it known.' He held the hard glitter of her gaze with his own stare. 'Arien from Brickletown.'

'Remember it, bannerman.' A smile ghosted across her lips and vanished so quickly he knew she had not wanted him to see it. Wrapping her shawl tight around her, she lay down on the floor in front of the hearth, her head pillowed on her arms. As far as he could tell, she was asleep within a breath or two.

Outside, a tricksy wind rattled the shutters, and a patter of rain sent water trickling from spout to water butt. He settled down to wait for Mongrave's return, but could not sleep. Not even another tankard of unwatered ale could help him doze.

He tried to calculate how long it would take to scale the wall that enclosed all the royal buildings, to cross the royal gardens, to climb up to the queen's bedchamber, to swap the babies and then return—carrying a newborn. With few conjury skills himself, he couldn't chance a guess. There would be ladders to weave, camouflage to conjure, power to craft in order to lift the inner bar on a shuttered window, and finally the sleep-weaving to send those caring for the new prince into a deep-knotted slumber. Few loremen could do half that.

Poor puppet queen, manipulated by people and forces she didn't even know existed. And he, a man who now answered to the Talodian name of Jordir Banlock instead of his own, was one of the despicable puppet-masters. His stomach roiled. Longing thrummed through him. For Kanter of golden skies and pearl-tipped waves, with its cities of lace-webbed towers and music that touched your soul...

What was left of it.

He had never dared to ask Mongrave how much of their land had already vanished to the encroaching tides of swarming esklet.

2

Sergeant Hervan of the King's Guard cursed under his breath. Why the ten hells was it that whenever he and his squad were called out at night, it rained? The street was cold, the gusty wind water-laden as it flapped his wet cloak until it snagged on his scabbard. But his orders had been clear: hire a palanquin and bearers, plus a linkman with a lantern, and get them and his men to Royalgate come midnight.

The four bearers now flattened themselves against the palace wall near the two palace guards in their sentry boxes. The linkman had cheekily settled himself inside the palanquin with the excuse that his lantern needed to be kept dry. All Hervan and the four members of his squad could do was hunker down as best they could against the side of the contraption.

His under-officer tapped its wooden door and muttered, 'A public litter. We're just here to coddle one of the King's whores, yet again.'

'Muzzle it, Cyrrin.' The man was right, though. Everyone knew that the stairs led upwards from the public street to the King's private chambers, and it was not the first time they'd been called to escort a palanquin away in the middle of the night. 'If His Majesty wants to bed every lass in the local whore-house, we see naught.'

Cyrrin snorted, but he did lower his voice to a whisper, though his peevishness remained clear. 'And with the Queen having birthed an heir just one night ago...'

'Well, that's a time she's hardly like to welcome the King to her bed, is she? Whereas he's in the mood to celebrate!'

'Damn it, Herv, we're better than this. Even if wife or daughter to a lord, which I doubt, they still be whores we

20

have to nursemaid! We're *soldiers*. Armsmen. God Saffrin's men!'

'You want a promotion to better things? Keep your tongue stilled. Someone's coming.'

The linkman sprang out of the palanquin, the palace guards opened the wrought-iron gates to the stairs, and Hervan snapped to attention. To his surprise, King Edwild himself escorted the woman down the stairs. There was no mistaking his stocky build and unruly straw-coloured hair shining in the light cast by the torch at the gate. The woman was enveloped in the voluminous folds of a man's woollen cloak and kept her head ducked, her face hidden deep in the shadow of a fur-trimmed hood. Only her shoes, bejewelled slippers unsuitable for a rainy night, betrayed her sex.

One of the bearers opened the door of the palanquin and the King helped his companion inside, whispering something into her ear as he did so. He shut the door and nodded to Hervan. 'Sergeant, take the lady to the royal entrance of Atticun's Temple. She is expected there. Wait until her visit is over, and follow her instructions with all courtesy.'

Hervan snapped a salute, but the King had already turned to stride back up the steps.

A quarter of an hour later the sergeant was helping the woman out of the palanquin into the private courtyard of the temple. Despite still being bundled in the cloak and having drawn her tippet up over her lower face, she was shivering. Mercifully, the rain had stopped.

In front of them, an archway carved with God Atticun's motto — *For the Greater Good of Creation* — was lit on either side by sputtering torches. A thin, pale man in a black gown stepped out of the shadows, bowed, and introduced himself as the secretary to the Lawseer, the Decasian Pantheon's Grand Archpriest, there to escort the gracious lady into the Lawseer's inner sanctum.

She was expected then... A whore, perhaps, but definitely not one from a brothel.

Sergeant Hervan opened the door to the palanquin and offered her a hand, but she ignored him as she descended to the wet pavement, clumsily clutching the cloak to her body from underneath. She nodded to the secretary and followed him through the archway.

Once they had disappeared and the palanquin bearers had settled down to shelter under an ornate archway, Petch — the youngest of Hervan's squad — asked in a puzzled fashion, 'What's a whore got to do in the Arch-God's temple? God Atticun's for the nobs, not for the likes of street-tail, nor us neither.'

Hervan snorted in ridicule. 'Use y'wits. She's no street walker. The King don't ask his guard to escort a common whore.'

'Then who is she?' Gappy, asked. He was the nosy one of the squad, always looking for the gossip.

'Got to be the King's current mistress. Someone of class. You treat her with real respect if you want keep your rank.'

'Doesn't explain what she's doing here,' Petch said. 'A loose woman coming to pray at God Atticun's feet? That don't happen!'

Hervan looked at him in surprise. Petch was the quietest of his squad, and rarely said much at all. He had a point, though. Such women favoured Jenat, the goddess of women and children. But still, a kingsman did as the King asked, and he certainly didn't ask questions.

'She's left summat in the palanquin,' Gappy added, peering through the window. 'Looks like a jewel box, if I had me guess.'

'None of our business. Leave it be. It's like to be something the King's gifted her.'

'Gift? Whore's price, you mean!' Cyrrin smirked, an expression rendered all too easy by the scar on his face, the result of an old sword-cut from the corner of an eye to the corner of his mouth. 'Paid off and sent away because the King has an heir at last and he don't want to upset his lady wife.' He nudged Hervan on the ribs with an elbow. 'And you too should have another brat by now, if I have the right of it? Due this double moon?'

'Any time now.' He smiled at the thought. A second son, he hoped.

'And you'll be hankering after leave to visit Breakedge to see the brat, I suppose.'

'Jealous, Cyrrin?' The question came from Folman, the fourth member of his squad. The bastard was just stupid enough to think needling the under-officer was amusing.

'He knows better,' Hervan snapped. 'Watch it, Folman, or you'll be off my squad.'

'Sorry, Sarge. 'Twas just funning.'

A wisp of unease niggled at Hervan, and he wasn't sure why. Yes, he had a proxy-wife and had a deep respect for her, but Cyrrin had no cause for jealousy. After all, his proxy-wife was for heirs, not for loving...

And dammit; it was starting to rain again.

*

It was a long time before the woman emerged through the archway once more. Escorted by the same secretary, she was still smothered in that cloak, using it like armour to signal she was unassailable. She left her escort and, head ducked, walked gingerly across the damp paving to where Hervan waited. He opened the palanquin door, sending a cascade of raindrops to the ground, and settled on the vaguest honorific he knew. 'Milady, we will escort you home, if you will tell us where...?'

'Oh, I am not going home, Sergeant. Yet. I wish to go to the Temple of Goddess Jenat now. You may leave me there.'

'But ... that weren't my orders, Milady. His Majesty surely wished you to be delivered safely ho—'

'The priestesses of the temple will see me safely delivered wherever I wish.' She added firmly, 'Now, if you will be good enough to assist me up the step...'

'The King's orders—'

'—were to follow my instructions. Your assistance, please.'

As neither of her hands were visible, he hesitated until she raised one eyebrow sharply in remonstration. He clutched at where he imagined her elbow to be under the folds of the cloak and steadied her while she climbed inside. 'To the woman's door, not the public gate, Sergeant,' she added.

He turned away and gave the order for the linkman and bearers. Internally his irritation burned. Petch was right, he was a soldier, dammit, and no one had warned him that would include mollycoddling a king's harlot.

When they arrived at the women's entrance, tucked unobtrusively away from the main steps of Goddess Jenat's Temple, the torch in a sconce outside had long since burned out. Hervan escorted his charge to the door and yanked at the bell-pull. The peephole slid open to reveal a pale face framed by the wimple of a priestess. 'I'm Sister Agrina,' she said. 'What is your need?'

'I need advice, Sister,' the woman said softly.

'Then you are welcome. But no man enters here.'

The King's mistress gave Hervan one last glance. 'I'm so sorry, Sergeant,' she said. The door opened then and she slipped inside.

Sorry? About what?

As he returned to give the linkman and the bearers the tokens they could redeem for the evening's work, his boots skidded on the wet paving. He steadied himself against the palanquin, and his glance lit on the empty seat within.

The box was gone. Whatever it contained, she had taken it with her. He frowned, and unease crept up his spine. Highborn ladies, even ones who had sunk low enough to go whoring, did not usually apologise to guards for anything...

PART 2

CAUGHT
IN THE
WEAVING

(Eighteen years later)

3

King Edwild's historian, a decrepit, nosey woman by the name of Lady Sianta, lacks both charm and a full set of teeth, but she is very persuasive. Which is why I'm writing this tale down instead of spending these precious final days doing something just as unproductive, like cursing the King, swearing at my fate, or weeping into the bug-ridden straw pallet in my cell. Lady Sianta also says she's the reason I have been transferred to this quiet cage, served by only one jailor, an unprepossessing fellow called Alzop, who delivers my food and water. Alzop is illiterate and so pious it's a wonder he even craps without the permission of God Saffrin. He's also never learned to speak because he's totally deaf, so he can't say much, can he?

Interesting choice of guard, Sianta.

This stone-walled den of mine is in a very quiet area near the top of the King's Keep in Templebridge, and I don't appear to have any fellow prisoners on either side. In fact, apart from distant noise that filters in along with the sunlight through a tiny window far above my head, I hear no sounds at all. The upper half of the door has a decent-sized, barred peephole so I can see out into the passage, but no one passes by. Ever.

In a rare moment of calm and hubris, I promised Lady Sianta I would record the events that led me, the son of a captain in the King's Guard, to this cell in the King's Keep, awaiting the day of my execution for treason. A closed court with an unsympathetic judge and evidence from my own kin resulted in a guilty verdict, or so I'm told. I wasn't there. Fate in the shape of spring storms keeps me temporarily alive, because they have delayed the return of King Edwild from his annual visit to several of the northern duchies, and it seems that executions require the King's signature.

Long may the weather remain mud-inducingly abominable.

I think Lady Sianta was pleasantly surprised to find that — although my accent is a southerner's, full of rolled r's that northerners say reminds them of someone hawking phlegm — my written hand is neat and my grammar faultless. Well, almost. As an aid to learning, my knuckles were well battered by the schoolmaster in a military academy run for the benefit of the border patrol. We're not all sand-brained in Southedge Duchy.

So here goes.

My name is Taygen Hervan-Gariane and this tale starts one morning in an ordinary street market in Breakedge, border city and capital of the duchy, which is some forty days' cart travel from Templebridge, capital of Talodiac. I was leaning casually against the pitted end wall of the crumbling row of houses in Market Lane. I'd just turned eighteen and thought I knew a great deal about how to look after myself.

Quite.

What a difference the turns of the moons can make!

I was using the time to assess the crowd that surged and ebbed through the cluttered mishmash of market stalls. Almost noon: the hour vendors had to pack up and leave. Mingled noise — the strident determination of those itinerant merchants disposing of the last of their over-ripe fruit and fly-blown meat, and the rowdiness of customers voicing their outrage at the cost. Everyone in a hurry, buyers with their hands full of purchases, vendors anxious to get out of there and tot up profits. Excellent time for a little petty thieving. An hour earlier I'd stolen a handful of plum-berries from a fruit-seller's table. I'd eaten them, but I'd kept the stone-hard pips.

(I admit it, you see; back then I was a thief. Ironic that I've ended up in jail not for thievery, but for the one thing I thought I'd never be guilty of: treason. *Me? Really?* I'd spent my childhood dreaming of being a King's Guard while earning accolades for my loyal bravery!)

I was listening carefully to the bustle. My mother always said I had the hearing of a hunting dog, but not even she knew how close that was to the truth, and I certainly never told my pa. Not a sympathetic man, my father. As a small boy, I was always stuffing things into my ears to escape the constant assault of sounds no one else ever heard: beetles eating a rotten log in the wood heap; neighbours having a whispered conversation four doors away; the padded feet of a dromedary caravan, still out of sight, plodding the sands of the Great Desolation. I would throw myself on to the floor, screaming — anything to escape the relentless clamour drumming nonstop into my head. Fortunately for my sanity, by the time I was five or so, I'd perfected a way of tucking the superfluous noise away into a muffled corner of my brain where it was little more than a distant hum, to be ignored if I didn't want to hear it. It's still there, that buzz, awaiting the moment I reach in and select the sounds I need at any particular time. Weird, maybe, but a handy knack for a thief.

My gaze was on a plump housewife with a basket over an arm as she attempted to round up three fractious tots of varying ages running hither and thither and paying her no mind. Noticing the way she'd shoved her drawstring purse into the pocket of her apron and left the ties dangling, I gathered myself ready. Then I realised how full her basket was and when I listened, I couldn't hear any chink of coins as she moved. She probably did not have much left in that purse.

Maybe the elegant youth sauntering between the rows of makeshift stalls was a better mark. I'd been watching him, too. And loathing him without knowing a thing about him except what I could see. Like me, he was somewhere in those

29

ill-defined years where everyone expects you to act like an adult, but seldom treats you like one. There the resemblance ended. I was broad-shouldered, muscled, stocky and brown. Not as tall as I would have liked, and usually I looked like an artisan's apprentice after a hard day's work — scruffy hair, a sprout of dark whiskers that needed constant shaving, dusty clothes, scuffed shoes that fit me ill. Mam fed me well, but there was never much coin for fancy clothing.

That other youth, though, he had to be an aristo if ever there was one. Everything I wasn't: tall, elegant, finely-boned, fair, well-groomed, smooth-skinned. True, his padded green velvet jerkin appeared to have been patched, but his clothing was too damn fussy by far. The jerkin was embroidered, for pity's sake. His shoes had buckles *and* ribbons. Pah!

Aristos were a rare breed in this runt-end border town of the kingdom, a place that seethes with merchants and greed rather than nobility and manners. Ye gods, how I despised fops. I'd have bet his hands were as soft as a babe's ... He interested me not because of his looks, but because he'd have coin to spare.

I headed into the press of people between the stalls, clutching the fruit stones. Master velvet-jerkin lingered in front of a makeshift counter laden with buckles and similar gewgaws. The stall holder, picking him as a chump for the culling, launched into his sales pitch. I slowed, giving myself time to spot the bulge where the fellow had stowed his purse: an inner pocket of the jerkin, just under his ribs on the right-hand side. Cautious fellow, then, but not cautious enough.

I eased my palm-blade into my left hand. Once I was close enough, I lobbed the fruit pips from my right hand up and over the fellow's head. They pattered down on the stall counter on the other side, distracting both him and the merchant. I slid my hand along the youth's jerkin in the lightest of touches, and the slick blade in its tiny wooden holder sliced the cloth.

The purse slipped into my hand.

I was about to hide it under the loose fold of my jacket when a commotion erupted immediately behind me at one of the stalls. I whipped around, thinking someone had seen what I'd done. But no, it wasn't that.

One of the plump matron's children, a tot of three or so, must have reached up and taken a ripe desert fig from the trestle table of a fruit-seller. A wiry man with huge whiskers and a loud voice, he now gripped the child by the wrist as he yelled, 'So you're the little snitch who's been filching my fruit, eh?'

She screamed for her ma and dropped the fig. It splattered on the ground, making him even angrier. He let fly a stream of filthy words I hoped she didn't understand, then raised his free hand to smite her.

I didn't stop to think. I dropped the purse and flung myself forward to snatch the fellow's arm just as it started on its downward trajectory. If it'd connected, gods only know what would have happened to her. His intention was overtly vicious.

'For Saffrin's sake, man,' I protested. 'She's but a babe! Not old enough to know 'twas stealing.'

The child wriggled out of his grasp and flung herself at her mother, who immediately whisked all three children away into the crowd, leaving me to face the wrath of the fruit-seller. I released his arm, and for a moment he glared at me with enough rage to make me wonder if the blow meant for the lass was about to clip me over the ear. I clenched my fists to tell him I was no cringer. He took a deep breath and lowered his arm.

Perhaps openly invoking the God worshipped by soldiers had been wise...

'Mind your own poxy business!' he growled and turned back to his stall.

I moved away, scanning the ground for the dropped purse.

And saw instead a well-shod foot. My stomach somersaulted as I raised my gaze to meet the cool stare of the young fop standing an arm's length away, head cocked to one side, shoe firmly planted on the leather drawstring of his own money pouch.

'Ah, think you dropped your purse,' I said, pointing a finger at it.

The fellow's gaze remained locked on me. 'How odd,' he remarked, his tone as frigid as a desert dawn. 'It seems I did. Funny; I don't recall being so careless.'

Not just finely-tailored clothes, but a sarcastic uppity accent too; words beautifully enunciated, leaving me feeling like an ignorant bumpkin. Definitely not born in Breakedge, or indeed anywhere in Southedge Duchy.

'Y'ought to be more canny,' I replied as he fingered the slit in his jerkin without moving his gaze from mine. 'Never know what shysters 'n' rogues abound in border towns like this 'un.'

'So I see.' Chilly as chipped mountain ice.

Walking away, I felt those grey eyes boring into the back of my head. I had no trouble hearing the words he muttered under his breath. 'Thieving prick.'

I tried to convince myself that the fellow couldn't be certain who'd been responsible for the way his purse had vanished from his jerkin, otherwise he would have raised a ruckus.

Quickening my pace, I left the market without looking back.

*

GLENDA LARKE

Breakedge is a serpent-shaped city slithering from east to west for several miles along the base of the Devil-Honed Hills, the shape sculptured by the availability of groundwater beneath. It doesn't rain often in the shadow of those mountain peaks. Within the serpent, skinny dirt laneways separate the jumble of tenements in the poorer areas. In the commercial part of town, roadways of sun-baked brick are wide enough to allow the turn of a laden wagon drawn by a team of shaggy, broad-horned talyaks.

Squashed thus between mountain range and desert, in an area where food is hard to grow and rain is greeted with spontaneous dancing in the street, the city has only one reason to exist where it does: it's the final destination of the caravan trade across the waterless plains of the Great Desolation. On the city's southern side, facing the desert, there are tether lines for the two-humped dromedaries, and an ever-changing jumble of tents erected by the nomads who ride those strange beasts.

When I was younger, I dreamed of travelling south along the yellow dirt trade road that bores across the vast flatness, as straight as a ray of sunlight, to link Talodiac with a far-off, unfamiliar world vaguely labelled on maps as 'Barbarian Lands'. As a lad, I wondered about that description, because the men who came riding along the yellow track on their shaggy beasts did not seem at all barbaric. They may have been taciturn and mysterious with their long white hair and tattooed faces, but they brought us trade goods from their lands that were eagerly sought-after: woven silks and etched silver, carved jade and facetted rubies, gaudy rugs, pungent spices, and even exotic caged birds. They call themselves the Dekadani and their sons travelled with them from the time they were six or so. I used to hang out with them whenever I could.

Traders aren't the only people that traverse the plains, of course. Talodiac's Border Rangers are tasked with repelling the frequent raids of desert Menkz marauders who come to steal, kidnap and burn. My elder brother Javelin, Jav for short, one of the finest men I'm ever likely to know, was a ranger. For much of my life, I thought I'd be a Border Ranger too, at the very least.

One can dream when one is young and the whole world seems to lie at your feet.

Our house, in the area properly known as the Proxy-wives' Quarter, colloquially called Sprogs' Cradle, was on the first gentle slope of the mountain on the northern edge of the city, right outside the Border Rangers' barracks. My father was a northerner and had grown up in the Riverland of the King's Duchy. He'd joined the King's Guard as a lad and was sent to Breakedge to help train the Border Rangers when he was not much more than twenty. That's how he met my mother. She's like me: dusky and dark-eyed and none too tall. She became his proxy-wife, and I was brought up around fighting men of one kind or another.

Mine was a natural enough ambition. Always hopeful a sprog would be a future recruit, rangers were impressed by my eagerness and trained me in their off-duty hours. The Master of Arms remarked I was a born armsman, with quick reflexes and a canny eye.

By the time I was twelve, I could handle a sword well enough to worry eighteen-year-old Jav in a fight. Unfortunately, it was around then that I was awakening to the knowledge that, although I had everything to be a fine recruit, I lacked the one attribute any armsman of the King requires: he or she has to worship God Saffrin. God of Peace and Warriors. God of Battle and Order. And, as we all know, to do that, you have to *be* saffrine.

The first time I looked at a girl and my body perked up nicely randy, I knew that lack, but it was a long time before I was prepared to admit it. In fact, when I was fourteen and Jav helpfully pointed out the obvious to me, I told him he had the brains of a baked turnip and stormed out of the house.

My rational mind knew that although anyone could *pray* to God Saffrin, he accepted as true adherents only men and women who do not love as most do. God Saffrin was for those who prefer man to man, or woman to woman, and suchlike. Or those given the incorrect body at birth. If God Saffrin did not accept you, how could you fight under his aegis to maintain the peace? By the time I was fifteen, a pretty girl turned my head and raised my cock easier than mountain ice melting in the sun. I can't say I regretted that, exactly … After all, that was the year I happily surrendered my virginity to a widow of twenty who lived in our street. I'd been sneaking into her bed ever since, whenever both invitation and opportunity arose.

But the truth remained. I was not saffrine, and by then everyone knew it. They smirked, but said nothing — at least not to my face. And I grieved with the knowledge that I could never be a soldier.

And now I've filled the first sheets of blank paper you gave me, Lady Sianta. Did you really think I could tell a story like mine in a page or two? I've barely started.

4

Another day closer to death and Lady Sianta has given me a new stack of linen paper and bid me be briefer. I think not. I'll make my script smaller instead. You future historians reading this will be cursing, I know, but damn it anyway. I want my story told properly, all of it. After all, what have I to lose? I'll be dead before we reach the season of the red moon.

Sianta has already read my first bundle and had much to say about my description of her appearance. Being somewhat disgruntled with my imprisonment, I did indulge in gross exaggeration, which I admitted. She is, she informs me, a mere forty-eight years old and in her prime, and I grant that description is probably closer to the truth than a word like 'decrepit'. In fact, she is quite a handsome woman.

Except for the teeth.

I wonder why she only comes to visit me in the dead of night?

*

The day I failed to steal the aristo's purse was the day everything came to a head. When I left the market, I stopped at a pieman's stall long enough to have a bite to eat and a tankard of ale, then I strode off towards the Proxywives' Quarter. I was uneasy, worried my bungled theft might have repercussions. Underneath all that, a slow burn of resentment at the unfairness of life smouldered in my gut. Good combat skills, plus the desire to serve the kingdom, should have been all that was necessary to be a soldier.

My father, Hervan, now a captain and long since transferred back to serve the King in Templebridge, was saffrine.

So was my brother. Why not me? Why not my sister? Not that she cared. She was married with her second child on its way, as proud of that as she was of her husband, the local chicken butcher.

I turned off onto the path through the orchard that led to our cottage. My mother, Gariane, had planted fruit trees there the same year she'd signed the proxy agreement with my father. A proxy-wife's cottage near the barracks had been part of the deal. The planting of the small orchard was her affirmation that she intended her adherence to that contract to be lengthy. The success of her fruit crops had become a matter of quiet pride; in that small patch, she grew rose-plums and pomegranates so big they split their skins, but most productive of all were the olives for oil. We three children were proof that she had kept her side of her bargain with my father to bear his children, but I think, to her, it was as much the orchard that told the world she was worthy of respect.

Pa transferred to the Royal Guard in Templebridge not long before I was born, but he returned every year on furlough to see us. As a child, I took the peculiarity of their marriage for granted; as a youth, I thought about it a lot. What prompted a lass, aged twenty, to agree to bear a soldier's offspring? How she and Pa had conceived three children when my father had no interest in women, I'd never had the gall to ask. My mother raised us more or less alone, foregoing any other male relationship, all the while knowing Hervan's only physical interest in her was her ability to bring his children into the world and raise them thereafter. What could possibly have made her take such a decision?

Poverty, I suppose. A lack of family ties. She couldn't read or write, my mam. She never told us about her life before she became a proxy-wife, except to say she had no other family members alive.

That afternoon I found her in the kitchen, stirring a mess of her plums in the preserving pan over the open fire. The tartness of the aroma made my nose twitch.

She looked up in surprise. 'Thought you was working all today?'

'Thought I was.'

She sighed and put down the wooden paddle on the hob. The smell of hot sugar and plum pulp was mouth-watering. 'Taygen, it's time we had words 'bout that. People talk, y'know. You h'aint been working for that carter over at the meat market, like you says.'

Ah, godless hells. She'd found out.

I avoided looking her in the eye by wandering over to stoke up the fire, shrugging as if it didn't matter.

'They say you done hang 'round the markets. There's talk you been heavy company with thieves.'

'No one's got the guts 'n' gall to call me light-fingered!' *Not yet.*

'None'd dare say that to my face. But folk've noticed how tight you be with Locksmith Spake. Dunno him myself, but I heared tell his elder son is 'bout as honest as a wasp stalking a grub. Then there's talk of wrestling matches at the talyak yards of an evening...'

'Nothing wrong with that.'

'They say you done bet on the outcome.'

I shrugged. 'So? I bet on meself. Haven't lost yet!'

'Oh, son, what kind of a life is that? Your Pa'll blow brimstone out his ears if he heared that gossip!'

'Well, he's not going to find out, 'less you pass on the tattle, is he?'

'I think he's already heared by now.'

My stomach heaved. Pa *knew*? 'What d'you mean?'

'He's here. Well, over at the barracks with your brother. He'll drop by soon.'

'Jav's never going to spread tattle—'

'No. But there's others who will. You think the rangers don't have their ears flapping 'round the town?'

'What's there to be worried about? There's naught to tell. I'm fine.'

'No, you're never. Tay, don't tell me I can't fathom me sons. At first, I didn't want to believe what I heared. But now? Friends with purse-snatchers? This brawling you done call sport — a crowd of rough-knuckles betting you'll break your neck?'

The contempt in her voice cut me to the backbone. If she'd been angry, then I might have argued, but her scorn just made me feel sick. Gods below, what a mess my life was, like a runaway night-cart careening down a hillside spilling its shit-load, with me not knowing how to stop it.

When I turned away from the flames to look at her, unable to hide my misery, her disdain vanished. 'It's all 'bout not being saffrine, isn't it,' she said, making it sound like a statement of fact.

I shook my head. 'No. Course not. I don't *want* to be saffrine! I *like* what I am.' A sudden thought occurred to me: had she found out about my trysts with Widow Lillia? I pushed that thought away. 'What I want is to be what I *am* and still be able to join the Border Rangers. Or to join the Duchy Patrols, or the Royal Guard! To be a *kingsman*. We all know redweaver sightings been increasing, and there's traces of red conjury all over Talodiac. Rumour says our forces are overextended. Why can't I do my part to defend us?'

She looked past my shoulder and fell silent. Another voice answered from behind me instead. 'You can.'

I spun around to see my father standing in the kitchen doorway. The snarling griffin of the King's Royal Guard on his linen surcoat and his sword at his side were enough to warn any stranger he was not a man to be trifled with. I felt a surge of pride. Tall, golden, powerful ... They were the words that came to mind when I thought of Pa. With sun-browned skin and sun-streaked yellow hair, a pugnacious jaw and powerful shoulders, he was an imposing man, worthy of being one of the Royal Guards.

He was also more than a handspan taller than me. Envy lurched inside my chest. Gods damn my wretched luck. I took after my mam. Short, swarthy, and as ordinary as a chunk of quarried rock.

'You *can* do your part,' he said. 'Just not as part of the army. Come on, Tay, you've known for years you're not saffrine.'

I shrugged.

He said, 'The rangers just been ordered to stop sparring with you and halt your access to the barracks. Time you found a suitable trade, lad.'

My breath caught. *Hells.* I dragged in more air before I choked. 'I — ah, well, maybe. I s'pose.' Blast it, I was *good* with a sword, and a damn fine taldeer rider too.

'Come walk with me,' he suggested, placing a hand on my shoulder and steering me firmly out of the door. Once in the street, he pointed in the direction of the barracks. 'Training pitch,' he said. 'Won't be disturbed there at this hour, and I got enough seniority to give you one last practice bout.'

I scowled, ungracious as usual. 'What use is that?'

'Knowing how to defend yourself is never useless.'

'Being a kingsman — it's all I ever wanted.' I sounded like a sulky child and could have kicked myself for giving voice to my immaturity.

'There be other jobs, just as challenging, that involve lawful strapping on a sword. Guarding trade caravans 'twixt

40

the duchies, maybe. Bodyguard to a merchant. Though I'm thinking you could do better. I chatted to the Border Ranger's script-master this morning. Impressed with your learning when you was still in the schoolroom, he was. And we know you can squawk words prettier than the rest of us if you put your mind to it!'

'The script-master? He used to say my penmanship reminded him of pig tracks through a wallow!'

'Pretty lettering is not all what makes a merchant or a jobber, or so I'm told. He sez you've a fine mind 'twixt your ears. Sez your words come out like they've been polished, when you've a will to make 'em so. You're smart, lad. Time you used those wits.'

I blinked, groping to find something sensible to say. 'You knew I'd never be a soldier, didn't you? That's why you insisted I learn writing and figuring when I was all of nine years old!'

'Seemed like it might be a good idea.'

Godsdamn, why did everyone else seem to have known more about me than I had? I sighed, alarmed at how dense I'd been. At least I enjoyed the learning, but hells, it was time I sharpened the wits. 'What's this trip of yours here all about?' Mam was surely beyond the age of birthing, and I was fairly certain that the Royal Guards didn't give family leave to a guardsman when his youngest whelp was already grown.

'Your mam sent word she was fussed 'bout you. When I heard an archpriest was being sent here, I offered my services as escort.'

The story stank. A kingsman didn't bother too much with their non-saffrine offspring. Nor did they just 'offer services' to an archpriest. Temples had their own armsmen to send on a task like that.

I must have looked disbelieving because he added quickly, 'And there was a squad of Royal Guards coming as well. I joined up with them.'

'A squad? What's afoot?'

'Routine,' he said. 'Someone thought I might be in a position to help find the miscreant they were looking for 'cause I know Breakedge.'

The stench deepened, but I knew when not to dig into the muck. 'Lucky,' I said dryly, striving to sound nonchalant rather than sarcastic.

We reached the barrack gates then, and he nodded to the guard on duty who snapped off a smart salute as we walked through. I turned the subject back to the arrival of the archpriest. 'Don't we already have enough archpriests here?'

He snorted. 'There's only one other. An archpriestess, and she's old enough to be rusted, and hardly ever leaves her hearth.'

I halted my blather in shock at my own ignorance. Breakedge had all ten Decasian temples represented, and I'd assumed that each had an archpriest or archpriestess in charge. Gods' light, we needed high clerics because they were the only ones who could see redweaving!

He noted my reaction and nodded. 'In the days when Breakedge had no signs of conjury, temples took our top clerics, the ones who could see redweaving, and sent 'em where they were needed more. Now someone's got prickles 'bout that.'

'Which temple sent another?'

'Dargan's.' An appropriate choice, seeing Dargan was the god of those who labour. Breakedge had no place for the idle rich; there was no landowning nobility. It was a city of hard-working merchants and labourers. 'Sent a real tough bastard, they have,' he continued. 'Glint of a fanatic in his eye. Seethes with hatred for redweavers. Anyway, naught of your concern. Let's have a gab about your future.'

Ah. I braced myself.

'I palavered with your mam. We've decided it's best you come back with me to Templebridge. Maybe we can get you 'prenticed somewhere.'

I floundered, not sure how I felt about that. Excited? Annoyed decisions were made without consulting me? Cautious, I asked, 'You have something particular in mind?'

'Just 'cause you don't belong to the cadre of God Saffrin, doesn't mean I won't set you up right. I got connections. If you don't want to be a private guard, then we could get you a place elsewhere. A counting house maybe. Or clerking with a merchant. We'll see.'

That sounded hideously dull. Templebridge, though ... Someone once told me that the city was twenty times the size of Breakedge. I couldn't even *imagine* that. Exciting? The very idea was breathtaking.

We'd reached the barracks training ground, so he disappeared into the armoury to procure the use of some practice blades and padding. I grinned to myself as I looked around. Clerking? I didn't think so.

But Templebridge...

A movement caught my eye just then: someone was up on top of the boulder-topped rise that overlooked the training ground. Bowmen often practised shooting arrows from there into targets inside the training field, so I scanned the outcrop carefully. No bowmen.

There was a fellow, though. Someone wearing a green jerkin. Even as I glimpsed him, he ducked away behind the tumble of boulders that adorned the crest like a giant's broken teeth, and disappeared.

43

THE TANGLED LANDS

*

Two hours later, when Pa brought the practice session to a close, I was both bruised and exhausted. I was also surprised. Last time he'd challenged me, I'd been soundly trounced. But that had been a year back; now I was holding my own. Well, almost. He still had the advantage of a longer reach and more experience, but he tired before I did. I was faster on my feet, better at weaving and dodging, and possibly I reacted more quickly. I thought so, anyway. He did disarm me once and slapped me in the ribs with the flat of the wooden blade, but for the first time I knew I'd impressed him. I think we both knew that with another year's training, I could be close to his equal.

The irony was almost too much to bear. There never would be another year of training.

As I stuck my head under the pump afterwards to wash away the sweat and dust, he said, 'You would have made a good armsman.'

I straightened up and shook the water out of my hair. 'Still could,' I said, bitterness dribbling through the words, 'if I was let.'

He shrugged. 'You know why it's done this way.'

Of course I did. Soldiers fought for the king, for the unity of Talodiac, for a noble cause. All that was true. But when it came to a vicious battle, when death was all around them, then the passion that gave them courage, that kept them fighting amidst the agony and the horror and the spilled guts — that was love. They fought best for those they loved. For saffrine males, that was often the men of their company, for it was always a soldier's privilege to serve side by side with his lover or lovers if he wished. I assumed it was the same in the women's regiments.

I'd idly wondered if sometimes a man might not do something stupid in the midst of battle *because* he worried about the beloved comrade at his side. And what about a man jilted by a comrade-at-arms; would that not influence his judgement? However, I knew better than to dispute the tradition of total saffrine loyalty to one's comrades, as well as to God Saffrin. It just didn't seem fair to me that a Saffrin lad or lass could follow whatever trade or craft they wanted, while someone like me was banned from the armed forces.

Frustrated, I picked up a pebble and flung it as hard as I could at the bowmen's bull's-eye. It left a mark in the centre of the target.

Pa quirked an amused eyebrow my way.

'When are you heading back to Templebridge?' I asked.

'When our task here is finished.'

'Can I help?'

'No. It's the King's business. I'll let you know when I'm returning. Until then, you stay out of trouble.' He flipped a coin in my direction.

I caught it, glad to see it was a double heavy silver, worth twenty ricks. I could get back in Mam's good graces and still have plenty left over. I smiled my thanks, but my thoughts were darker. There was something afoot that I was not privy to, and I never liked not knowing what was going on. Ignorance, as I had discovered several times to my cost, was dangerous.

He handed over his sword to me then, the real one. 'Clean this for me, will you? Shine up the belt and all.' It had been a favourite job of mine when I was a youngster, but there was a strange kind of finality to his request, as if he were saying we'd would soon be parting.

I took the weapon with a nod and headed out of the gateway, ostensibly to head home. Once out of sight of the guards on the gate, though, I left the road and slipped into the dirt lane that wound up through the Proxy-wives' Quarter to the back of the rise overlooking the practice grounds. I buckled on the sword to save me the trouble of carrying it, and yes, I knew that carrying any offensive blade more than a handspan long is forbidden by law to an ordinary citizen. However, as those in charge of enforcing such a rule in Breakedge are the Border Rangers, all of whom knew me and my pa, I wasn't worried. If any of them saw me wearing Pa's weapon, the worst I'd get would be a halfhearted cuff across the head for being cheeky.

What *was* niggling at me was that glimpse of a green jacket on the person on the hill, and the way he appeared to duck out of sight in a hurry. It could have been anyone, and surely they would have been long gone, but I had to look.

So, Lady Sianta, are you still interested in this tale of mine? If so, do you think I could have an extra blanket? It's rime-ice cold in here. I swear, the ink you gave me was friz this morn.

5

When I crested the hill, I really didn't expect to find the watcher still there.

Yet there he was, the aristo, leaning back against a boulder in such a way as to have a wide, unobstructed view of the barracks below, even as he himself was half-hidden. There was a touch of arrogance in his easy confidence that no one would challenge his right to be there watching the barracks and observing the rangers going about their business. A quarterstaff was propped up on the boulder by his side.

Intriguing. I hadn't pegged him as a fighter.

The barracks school had drummed into us lads the idea that details were important when assessing a potential enemy, so I noted the neat way he'd tied back his fair hair at the nape, the cleanliness of his fingernails, the quality of the cloth of his breeks. He even wore a green linen kerchief neatly tied around his neck — an affectation if ever there was one.

Possibly I made a sound, because he turned his head to look at me. 'Ah,' he said, not bothering to straighten up, 'the purse-picker from the market.'

'You followed me,' I said, blurting the words like a lackwit.

He arched an eyebrow. 'Nonsense. Why would I have even the faintest wish to pursue our acquaintance? You ruined a perfectly good jerkin with your clumsy slicing.' He flicked his fingers in my direction as if in dismissal.

'Ruined it? You're wearing it!' I couldn't even see where the cut had been. Gods be blethering, he must have already got someone to stitch it up! I took a couple of steps closer. 'You've been watching me and my pa.' Come to think of it, even our house was visible from where he stood.

'Well, if that was your papa you were sparring with, I don't deny that. He's a pretty swordsman, worth watching, wouldn't you say? Although I can't help feeling *you* are wasting your time.'

I bristled. 'Which tells me how piddling little you know about swordplay.'

'Oh, I don't doubt you could hold your own in a practice bout. But you worship the wrong god for real soldiery, don't you?' He glanced at Pa's blade. 'And bearing a sword in the streets is against the law for us non-saffrines.'

I gave what I hoped was a contemptuous snort.

'Someone who can never be a soldier best look for other weaponry,' he added. 'Something that's legal.'

'Like yon stick?' I asked, infusing the words with a tinge of contempt I didn't need to feign. I was annoyed, though. How could he possibly know I was not saffrine? Maybe that was a stab in the dark. I was none too sure about his assertion that he was non-saffrine, either.

He smiled and straightened, reaching for his polearm. 'That's right, one like this.' He thrust it at me, and I stepped sharply back out of range. 'Finest ash, harvested at the right time and correct age, well-cured and honed.'

An ash was, I guessed, some kind of a tree. Not one that grew in Breakedge, for sure. 'Cut a man with a sword and he's either dead, or in a real pickle,' I said. 'Hit a man with a stick, and all he has is a bruise.'

'Or a broken limb. Possibly even a fractured pate. And don't forget, the swordsman has first to get close to his opponent before he can cut him.' The end of his weapon wove patterns in the air, swishing near enough for me to feel the wind of it, all while he was well out of the range of a sword. 'Come on, master purse-picker; see if you can tickle my nose with the tip of your blade.'

I resisted the temptation to take another step backwards. 'Why would I want to do that? I've no argument with you.' I also had no desire to compound my misdemeanour of wearing arms within the city limits into a major crime by using it.

'*I* do have an argument with *you*, though,' he said. 'You stole my purse.'

'I did not,' I pointed out. 'You still have it.'

He jabbed at me again, and this time I didn't get out of his way quickly enough. The staff thwacked me on the hip, hard enough to hurt. 'Come at me with that blade of your father's,' he said, 'and I'll show you the benefits of using a pole.'

I moved further out of range. 'I'll take your word for it. I was taught to choose my battles carefully, and brawling over the merits of stick or blade is hare-brained at best, cockeyed dunderheaded at worst.'

His stance remained threatening. His hands slid up and down the pole as he jabbed at my throat. Shades of a god's shadow, but he could make that stick of his dance! 'What's your name?' he asked.

I knocked the end of his staff an inch to two to the side with the flat of my hand. 'Make up your mind. Are we having a fight or a friendly chat?'

He lowered the pole with a shrug. 'Just testing you. I like people who can't be goaded into a stupid fight.'

'Well, I don't have a very high opinion of a nick-ninny who does the goading!'

Another shrug. 'I'll teach you how to use a quarterstaff, if you like.'

I blinked. 'Why the pickled pig would you want to do that?'

'Because I watched you sparring down there, and I think you'd be good at it. You need something else, because no ranger's sword is ever going to be yours, and you know it.'

49

I stared at him in disbelief.

'All right. The real reason: because you dropped my purse to save a child from a vicious blow that would have hurt her grievously. And you did it knowing you could have been in a sticky pickle with the law as a result.'

He might have thought that explained his offer, but *I* didn't. 'And what makes you so sure I'm not saffrine?'

'Oh, that's easy. The way you looked at me. Or rather the way you *didn't* look. Believe me, I *always* rate a second look from a saffrine male.' He grinned at me with a look that was pure mischief.

I rolled my eyes at his arrogant certainty, even as I acknowledged to myself that he might have had a point. He was an attractive fellow, with a lithe, athletic body and a sweet smile when he tried. Jav would have found it tough to look away, for a start. And others might have seen him as competition ... However, part of me was as suspicious as a talyak smelling the blood in a knacker's yard. Who the ten heavens was this fellow? I was certain it was no coincidence that he'd turned up here just as I arrived below with Pa.

'What's *your* name?' I asked.

'Haze. Wayfaring family. You wouldn't know them.'

He was probably right. Most wayfarers used a regular circular route plying their trade from town to town and never stopped long in any one place. Many acknowledged no surname but Wayfarer.

'Where are you living now?' I asked.

He snorted. 'Where our sort usually live: on the outskirts of town. Along with the milkmaids, swineherds and gong-farmers. If you want to have a lesson with staves, I usually work out on the cow meadow around dawn. You still haven't told me your name, by the way.'

'Taygen Hervan-Gariane.' I snapped it out, oddly aware I was losing control of the conversation and more certain than ever that not every wag of his tongue was honest.

'I heard in the market this morning that kingsmen had come in from Templebridge,' he said. I didn't comment, so he added, 'Your father's wearing the King's Guard's griffin, not a rangers' uniform. Is he one of them, then?'

'None of your business.'

He cocked his head, regarding me with the same critical assessment one gives a bowl of questionable potage served up in a noisome alehouse.

'I still don't get why you'd want to teach me anything,' I said.

'You stole my purse, and you were damned clever about it. Practised. Yet you're the sprog of a kingsman.' He pointed at my father's scabbard on my hip. 'Embossed griffin's head at that, that means your pa's an officer. Captain Hervan, I warrant. You live in a Sprogs' Cradle. You were born lucky, but you're messing up, aren't you? Lifting purses like a slum brat who knows no better! After watching your swordplay, I reckon you're beset because you can't be a soldier like your pa.'

I flushed. How could he possibly know so much about me in such a short time? It was uncanny. *He* was uncanny. Unease skittered up my spine.

'Go to godless hell,' I said, and walked away.

He called after me, 'Just after dawn, tomorrow!'

I didn't look back.

*

My thanks for the extra bedding, Lady Sianta! I shall sleep warmer tonight, and yes, I will indeed attempt to speed up the telling of my tale. Though, to be quite frank, I wonder if your concern is not prompted more by your worry that I won't have penned the full story before the King returns and puts his signature to the order for my hanging.

*

I'd no sooner unbuckled the sword belt and laid it down on the kitchen table after my conversation with Haze, than Pa entered the house in a hurry and grabbed it up. 'Just had word,' he said over his shoulder as he headed out the door, 'the new Dargan archpriest has already seen some signs of redweaving. Wants us along in case his men need back-up.'

Of course, I followed him.

Out in the street four men waited, all King's Guardsmen. I recognised one of them, a fellow with a scarred face by the name of Cyrrin. I'd met him once before when Pa had brought him to the house. I'd been about ten at the time, and Ma hadn't wanted him around. I was so wet behind the ears, it took Jav to explain to me that Cyrrin was Pa's lover. Seeing him now told me that Pa's story of joining up with a random squad of kingsmen was pig's swill. These were *his* men. Under his command.

Once he'd joined his squad, they all ran to catch up with some other men further down the hill wearing the uniform of clergy guards. I couldn't see their breast insignia, but I guessed it would be the hammer-and-saw symbol of God Dargan. They jogged down the road two abreast, in step, their precision more ridiculous than impressive. As they weren't kingsmen, they weren't allowed to carry swords or pikes. Instead, they had sheathed daggers at one hip, and truncheons stuck through the belt on the other. I followed, but hung back until both squads had halted in front of the unadorned façade of Dargan's Temple, right opposite Goddess Amaranthal's temple. When a group of youths passed me on their way there to pray for artistic inspiration, I tagged along until I could hide myself amongst the flamboyant statuary that decorated the temple's entrance. Peeking out from behind a colourful representation of the goddess and her attendant porcelain cherubs, I watched what was happening across the street.

God Dargan's new archpriest, swathed in grey robes bearing the Dargan symbol, came down the steps from the temple. I now knew that besides one decrepit archpriestess, he was probably the only person in the city who could see redweaving. My hearing captured his words without having to strain. I expected deep concern, consternation perhaps, but what I heard was anticipatory glee. 'Red traces everywhere,' the fellow told Pa. 'I've found one place smeared with their foulness. We can root them out.'

'Not my task, Most Reverend,' Pa said. 'Would be my advice to inform the Lord Mayor's town law-proctors, or the Border Patr—'

'Dargan below! Are you going to quibble about who kills these evil conjurers invading our land? Afraid, are you? I have enough god-granted ability to warn of any conjuries they cast in your direction, I assure you!'

'My priority has to be the King's busi—'

The archpriest came at him like a thwarted bull talyak, thrusting his nose into Pa's face. 'And redweavers aren't the King's business? Right, then. You tuck your balls between your legs and head home, while I take on this nest of snaggle-toothed aliens.' With that, he strode off down the street.

'Flea-witted bastard of a god-licker.' Pa's curse was soft but heartfelt. It was also tactless, and I could only hope no one else heard. He sighed as the Dargan squad set off after the archpriest, but he ordered his men to follow nonetheless. I tagged along some distance behind as they all headed towards the desert edges of the city.

Arms swinging and robe swishing around his ankles, the archpriest marched as if in testament to his righteous purpose. He turned into a smaller laneway, which led into another and another, each meaner, dirtier and more deserted than the last. When he finally halted, I knew we'd arrived somewhere near the outer southern rim of the city where crumbling buildings were never repaired, the drainage stank, and the night-soil was rarely collected. This was home to the worst of Breakedge's citizens: the drunk and the drugged and those who lived outside the law. The alleys only came alive at night. To my shame, I must admit I was no stranger there.

I'd dropped back to avoid being seen by Pa, so when the archpriest halted to whisper something to him, I was too far away to catch the words. The cleric took a step to his left and disappeared. His squad followed and Pa gestured his own men after them. From where I was, it looked as if they had all vanished into a wall.

I hurtled down the alleyway to where they'd been, only to skid to a halt because I almost missed the narrow entry into a cramped passage between high, mud-brick walls. I peered into the dank murk that smelled of piss. Enough light filtered down from a crack of sky above for me to see a blind alleyway, about forty paces in length, ending in the blank wall of a building. Pa, the archpriest and the armsmen were all gathered at the far end, outside a doorway to the left.

'They've got to be in there,' the archpriest was saying in an undertone. He scuffed at the filth underfoot. 'The redweaving dusts everything like the first autumn snowfall.' A useless description as far as I was concerned. I'd never seen snow.

Even once my eyes adjusted to the gloom, I couldn't see anything out of the ordinary and it occurred to me that we placed a dundering heap of faith in the higher clergy of the Decasian Pantheon. They *said* they could hear the gods speak, and as far as I knew, they were also the only folk who *said* they could see redweaving conjury. What if some of them — or all of them — were liars?

All right, a ridiculous notion, I suppose.

Just then Pa glanced back up the passageway, spotted me and scowled. When he beckoned, I knew better than to disobey. I jogged up expecting a scolding, but all he did was ask if I could hear anything. Typical. The King's business came first. He did know I had excellent hearing, although he had no idea of just *how* good, and I had no intention of ever telling him.

I listened, but the mud-brick walls were too thick and I didn't have to lie. 'A young child whining. Two people talking, one a woman. Could be coming from anywhere in either building on either side. Can't hear the words.'

'Right. Now go home. This is not your affair.'

'Is it yours?'

'Taygen — *go.*'

I went. Well, I retreated to the entrance to the passageway, anyway. When I halted there to glance behind, the armsmen were breaking down the door with their truncheons. Given the rickety nature of the wood, it was easily done and they all plunged through the doorway, the archpriest and his men to the fore, Pa and his men following, swords drawn.

I dithered, reluctant to walk away.

My father was facing a conjury he had no skills to combat and couldn't even see. I'd heard it could make you see things that weren't there and hide things that were; I'd heard it was so poisonous that just breathing the red mist was fatal. Other people said it sent you mad. Or worse.

I stayed where I was.

Almost immediately something weird caught my eye to the side about halfway down the alley between me and the door, a wavering in the air like a scarlet heat shimmer. It wisped upwards from the bare earth at the angle where the wall met the ground. Behind it, something began to coalesce. That took on colour and form, then solidity. A head, emerging from the dirt.

My heartbeat throbbed in my ears. I was as scared as it was possible to be and still stand upright.

The head of a living man.

Impossible, and yet there he was: a head, then shoulders and torso, all rising up *from inside a hole in the ground*. Too shocked to run, too stunned to call out, I stood slack-jawed. He emerged whole from the hammered earth as if he'd climbed an invisible staircase at the base of the wall, all without disturbing a grain of dirt. A bearded, grim-faced fellow, maybe thirty years old. Looking straight at me.

Followed by a woman, clutching a toddler to her chest.

Then a boy of ten or so followed, wide-eyed. Terrified.

Three people with a child-in-arms stepping up from inside the earth, until they were standing at the edge of the narrow lane, one behind the other, a bare ten lengths from me. I went cold all over, knowing I must have been looking at a redwoven gateway.

*

It's late and my candle is guttering. I'll write some more tomorrow. Perhaps a better quality candle, or an oil lamp, would encourage my productivity, Sianta?

6

I find myself reluctant to write about what happened next, as if some things are better kept tucked away in memory and not aired too often. I was brought up to believe that the Netherfolk were possibly mythical, but definitely evil. I'd heard all the stories. Folk spoke of mischievous beings, not *quite* human, born in Lands of the Beyond, folk who entered the world of Talodiac through hidden, glowing gateways. Their men were said to entice beautiful maidens to follow them to that netherworld; their women were said to steal children while leaving their own deformed young behind in the cradle. I'd heard all kinds of muddled, inconsistent tales that didn't make much sense, but all stories of the clergy of the Decasian Pantheon had one consistent detail: redweavers slipped into Talodiac through gates woven of writhing cords of red magic. Worse still, most of their tales said redweavers could weave illusions that seemed real.

No one ever gave me a *sensible* reason backed by evidence as to *why* the Netherfolk came.

A week or two before I saw those folk come up out of the ground, I'd asked an old friend of mine what he knew of Netherfolk. My mother had sent me to buy some dromedary dung from the Dekadani traders down at the border, and Chendak Polor, one of the Dekadani lads I had played with as a child, was there with his family of traders.

Annoyingly, Chendak was at least a head taller than me now, and if that wasn't enough, he had a smile that would charm the spots off a desert hyena. With the skin colour of a talfawn, and heads of long hair as white as clouds, I reckon the Dekadani people are the most handsome folk I'll ever see. If he'd had a sister with those looks, I'd be...

Never mind.

Five years had passed since we last met, but he greeted me as an old friend and took me along to his tent, where a young lad of his family produced hot bowls of spicy tea laced with palm-toddy. We reminisced for a bit, then I asked him if he knew anything about redweavers.

'Heard say, you got some o' thems in Breakedge,' he said. 'We only got legends. Remember them tales I telled back when? 'Bout mirages?'

I nodded.

'Strange folks popping out of nowheres, sudden-like. One I remember: Dekadani fella coming home from desert trading, finds he got 'nother fella inside his tent. Fella looked just like him, but wasn't him. Was woven to look like him.' He shook his head. 'Bad magic, that.' He poured me another bowl of tea.

A chill skittered down my back. We had nightmare yarns too, of Netherfolk pretending to be like us. 'If the Netherfolk were real in your history, and they disappeared, do your stories say where they went?' I asked.

He'd laughed then. 'Dekadani God, he much more big than your many gods. He help. Redweavers run and no more come back. They got red doors to elsewheres now. Here maybe.'

That was now more than just a sobering thought.

*

I stood there at the end of that alley, incapable of movement and watched that family step out of the earth. Fear, horror, shock — I felt them all, but it was disbelief that punched me in the chest, leaving me motionless, hardly able to breathe.

How was it possible? Even with all I'd heard of redwoven gateways, part of me had not believed in them until that moment when I saw people appearing out of nowhere, emerging from where there was no door, no gate, nothing except a reddish hole — at least not to my eyes. The man was ill-clad and unhealthy-looking. He slipped his arm around the waist of the woman as she stepped out on to the surface of the lane. The lad behind her was as skinny as a stick insect. The smaller tot was a girl, and the woman clutched her protectively against her shoulder. It hit me how thin they all were. Underfed, certainly; perhaps even close to starvation.

We stared at one other. I was blocking their way out of the alley.

Shocked, I didn't move.

Thoughts skittered through my mind. Maybe they were just … dream pictures. Not real. Just lies of a redweaver conjury. Before I could gather myself sufficiently to do anything at all, the man decided to barrel his way out into the alley by running me down. He let go of the woman and aimed his shoulder at me, driving forward. Not only real, but desperate, off balance and weak. His family followed.

Just before he reached me, I stepped out of his way and stuck out a foot to halt his flight, more an instinctive reaction than a planned one. He sprawled at my feet, a wreck of tangled limbs and tattered clothing. The woman yelled something — his name, I guessed. Ashamed of what I'd done, I bent to help the fellow up, but even as I made the gesture, the Dargan priest emerged from the door at the end of the alleyway. He stared at us, then roared, 'Redweaving! A gateway!' His soldiers poured out of the door behind him in answer, truncheons in their hands, followed by my father and his squad.

The man accepted my arm.

The archpriest yelled, 'Make sure you get them all!'

His soldiers pelted up the lane. Pa and his men stayed where they were.

The woman turned to look.

'There's a child! Have a care—' I shouted the words. No one took heed.

The first of the archpriest's men swung his weighted weapon against the woman's skull with such power he nearly split her head in two. She collapsed without a word, blood droplets arcing through the air in scarlet rain. The child dropped out of her arms, her tiny hands flinging up, her mouth opening in surprise. Her body hit the ground and the shock of her fall silenced the cry she had been about to vent.

The lad gaped, unable to comprehend the horror and not even noticing when the second of Dargan's men drew his dagger. A flick of a blade later and the lad's life ebbed away in a welter of blood pumping from his severed neck. His father hauled himself upright in time to see it happen.

I saw his face.

I saw him take a single desperate step towards the little girl.

He ignored the Dargan armsman coming towards him, didn't take any action to avoid the blow. He saw nothing except that small child on the ground in her skimpy torn frock, and the scrabbling of a tiny hand that said she was still alive.

Far too late, I screamed at Pa, bellowed at him to stop the slaughter.

But Pa remained where he was, locking his gaze on mine as one of the armsmen stamped his heel on the girl's neck. Brutal, but final. They were merciful in their death blows, I'll give them those templemen that. As merciful as they were merciless in their intent. It was all over in less time than it would take a cock to crow. Four people dead. A family eliminated. Blood everywhere. I was spattered with it. Gods, so much blood. Still pumping from the dead, thick, the smell as rich as molten metal in a forge crucible. So ... *human*.

When I think about it now, I realise a brutal archpriest had turned these artisans and labourers into his personal

guard of brutal killers, out of fear and ignorance, I suppose.
Even as I watched, he smiled and nodded to his armsmen.
'Good work, men. You have earned Dargan's blessing this
day. Fear not, I will unweave this godless gateway to the
Netherworld.'

Go home. Hervan, grim-faced, mouthed the words at me.
Go home.

Behind him, Cyrrin's face was impassive. The other three
kingsmen were all staring at the ground. Clearly, none of
them were happy about it, but none of them had intervened
either. I could almost hear Pa saying, *Not our business, son...*

I turned and staggered around the corner into the wider
lane, where I threw up in the gutter, again and again until
there wasn't even bile left. Nothing was going to change my
besmirched soul, though. Nothing ever will. In death they
weren't redweavers, or alien creatures. They were just a family. *They were us.*

I did indeed go home. Moreover, for the first time in my
life, I had second thoughts about the desirability of being an
armsman, even as I tried to convince myself that the human
guise of that slaughtered family was all a sham. Perhaps underneath they were monsters. Or human, but just not quite
like us. Taller, thicker, uglier, darker, hairier? Who knew?

No, wait. Someone *did* know.

The clergy.

Well, at least their top rung: The male gerents and the
female gerentias. Each temple where a deity resided had one
such. And after them, the more numerous arch-clergy —
goodness knows how many. They all must know too, because
they were the ones who could see through the illusions of
redweaving. Or so I'd heard.

I repressed a shudder. There had been something so ...
human-like in the way that desperate redweaver father had
reached for his daughter. If his magic was so powerful as to

open a door in the ground, how come he and his family were dead?

*

Mam was not in, and I was glad of that.
    I stood under the pump in the yard, clothes and all, and washed away the evidence of a brutal crime. After hanging out the wet clothing, I entered the house. When I sat down in dry clothes at the kitchen table a little later, my hands wouldn't stop shaking. I'd seen people die before; I'd even seen a couple of fellows killed by street violence. But never with such cold, efficient brutality, such lack of compassion. Never like that.

Never *children*.

On the say-so of one man, who reckoned they reeked with an evil conjury. All I had seen was poverty.

I was still sitting there when Pa came home. He had blood on his shoes. He took off his sword belt and lay it down on the table. 'Never did get that cleaning.' The stare he gave me then made me feel as raw as a boy not yet graduated to trousers. 'I did tell you to get on home.'

'Yes. Wish I had. I'll never be able to — to *un*see that. Not so long as I live.'

'They were redweavers. Aliens on our soil. Intruders. Here to harm us. Or scrounge from us.' He shrugged. 'Not pleasant. But necessary.'

'Says who? That archpriest? He revelled in the blood! He *enjoyed* himself!'

My vehemence shocked him. 'You can't doubt they were redweavers, surely?'

'How do we know? They could have been running *from* redweavers!'

'We did see 'em emerge through what must have been one of them woven gateways, though. To me, looked as if they grew outta the ground! Taygen, we're ordinary folk. The gods give the ability to see redweaving only to arch-clergy.'

'Who are always men and women of integrity,' I said, my sarcasm as sour as it was thick. 'And if redweaving is so hideously dangerous, why didn't the gods give all of us that perceptive sight? And why didn't that fellow use his to protect his family?'

Pa's glare was that of a man affronted. 'Mayhap the gods choose as priests them that can see the weaving. Mayhap them that are worthy of such a skill get it. Either way, none of our concern.'

'But how do we know the archpriests and gerents tell the truth?'

'Drop it, Tay! Each of 'em is chosen by the god of their temple for that position. How can we possibly question their honour?'

When I didn't reply, he sat down opposite me and added, more gently, 'Listen up. I can tell you what I *have* seen meself, first-hand, with me own eyes. A woman, newly given birth to a healthy baby, crazed because the babe had been stolen from its cradle alongside her bed — while evil magic kept her unable to move. She lost her mind. I saw her husband unmanned with grief. That is what they do, them redweaving muckers. Netherfolk steal our children, for what purpose we don't even know! They get into our world through their bloody woven gates, live among us unseen, and more and more of them are arriving. They are hunted down, but the redweaving fades once they leave the gate behind, and how the ten hells can we recognise them, 'less they use their conjury again? And them so clever at mimicking our speech, at learning our ways, till we can't be sure whether they are them or us. Make no mistake, they're *not* us, and they never will be.'

'Can they *all* use conjury?'

'Who knows?' He sighed. 'We know so very little about 'em. When they first arrive — like that family today — they glow red to those who see conjury. Their clothes are sometimes of a different cut, and for all that they speak our tongue, their accent is rough and foreign to our ears at first — like them sailors from the west islands — till they learn to change and fit in.'

'What's the harm in them then?'

'They don't worship our gods. They don't care 'bout our ways. Or follow our traditions, and that's just for a start.'

Another thought struck me. 'What if those children who died today were not theirs, but *ours*? Stolen from our mothers?'

'The archpriest would've known.' He tried to sound sure, but it was doubt I heard in his tone. 'None of our business anyway. We are kingsmen, and we don't deal with such, for all that we are worship God Saffrin. These invaders are the business of Gerent Battleseer's cohorts and his taldeer troops.' He stood and picked up his sword belt again. 'My men and me need to search for our own quarry and leave redweavers and their like to them. I don't know when we'll be leaving, Tay, so you best say your goodbyes to your friends and be ready, all right?'

With that, he was gone.

I sat there for a while longer, feeling sick. Somewhere deep in my soul, I knew my relationship with my pa had subtly changed. In the space of a day, so much had happened. Too much. Pa had given my life focus by showing me the glimmer of a successful future ahead in Templebridge, then that wretch, Haze, had shaken me to the point where I feared that future was already in jeopardy. Why had the fellow followed me?

No, wait a moment. Maybe he *hadn't* followed me. After all, he must have stopped to have that jacket of his mended ... Besides, I hadn't seen him, and watching my back was second nature for me since Spake the Locksmith had drummed it into my skull when I was all of eight years old. Gods, *Spake*. If he heard about what happened in the market...

Ah, perhaps I'd better explain that, Lady Sianta.

The year I turned eight, Mam was desperately ill. My older sister, Salli, rarely left her side. Pa was in Templebridge. Jav was training with the rangers and wasn't home much, so no one looked out for me, and I more or less lived on the streets.

One day I'd wandered into Spake's smithy where his workman fashioned his locks. I ended up earning a rickling coin for sweeping up. Locks, and how they worked, fascinated me, so from then on, I hung around the locksmith's doing odd jobs and running errands, while I learned everything there was to know about keys and deadbolts and combinations.

I didn't know then that Locksmith Spake was the spider at the centre of a sticky web that reached into every alley, every gutter, every cellar and every taproom in Breakedge, from the camp of the desert caravaners to the herder huts on hill slopes. By the time I realised the web existed, I'd been caught up in the glue of it, his network of spies and thieves and informers. I liked the excitement, the adventure. It began with me carrying messages for him and progressed to light-fingered skills. Life under Spake's watchful eye was never dull, and I scarcely noticed the moment when I slipped from honest tasks to the wrong side of the law.

I sat there at the table in Mam's house that day, though, and considered my past and my stupidity. For years, I'd been clever enough to escape notice, but now Mam had made it clear folk had begun to talk.

Worse, what if Haze the wayfarer accused me of attempted theft before the city magistrate? My mood spiralled downwards. I tried to convince myself that the death of the redweaver family was just colouring my thoughts from a grim palette, but I couldn't rid myself of that memory. If those pathetic folk were redweavers, they were hardly a threat. Easily killed, now dead. *And my father had sanctioned it by his presence.*

In the space of one day, not only had my world begun to crumble, but I had no idea how to regain my balance on the disintegrating ruins.

7

When Mam came back, I couldn't bear the thought of normal conversation, so I told her I had an errand to run. I walked out of the house and headed for the person most likely to know something about Haze, even though he was the last person I wanted to consult.

The locksmith. Spake.

By the time I arrived at his workshop, I'd decided I might be looking at what had happened the wrong way around. Perhaps Haze had known who I was and where I lived *before* I'd tried to rob him. I couldn't think of any reason *why* he might have known me, though. In fact, it was an even more unsettling thought because it meant that *he* might have been spying on *me* in the market, not the other way around.

Master Spake wasn't in the shop, so I nodded to his eldest son, Fredar, who was chatting to a customer at the counter, and continued down the steps into the smithy behind. The moment Spake saw me he came barrelling across the room, head lowered and shoulders thrust forward like an irate talyak bullock.

He stopped just short of knocking me down. 'You pin-witted pisspot!' he bellowed, spraying spit all over my face.

I winced, while the three workers in the room did a rotten job of pretending they hadn't heard.

'You botched a purse-pick,' he said, hands on hips. 'And you were *caught*.'

'Not exactly,' I said. I wasn't all that surprised he already knew what had happened in the market. Every street urchin collected coin from him for that kind of gossip. 'The mark laid no charges.'

He leant forward even closer and said into my ear, 'Just as well. Otherwise, it might have gone ill for you.'

I shrugged, all bravado. 'That would have been my problem, not yours.'

That was true enough. He'd trained us as thieves when we were lads, he'd fed us with information from his numerous spies, and he'd fenced the valuables we stole. Three-quarters of everything we'd lifted went to his coffers, but we all knew if we were caught, we were on our own.

After realising several years earlier that he took special delight in corrupting the son of a kingsman, I'd begun weaning myself away from the smithy, pleading my studies with the rangers and the barracks school as an excuse. Spake had let that happen, but he also reeled me in every so often, just to remind me who was in charge. At the time, I was in far too deep to betray him without implicating myself, which scared me witless. I was desperate not to bring shame to my parents.

Spake wasn't finished. 'You're too smart to be caught out like that! And all to protect a pilfering brat from a clip over the ear?' He reached up and pinched my earlobe between thumb and forefinger, hard. 'Sentimentality is lob-cock stupidity. Ain't I taught you that much?'

'Indeed, you have,' I said drily and pulled my head sideways until he let go. 'Do you know who the mark was? He dresses and speaks like an aristo.'

He snorted. 'Lad, you ain't laid eyes on a real genteel mincer! That lad's just a stitcher's son. Or nephew. Whatever. They travel together, anyway. She sews his clothes with fine threads and he swans it over us mucky pigeons, is all.'

'Where do they live? I haven't seen him around before.'

'Rented Old Tom the Pewterman's cottage, down by the cow meadows. Came in 'bout a month back with the last lot of wayfarers, him and the lady high-nose. You steer clear of 'im. Don't want nobody getting none too interested in how someone accused Cap'n Hervan's lad of picking pockets, unnerstand? I got a big caper for you coming up and I don't want nobody looking too hard your way.'

'I don't think a job is a good idea right now,' I said, appalled. 'My pa's here.'

'Think I don't know that?' He grinned at me, baring a mouth full of broken teeth and purple gums. 'That's the whole point. Who's goin' to think you'd be up to mischief when your pa's in town, eh? This is a big caper, Taygen. Biggest yet. I need someone who can open a Cratchett chest.'

Puke on 'im!

Cratchett chests, named after their maker, were huge and heavy. Being imported from Templebridge by talyak bullock wagon made them hellishly expensive. We all knew exactly how many had ever made their way into Breakedge — and who owned them. They were too heavy to steal, double locked by a mechanism that took at least two hours to manipulate, if you were both skilled and lucky. We knew that because Spake owned one and had set his sons and me to working on how to open it without the key. As a result, we avoided them. There were easier targets.

'Why me?' I asked, taking a step backwards away from him. 'You can do that yourself!' And so could any one of his three sons, for that matter.

'And who'd be the first people under suspicion?' He followed me and jabbed a pointed finger into the base of my throat. 'The only folk in Breakedge who know how to fiddle a Cratchett be right here in this room, right now. And the only person the city burghers would never believe had lock-picking skills is *you*. The rest of us will have an unassailable alibi on the night in question. We're all going to be consorting with them burghers themselves!' The grin he gave me brought bile to my throat.

I had no idea what he had planned, and I didn't want to know. 'Count me out,' I said as I back-pedalled some more.

He wasn't going to let me off so lightly. Grabbing me by the shirtfront, he yanked me closer until we were almost nose to nose, then shook me with unexpected ferocity. He was stronger than he looked. A whiff from his rotting mouth almost had me gagging. 'You don't get to say no, you totty-head. You're mine, body 'n' soul.'

Sweat broke out on the back of my neck. The other workers in the smithy were sliding glances in my direction while they worked, doubtless glad they weren't the object of his ire. 'Sorry, Master Spake.' My voice was annoyingly husky, but I persisted. 'Not while my pa's in town, anyway. After he's gone, perhaps.' By which time I'd be gone too.

He dug his nails into my neck and whispered, 'You'll do this job, or I'll tell Pa exactly what you been up to. And I promise yer, I'll come out of it as pure as the dew on a lamb's nose. You, on the other hand ... Remember Melken? I had him framed as neatly as a picture!'

My mouth went dry. Melken had been one of Spake's apprentices and he'd been hanged for theft. I'd wondered at the time whether he'd possessed sufficient wits to commit the crimes he was accused of, but the evidence had been overwhelming.

And, it seemed, a lie.

I nodded, not sure I could speak without betraying how much he scared me. He flung me backwards, and I played along to give him the satisfaction he craved. I flung my arms out, half twisting as if I lost my balance, ending up spread-eagled in a clumsy, inelegant tangle across his desk. I slid to the floor with a thump, followed by a shower of his account books, papers, tools and other paraphernalia. I rubbed my head and groaned as if I'd banged it on the way down.

'Troyn,' he snapped to his middle son, 'get this heap of shit out of my sight! Don't come back here, Taygen, until I need you. Templeday Eve.'

Inwardly, I winced. That was three days hence, the day of the annual Burghers' Ball. That was it, of course. He and his sons had wangled tickets to the ball where they'd be seen while the contents of a Cratchett chest were being stolen on the other side of town.

Scattering papers, I scrabbled to my feet. As Troyn grabbed my arm to pull me towards the stairs, I heard Spake ordering another of his sons to clear up the mess I'd made.

*

It's funny how fate always seems to kick you in the teeth when you think you have your future nicely planned. As I left the smithy, attempting to look both meek and chastened, my world felt cramped, as though the very buildings were closing in, the roofs louring, the walls entrapping, their shadows shrouding any chance of a brighter future.

At least I now had an inkling of just which Cratchett chest Spake was intending to rob. He loved plans and maps, and he loved to sketch possible entry points to targeted buildings and escape routes through the streets afterwards. My theatrics had paid off. The plan had been on the table. I'd carried it to the floor when I fell and had a good look at it while I lay there rubbing my head. I knew the building.

Not that I felt much happier knowing. Spake had tired of petty thievery and was aiming higher than I had considered possible. The Breakedge Counting House? He had to be joking!

*

Old Tom the Pewterman might have existed once, but I never knew him. I knew his house, though; one in a row of adjoined two-roomed huts built along the edge of the common land. Usually rented by wayfarers passing through, they were not fancy enough for someone like Haze of the green velvet jerkin to live in — or so I would have thought. After leaving the locksmith's, I headed out that way, although I'm not sure what I expected to achieve.

A thick hedge ran along the back of the houses, between them and the adjacent grazing land, so it was easy to sneak up to the rear. The backyard was no more than a dusty patch a couple of paces wide, containing a pump, a rickety pit latrine, and an ageing mulberry tree. In the dusk of evening, I couldn't see much detail, but the back door was open to let in the cooler evening air, and the room beyond was candlelit. Wax, not tallow, which told me they had money to burn.

I heard Haze's voice, sounding thoroughly fed up.

'Please, not again!' he was saying. 'Why?'

'They're here for us.' A woman's voice, his mother I assumed. Or sister? Aunt? Lover?

'You don't know that.' Haze again.

A short pause, then, 'No, I don't. Not for sure.'

Accents fascinated me, possibly because of my odd hearing. Even when I was a brat still wearing a smock, I could always tell who was an outsider. I'd ask complete strangers why they spoke so funny and where they came from.

Haze's accent had already interested me. Educated, definitely; effeminate in tone perhaps — yet with the arrogant edge of a confident male. There was also a confusing mix of the soft burr of fishermen and harbour folk of the littoral states, and the crisp pronunciation of traders and merchants of cities. All places I'd never been to in person, but their citizens travelled, even if I didn't. The woman had an accent similar to Haze's, telling me they had similar histories.

I didn't move. There was a long silence before Haze spoke again. He'd lowered his voice, but his tone was impassioned.

'I can't do this anymore, Innata. I can't, not without knowing why.'

As he called her by name, she probably wasn't his mother. Or aunt, either. Sister maybe. Or friend. The name itself told me nothing. The very first Innata was a mythical heroine, a warrior and founding mother of a ducal line from the days of Talodiac's beginnings, and every family in every duchy had at least one Innata in it somewhere.

The woman's voice again, sounding resigned. 'Yes. It is time. But not now. Now we have to pack and leave.'

'Taygen is coming here tomorrow morning. I said I'd teach him to spar with a quarterstaff.'

'Taygen?'

'The fellow I mentioned yesterday. Captain Hervan's younger son.'

The hair rose on the back of my neck.

'His *son*? *Coming here*? Are you oakum-stuffed?'

'Not to the house,' Haze said, apparently unfazed by her reaction. 'I'm meeting him on the pasture, if he comes, and I think he will. I baited the hook well.'

'*Why*? Why would you do something so blamed dangerous?'

'Because you're scared of Captain Hervan. I thought I might be able to find out from his son why the squad of royal soldiers came to Breakedge. I can understand the god-guards for the archpriest, and Hervan's presence would be easy to explain if he was alone, because this is where his proxy-wife raised his brats. They all still live here. Hervan might come to see them. But he brought a squad with him, and that's another thing altogether.'

'Oh, sweet Jenat. If I'd known you'd be so silly ... Haze, you don't understand!' The woman's voice trailed away.

'You act as if they came to find you. But you won't tell me why. For all I know, you might just be irrationally crazed. I'll find out if Taygen knows why his pa has brought his squad. Then at least we'd know if you're jumping at shadows.'

'Oh, you— You're a dunce poking the gods with a needle! Why can't you leave well enough alone?' So packed with anguish was her tone, it sent shivers down my back.

Annoyed I couldn't see her, I hunted for a weak spot in the hedge.

'Are you any better?' Haze asked. 'Where's the sense in refusing to tell me why we have to move all the time? I'm an adult and I've never spent more than a few months in any one place my whole life. I'm sick of it! I don't have friends, or a home, or a future. I'm done with a wayfarer's life. It's not for me.' There was another long silence before he spoke again. 'Taygen and I are sparring tomorrow.'

'It's more likely the fellow will guide Hervan's squad here in the middle of the night!'

'Why would he do that? Taygen's got no idea you and I have any connection. He knows nothing whatsoever about me!'

Innata didn't answer.

I found a gap in the hedge and squeezed my head and shoulders in further so I could see better through the leaves. A woman leant against the jamb of the open doorway with her back to Haze and the room. In the fading light I didn't see much of the detail apart from her slim figure and dark hair. From the conversation she was the elder of the two. Her clothing was that of a burgher's wife or daughter: plain, neat, probably good quality, for it had a collar and cuffs.

'We leave tomorrow,' she said. 'After I visit the dressmaker.'

'You can leave. I'm not sure that I'll go with you.'

After hearing that, I expected some kind of explosive argument to ensue, but neither of them spoke again. Haze came out to pee inside the latrine — pickle me, I would have just watered the garden! — and returned to the house, after which I heard the clink of dishes, the splash of a drink being poured and other everyday sounds. I decided not to wait for any resumption of conversation, but set off back home instead.

That mincing dandy Haze was going to pick my brains for information, was he? Well, he had another think coming...

*

When I reached our cottage, I found my whole family there, full of chatter and laughter, and supper on the table. My sister, Salli; her husband and their baby; my brother, Javelin; my Pa and my Mam: with all of them crowded into the downstairs, nothing much was required of me except to eat my supper and offer to burp Salli's baby when she released him from the breast. The realisation that a family gathering like this was unlikely ever to happen again brought a sharp sense of loss, surprising me. Did I really want to go to Templebridge? When I said as much to Jav in an aside, he just laughed.

'Think, how much time do I get to spend with the family when I'm right here in Breakedge?' he asked. 'Could only come tonight 'cause Pa fixed it for me. Otherwise, I'd be out on patrol, south side of town.'

'Trouble?' I asked. On the other side of the table, Pa's proud gaze never left Jav, even though his conversation was with Salli. I tried not to be jealous. Truth told, it was not difficult; Jav was a good brother to me, kind of heart, generous. He was easy to like.

'Reports of vagabonds appearing out of nowheres, down by the lye factory,' he said. 'Haven't been able to find 'em yet, though. Still, we have to keep an eye out. The moment summat like that happens, folk start muttering 'bout redweavers and Netherfolk.'

'Is that what they are?'

He shrugged. 'Gods know, but the gabble 'bout their increasing number has grown louder all over Talodiac these past few years and, yes, some red bastards been winkled out and executed. If redweavers want to live undetected, Breakedge would be a good place to come to. Pa's right. We need more archpriests who can see their conjury.'

Before then, I hadn't been much interested in redweavers. There'd always been scares about them and their evil spells, but I'd never actually met anyone who admitted to being ensorcelled by one. Even now, what I'd seen seemed more tragic than frightening. I changed the subject. 'Do you still have that quarterstaff of yours?'

'Sure. You want it? I have no use for it now, but it's a good pole.'

I nodded.

'I'll leave it by the front door tomorrow morning at dawn, on our way out.'

He left shortly afterwards, at the same time as Salli and her family. Mam excused herself and went upstairs to bed, leaving Pa and me chatting over the last ale in the pot. I fully intended to tell him about Haze and Innata, even toying with confessing my whole sorry predicament with Spake, but Pa turned the subject to weaponry and what arms I should carry for safety, so I asked his opinion about carrying a quarterstaff. Rather to my surprise, he thought it a good idea. 'But,' he added, 'if I was standing in your boots, I'd train up the skill you've had in wagon loads since you were 'yak-calf high.'

I blinked in surprise, not knowing what he meant.

'Throwing things,' he said.

I laughed, remembering times when I'd aroused ire in the family by pelting Salli with dried gopi nuts, or lobbing stones at neighbourhood lads, or hurling mud-balls at Jav. 'You can't be serious,' I said. 'Defend myself tossing pebbles?'

Wordlessly, he handed me a pewter spoon from the table. 'Throw that,' he said. 'Land it on the fourth step of the stairs, with the handle facing towards us.'

I shrugged, took the spoon, and spun it across the room. It landed exactly as he'd asked. I did have an instinct for that sort of thing, a knack of being able to weigh something in my hand, sense how it would spin and then adjust the throw to fit the distance. It was a kid's trick I'd honed with practice, not something for an armsman.

Elbows on the table, he leaned towards me. 'In a fight, anything can be a weapon, and you got a knack, not only for whackin' whatever you aim at, but for hitting it with the chosen end of your missile. Any idea how hard that is? Work on that, and you'll always have a weapon to hand, 'cause you can always find something to throw.'

I'd never thought of that ability as a mode of combat or defence, and I half believed he was joshing me, but I tucked the idea away for further thought and brought the subject back to why he was in town. 'I know Breakedge better than you. Why don't you let me help you with whatever has brought you here? You looking for someone? I know all the hiding places, I know who the snitches are, I know who to ask.'

He grimaced. 'Eager to get rid of me, are you?'

'Hardly.' The opposite in fact. He had a squad at his back and, as a last resort, I was going to have to swallow my stupid pride and ask his help to save me being swept up in Spake's nastiness.

'I told you,' he said, 'I'm on the King's business, and tattling is one thing a kingsman doesn't do if he wants to keep his head perched on his neck. 'Sides, would be besmirching me honour.'

'But if you're looking for information, you have to ask questions of someone! Why not me? At least you can trust me not to babble like a leaky bucket!'

'Maybe so,' he conceded. 'Tell me this: who's the best goldsmith in town, the fellow who makes the best jewellery? And second, which tailor or dressmaker uses the most skilled seamstresses?'

I wasn't sure if he seriously wanted to know, but I gave him straight answers anyway. 'Master Colper is the goldsmith you'd want. Best by far. The rest are just pawnbrokers and jobbers doing repair work. The tailor? They'd all be in Needle Street, I bet. Easy enough to find out.'

'My point, exactly. Got the information we needed today, from a seamstress. As I said, this is the King's business. Fewer folk who know just what we want, the better, and that includes stickybeak sons!'

'Well, I do have some informatio—'

He tossed down the last of his ale and stood. 'Forget it, Taygen. I'm off to bed.' With that, he picked up his cloak and headed out the door to return to the barracks.

I couldn't make up my mind if I was hurt or just plain furious at the dismissal. Well, if I'm to be totally honest — and I suppose one ought to be when one's neck will soon be heading in the direction of a noose — I was more scared than wounded, and more sick in the stomach than angry. I was dead tired too. Too much had happened that day for me to process it all.

There you have it, Lady Sianta. The exact moment my treason began: when I should have told my father, believing him to be an officer of the King's Guard, of an overheard conversation that concerned him. I chose not to do so, partly because he'd hurt my feelings and partly because I was consumed by my own troubles. Strange, all I've written so far occurred not so long ago, yet now it seems another time, when I was still a guileless pup.

I am not that person any more.

8

Haze was already on the grazing common behind his house when I arrived the following morning, in his shirt sleeves, wearing another neat kerchief around his neck, a different colour this time. He liked his fancy garnish, did Haze. His velvet jerkin had been tossed on to the grass. I watched him practice a sequence of manoeuvres with the graceful agility of a leaping taldeer: elegant, yes, but also powerful. I wasn't the only watcher; several of the milkmaids on the far side of the common took time off from their morning tasks to stare at him, in ways I would have enjoyed had they been looking at me.

When Haze saw I'd arrived, he grinned and beckoned me over.

'You have an audience,' I remarked.

'A bunch of gigglers.' He didn't bother to glance in their direction. 'Ah, you've brought your own staff! That makes things much simpler. Shall we start?'

I expected he'd be more interested in picking my brains about my father. Instead, he ran through the basic moves of fighting with a quarterstaff. I expected that I'd soon end up being the butt of his expertise, emerging from the practice a mass of bruises and battered pride, but that didn't happen either. He was a good teacher. He had me imitating his moves again and again until my movements were smooth and controlled. Lunging, defending, blocking, attacking. One hand, both hands, holding the staff in different places, palms up, palms down — all more complicated than I'd thought it would be.

About an hour later, he said it was time to put some of what I'd learned into a fight situation, but even then it wasn't a free-for-all. He told me how he would attack, and how

I should defend myself. Which sounded a lot easier than it proved to be. His attacks were real and hard. My wrists ached, and in spite of knowing how to block particular moves, I took a battering, which elicited a frown rather than a grin, as if I was proving a disappointment. He lectured me each time I made a mistake, and then made me repeat the move until I had it correct.

'Stop being so worried about your nuts,' he said at one point when I'd kept my guard too low. 'I've no intention of threatening your private treasure chest in this first session. That comes in lesson five!'

A couple of milkmaids walked past with their pails full, laughing. Haze rapped my knuckles when my attention was diverted.

Annoyed, I switched my hold and launched into an attack, jabbing at him with one end of my staff. He stepped back sharply and trod in a fresh cowpat. As his feet slipped through the mess of green muck, he flung up his arms in a vain attempt to maintain balance, only to thump down hard on his backside instead.

Already off balance, still leaning into my attack, I fell forward over his body. Our two staves went flying. I'd tried to save myself, but ended up with my hands on his chest and my nose buried somewhere in the region below his navel, only to be tossed off on to the grass with remarkable speed. I sat up, my mind a muddled mix of impressions, none of them making sense, not right then.

The milkmaids left, almost doubled over with laughter.

I stared at Haze, nonplussed.

And bless me if he didn't turn red.

Bright red.

'Sweet Saffrin!' I blurted after a startled, speechless moment. 'You're a *girl!*'

He — no, *she* — picked up his — *her* fallen staff.

'Girl?' Her lip curled. 'I think I'm old enough to be considered a woman. If that sticks in your craw, then try "female".'

'You're a — a hoodwinking *minx* is what you are!'

And I'd been as blind as a flea in a rabbit hole. Saffrin's balls, she must have been laughing at me. What a hickgoose I'd been! Gritting my teeth, I levered myself up, trying to brush the cow manure from my knees and still cling to a vestige of dignity.

'I think we had both better wash at the pump,' she said, turning to look at her backside. She was definitely in a worse state than I was, but that was cold comfort. Without another word she headed down the slope towards their hut with her staff and her jerkin in her hand.

I trailed after her, trying to make sense of what had happened, my thoughts all over the place. She'd said she wasn't saffrine. If that was true, she wasn't presenting herself as a man because she felt herself to be male; she was a woman in disguise. A deliberate deception, even to the extent of walking with a man's gait, wearing her hair short in a man's style, taking a man's name, wearing a man's clothes.

Damn him.

Her.

True, I could now see a few things that might have given me a clue: a voice that was pitched a shade higher than an average male, the kerchief that presumably concealed her lack of a man's voice box, and the line of her jaw, perhaps a little feminine now that I thought about it.

Confound it, though, she was one tough girl. Female.

I jogged after her until we were side by side. 'Why,' I asked, 'was this mummery necessary? If you were just trying to make a fool of me, you succeeded, but what was the point?'

'Oh, for pity's sake, why would it be about *you*? I've been travelling this way for years — because it's *safer*. That's all. My elder sister and I travel together. She's been looking after me since she was fourteen, when my mother died giving birth to me and our dad scarpered. When I was small, we were always lucky to find decent wayfarers who added us to their family. But later, with me sprouting tits and hips, we'd just be two women alone, rabbits for the gutting. Plump pigeons for the dining. On the road, no one cares much for women foolish enough to travel without a man's protection. When I was ten or so and shot up in height like a weed in the crop, I started dressing as a boy and learned to stick fight. Didn't make me entirely safe, of course, but it did help.'

All logical enough, but far too smooth. It sounded like a practised story.

'What is your name?'

'Hazelle.' Still no parent names to give me a lineage. 'I'd be obliged if you would continue to call me Haze.'

We strode on in silence to the door of her house.

The only access to their backyard pump was through the cottage, so I took a good look around as we went. A single room containing a table and two chairs in the middle, a webbed bed frame with quilts neatly folded and a brick fireplace at the far end with a flue in place of a chimney. The floor was beaten earth. Only one personal item really attracted my attention: an embroidery hoop on the table with a half completed pattern on the linen cloth it contained. Salli did piecework for a dressmaker, but nothing as fine as this.

When we stepped out into the backyard, I asked, 'Your sister's not home then?'

'Obviously not.' She swung a bucket under the pump and reached for the handle, but I was there before her. She snorted then, saying, 'Ah, a proper gentle-fellow! Brought up mannered, I see.'

The pumping produced a miserable tickle of water, which is normal in Breakedge. She stripped off her shirt so that she could wash the back of it, displaying a chemise with lacing designed to confine her breasts tight to her torso. More deliberate deception. Lucky for her, she wasn't overly endowed in that area.

I looked away, feeling vaguely cheated by her deception and stupid for not having seen through it. As I attended to my own clothes, I thought of Pa speaking of dressmakers and seamstresses, of Haze's sister speaking fearfully of Pa, to the point where she wanted to leave in a hurry. All just a weird coincidence, or something more? To me, it sounded as if Innata possibly thought Pa's squad of Royal Guards might have come to Breakedge looking for her, and her little sister was unaware of why. A heaviness settled deep in my stomach akin to a meal of unleavened dough. Right then, I would not have wagered a rickling on the odds that Haze had been in my vicinity in the market accidentally. She could have been following me, because I was Hervan's son.

Damn it, why hadn't Pa told me who he was looking for, and why? I was the rabbit caught between a hunting fox and a hungry lynx, not knowing which way to run. My loyalty ought to be to my father and the King. Haze had not been honest with me, so betraying her and her sister should not have mattered.

Yet...

'Does your father come to see you often?' she asked as she washed off the last of the cow manure.

She appeared oblivious to her state of undress, so I tried to copy her dispassion by neither staring as I wanted to do, nor turning my back. If she could be so indifferent to my gaze, I could at least pretend nonchalance. 'No. Not anymore.'

'Why is he here, then?'

'Who knows? He never tells me his business.' I shrugged. 'Does your sister confide in you?'

She froze momentarily and I knew that I had caught her off guard. 'I suppose not.' A grudging admission.

'Annoying, isn't it?' I smiled at her, but she did not reciprocate.

Instead, she said, 'I've heard of your father before, you know. Wayfarers talk to one another, pass on the gossip, that sort of thing. Hervan's supposed to be a captain in the Royal Guards, yet he and his squad travel the kingdom from duchy to duchy, asking questions. Kingsmen, certainly, but not Guardsmen. People say they've been hunting someone for years.'

I tried to pretend I wasn't shocked to the sole of my boots. For *years*? Pa never spoke much about his duties, but he'd certainly implied that his squad were King's Guards.

He'd *lied*? For years?

'People gossip,' I said, scrubbing at my own clothes, wanting desperately to deny what she was saying. 'I wouldn't take too much notice of wayside jackanapes' chatter if I were you. Unless, of course, it's you he's looking for.'

She snorted. 'Do I look like a miscreant worth chasing from the time I was in a toddler's skirts?'

'Your sister, then?'

'Innata is a stitcher of embroidery!'

By this time, I'd removed the worst of the manure. I bent to pick up Jav's pole. Hazelle's quarterstaff was propped up against the wall of the house, out of her reach.

'Maybe you two are redweavers,' I said, tightening my grip on the pole in case she reacted. 'Pa helped an archpriest get rid of some of them yesterday.'

She looked across at me, at ease and laughing. 'Ah, how I wish. Reckon possessing a conjury or two would be an advantage when some cockchafer gets antsy at the sight of a lass on her own.'

She was still half-dressed, and apparently unaware of my attempts not to stare at her chest while my unruly thoughts wondered how big her tits would be if they weren't so confined.

'I have to be off,' I said eventually. 'Thank you for the lesson.'

'Come again,' she said. 'I'm always there in the field in the mornings.' Not a word about her sister leaving Breakedge.

I nodded, though my goal just then was never to have anything more to do with her. I had to tell Pa everything, even if his reticence about his mission annoyed the piss out of me.

*

As I plodded up the narrow laneway that led back into town, stray theories about Hazelle and her sister bubbled about in my brain like ingredients in a hot stewpot. If what Hazelle said was true, then it was hard to see why either she or her sister would be targeted by kingsmen.

But then, she might be lying. The conversation I'd overheard the night before bothered me. Innata was afraid of my father but wouldn't even tell her sister why.

I gave up thinking about it and turned my mind to what to do for the rest of the day.

It was still early. Another gaggle of milkmaids ahead of me were making their way back into the heart of the city, lugging their full pails to Tedman's Dairy. It wasn't until the lane opened on to one of the town alleyways that I encountered someone coming in the opposite direction. A single woman bothered by the attentions of a stray dog that must have sniffed something edible in her marketing basket.

Frowning, she switched her load from hand to hand to discourage its interest.

Innata? She was the right height and build to match the woman I'd seen at the cottage, and she was heading in that direction. If I'd had to guess her age, I could only have said somewhere over thirty. She didn't resemble Hazelle much, though. Everything about her was more delicate: features, figure, hands. Not a woman who would grab a quarterstaff to defend herself.

The mongrel lowered its head, bared its teeth and raised its hackles. The growl in its throat rattled nastily.

As I drew level, I swung the staff up and shook it under the dog's nose in a threatening gesture. It slunk away, tail down, giving a single wary look over its shoulder that might have melted my heart in other circumstances. I glanced back at the woman to find her gaze fixated first on my staff, then my face. Her blank expression merged into something that bit through to my heart. All I read there spoke of terrible pain, a grief so deep it could have no other voice, as if no words would ever be enough. We both halted, marooned in a sliver of time while her pain spoke to me, yet neither of us said aught.

Then she turned, intending to continue on her way.

'Wait!' I said.

She stopped and turned to look back at me, shoulders tensed, misery writ in every bone of her body, even as her defiance raged at me from her eyes.

'Tell me why Hervan — my father — hunts you.' *Please.*

Why did I ask? Not because I necessarily thought it was true, but because her face told me that she was convinced he did. Moreover, she believed her freedom was over.

And me — well, now I'd glimpsed her pain, I wanted a reason not to tell Pa about her or Hazelle. I don't know what sort of a reply I expected, but it wasn't the one she gave.

Her lips curled slightly into the merest suggestion of a mocking smile. 'If only I could,' she said. 'Are you going to tell him where to find us?'

'Not my business.'

She gave a disbelieving smile. 'I've never done aught to harm either of you,' she said and walked away.

I stood there like an idiot, watching her. She didn't look back.

I knew I should tell Pa about her, even as I would hate myself for it. If he was hunting her, then it had to be for a crime against the King. A thief or an ordinary criminal could be dealt with by local assizes or one of the God Courts. Only treason against the Crown would involve a squad of kingsmen.

But that wasn't my only problem. There was Spake. I had to talk to Pa about him too ... Gods Decasian, I couldn't imagine how I would find the words for that!

Perhaps I'd do better to ask Jav for advice first. After all, what else are elder brothers for, if not to help out their witless younger siblings?

*

A nd what d'you know. I still have paper left. But the lamp is dimming, and it's too dark in this blasted cell to see what I have writ. Never mind, you will be here soon, as it seems that it's your custom to come a-visiting me only in the middle of the night, isn't it, Sianta?

I wonder why that is.

9

Halfway home I ran into one of Master Spake's runner boys.

'Oi yay!' he cried when he saw me. 'Reckon you walkin' barefoot towards a heap o' coals, Tay! Master says you got t'be on the ready when he asks, else your pretty sister gets her skirts ripped by them that's not her lawful wedded fella, if y'get me meaning.'

I jabbed my quarterstaff at him and he skipped out of range into the crowded street. I would have clobbered him hard if I'd had the chance, and he knew it.

Those *bastards!*

Salli, who knew nothing about my stupidities? They were *threatening* her — mother of a suckling babe? I swallowed bile, the bitterness a burning reminder that there's always a price for idiocy. Curse me witless, I *knew* what Spake was capable of; I'd seen him beat a boy to pulp just for giving him cheek. What the ten hells was I going to do? *I* could leave the city, but Salli couldn't.

Panic beat its wings against my ribs and sucked my mouth dry. I hunched my shoulders, ducked my head, and plodded on to the barracks.

The guard on duty at the gate informed me that Jav wouldn't be off duty until late evening and there was no way I could see him until then. Pa and his squad, on the other hand, were down in the city. The fellow thought they'd headed for the artisans' quarter, so that's where I went next. When I hadn't found them by midday, I gave up the search and returned home. After helping Mam with the chores around the house, I walked out into the orchard to chuck things. If Pa thought throwing stuff was a useful skill for a grown man to have, then I was willing to turn a boy's trick into a weapon for a man not permitted to wear a sword.

Two hours later, fascinated by the trajectories, learning as much from the failures as from the successes and nursing a sore shoulder as a consequence, I picked up one of the items I had been using to practice, intending to throw it at a mark on the trunk of an olive tree.

'Taygen!'

I turned to see my mother standing in the doorway, hands on hips, her face fixed in horrified disbelief. 'What rot done got into your brain-box? That's the kitchen poker!'

'Sorry,' I muttered, sounding like a lad barely out of his toddler pinny.

'And if you've damaged any of my trees—' Her lips pursed up as if she'd sucked a sour lemon.

'No. Of course not.' Well, not much...

To be honest, mostly I was impressed by the success I'd had at hitting targets exactly the way I'd intended. I was *good* at this.

*

Pa came back late that night, with his squad. I was waiting for him on the roadside near the barracks. There was enough starlight to see the look on his face when he caught sight of me: right royally pissed off. We weren't supposed to approach Pa when he was on duty.

He waved his men on into the barracks and waited until they were out of earshot before he growled, 'What have you got to say for yourself?'

'Pa, think I got information 'bout the person you're hunting. I know wh—'

'I'm on the King's business, and you don't stick your snotty nose into it.' When I opened my mouth to protest, his next words were spaced out like whip cracks. 'Is. That. Quite. Clear?'

'But—'

'Did you not hear me?' he thundered.

I couldn't understand what had got into him, but I knew when I was beaten. 'Yes.'

'Yes, what?'

'Yes, sir.'

'Go to bed. First thing tomorrow you pack yer things. A few essentials to take to Templebridge. Change of clothes, blanket, best boots. We'll have just one talyak bullock and a cart for packs and supplies. I got yer a gelded taldeer of your own, but you can't fit much in saddlebags. Bear that in mind. I got a furred cloak for you, too.'

'We leaving tomorrow?' Lord gods, when was I going to have time to do something about Spake? Tomorrow night was the Burgher's Ball when I was supposed to be stealing from the Counting House.

'Not tomorrow, no. More like we'll be off the day after. Early.'

He turned on his heel and followed his squad into the barracks.

I stood there, fuming because he'd refused to listen, a stupid lump of hurt in my throat. Even so, I was excited as a sprog with a full honey jar all to himself. I was going to Templebridge and a new life. A voice in my head said it was more than I deserved, but I dimmed its whisper.

Returning home, I sorted out what to take, all the while chewing over everything I'd learned that day. If Haze was right about my father searching for someone for years, then his quarry must surely have committed some heinous crime against the monarchy. It was hard to believe that someone was Innata, but if it was, she deserved her fate and I had to find a way to tell Pa what I knew, even though his resistance to listening to me was beyond weird. Of course, maybe Hazelle was a liar and none of this was anything more than garbage.

Was she worth one more try on the off chance I might learn something of value to Pa? I decided she was, even as I acknowledged that what to do about Spake and his venomous threat towards Salli was a far worse problem. Reluctantly, I had to admit I was out of my depth.

So I went to see Jav.

Luckily, the guard on the gate knew me well and was obliging enough to send a message to my brother. From Jav's scowl when he came, he was not overly pleased.

'I've only got to the next bell,' he said, tone ungracious, 'then I'm on mess duty. What's wrong?'

I'll paint a thick fog over much of that conversation.

Suffice it to say, I was on the receiving end of a big brother's scorn for ever having anything to do with Spake. We parted with Jav cursing me roundly in language I won't repeat here, but conceding that he would *perhaps* make sure Pa came to my aid, *if* I could think of some miracle that would put Spake in jail instead of me. His final words as he left to go on duty were, 'And you better think of something quick or I'll slaughter you myself!'

He said all that without me telling him that I was due to break into the Counting House the following night, or that Spake had threatened Salli. Yes, that's right; I was a coward.

*

A nd there, Lady Sianta, I will halt my story until you supply me with another bundle of quills. Oh, and thanks

92

GLENDA LARKE

for telling me that they don't hang common folk for treason, only aristos, and so I am to be crushed to death by having rocks piled on my chest, one at a time until I die. Slowly. For some reason or other, I'd assumed treason merited hanging. Ah well, I guess there's not much I can do about it, is there?

I await your next midnight appearance. I guess you don't like being seen sneaking into a prison on a regular basis, hence the night owl visits in a voluminous cloak. So, the question is: who are you afraid of, Sianta? Or perhaps: what are you hiding?

10

Ah, that was an interesting chat we had last night, Sianta. And no, I am still not prepared to tell you all I found out about Haze. You'll have to wait until I've written it down. One should never spoil a good story by asking for the end first!

So, on with my tale...

After an almost sleepless night spent making — and largely discarding — plans, I reached the cow meadow in the grey pre-dawn light, thinking I'd arrive there first. I didn't. Haze was waiting. I watched for a moment as she practised with her quarterstaff, whirling it through an early morning mist that still tendrilled across grass wet with dew. As if she had not a care in the world.

When she saw me, she welcomed me with a smile. 'I wasn't sure you'd come back after what happened yesterday.'

'What's a little cowpat between friends?'

'Revealing, maybe?'

It had certainly been that. 'To be honest, I wasn't sure that *you* would still be here.'

'Why not?'

'Oh, no reason really. It's just that I bumped into your sister yesterday on the way back and she looked ... scared. Does she know I'm Hervan's son?'

'Scared? Innata's scared of nobody. And yes, she knows. Why would that worry her?'

I shrugged. 'My mistake.'

'You haven't been telling Captain Hervan that offal about us being redweavers, have you?'

'That was a joke. A poor one. Believe me, I don't joke about things like that to my pa.'

'I should hope not. Shall we spar?'

We worked through the routines she'd shown me. I was just beginning to relax into the rhythm of the movements when everything went cockeyed. She began spinning her staff so fast over her hands that it became a blurred circle between us. I stepped back. Or tried to. The moment I shifted my weight on to my back foot, the end of her pole shot between my legs to trip me up. I used my own pole as a crutch to halt my fall, so she used hers as a lever to make sure I lost balance. In a state of rueful shock and unable to save myself, I toppled flat on to my back. I had just enough nous to hold onto my staff, but she was still too fast for me. She rammed her pole down across my throat, her hands gripping the wood on either side, applying enough pressure to make breathing difficult, but still possible. Worse was the positioning of her left knee pressing firmly into my groin. Most of her weight was on the other knee at my side, but the promise of possible agony was there.

Her face was a handspan from mine and I had no idea how I was going to free myself.

In the end, I groped for humour. 'You win,' I said. Well, more gasped than said and, yes, it was a sad attempt at being funny.

Haze scowled. 'Oh, rest assured of that. I have an idea this is going to be horribly painful for you.' No humour in her reply.

'Aaagh— Ah, really? Not necessary, I assure you!'

'I hope not. All you have to do is tell me what you know that I don't.'

'L-lots of things, I imagine. I love mangel-wurzels, for example. I can't hold a tune. Sound like a cat in heat if a try to sing. I—'

She leaned more firmly on the quarterstaff, making it harder for me to breathe. 'I'm not in the mood.'

My right arm was trapped under the staff, along with my neck. I flexed my left arm, which was slightly less compressed because I had fallen with it in a more outstretched position. If I could yank it from under the pole, maybe I could box her on the nose with my fist. Or something.

She felt the tensing of my shoulder muscle and reacted by pressing her knee a little harder into my balls. 'Don't you dare,' she said. 'Is Hervan coming after Innata?'

'I don't know,' I said, the words rasping in my throat. 'He doesn't tell me the King's business. He really doesn't.'

'Then what made you think he's a threat to her?'

'I don't know that he is! If you must know, it was Innata who said he was, not my pa. I heard her. I — I was spying on your house the other night when you were talking about it.'

Her eyes widened. 'You sneaking mizzler—' She was really angry now.

'I thought *you'd* been spying on *me*. And you were, weren't you? You know, tit for tat.'

She deflated like a ruptured puffball, rolling away from me, all fight drained out of her. I pushed the quarterstaff away and sat up, rubbing my bruised throat gingerly.

'You were *listening* to us? You ... you utter rag-bag!'

I swallowed. It hurt, so I nodded instead of saying anything.

She lay there for a moment longer, then stood, brushing the grass from her knees. 'It's true, isn't it? He really is looking for her. It's the only explanation for the way she's been acting. But why?'

'You don't know?'

'No! If you were spying on us the other night you must know that! Has he found out where we're staying yet?'

'I told you, I don't know. And if I did, I wouldn't tell you. Look, my pa's a kingsman. I trained with the Border Rangers and schooled in the barracks' classroom. My ma is a proxy-wife. I'm not about to betray everything I was brought up to revere. Like Talodiac. Like my fealty to my king. I don't change my loyalties with every swing of the wind.'

She gave a puzzled shake of her head. 'And yet this patriotic son neglected to tell his father the kingsman that he knows where Innata lives?'

'I would've if he'd let me,' I admitted. 'But he didn't.'

'Saffrin's balls, Taygen, you are so *weird*.'

I could have said that she was equally strange to believe anything I said, but she didn't give me a chance. In fact, she turned and unexpectedly raced away in the direction of her house. I bent to retrieve my quarterstaff before dashing after her, but she had too much of a lead for me to catch up. By the time I'd arrived at the door of Tom the Pewterman's house, she was on her way out again.

'She's not here.' She sounded calm, but the look in her eyes told me fear was shredding her equilibrium. 'And her sewing is missing. She's gone to deliver her embroidery to the dressmaker.' She dragged in a deep breath, then whirled away, running up the path towards the city edge. I tore after her yet again. Gods, but she was fast!

She yelled back at me over her shoulder. 'Your father didn't ask you because he already knows how she makes her living, doesn't he?'

Useless to tell her I hadn't told him. I caught up to run alongside, asking between breaths, 'Maybe time's come for you to cut the apron strings? If Pa really has tracked Innata on the King's business, then he'll either lug her back to Templebridge to pay for whatever she did, or he'll kill her now. King's orders. Either way, there's nothing you can do to stop it, honest. You'd do better to quietly find a wayfarer caravan heading north.'

I was still trying to patch together their whole story. Difficult, because there were so many elements that didn't add up. Surely, if Hervan really had been searching for Innata for so long, he would also be aware she was travelling with someone else. Moreover, if Innata was so important that tracing her whereabouts warranted a squad of five searching for years, Pa should have the resources of all eight duchies at his disposal. Why had no one been able to find her before this? Surely his squad couldn't have been the only people looking for her! And what could they possibly want her for, anyway? It didn't make *sense*.

Maybe nothing about Haze's story was true. I suspected she could have looked me straight in the eye and fibbed without as much as the quiver of an eyelid. Damn Pa for not confiding in me!

The number of people on the streets slowed us when we hit the edge of the town, but Haze did her best to barrel through to Needle Street. I followed, knowing her attempt to warn Innata was a useless gesture. Pa had enough information, gleaned from who knows where, to have dressmakers, tailors and jewellers under watch.

Needle Street linked two main thoroughfares and at this hour of the morning was particularly busy. At the northern end, half a dozen shabbily dressed men were playing flip-coin in the street, betting on the throws of a pair of rickling pieces. I recognised two of them as Border Rangers.

Haze plunged on without hesitation and I tucked myself behind her, head turned away from the gamblers. Halfway along the street Innata emerged from a doorway, basket on arm. She didn't notice us, but headed our way, walking as briskly as possible in the throng of people. Through a gap in the jostling bustle behind her, I glimpsed the red of a guard's surcoat. Several surcoats.

I grabbed Haze's arm and yanked her back. Before she could protest, I had hustled her against the wall of a building on our left. 'Hervan,' I whispered into her ear as she opened her mouth to ask me what the blazing hells I was doing. 'There, with his squad.'

She tried to shake me off, elbowing me in the ribs. 'Let me go,' she snapped. We scuffled momentarily as I tried to keep her from linking up with Innata.

'Gods below, will you stop it!' I hissed into her ear. 'Don't draw attention to yourself. Those gamblers over there are rangers. Hervan has help.'

She stopped struggling then and swore at me instead. I blinked, taken aback by her familiarity with the words ripping from her tongue. From behind Innata, Hervan snapped out an order. Haze wouldn't have heard him in the babble of the market, but I did.

'Arrest her.'

The gamblers had abandoned their game and were already heading Innata's way, but two of the kingsmen, both carrying halberds, reached her first. One of them grabbed her by the right shoulder from behind. I found out later his name was Folman and he always was a bit of a bumbler.

I think he expected Innata to turn towards him, or possibly try to escape forwards. Instead, she jerked backwards in shock and twisted at the same time, just as the second guard, a fella called Petch, lowered his halberd on her left side. Then, in a mere sliver of time, everything cascaded into a horrendous disaster.

It was an accident. Petch didn't mean to cut her. It was just that his blade was viciously sharp and she jerked right into it as she turned. It caught her on the side of the neck and her skin parted like roasted goose under a carving knife.

In a flash, the street changed. Several women screamed and almost everyone froze, at least for a moment. Innata gazed in a puzzled fashion at the blood drenching her sleeve, dribbling down to her hand. A heartbeat later, the crowd fanned out away from her as skittish as startled pigeons. The appalled expression of the two guards responsible reflected their awareness of the magnitude of the disaster. Petch actually flung his halberd from him as if he wanted to disown what he'd done. Even Hervan, a step or two away with his remaining two guards, looked stunned.

Innata swayed, gasping. Her hands clutched at her neck. Blood flowed through her fingers. People began to skedaddle in earnest then. Everyone knows it's best not to meddle in the business of King's Guards.

Pa slammed Petch with a single backhanded blow, sending the fellow crashing to the ground. Innata sank to her knees, gently folding up like a rag doll. Folman caught her and lowered her the rest of the way to the ground. Haze moaned and started towards her sister. I jerked her back again, wrapping my arms around her from behind, speaking into her ear all the while.

'Think! You can't help her. They can. It was an accident. Let them deal with it.'

'They've *killed* her!' The words were no more than a shocked whisper, poignantly muted. Her muscles tensed as her hand clawed around her quarterstaff. If she could have swung it — at me, or Pa or any of the guards, she would have.

I held on tight, clamping her arms to her sides and spoke from between gritted teeth straight into her ear. 'Look at her. She's not dead. Look at Hervan's face. He's devastated. They'll take her to the healers at Goddess Hetha's Temple.' It was the woman's only chance. Gods, but there was blood everywhere…

Haze quietened then, into a deadly calm.

'I'm going to tell you what to do right now,' I said, still in a whisper. 'Go to the temple. Pretend you have terrible toothache. The attendants will take you into the inner ward where the healing rooms are. When Pa and his men bring Innata in for treatment, you'll be forgotten. Play it by ear. Find out how bad she's hurt. Might even be able to speak to her, 'cause the guards won't be allowed into the ward. If my pa bullies his way in, press your kerchief to your face so he won't get a good look at you. Understand? Be clever, Haze. Find out as much as you can.'

I felt her body relax a little. She dragged in a rasping breath and nodded. 'Let go of me.'

By this time, folk who'd heard the screaming were pouring out from the shops and businesses to see what was happening. The rangers did their best to clear the street, but in the moments following there were so many people between us and where Innata lay that we couldn't see her.

I released Haze and she turned to face me. I said, 'I'll see my pa later today. I'll find out more then. I'll meet you after dusk, on top of the hill near the barracks. I'll tell you everything I find out. I wouldn't go home, if I was you.'

There was nothing to read in the look she gave me then. It was as if she had wiped every emotion away, leaving only an empty shell.

'I won't betray you. Trust me.'

She nodded again, her sudden calm almost unnatural. 'Why are you doing this?' she asked.

'I have no piddling notion,' I said, and that was the truth. I ought to have handed her over to my father. I ought to have been supporting the kingsmen, no matter what.

Gods, but she was iron-willed. She stared at me for a moment longer, then walked briskly away without even glancing back to where her sister lay.

I did, though.

I retreated into a doorway and kept watch. No one was looking my way and I was almost certain that neither Pa nor his squad had glimpsed me or Haze. Cyrrin hurried past, probably on his way to alert Goddess Hetha's Temple to expect a wounded woman. Folman dived into the shop of one of the tailors, to emerge a moment later with a length of cloth. He used it and a couple of halberds to fashion a make-shift pallet. Shortly afterwards the squad hurried past carrying Innata, with Pa to the fore bellowing at everyone to clear the way or they'd feel the flat of his sword. Petch looked sick.

*

I returned home. Morning chores had to be done, but my head whirled with problems, each one of them clawing away my peace of mind. If I just disappeared with Pa, Spake might come after my sister in revenge. How the godless hells could I stop him if I wasn't even in Breakedge anymore? How could I aid Haze without betraying my father and my king?

Why did I even want to?

Questions, but no answers. I didn't even know if she trusted me enough to turn up come nightfall.

After choosing odd-shaped and unbalanced items from the house and garden, I went out to hurl these projectiles at a mark on the garden wall. Encouraged by how fast I improved, and how much fun it was to weigh a new missile in my hand and assess its trajectory beforehand, I almost missed the moment my father and his squad returned to the barracks. It was midday when he finally put in an appearance back at our gate, and he was alone. When I approached him, he looked exasperated and said, 'Our departure is delayed. I'll let you know when.'

He turned away as if to continue on to the barracks. I said hurriedly, 'I heard your men beheaded a woman down in Needle Street.'

He gave a snort of disgust. 'Gods below, gossip is the piss of the uninformed. No one was killed. 'Twas an accident.'

'And the woman?'

'Under guard 'n' being healed.'

'A prisoner? Will she be going with us to Templebridge?'

'That's the idea.' He sounded as if he was speaking between gritted teeth. 'With the help of Goddess's healers, she should be recovered enough by day after tomorrow. Be ready at dawn.'

'Who is she? You and four of you squad came here all this way to capture a single woman? What's so special about her?'

'She's a traitor to the Crown, been wanted for years. And 'tis none of your business. Saffrin spurn yer, Tay! Learn t'keep that mouth o' yours shut. Not yer place to question yer elders!'

'Pa, I—'

He turned his back on me and walked away. The bastard. I watched until he'd entered the barracks, an ache in the centre of my chest. It really hurt.

*

I was up on the hill at sunset, even though merely by being there I was making a commitment. I was betraying my father and my king and to this day I'm not entirely sure *why*. Because Pa wouldn't tell me what was going on? Because a perverse part of me believed Haze knew nothing of any treasonous plot and was therefore an innocent party? I even wondered if Hervan had the wrong woman; if Innata was innocent. Mostly, though, I suppose it was because I liked

Haze. And no, before you jump to conclusions, it wasn't because I was wondering how to get into her trousers. She was a damn sight too prickly for me to think that was a good idea. Still, she did fascinate me. For the first time in my life, I'd met a young woman I wanted as a *friend.*

If I'd known it was going to lead me to this prison cell, doubtless I would have done things differently.

When I arrived at the top of the hill, she wasn't there. It was a warm and pleasant evening, with the perfume of trumpet flowers heavy in the night air and all three moons hovering over the city like wax-paper lanterns. I made myself comfortable leaning against one of the boulders and wondered just how to deal with Spake.

By the time Haze arrived, several hours later, I had the bare framework of a mad plan born of desperation. I must have been insane, and if I'd had to put that particular idea into action, I doubt I'd be here now; I'd be dead. Fortunately, Haze drove all thoughts of it from my mind when she arrived. She was in such a terrible state I thought Innata must have died.

She clutched my arm and her hand was shaking. 'C-can we go somewhere private? Where there's some light. I have something that I want — that I *need* to show you.'

I eyed the bag she had slung over her shoulder. 'We can go to my house.'

'Your father—'

'He doesn't stay there, and my mother'll be sound asleep. Even if she hears us, she won't take any notice. She's used to me having friends over to chat and drink an ale or two.'

Once I lit the lamp in our kitchen a short time later, I was shocked to see how pale Haze was. She had a tight hold on her emotions, though, so I couldn't tell if she was scared, or shocked, or grieving, or bubbling over with rage. I waved towards a chair at the kitchen table and she collapsed into it.

'Is it Innata?' I asked as I went to pour her a drink.

'Yes. No. Yes. I mean, she's hurt, badly, but they say she won't die. The blade missed the jugular.' She dragged in a deep breath. 'I did what you suggested. No one took much notice of me, but I couldn't talk to her privately. The temple healers saved her, but she's very weak and in a lot of pain. She's still in the temple sick ward, but your festering father's left a heavy guard in the anteroom. He said he'd arrange a litter if she can't walk.'

'That's good news, surely.'

She shot me a sour look and downed half the contents of her mug. 'Good news that she's a prisoner about to be taken to Templebridge? Which is what I overheard. He saved her for a reason, didn't he? And I'll bet it wasn't to shower her with royal honours.' Digging into the bag she carried, she drew out a packet wrapped in oilcloth, which she laid on the scrubbed bare boards of the table. 'Everything I once knew is spinning every which-way, till I don't know if the sky's up or down. I don't understand what's true—'

I stared at her in total bewilderment.

'I have to trust you,' she whispered. 'You, the son of the man who's taking her to only-gods-know-what fate. You're the only person I know in this wretched city.'

'That's not true, surely. You're a wayfarer.' Wayfarers always travelled in groups for protection. She and Innata would never have crossed Southedge Duchy alone to come to Breakedge.

'I wouldn't trust any one of them with this. At least I know you won't sell what I'm going to tell you.'

It seemed a good time to be cautious. 'Are you sure? Have you forgotten how we met? I'm not exactly pure spring water, Haze. I can't make you any promises when I don't know what you're about to say.'

'I know. I'm damned if I even know why I trust you, except that you risked a lot to stop that awful man walloping that brat in the market.' She fiddled with the wrappings as if she couldn't decide whether to show me the contents or not. Finally, she launched into her story.

'Innata told me that if she died, I was to go and dig up her tin box. She always buried it whenever we stopped for any length of time. I thought — I always thought it was just her money. And her jewellery. All the years we've been travelling, whenever she couldn't make enough money with her embroidery, she'd sell a gem or some gold prised out of a piece of her jewellery. There always seemed to be an endless supply. I never really saw what was in the tin, though. I thought maybe she'd once been rich, and had run away. But she never, ever explained.'

'You're not her sister?'

'I don't know. She's never said.'

'So you lied to me?'

She shrugged. 'Maybe. Maybe not. I like to think I am her daughter, but she won't say because, well, maybe my father was not a nice man. Or maybe she didn't know who my father was.'

I blinked, surprised by her casual acceptance of a possibly murky family history. She took a steadying deep breath. 'I feared Captain Hervan's men might do something to make her tell them where she'd hidden her valuables, so after I left Hetha's temple, I dug up the tin box from under the hedge at the back of Tom the Pewterman's cottage.' She grimaced. 'And then I heard Hervan's men come to the front door. I took the tin and fled into the meadow. I hid in one of the empty cow byres and watched while they searched the cottage. They even ripped up the thatched roof! I waited until they were gone, then looked at what was in the box. There was some money. Also some rings, brooches, gold chains. And then there was *this*.'

She unfolded the oilcloth to reveal the most beautiful piece of jewellery I am ever likely to see in my lifetime.

I gazed at it. And gazed some more.

'Do you know what it is?' she asked.

I nodded. 'It's a carcanet. A jewelled collar. Worn like a necklace.'

'Not an ordinary necklace.'

'No. This one's got a pendant as well. Which is ... unusual.'

'Of a creature half lion, half eagle.'

'A griffin. The King's symbol.'

'She ... she must have stolen this.' She ran a finger around the glorious gold collar studded with diamonds, to where the pendant dangled at the front. And what a pendant! Faceted blue sapphires and rubies, linked by delicate bands of silver to shape a griffin in flight ... No. Not just any old necklace.

This was the Griffin Carcanet.

11

My jaw sagged. Sweet Saffrin, *Innata had stolen the Griffin Carcanet*? I hadn't even known it was missing. I was a thief, remember? Trained by Spake to know my jewels, and I'd heard of the most glorious carcanet ever made.

I sat there, staring. The beaten gold at the back of the collar had been unobtrusively plundered, with the two smallest plates missing as if someone had wanted to cash in unidentifiable gold in a hurry. The griffin itself, worth much more, was still whole, its gleaming ruby eyes shining and all its dark emeralds as deep-coloured as a midnight summer sky, a gorgeous creature made to nestle in the cleavage between a woman's breasts.

'Did you know Innata had this?' I asked, my voice a squeak.

'No!' She was indignant, but her voice wobbled. In that moment she was not the confident young woman I'd known. 'I'm—I'm guessing those blue chunky pebbles with the flat tops are sapphires, and those sparkly bits are probably not glass.'

I took a deep breath. 'It's called the Griffin Carcanet, made to be bestowed on the King's consort on the day she births an heir. Innata must have stolen it. That's why my father has been looking for her and why he wants to take her back to Templebridge.' I sighed and fingered the sapphires, trying not to drool. 'We'll be leaving the day after tomorrow.'

'I'll offer to give it back if they'll let her go. They will, won't they? I mean, it must be worth a great deal.'

'A fortune. And it's symbolic too, which is even more important. Every duchy donated diamonds or sapphires for the collar when they all united into the Kingdom of Talodiac. If you think Pa will let you go free, you're dreaming.'

'Then stop being such a prattling poser, Taygen, and tell me what I should *do!'*

That was rich. She had never given me the slightest encouragement to tell her what to do before. 'You can't think he'll let you bargain with him if he knows you have it! He'll just get his under-officer to torture you until you give it up.'

She was silent, biting her lip while she thought that over.

'How long do you think Innata has had this?' I asked.

'How should I know? My early memories are when I was maybe three. Innata and I were together then. All my memories are of wayfaring, but she knows so many things. About gentry life, about the nobility, about things like having servants and riding taldeer. Even her sewing — fine embroidery with silken thread. That's what rich women do, isn't it? Sew pretty things.'

'I wouldn't know.'

'She taught me how to behave in uppity society. Not that I ever had much chance to make use of it. She was constantly changing the colour of her hair, or using different names, always spinning different stories about which duchy we came from. She'd assume a different accent to match the story; she was good at that. She told me I was her sister, but with fellow travellers and people we met, the tale varied from town to town, and so did our names. Sometimes I was her daughter or her niece, or her nephew or her son. Sometimes she dressed as a man, or pretended to be a cripple, or posed as a dribbling idiot led around by her doting daughter: me. Sometimes we travelled with others and she'd pretend to outsiders that they were our family...' She stopped suddenly as if she'd just recalled something.

'What?' I asked.

'When I was very young, I remember often being cared for by Goddess Jenat's templewomen, no matter which duchy. We'd stay a few days, sometimes weeks, at a temple somewhere, and then be on our way again. I remember Innata joking once that she knew every one of Goddess Jenat's archpriestesses... I remember them as elderly ladies. Always kindly. Patting me on the head, and telling Innata that she shouldn't worry about me; I was in fine health, robustly normal, apparently.' She smiled. 'I also remember that when we left, we were given new clothes. They were inordinately concerned that we were well clad!'

'That's weird. They can't have known she stole the car-canet.'

There was a pause, just a tad too long, before she nodded. My instincts kicked in. She wasn't telling the whole truth about something, but what?

She said, 'I suppose not. Those stays grew less frequent as time went by.'

'And my father? When did you first hear about him?'

'Innata would mention kingsmen from time to time. Say how afraid of them she was. I think she did that just so if ever I saw any I'd walk away. She never told me why.'

'Did she mention *anyone* else from her past?'

'A man with deformed hands. A missing thumb. I don't know why he was so important to her. But she was always looking for him. Always. He was why we were always moving on.'

'And she never found him.'

She shook her head. 'No. We followed leads that seemed good, and a couple of times she thought we got close. But in the end—' She looked down at the table, evidently not wanting to meet my gaze. 'She never explained. She told me his name was Kaillan Riverdell.'

All I could think of was that my father had been sent, with his men, on a secret hunt for the carcanet and the woman who had stolen it. But then, any sensible thief of such a recognisable jewel would have carved it up and sold each gem separately. Why hadn't she?

I gave a sigh and said, 'Hervan is going to take her back to Templebridge as a prisoner. He hasn't told me who she is, or what she's supposed to have done. He wants me to go with him. To learn a decent trade. I'm guessing we'll leave as soon as she is well enough to travel, and he's indicated that'll be the day after tomorrow. He won't hurt her, you know. He was furious when she was cut like that this morning. It wasn't meant.'

'But if she stole this'—she tapped the carcanet—'she's doomed anyway, isn't she?'

'I—I would say so.'

I poured her another drink and she took the tankard gratefully and quaffed half of it straight down. She wiped her mouth with the back of her hand and asked, 'Why didn't the King just ask Hervan to kill her when he found her? Less, um, *messy* that way.'

'I imagine because the King needs to see her dead. Or possibly he wants her handed over to men who will have her tortured to find out what she did with ... this.' My turn to tap the carcanet.

She gave a sharp intake of breath. 'They would do that?'

'Probably.'

'Then I'll give it to them!'

'Then they'll happily murder you both.'

'Oh.' She pulled a face. 'Are you going to mention this to your pa about me?'

'I don't think he's in the least bit interested in you. If he was, you'd already be under lock and key, because they sure

111

as temples are stone know Innata came to Breakedge with a young man. He and his men are not stupid, but as you switched between being a lad and a lass over the years, they probably don't think you're the same person who's travelled with her all this time. They'd rather her latest travel companion just faded away. Less complications.' I sighed. 'Pa's men so mucked this up. They wanted to hustle her away quietly, but ended up with a bloody mess in a public place.'

She was silent, debating the honesty of my words, I suppose.

'Look,' I said, 'let's assume for a moment that my father and his squad were handpicked for this job, to catch the thief of the carcanet. I can tell you what they would have been told before they started: "Bring this woman to us as quietly as you can, and with as few people knowing as possible." Believe me, the last thing they wanted was for her to be wounded like that. And the second last thing? To seize someone she was travelling with who may have friends who'd make a fuss.'

I touched her hand. 'Haze, my advice is to go away, quietly, and lead your own life as best you may.'

'She's the only person who ever looked out for me. And you're telling they are going to hand her over to people who will torture her!'

'She told you a lifetime bundle of lies.'

'She raised me and she's the only person who will ever be able to tell me who I am. Would *you* walk away if you were me?'

She had a point, but I didn't need to be sucked into her life.

'There was something else in the tin.' She fiddled in her pocket and drew out a small piece of parchment which had been folded in half. She spread it out on the table to show me the words written there:

Baffle : Innata

112

'That's Innata's writing.'

I shrugged. 'It means nothing to me.'

'Baffled means bewildered. To baffle: to confuse.'

'I'm aware of that.'

'I think she left it for me to find. It has to be important.'

'Well, I'm sorry. It means nothing else to me.'

I should have known she wouldn't let me off that easily. She plucked the remains of the carcanet up from the table and dangled it in front of me. 'Rescue her and I'll give you this carcanet thing.'

'*What?*' I threw up my hands and laughed. 'Don't be ridiculous. For a start, I could take it from you now if I really wanted it, and there's not a rot-pickled thing you could do to stop me. In fact, I ought to. It's not yours.'

She eyed her staff where it leant against the wall.

I looked up at the ceiling meaningfully, cocking my head and smiling slightly.

'You'd call for your mam for help?' she asked, incredulous.

'If I needed to. And if you think that's noodle-headed, it's because you don't know my mam.'

She jiggled the carcanet, uncertain if I meant it, but I knew that the last thing she wanted was anyone else knowing this story. The diamonds caught the lamplight and sparkled like frozen sand grains catching a desert dawn.

'You're asking me to commit treason,' I said, trying not to stare at it. 'Encouraging me to fight my own father and four seasoned soldiers, all to save a doomed woman who's on a mad quest looking for a man with crippled hands! Why would I even *want* to do something as crazed as that?'

She waved the necklace under my nose.

I plucked it away from her. 'That's not yours. It belongs to the Crown.'

She snatched it back with one hand and grabbed up her quarterstaff with the other. 'You want to fight about it?'

I glanced at the stairs. My mother was not a light sleeper and she was used to my having a drink with friends in the kitchen from time to time, but I doubted she would sleep through a full-scale brawl. 'Of course not. I shall just tell Hervan you have it instead.'

A stand-off. Her glare deepened and I smiled back, pretending indifference. She dangled the necklace. The diamonds of the collar were tiny stars of red and silver and gold dancing in the air. Damn it to Atticun's hell, but they were enticing.

I thought of Spake and what he wanted of me. I considered his threat to Salli. I dreamed of how much I'd like to see that slimy heap of a thug get hung upside down in a dungeon forever. And yes, I thought of Innata the needleworker and remembered the fear and the rage I'd read in her eyes. I glanced back at the words on the paper, inscribed with a stylish penmanship one never saw in Breakedge except perhaps on legal documents and royal edicts that originated in Templebridge. Or, perhaps, penned by gentle-bred wives of merchants.

Gods. How did I ever get mixed up in this?

'All right,' I muttered, capitulating.

'All right what?'

'Give me the carcanet, and I'll rescue Innata. No, wait, let me amend that undertaking in the interests of honesty: I will make every effort to rescue her if I can do it without taking the kind of risk that will end up with my neck in a hangman's noose. That's about as far as I can go with promises.'

She stared at me, considering, then rose, still clutching the necklace. She circled the table once like a cat on the prowl, then a second time, after which she sat down, frowning. 'I can't trust you, though, can I.'

'It would be rather stupid,' I agreed, sounding more cheerful than I felt. Come to think of it, I wasn't too sure I trusted her, either. I had a niggle somewhere in the region of my stomach that was telling me she was hiding something. 'Of course, I could just go to the barracks right now and tell my father everything, with or without the necklace. Look, I think we can work something out between us.'

I didn't tell her what influenced me most: unless Haze had lied, Innata had been helped for years by Goddess Jenat's many archpriestesses in duchies across the land. And for that to happen, the original decision to aid Innata could only have come from the Goddess Jenat's Gerentia, the highest and most influential archpriestess in the kingdom of Talodiac. The thought rattling around in my pate was this: who the hell was I to gainsay the path approved by the most powerful of the goddesses? I might have been an idiot, but I wasn't lack-brained.

I *was* missing something. Something fundamental. Obviously, there were parts of this story still untold...

Blue hells, what a mess this all was.

Hazelle laid the carcanet on the tabletop. Emeralds and rubies are pretty, but diamonds? Diamonds are king.

I drooled.

'Done,' I said, picking it up. 'I'll do my best.'

*

Yes, yes, I know, Lady Sianta, I still haven't finished — however, I *am* getting to the crux of how I ended up in this cell. But you knew much of this anyway, didn't you? There is no way I would have been allowed to record my tale unless you already knew at least the bare bones of it. For some reason, someone trusts you not to say a word. I wonder why they think you'll do no more than record my story? There's much about you and your position here that's a mystery, isn't there?

That word baffle... I wonder if that means anything to you?

Gods know why you want any of this written down, though. A written secret can so easily become a secret that's read. I don't suppose I'll ever find out what this is all about, either. Which is *so* annoying...

12

Hazelle spent the night wrapped in a blanket on the hearth in front of the dampened fire in our kitchen. In the morning, she was gone before either Ma or I were awake. She'd told me she was going to buy herself a taldeer and asked if she could leave her pack behind to collect later. 'I'll be following Innata, no matter what,' she'd told me, 'and I'll need a mount.'

I'd given her the name of the least rapacious of the stock dealers and put some bread and cheese out so she could break her fast, a tacit acknowledgement that it was probably better she was gone before Ma rose in the morning. By the time I came downstairs, she'd done just that, leaving the blanket neatly folded on the table. Ma had gone off to the market without waking me or wanting an explanation for the pack in the corner of the kitchen.

I hadn't slept much. I'd spent most of the night awake, planning not only how to wriggle out from under the blade of Spake's rage, but also how to save the family from his wrath after I'd disappeared.

As I broke my fast and contemplated Hazelle's pack, I wondered why she trusted me as much as she did. The logical thing for me to do was tell my father everything I knew. She wasn't to know how angry I was with him, or how often he'd brushed me aside. For some reason her trust left me uneasy, as if I ought to look over my shoulder to see what trouble was brewing there. I shrugged and ceased resisting the urge to peek into her pack.

I slung it onto the table and carefully took everything out. No money, no jewellery. Nothing except a few items of clothing for men and women, a woollen cloak, a leather flask, a knife, a bowl, a spoon, a candle, thread, a dressmaker's bodkin — the bare minimum of essentials for travel. I put it all back the way I'd found it, but I'd no doubt she would know it had been searched. But then, would she have expected anything else?

The next thing I did was to prise four of the more modest diamonds out of the carcanet collar, and chop off a few nice chunks of the gold. After all, what's the point of being a thief if you don't help yourself to the treasure when it falls into your hands? A horrible thing to do to something so sumptuously beautiful, but I did make sure all the damage was at the back. I walked down to Goldsmith Lane and exchanged the gold for coins, half at a jeweller's and the other half at four different moneylenders. At least I would leave a considerable heap of coins for my mother when I left.

After that, I planned just how I was going to save my neck — and my sister's — from that slimy piece of foulness, Spake the Locksmith. I had the semblance of an idea although I reckoned the chance I could succeed was just about the same as that of dying in the attempt. Mind you, there was also a strong possibility that if I did succeed, Pa would kill me anyway.

The remainder of the day was spent readying myself for the trip to Templebridge. When Haze came to reclaim her pack late in the afternoon, I surrendered it and told her my news: Pa had sent me a message to say we were leaving an hour after dawn on the morrow.

'Innata will travel on the back of a cart. Our journey will be slow and there's no point you trying anything until she's back on her feet,' I told her. 'Pa said he doesn't expect her to be able to ride for another five to ten days or so. The wound was stitched and is healing well, but the loss of blood has left her too weak to walk more than a few steps at a time.'

She nodded. 'Then I'll leave tomorrow too. I've bought two mounts. One is for her.' The look she shot me was full of meaning: it was up to me to free Innata.

'Join a caravan for safety in the meantime. Worth the money.'

'You trying to tell *me* something about how to travel?' Her arched brow was pure mockery. Abashed, I was silent, so she added, 'There's five wayfaring families leaving tomorrow at dawn. I've travelled with one of them before.'

'Where do you want to meet up with us?'

'Crowbridge,' she said, without a pause. 'Everybody has to cross the Crowlick River if they're going to Templebridge. I'll keep a watch at the bridge for your arrival. There's a wayfarers' camping area and a kingsmen's campsite this side of the bridge. By then you'll have a plan on how to rescue her, and she should be well enough to ride.'

'You really believe I'll keep my end of the bargain?'

'I do.' She looked grim as she shouldered her pack. 'I've paid you in advance. A king's ransom. I think you're a man who keeps his promises.'

Gods only know where she got that idea from. She'd handed over a necklace collar worth more than most people could earn in several lifetimes, apparently sure I would betray everything I had been brought up to believe in: loyalty to king and country. Her blind trust in someone she knew to be a thief was just extraordinary.

'You're daft,' I said.

'Am I?' She gave a faint smile. 'Maybe I'm just desperate. And maybe you ought to wonder what I'm capable of, should you not uphold your side of our bargain.'

Her smile widened into a feral grin. Did I believe the promise of retribution behind that smile? I rather think I did.

*

A message was delivered to me at our house late in the afternoon by Lomnot, one of Spake's runners, a grubby, barefoot errand boy with missing front teeth and a lisp. 'Tonight,' he said. 'Thpake's back room, ten bells. You don't turn up, t'will be yer kin...' He drew a finger across his throat. 'You follow?'

'Yeah, I follow,' I growled. 'Tell Spake I'll be there. Now get out of here.'

He jerked his head back towards the road. 'You won't get lonely,' he said. 'Thpake'th left friendth, to keep an eye on ye, like.'

I poked my head out of the door and groaned inwardly. There were no less than six of Spake's runner lads lounging around in the laneway, kicking a makeshift ball of weed and twine.

'An' don't forget your back neighbourth. Them's very friendly with Thpake.' Lomnot nodded past our house through the orchard to the drystone wall that separated the proxy-wives' quarter from ordinary residents. The house on the other side belonged to Bronkine, whose sons had made a practice of stealing our fruit until Jav had broken the arm of the eldest lad. That had not endeared us to the family as a whole. Spake's lad grinned and left, receiving a friendly slap on the backside and some ribald comments as he passed the louts on the road.

I should have been drowning in despair, but my mood was tinged with an odd relief. Things were coming to a head. Win or lose, at least the horror would be over soon.

Or so I thought.

*

I entered the house and wrote a note to Pa, an epistle that was three parts confession concerning my connection to Spake, and one part possible rescue plan. I was sealing it with candle wax when Ma came back from a visit to a neighbour. Her eyebrows shot up. Writing letters was not something we ever did, let alone ones that needed to be sealed.

'What's all this about, then,' she asked, hands on hips.

I took a deep breath. 'Um, bad news.' I tapped the letter. 'Either Pa or Jav has to have the information in this as soon as possible, early tonight certainly, but no one must know. Problem is, the house is being watched...'

She folded her arms across her chest and the mild pucker of her lips morphed into a glowering frown. 'Spit it out!'

'Um, I think the less you know the better. Then if anyone asks—'

'You lackwit! What gormless thing you done now?' Her pale face made me feel far worse than her words did.

'Ma, someone is threatening Salli and her family if I don't do what he asks—'

She gave a sharp intake of breath and paled. 'It's that devil Spake, isn't it? I done told you his honey words was poison—'

'I know, I know. I'm sorry, but can we discuss how daft I've been some other time? Right now, I've got to work out how to get this letter to Pa, or at the very least to Jav, in time for them to rescue my sorry arse tonight.'

She paused then, to think, before asking, 'The house is being watched? D'you mean them louts I passed on my way in? The ones playing street ball?'

I nodded.

'And out the back?'

'Need you ask?'

'Bronkine? He's in Spake's pay too?' She sat down heavily on one of the kitchen chairs and her silence dragged on for an excruciating time. Finally, she said, 'Let me go through this once more. You can't be seen going down to the barracks, but the letter got to get there. Soon.'

'That's right. My guess is that there'll be other watchers down by the barracks and along the way into town too. Getting this letter to Pa or Jav is so important that lives — yours, Salli's — might depend on it.'

'No chance you're hiking a bit of a pester into a plague?'

I shook my head, feeling about as small as a mealworm at the bottom of an empty barrel. 'Well then,' she said, as if her next words were self-evident, 'we'll get folk to come to us instead. We'll fire the orchard come dark. That'll get half the barracks up here, quick smart.'

'*What?*'

'That mix of old straw and the fresh, dry dung under the trees? Burn easy, that lot.'

'You can't be serious!'

'Rather lose me orchard than a son or a daughter. A fire'll give me a chance to slip a letter and a few words to Hervan or, if he don't come running, to one of the rangers who do. They'll come up right smartly from the barracks to fight the fire.'

'Ma, you *can't!* You might lose the *house.*'

What she was suggesting was appalling. This was a city where everything was dry and water was scarce. Fire often ripped along the city's edges where wild-grass grew and died. Wind whipped sparks and burning ash through glassless windows to burn homes from within, and such a conflagration could spread as fast as stampeding taldeer.

I opened my mouth to protest, but she spoke over me. 'After dark, all our neighbours will be home. They'll help you fight the fire. Soon as them flames take hold, you call in those louts out there to help. And they will. They'll be just as

122

frightened as you are. While everyone's all busy fighting the flames or keeping an eye on you, I'll get whatever it is you done writ here to yer Pa, one way or t'other.'

'Ma—'

She cut off my protest with a chopping gesture of her hand. 'Seems you done made a reeking mess of our lives, lad, and I'll not take your mouthing as worth hearing right now. For this once, you'll do what I say. And after — you'll go to Templebridge with your pa and you'll not come back till you're a man 'stead of a half-baked boy with a turd on your shoulder 'cause you didn't get to be what you wanted.'

By then, I was close to choking on the swelling lump in my throat. She'd never spoken like that to me in my life and every word was a whiplash of hurt.

I nodded dumbly.

*

Sitting here in this cell, I think about my mother a lot. Of all the things I've done, and considering everything that's happened, how my actions wounded Gariane will haunt me till the day I die.

Lady Sianta, I would wish that she never discovers I was executed for treason. It would add to her already intolerable grief. She is devoted to God Saffrin, you know, believing him to be more the God of Peace than of War. Her role of proxy-wife to a soldier is part of her devotion. She thinks Hervan is a servant of peace, so he has the right to further his family line and God Saffrin will reward her for anything she sacrificed to provide him with that family. She deserves better than to be burdened with the shame of a son executed as a traitor.

Now, let's get back to this knotty problem of just who I am writing this tale for. You have told me that the manner of my death will never be made public, given that the King would rather keep — ah — certain events secret. You've also said an accurate account is important for history and that it remains the property of the Historians' Guild. You have now just informed me that this document will only come to light one hundred years from now.

You implied that the King knows and sanctions what I am writing. Yet we all know, surely, that words can be read by those for whom they are not intended...

But then, I suppose all this matters little to someone sitting in a cell awaiting execution.

Never mind.

13

We were lucky.

The moonrises were late that night, and the wind was light.

Just before dark, Ma poured oil around some of the trees. As the sun set and the gloom deepened, her actions appeared no different to her usual evening watering. Spake's louts watched with only desultory interest.

When she came back into the house, her face was as grim as I'd ever seen it. Those trees: she had planted most of them more than twenty years earlier. She'd nurtured them through droughts and desert winds, through the two great sandstorms of my childhood, and the flood years when torrential rain had fallen on the mountains and water had rampaged down the slopes into Breakedge carrying earth and scrub and rocks on its back. Ma's orchard had survived all.

I opened my mouth to say yet again how sorry I was, but she stopped me with a single glance.

Spake's louts were still hanging about in the street, talking loudly and obscenely about their conquests and how that sniveller Taygen Hervan-Gariane should give them the respect they were due. As the sun disappeared, they lit a fire at the road edge and produced kesta leaves to burn. I'd tried kesta a few times, but soon decided the dreams and pretty colours were not worth the kiln-dry mouth, let alone the axe-split headache of the following day.

'Good,' Ma remarked, knowing the fumes would keep them befuddled. 'I think the time is right, lad. Get to it.'

'Maybe there's no need to fire the orchard,' I ventured to remark. 'They'll be half drunk on the kesta smoke.'

'And what is it I done heard about that evil stuff?' she asked in a whisper, her sarcasm oozing through. 'Makes you reckless, I heard tell. Makes a man aggressive and jumpy.'

'Exaggeration,' I said, but she wouldn't have it.

'Burn the orchard,' she snapped, dousing the lamp and cracking open the back shutters. 'You don't take a risk with the life of your sister's family, understand? I'm ready to go now. Start the fire.'

I sighed and watched as she slipped out of the back door as if going to the privy. Using a kitchen ladle, I lobbed hot coals from the kitchen fire through the window onto the ground beneath the trees outside. As soon as one of the coals hit a patch of oil, flames darted across the ground. I stayed there for a moment, watching, scarcely able to breathe. Each flicker of new flame scorched my soul.

As the first twist of fire licked its greedy way up the trunk of an olive tree, I turned away to the front door. I wrenched it open and ran outside yelling for help at the top of my lungs. Grabbing up the pail of water I'd placed by the door in readiness, I continued to shout. 'Fire! Fire!'

I don't remember much about the next few minutes, except how fast everything happened. I couldn't see my mother, so I knew she must have left undetected, and that was the main thing. Spake's layabouts came to help without even pausing to consider how the fire might have started. One of them even ran to the neighbour's house and banged on the door for help. I tore back inside to grab the broom and an old padded quilt I'd already placed just inside the door. I chucked them to the lads for beating the flames out.

The wind was like a devilish sprite, blowing sparks everywhere. As fast as flames were doused by a bucket of water, others sprang into life to devour the fruit trees and whoosh up into the olives. Our neighbours were now everywhere beating at the flames, yet still the fire spread. My eyes wept in the smoke, my throat was scorched raw, my boots smoked as I stamped on those living tongues of flame and swept soil over the embers.

One of Spake's louts attached himself to me, making sure I didn't speak to anyone without him knowing, but the only person to inquire after my mother was one of our neighbours. I told him she was fighting to save her favourite olive trees on the other side of the house.

It seemed an age before border rangers from the barracks arrived, armed with fire brooms and sacking. By then, the fire raged out of control. They attacked it with little regard for their own safety, risking burns and the fall of flaming branches, with all the courage and competence of military men fighting an invader. Even so, it felt like an age before the flames were gone, the house saved, and all that was left of the fire was an ash-covered ground and smoking trees. After thoroughly checking that there were no hidden embers still glowing, they made arrangements to return the following day.

'We'll wash the ash from the house walls, for a start,' one of the junior officers promised, even as he rinsed a nasty scorch on his forearm. 'And chop the fallen tree limbs into firewood for you. If you think there are any trees that need uprooting, we can do that as well.'

Their regard for Ma and me was genuine and raked me with shame. They didn't care that we weren't saffrine; we were part of their military family, and every one of them had been prepared to risk their personal safety to protect us. Now they were all agreeing to return, even though it would mean giving up any spare time between their duties. Every expression of their concern gutted me with guilt.

Ma had returned sometime during the havoc, giving me a curt nod when our paths crossed, enough to tell me the letter had been passed on safely. Jav was there too and from the look he gave me, I knew he'd read my letter.

'Pa's organising things for later tonight,' he muttered in my ear.

Later he spoke to Ma and me, making sure we were unharmed and the house was safe, all within easy earshot of one of Spake's louts lurking nearby. From his icy glare, I knew he was beyond furious, but he gave no indication of it to the eavesdropper. He even thanked the fellow for coming to our aid, clapping him on the back. 'I'm sure my brother here will give you some coin to buy a drink as a way of saying thank you!' he added as he left, heading back towards the barracks.

I gave a sickly smile and a nod.

After everyone had left except for Spake's lads, Ma walked through looking for damage by the silver light of the triple moonrise, touching the trunks and scorched branches with grieving tenderness. I waited for her just outside the door, but when she returned to the house, she didn't glance at me. All she said was, 'The house didn't burn.' The flat dullness of her words, the way she looked at her fingers and then rubbed them down her apron to rid them of ash... it was enough to make the gods weep.

She turned away and climbed the stairs to her bedroom without another word.

The watching lads, now sitting on the garden wall, appeared bored. 'Thanks for the help,' I said, managing a smile without gritting my teeth. 'Shall we have a drink until it's time to go to the locksmith's? We have some excellent ale.'

I figured that a band of guards mellowed by drink would be less of a danger when things turned nasty later on, and I ushered them inside.

*

128

It was bitterly cold out in the street that night, a raw desert chill that creeps into your bones before you're even aware the heat of the day has faded. I put on my coat and allowed Spake's fellows to deliver me to the locksmith's at the agreed hour. Their usual mockery had been reduced to a more sympathetic commiseration, as if fighting the fire had linked us in some sort of comradeship. They were wrong.

They took me to the back entrance of the locksmith's, which led straight from the back alley into the workmen's area in the basement. Grogor, Spake's youngest son, opened the door and the blast of hot air from inside was welcome. A portable forge on iron legs in the centre of the room served a dual purpose: it could generate enough heat for small locksmithing jobs and, on a cold night like this, it heated the room and warmed the shop and bedrooms above.

Grogor flapped a hand at my escort and they melted away into the darkness of the streets once more. I stepped inside and shrugged off my coat. On the wall alongside the door, a row of warmer and more elegant overcoats hung on brass hooks. Gold buttons and fur trimming on the one closest to the door told me the owner was Spake; he'd obviously brought out his best to wear for the Burgher's Ball. I hung my shabby overcoat next to it. Grogor barred the door and waved me further into the room.

Five other men were gathered around the table in the centre, and as one they turned, their stares unwelcoming. Spake was flanked by his other two sons, Fredar and Troyn, all dressed up in their best finery and sporting a king's ransom in jewels and silks. The remaining two fellows I'd never met, professional sluggers at a guess. Heavy men, broad of shoulder and hard of face. One was vaguely familiar to me from my wrestling days down in the talyak bullock yards.

'Come in, come in, m'lad,' Spake said, waving me over to the worktable and turning on a fake smile that sent a shiver up my spine. 'We've much to do afore we leave. Me and the

129

boys are due at the ball in an hour.' He indicated the two bruisers. 'These two will make sure you get to where you're going later.'

Grogor and his oldest brother, Fredar, crowded in on me more like guards than accomplices, until I stood at the table facing Troyn, the best-looking of the trio. He dimpled at me from the other side, next to his father. People who didn't know him found him charming. He wasn't.

The bruisers, arms folded, stepped back next to the forge fire where the coals still glowed red. The tools of a black-smith's trade — anvil, bellows, hammer and vice — were neatly laid out on a nearby bench against the wall. I was nervous, thinking they looked more like instruments of tor-ture, but Spake was still smiling. 'Fire's just to keep us warm, lad,' he said. 'No more than that, eh?'

He indicated a plan that had been spread on the table top, so I gave it my full attention. It was a labelled drawing on linen, and a cursory glance told me it was the plan I'd already glimpsed before of Money Street, Treasury Square and the Breakedge Counting House, where the city kept all the tax money and the city's finances.

Spake tapped the linen with a forefinger. 'Lookee here. Front door of the Counting House. We have a copy of the key.' He fished in one of his many unobtrusive pockets and laid a key on the table. Ornate and beautifully wrought, it was as long as my hand. Spake tapped the side of his nose. 'How we got the original loaned to us to make this one is best not talked about. All you need to know is that this key will get you in the front door.'

'There are two town guards on the entrance all day and all night,' I pointed out. I also knew the edifice had no win-dows on the ground or first floor. The high windows of the third floor were barred. A central air well in the middle of the building provided fresh air and some sunlight into lower inner rooms, but it too was barred and inaccessible. The place resembled a prison and probably used more lamp oil in a day than most people did in a year.

'Just before you roll up at the door to insert that key in the lock tonight,' Spake continued, 'there will be a gods-awful bang at the back of the Counting House. Like a clap of thunder, y'know. So huffing rowdy, in fact, the guards'll piss their breeks. It'll come from here.' He pointed to a spot on the map. '*Boom!*' he cried, then ran two fingers across the parchment in illustration.

I blinked, wondering if he was japing me. He was like a child with a new toy, barely suppressing his excitement.

'The guards'll race around the back to see what's afoot. Along the way, they'll pass the only other door, the servers' entrance.' He indicated a side door on the plan of the building. 'Triple barred from the inside every night. Checked by the night watchmen on their rounds. The guards'll notice nothing wrong there and so they'll continue on to the rear. Got that?'

I nodded.

'While they're gone from the front,' he continued, 'you'll enter the main door using this key. You'll lock it behind you. You then have a couple of hours to open the Cratchett safe, take out as much gold coin and gems as you can carry in this—' He reached down under the table and held up a sack.

'How will I get out?' I asked. 'Noise or no noise, the guards won't leave the front door unguarded for long.' In fact, I could see a number of holes in the plan. What if only one guard left his post, but not the other? What if both of them didn't respond to the noise?

Spake smirked, reminding me how much I loathed him. 'Listen, lad. Do like you're told, and this'll all be simple as a breeze. You get caught and blab?' He shook his head sorrowfully. 'Your sister's house'll burn, with them inside, I feel sure. Got a feeling 'bout it, I have. You know me.'

And I did. So perhaps, did the two guards who would be on duty at the Counting House. The hair stood up on the back of my neck. I realised I was actually holding my breath, as if not breathing was safer. I licked dry lips and exhaled.

Spake reached across the table and patted my cheek. 'You get out by the servers' door. My two friends here will be waiting for you,' he added, pointing to the bruisers. 'You close the door behind you. You bring this front door key back with you, of course. When the robbery is finally discovered, the implication will be that one of the Counting House clerks had hid himself inside the building overnight...'

I never did get to hear anything more of their plan.

A thunderous banging vibrated the door I'd entered by, followed immediately by someone pounding at the front door upstairs. We all jumped in shock, then, briefly, no one moved at all. That momentary stupor was shattered as the back door crashed into the room and fell flat in a mix of wood and metal, followed by the head of a battering ram, a shower of splinters and what appeared to be an army, led by my father.

The Spake family dived in all directions, grabbing for tools to use as weapons. I just dived, not so heroically, under the table. A sensible choice at the time, seeing as I wasn't armed and I didn't want to appear at all belligerent to the attackers, but it did mean I only viewed the participants from the waist down.

Hervan had brought along his four kingsmen and seven men of the border patrol. That much I knew from recognising their footgear. Jav was easy to spot; he had a cockeyed way of fastening his boot buttons. They had the advantage of surprise and should have flattened the four members of the Spake family in the first rush.

But, well, things sometimes don't always work out the way you think they will.

When I poked my head out, planning to make a grab for the plans on the table, I was just in time to see Spake swipe them from the tabletop and fling them on the coals of the forge fire. The parchment curled brown and flared into flames before I could scramble to my feet.

Fredar, the hefty not-so-bright one of the family, snatched up the long-handled fire paddle. He shoved it into the fire, scooping up a heap of red-hot coals to use as missiles. I lunged out from under the table to grab his ankles. He swung around, the heaped paddle skimming my head as I ducked. He heaved the coals across the room, aiming — I think — for Pa. I yanked him off balance. He fell backwards against the forge. Even though it was mounted on four sturdy legs, it wasn't designed to have a man with shoulders as broad as a talyak crash into it. It tipped, the two closest legs lifting off the floor.

By this time, the room was the scene of a pitched battle, people grunting, wrestling, swinging. I was only vaguely aware of what was happening elsewhere, but in front of me I could see Jav on the other side of the forge. He wrestled Troyn to the floor just as Fredar toppled against the hot metal side of the fire bowl.

The whole apparatus teetered.

The glowing coals shifted, sliding away from me towards where Jav and Troyn rolled on the floor in a no-holds-barred battle. Fredar screamed. He tried to jerk away, further unbalancing the forge. On the other side, Troyn rolled and knocked against the base of the legs, providing the final nudge that spilled the coals over himself.

And over Jav.

The world changed.

THE TANGLED LANDS

The air split, shredded on high-pitched human agony. My breath bubbled in my throat as I choked on the stench of burning flesh. Catastrophe unfolded, opening up in sound and sight and horror and realisation.

I can never forget. Charred meat smell. Crisping hair. Shrivelling skin and melting eyes, etched forever on my soul.

Memory imprinted in an eternal purgatory at what my arrogance and stupidity had wrought.

The fight was all over then, and we had won.

And lost.

*

Lady Sianta, thank you for reassuring me that my execution is to be done on the quiet. And yes, I do have a faint feeling of satisfaction knowing that at some time in the future, people will know my story. Perhaps many will even feel that I had right on my side, or at the very least, that my treason was well meant.

And yes, yes, I know I'm running out of time to tell the rest of my tale now that the King is on his way back to Templebridge. How many days will that give me? Too few, I know. I lose track of time here, one day in a cell is so much like another.

And no, I won't write any faster to please you. Or to please the Historians' Guild.

14

Troyn, the handsome one, was dying, taking his few last tortured inhalations into fire-scorched lungs through a charred hole in his throat. The foetor of his burning drenched every breath I took.

Spake was hog-tied on the floor, wrists tied to ankles, foully cursing us all to godless hells, until one of patrol slammed the hilt of his sword into his teeth. Fredar was huddled on the floor, rocking to and fro in agony, moaning. His tunic had burned away, baring a reddened blistered back. The two bully boys were dead. The four men of the King's Guard were bruised but otherwise unharmed. One had a bloodied sword. So did my father.

Pa was staring blank-faced at Jav.

I wish I could forget that look. That absence of expression. All his pride in his favourite son, all his dreams, all his joy in having an heir so replicated along his own lines — all withered in a bitter blast of horror and grief and acknowledgement. He knew, as I did, there was no coming back from what had just happened. Jav might live, but he would never see again, not well enough to be a soldier. His rugged golden looks would never again turn the heads of lasses in the street or speed up the heartbeats of other saffrine lads.

Pa looked at me and his blankness evaporated as his grief for his older son was swamped by disgust for his younger one. It was I who looked away. I knelt at my brother's side, held his unblemished hands. 'It's me,' I said. 'Tay.' I wanted to tell him it would be all right, but the lie wouldn't come.

He groaned, a horrible, tortured sound. I was pushed aside and could only watch as his fellow Border Rangers carried him out of the room on the tabletop, whisking him away to Hetha's temple and the healers. In my heart, I knew their healing would not be enough. An archpriestess, or the goddess herself: perhaps they could have wrought a miracle restoration of my brother, but they both dwelt in Temple-bridge. In the King's city, in the shadow of a deity, miracles could happen.

But not in Breakedge.

Wanting to be with Jav, I started to follow the rangers, but my father jerked me back by the arm. 'No. You have a case to answer.' His voice rasped. His bruising grip above my elbow was savage. He wanted it to hurt.

The words brought me rudely back into the present. Others had entered the room after it had been secured. Among them were some of the city's senior council members, wearing their robes of office, garb normally donned for social events. One of them was the city's senior judge, Allian Tondor-Hessa, the man whose job it was to enforce the King's law. I'd never met him, but I'd seen him officiating at enough town festivities and court cases to know who he was. He stood by the door, arms folded, face solemn, foot tapping slowly. His stance sent a shiver up my spine. All I wanted to do was bolt. Flee to Hetha's temple and beg them to save Jav...

'Captain,' Judge Allian snapped at Pa. 'You promised you'd have proof of an intended robbery of the Counting House?' He waved a hand around the room. 'All I see is some of our respectable artisans either dead, injured, or tied up like vermin. What explanation do you have for this outrage?'

Pa saluted him, a courtesy rather than an acknowledgement of inferiority. 'I regret to say that these are the men who planned the Counting House robbery. This lad of mine'—he nodded at me—'very bravely pretended to be a miscreant, and was made privy to their intention. He informed his brother immediately.'

Spake screeched a denial.

'And your proof?' The judge used a tone that told me he didn't believe a word of it.

My heart flipped over. Spake's meticulously drawn plan was now no more than ashes on the coals.

Pa glared at me, his look telling me I'd better produce something tangible right then. For a moment my brain seized up. All I could think of were things that might implicate me in ways I didn't want, and then I remembered how I was supposed to enter the Counting House.

'There's a key,' I said. 'It was on the table. It will fit the door to the Counting House.' The tabletop had gone. My mouth went dry. 'It will be here somewhere.'

Hervan snapped out an order to search for it. When I moved to help, he yanked me back and muttered in my ear, 'Not you, you lackwit.'

The soldiers started a hunt, but the floor was a mess of blood, smouldering coals and scattered tools. The stench of burned flesh made my stomach heave. Hervan called for more lamps to be lit as his men and the Border Rangers scoured the room for the missing key and any other evidence of the intended crime.

One of patrolmen found a pot of Dekadani black powder and a fuse, which answered the unspoken question I had about the diversionary noise Spake had planned, but it was hardly proof of anything. Fortunately, a little later the key was found under Grogor's body. Pa handed it to Judge Allian, who handed it on to another man, who turned out to be the Counting House's chief accountant. When he examined it, the colour drained from his face and his choked, 'Sweet gods, this key should not exist,' said it all.

'Tell them to check the coats hanging up on the wall,' I whispered in Pa's ear.

His glare of suspicion was savage enough to make me wince, but he gave the order for the coats to be examined.

When a young ranger held up Spake's fur-collared garment in one hand and the Griffin Carcanet in the other, everyone turned to look. Hervan's vice-like grasp on my arm tightened still further.

'That—' the Judge began, then swallowed before gathering himself enough to ask in a tone of disbelief, 'A carcanet? With the royal griffin?'

At my side, Hervan was as taut as a bow string. 'I believe one such was stolen from the palace around the time of the late Queen's death.'

'I've never seen that before in my life!' Spake yelled. 'This is an outrage!' He struggled against his bonds, his rage building with his indignation. He glowered in my direction. 'You did this! You—'

'Don't be ridiculous,' I said coldly. 'Where would I come across such a thing? I've never been out of Breakedge!'

'Nor have I!' he yelled.

One of the guards clouted him over the head.

'I will question this man and his sons,' Pa told the judge. 'Tonight.'

'This is my jurisdiction—' the judge began.

'Are you about to tell me your jurisdiction supersedes the King's?'

Judge Allian opened his mouth as if to protest, thought better of it, and said instead, 'No. No, of course not, Captain. It shall be arranged.'

'Tonight. Right now, in fact. We are due to leave in the morning.'

There was a smidgeon of hesitation, but in the end the judge inclined his head. 'Of course. They will be taken to the prison now.'

Pa released my arm, murmuring quietly into my ear, 'Go home and pack. Say goodbye to your mother and meet me three hours past dawn at Belan's fields.'

'Jav—' I began.

Words grating from between gritted teeth, he pelted his fury at me. 'Don't you *ever* mention his name again in my hearing. Not ever, for as long as you live.'

With that, he strode across the room and snatched the carcanet from the patrolman's fingers. 'This is the property of the Crown and will be returned to the King's treasury.'

I slipped out of the room, tears hot on my cheeks.

I didn't go straight home, of course. I deviated to Hetha's temple to find out how Jav was and hung around until one of the healers told me he was out of danger. They had lessened his pain, placed him in a healing sleep and no, I couldn't talk to him. And no, they couldn't tell me if he would ever regain his sight. They bade me return in a day or two, when they would know the full extent of his injuries.

I left, knowing there would be no returning for me. I did not see him again, and now I know I never will. My brother's life and health were wrecked because I was stupid enough to ever listen to Spake.

Something inside me shrivelled, a spark of confidence and pride I had once borne, but never will again. I am a better person now, perhaps. Certainly, in my heart, there's a grief I'll never leave behind.

My brother, though, one of the finest men I'll ever know: he will go through life maimed. No acknowledgement of guilt or repentance will ever take away one iota of his pain — or of mine. The difference is, I deserve mine.

*

The travelling party was small.

Pa, his four guardsmen, myself and Innata. There was no woman in attendance for Innata, no servant for her. We had two taldoe as pack animals, and the others rode gelded stags because no King's Guard would ever have mounted a much more manageable doe. Being gelded might have stopped them fighting one another to the death in the breeding season, but they were still cantankerous beasts, still able to grow their massive antlers as wide as my outstretched arms. Their advantage for military men is that they love to run. Our lack of speed made them even more irritable than usual.

Our slowness was dictated by Innata's need to be transported in a talyak-drawn cart and talyak are ponderous even when they are not pulling a load. This one was content to walk for hour after hour, leaning its vast chest into the harness as it plodded along, but no one would have called it speedy.

As for Innata, she needed help to mount and dismount from the cart and could do no more than hobble a short way from the camp, leaning on someone, to attend to her bodily functions. Our lack of speed meant that Haze, who'd left just before us, would be waiting in Crowbridge for days before we arrived.

Hervan set the rules for me right at the beginning, even as we saddled up on the first morning. 'You do not talk to that woman,' he said, jerking a thumb at Innata. 'Not a word, ever. Disobey and I will have you flayed till your skin is ripped from your back. Understand?'

I nodded.

He glared.

'Yes, sir,' I amended.

'You'll work your arse till it aches. First up in the morn, last to doss down come night. You'll cook, and meals had better be good. You'll tend to the taldoe and the talyak. You won't be riding; you'll be driving the cart. You will inspect and care for all tackle. Everyone's. You will keep yer mouth shut and not speak 'less spoken to. Understand?'

'Yes sir. Might I ask...' I hesitated, faltering as I remembered our previous conversation.

'He lives,' he snapped. 'Blinded. No thanks to you. He'd be better off dead!'

The bile in my throat burned like a red-hot coal. 'Spake?'

'He and his third lad regrettably died under questioning.' He shot me a hard look. 'Still denying they knew anything 'bout the jewel in Spake's pocket.'

Regrettably. Right.

The look he gave should have frizzled my hair. I waited for the questions: *How did Spake get it? Is that why you wanted the coats searched? Did you put it there? Was that the first time you saw it? Had you ever met Innata?*

None of those questions ever came. Instead, he asked, 'Do you know what that jewel was?'

'The Griffin Carcanet? I knew there was such a thing. I had no idea it had been stolen until I saw it.' An honest answer, if disingenuous. 'I've heard Spake is the city's receiver of stolen goods.'

Did Pa know I'd met Innata before? Did he even know there *was* a Hazelle?

Perhaps he assumed I'd somehow got my hands on the carcanet that night before he arrived with Jav and his men, and that I'd placed it in the locksmith's own coat pocket in order to ensure the fate of the Spake family. On the other hand, maybe he decided that I suggested searching the coats because it was a sensible thing to do, and no one had yet done so. My guess now is that he believed I'd seen the jewel some time at Spake's, and I tried to tell him about it on those occasions when he'd refused to listen to me — but he didn't *want* to know for certain. Because he now believed if he'd listened to me, the night Jav was maimed might never have happened. If he'd listened to me, everything might have been different.

And so, he didn't pose the question.

Inside, all I could think of was that my mother and Salli could now live secure, aided by money I had received from the sale of bits of the carcanet. But Jav? Dear gods, the blame was mine. *Is* mine, for the claws of guilt tear at me yet, from where they ride eternally on my shoulder.

Jav, I am so, so sorry.

15

Yes, yes, I know, Sianta. Maybe you can tell the King when he arrives back in Templebridge that I am writing as fast as I can. I am sure you have some influence somewhere, right? I didn't appreciate your scolding last night. Either my story is more important than my execution or it's not. Bear in mind that your nagging is *not* helping my creative endeavours.

*

The trip was hell.

No one spoke to me except to give orders. I read their condemnation in their eyes, especially from Cyrrin. They all knew that somehow or other it was my fault my brother had been harmed. Hervan was the only one of them who had been lucky enough to produce a saffrine son, a fighting man, a warrior like them, and Jav's fate seared them all. However Spake had died, it would not have been pleasant.

Cyrrin had been Pa's saffrine partner since before I was born. In the past I'd found him cold and uninterested in our family; now his contemptuous anger burned at me from his eyes — and his message was pity help me if I didn't perform my tasks to his near impossible standards. Gappy and Folman were not overtly nasty, but they did as Cyrrin told them, and regarding me, his orders were far from pleasant.

Petch was different. At a guess, he was too consumed by his guilt over his accidental harming of Innata to think of much else. Even so, he always made sure that I received my share of the evening meal. He'd greet me with a nod in the morning, and was decent enough to help with my chores when neither Pa nor Cyrrin was looking, at the risk of being targetted himself. Pa made it clear I was not welcome to sit and eat with any of them; I had to wait until they'd all finished and it seemed that no one was to speak to me except to give orders.

Loneliness and guilt cloaked me, cold and intractable.

Jav.

His burned face. His screaming, the echo of it tracking me through the day, chasing me into sleep and inhabiting my nightmares.

They all treated Innata with a formal respect, although at times I thought that was threaded through with resentment. Petch alone was unfailingly thoughtful, addressing her as 'Milady', helping her in and out of the cart, fetching her padded stool for her to sit on, providing her with the best of our food, even fluffing up the padded quilts on her makeshift bed before she retired for the night. Once he even picked her a bunch of wild flowers. When she needed to seek privacy for her ablutions, he would offer her an arm to lean upon and take her to a more secluded spot, then leave her alone until she called for him to help her return. I half expected Pa or Cyrrin to object to these courtesies, but they never commented, convincing me that she must have been a woman of status, for all that she'd posed as a wayfarer. The runaway wife of a nobleman, perhaps? A court lady, perhaps even the King's courtesan, who had stooped to theft?

Hervan had told her not to speak to me, and at first she obeyed, merely nodding her thanks whenever I did anything for her. When I drove the cart as it bumped and rocked along over the ruts in the road, I softened the boards of my own seat with my sole blanket while Innata lay down behind on her bedding. When we stopped for the night, we never camped with other wayfarers, seeking instead a place more private. I was ordered to attend to Innata's needs at night, if need be, so I slept underneath the cart. On the first night, she was feverish and asked me to fetch some water so she could swallow the potion given her by the nursing sisters at Hetha's temple. Wordlessly, I did as she asked and returned to my pallet.

Sleep was elusive, and my thoughts roiled with unpleasant memories. After a while I heard the faintest of whispers from Innata and cocked an ear to listen.

'The twill and the rose. Twill, a type of weave. Rose a shade of red. You were arrogant, Kaillan. And brazen.'

I went to sit up, narrowly escaping knocking my head on the underside of the cart before I realised it must be her fever speaking. Rolling out from beneath the tray, I stood up to look at her. There was moonlight enough to see she appeared to be in a restless sleep. The camp was otherwise still, although at least two of the men were snoring. I leaned over to touch her forehead. She didn't wake, and her skin was clammy.

'Clever then, not so much now,' she whispered. 'My father taught me early to read subtleties, to recognise mockery when it was intended.' She groaned, and her hands pulled restlessly at the blanket covering her. 'They will torture you until you die. The only person who can save you is *me.*'

I touched her shoulder. Not wanting to disturb my father and be scolded for talking to her, I whispered softly into her ear. 'Milady, wake up. You dream.'

She didn't wake, but pushed me away. 'I'm a *mother,* Kaillan. No one murders a child in my care. This boy will be cared for.' There was real anger in her tone, but fortunately little volume. The rest of the camp slept on. Her eyes snapped open then, and she grabbed at my hand tight, asking, 'How could he be so cruel?'

Gods knew who she thought I was, for she wasn't seeing me at all. She was reliving her past, resurrecting it in a fever dream. 'They broke his fingers; did you see? Cut off his thumb ... I kept my pledge.'

'Who are you?' I asked, whispering.

Not really expecting an answer, I was surprised when she did reply, not that it made much sense. 'I can't say. The baffle, you know. Gerentia Iria did that to me. To protect the secrets of sanctuary.' A tear trickled down her cheek. 'I am so tired of fighting, Haze. I'm tired of looking for him, but I cannot stop.'

'Try to sleep now.'

'No,' she said. 'I need to *win*. And I have to find Kaillan, of course.' After that, she drifted back into a more natural sleep. I kept watch for a while, and didn't return to my pallet until I was sure her fever had dropped.

Even then I lay awake, trying to work out what she had been referring to, but none of it made sense. Haze had mentioned the name Kaillan Riverdell, but what were the twill and the rose? Or the secrets of sanctuary? The word baffle, though... When Haze had shown me that word written down, I'd thought of something that mystified, or bewildered, but now Innata had just said *the* baffle. As if it was a *thing*. That sparked a memory. I'd heard that word before. I remembered Spake's furnace, the stone one built outside in his yard. A metal door inside the flue could be closed off to reduce the supply of air, which then dampened down the fire. That metal door was called a baffle. Not something that *puzzled*, but something that *muted* ... And Gerentia? That was the title given only to the most senior of the archpriestesses of a goddess. There were five goddesses, thus only five gerentias.

In the cool of the night, I shivered, and wondered. What was it that had been done to this woman, and by whom?

*

146

The first time I looked as if I wasn't busy, Cyrrin made me exercise by running on the spot. After that, if I had nothing to do, I practised hurling a variety of projectiles or worked on routines with my quarterstaff, telling Cyrrin that Pa had asked me to practice those skills. On the first day, Petch watched. On the second, he produced a pole of his own and worked out with me. He was twice my age, but still supple, and egged on by Cyrrin, he could have left me much more bruised and sore than he did. Instead, he held back, even whispering advice as we sparred so I could avoid the worst of his blows. When he saw me wincing nonetheless as I crawled into my bedding that night, he surreptitiously tossed me a jar of taldeer liniment for my aching muscles. 'Works for taldeer,' he muttered with a mischievous grin. 'Should work for a stubborn Southerner!'

I nodded my thanks and he started to turn away, but then changed his mind and waved a hand to where Innata already slept on the tray of the cart. 'Do yer best for her, Taygen,' he whispered. 'She don't deserve none of this. Never did, not any of it, poor lass. You treat her like a lady, if yer can. Just don't let Cyrrin see. He blames her and 'ud see her dead if 'twas up to him.'

With that, he scurried away.

I watched Petch carefully afterwards, and noted a dozen ways he tried to make life easier for her and, more surprisingly, for me too. Wild lavender would appear on her pillow, or an extra helping of stew remained in the pot when I came to wash it, left there for me. He risked Cyrrin's ire, but he continued his kindnesses anyway and was clever enough to hide them.

As the days passed, by the time I sought my blanket at night I was exhausted. At least Pa didn't include me in the night shift when the others had to do their turn at guard duty. I was grateful, even though I knew it was because my own father did not trust me.

Late on the third afternoon, I made my first move. The sun was low in the sky, but Innata had asked to have her stool placed in the shadow of the cart to avoid the glare. As I walked past her on my way to collect firewood, I said quietly, 'Hazelle is on the road ahead of us.'

When I returned, back bowed under the weight of the wood I carried, I risked a second sentence. 'She's waiting for us in Crowbridge.'

Neither time did I look at her, so I had no idea if she'd reacted.

As I handed her the evening meal that night, she smiled and thanked me. When Hervan frowned at her, she said quietly, 'Good manners were drummed into me as a child, Captain Hervan. They are hard to relinquish. Moreover, I see no reason why I should change.' Her tone was neutral, her demeanour pleasant, yet he had been chided, put in his place in the gentlest of ways. Perhaps to reassert his authority, he then stopped me from sleeping under the cart, saying that she was well enough to shout for help at night if it was necessary.

I watched Innata surreptitiously whenever I could. She was unfailingly courteous, but also intractable. Pa would inform her that he wanted to be on the way in the morning an hour after dawn, but she was never ready. If there was a stream nearby, she would take her time washing. If it was just a matter of relieving herself, she never hurried. The one time Hervan told her she was too slow, she informed him in a tone as icy as a desert night that it was the carelessness of his men that had caused the injury, thus ensuring every movement was painful and laborious. Pa reddened, Petch looked sick with guilt and even Folman winced. I had to swallow a smile at her courage. I couldn't make up my mind whether her shambling walk leaning on the arm of one of the men was all for show or not, but it didn't take me long to see that

148

she was a woman of both wit and courage, and it would be a mistake to underestimate her.

I was beginning to like Innata — a lot. But I also wondered ... Why did my father and his men treat her as well as they did if she was indeed a thief? Moreover, one who had stolen something as valuable to the Crown as the carcanet? Perhaps they didn't dare mistreat her because they knew, or suspected, she was from an important Talodian family.

The next time I had a chance to speak to her without anyone else hearing, I said, 'Haze intends to rescue you in Crowbridge. I said I'd help. If you need to say anything, I have excellent hearing. Whisper, and I'll hear you, even at a distance.' Her eyes widened ever so slightly, but she said nothing. After that, I didn't speak again. I had nothing to say that was important enough to risk conversing and I kept away from her, except when I was driving the cart. Even then, speaking might have been a risk. If the road was wide enough, one of the guardsmen—usually Folman, who was not very bright but followed orders to the letter—rode beside us. Where the way narrowed, he'd drop to a position immediately behind the tailgate.

The journey soon took me away from the familiar. I'd never left Breakedge before and I stared wide-eyed at all that would have been normal to the others. Across the Devil-Honed Hills and into the Breakheart Mountains, we passed through tracts of grassland. In the folds of the slopes, an occasional string of motionless pools, beaded with trees along the edges, waited thirstily for the next rainstorm that could have been as much as half a year away.

The vista on the other side of the pass into Calbeck Duchy was such a contrast it staggered me. Trees, taller than any house, were packed together like people crowding into a market square to see a mummery. Water was so profligate it tumbled and gushed down the slopes, thundering in our ears until the men had to raise their voices to be heard. Rain became so frequent that the novelty of it soon wore off and left me miserable and wet and cold. At least now there was shelter for the night; miserable wayside dosshouses, unmanned, where my travel companions, Innata included, slept on the floor around the central fireplace, sometimes sharing with wayfarers or traders who were fellow travellers. I was relegated to the stable to keep an eye on our mounts. In the morning, Cyrrin was there to kick me awake.

At least the road was mostly downhill from the pass, winding in tortuous bends between two sombre walls of trees into the valley of the Crowlick River. I wasn't used to the cloudy sky, the damp, the dark understorey, the noise of falling water. I longed for distant vistas and far horizons, for blue skies and the heat of a bright sun.

With the constant rain, the state of the road deteriorated and our progress slowed. Several times the cart was bogged and had to be unloaded and dug out. The talyak was stoical, doing its willing best to move us through the sludge. The taldeer were more finicky, hating the way the mud oozed up the cleft of their hooves. They squabbled among themselves and balked at the worst of the mud patches.

The change in conditions reshaped us from a coherent party into a disjointed string of individuals trying to cope with treacherous slippery conditions, which made it easier for Innata and me to talk. Over the days it took for us to descend the mountains to Crowbridge, we snatched moments when the riders behind us were out of sight around a bend, and those ahead of us were out of earshot.

'Does Haze have a plan?' was the first thing she asked.

'I don't know,' I replied, glancing over my shoulder at her. 'She said she'll find us when we arrive in Crowbridge.'

'Then she will. Be alert. If you see her, tell her I'm fine. Well enough to ride.' She paused, drawing the hood of her cloak around to hide her face. 'Why are you helping us?' It wasn't hard to detect the suspicion in her tone.

I stared straight ahead. 'You could say she paid me.'

She was quiet for a moment, assessing that. Then, 'What with?'

'The Griffin Carcanet.'

I couldn't see her reaction, although I heard her sigh. Then, 'Captain Hervan told me he had obtained it. I wondered how, as he didn't mention Hazelle. I was worried for her, so I'm relieved you're the one who gave it to him.'

'Not exactly. Let's say, I let him find it.'

'And yet your father despises you! You are beginning to interest me deeply, young man. Do you know who I am?'

'No.'

'You puzzle me. You're the son of a kingsman who's spent half a lifetime hunting me and yet you're going to help me be rescued? Why?'

What could I say? That I was childishly angry with my father for his dismissal of my earlier help? That I *liked* Haze? That I'd needed the carcanet to save my arse from the fix I had got into — and once I agreed to something, I kept the promise?

In the end, I blurted another truth, 'Because, from what Haze said, Goddess Jenat's archpriestesses helped you escape my father and his men for *years*. Whatever you did, it must have had the sanction of a goddess. Who am I to question the decision of a deity?'

She gave a low laugh. 'Who indeed? Just who are you, Taygen? A young man so despised by his father that he is not given a voice to speak. What is it you did?'

Self-hatred flooded back and the words, when they came, were forced. 'Ruined my brother's life. He is blind, no longer able to serve God Saffrin, his dreams wrecked, all because of my foolishness.'

She was quiet for a minute or two, choosing her words with care. Then, 'Life can be cruel. I once watched, helpless to stop the unthinkable happening. I can give you some advice, if you like.'

I shrugged.

'Don't feel sorry for yourself. Your brother suffers and you cannot change that. But you have your youth and your health. If you cannot help your brother, then help others. That may be your only way forward.'

I snorted. Trite words. Easily said. For me, there *was* no way out. And not suffering? Did she not know there are so many ways to suffer? Then I wondered what she had been through. 'Is — is that what you have done? Helped others?'

'I learned.' Still careful with her words, she was silent for a moment, then added, 'It's hard for someone as bereft as I was to turn their back on another such.'

Folman rode up closer then, and we ended the conversation until we had another chance that afternoon. By then, I thought I truly understood. The baffle was a barrier that halted any words that could reveal her past history, even to her sister. Anything that magical had to have its source in a deity. It must have been imposed — at a guess — by the Goddess Jenat's temple to protect their secrets.

'When feverish, you mentioned a baffle,' I said to her, once we had another chance of conversation that afternoon. 'Is that perhaps a barrier to speech? A way of silencing you?'

Tears welled in her eyes. She clearly wanted desperately to say something, but could not.

'I'll tell Haze,' I said. 'I'll explain it to her.'

She reached over and squeezed my hand. 'Thank you. Thank you.'

'I'm sorry. It is cruel what it has done to you. If there is any way I can help you now, tell me. All you have to do is whisper.'

*

'We may make the military camp this side of Crow-bridge before nightfall.'

Her voice startled me, though the words were barely murmured. She had been silent for several hours, even when we could have spoken unobserved. It wasn't raining, but bands of mist drifted past, cold and clammy. Ahead of me, Pa was hunched low in the saddle with the hood of his cloak over his head. Rivulets of water trickled down his back. Ahead of him, Cyrrin. I didn't bother to look behind to check on the others. Innata faced backwards and would not have spoken had there been any chance any of them would notice us talking.

'I've no idea of where we are. I've never left Breakedge before,' I said. As a lad I had spent hours in the map room of the Border Patrol barracks, and I had an excellent map-based knowledge of the geography of Talodiac. My problem was transferring that knowledge to the reality of a winding track through mountains in poor visibility. 'I've never been out of the Southedge Duchy. Is the weather always as pukey as this?'

'At least it's not as boring as Breakedge's.'

'Right now, I could do with boring as long as it was sunny.' I was heartily weary of being cold and damp.

'Boring does have its advantages,' she said. 'If I were you, I'd be careful around Cyrrin. That man hates you even more than you realise. He's a twisted soul.'

I said nothing, so she changed the subject. 'Do you know what would happen to me if we got to Templebridge?'

'No.'

'I do. I would be quietly murdered. Once my body is shown to the Lawseer...' She struggled to say something more, but the words would not come. The baffle was working its spell.

I blinked, nonplussed. The *Lawseer*? Why on earth would the most important male cleric in the kingdom want to see her dead over a piece of jewellery? *Oh, Haze, we must have got it all wrong.* This can't be just about the theft of a pretty bauble!

Finally, Innata did manage a casual comment that, as far as I knew, had nothing to do with anything. 'I've heard the King has another bride in mind.'

I nodded. 'We did hear rumours in Breakedge. But then, we've heard the same rumour for years. A king without a wife is as odd as a rooster without a flock of hens.' There was nothing she could say to that, so I changed the subject. 'Is Hazelle your daughter?'

'I didn't give birth to her.'

'Your sister?'

She didn't reply.

'You can't say who she is, can you? Because of the baffle. I'd seen that word before you mentioned it in your fever — you wrote it down. Haze showed me.'

'Did I say anything else in my fever?'

'You spoke of someone called Kaillan. And how you were looking for him.'

She was silent.

'You can't say any more?'

'No.'

'I think he must be a redweaver.'

'What makes you think that?'

154

'You rambled in your fever. You spoke of rose, which can be a shade of red, and twill, which is some type of weave. Redweaver. And then you mentioned his name.'

She gave a soft laugh. 'Do you know how funny that is? All those years of not being able to speak! All that time struggling to solve a mystery when I couldn't form the words — and along comes a fever and I blab it all out!'

'Well, most of it was muddled up and didn't make much sense. Who did it to you?'

'Ah, that's one of the many things I can't tell you, alas. I hope you are not going to get into trouble because of Haze and me, Taygen.'

'Oh, I'll be all right. I can't be blamed for whatever Haze does, can I? She'll rescue you here and I'll just ride on with my pa to find a job somewhere in Templebridge.'

Just then the clouds cleared, and I glimpsed smoke rising into the sky from hundreds of chimneys in the valley below. Crowbridge.

Somewhere down there, Hazelle was waiting.

How was I to know that I was about to set foot on the path to this cell in the King's Keep?

16

Ah, Lady Sianta, you have just left me with this stub of a candle after telling me the King has returned — and so my remaining days alive are few. And thank you for explaining that he's waiting for the midsummer celebrations, when everyone is so involved with festivals and feasting that my execution will pass unremarked.

I think you have been lying to me though, Lady Sianta … I've doubted for quite some time now that His Royal Majesty has any idea that this particular story is being written down. Do you perhaps have a greater allegiance to the truth of history than you may have to a single person? Or do you serve a different master, someone *not* the King?

Either way it's a dangerous game you play, and I can only admire you for it.

Words appear to be failing me. Somehow there was always part of me that assumed I would be able to extricate myself from this mess. I'm sure you know how I've tried. I've seen you staring at those deep scratches into the mortar between the stonework, for example, evidence of my attempts to reach that tiny square of a window high up on the outer wall. A window doubtless too small to wriggle through, even if I could reach it.

Such a pity the cell doesn't have the kind of lock that can be opened from inside. I'm good with locks, but if you can't reach the keyhole, there's not much to be done.

I've even spent hours seeking to find the chink in the armour of your soul that would persuade you to free me. But alas, you are apparently steadfast in your support of a king who turned his back on his duty and all decency. Oh yes, I know much of the real story now. My father ordered Cyrrin to bring me here, trussed up like a goose for roasting, and that bastard of a man took great joy in telling me along the way as much as he knew. I haven't written that down yet.

But does it not bother you that all that was decided in the past was done with the approval of Goddess Jenat? Some say the gods judge us as we enter the flow of the eternal Red River on the way to the possibility of everlasting life. Most certainly believe it foolish to disregard the advice of gods! You've never told me which one you worship, although I have asked you several times. I wonder why not?

But enough of such things.

Let me now continue my tale so that those generations still to be born will know me when they read these words, and perhaps they'll tell their children of Taygen Hervan-Gariane.

Well, that's what you say will happen, anyway.

*

Two hours before sunset and still a mile short of Crowbridge, we passed the town's wayfarer camp under some trees. A little further along, we turned off through imposing gateposts in a stone wall, each carved with the griffin royal. Scruffy wayfarer urchins of varying ages sat in a line along the stone wall bordering the road, drumming their heels and lobbing stones at the pied crows poking around in the taldeer dung in the grass. The oldest of them was a lanky lad with spiky, unkempt hair and a foul mouth. When Pa glowered at him, he hawked and spat in our direction. Innata laughed.

The field beyond the wall was set aside as grazing for the sole use of mounts belonging to the Kings' soldiers, couriers, or officials. A narrow building had been constructed along the top of the slope to house mounts and men. It was empty when we arrived, except for an elderly caretaker, a pensioned soldier. The pasture field below was hemmed in by the wall on one side, hedges on another two and, at the foot of the hill, by a tributary of the River Crowlick. Pa intended we stay for a couple of days to rest and feed our mounts after the arduous mountain crossing. Luckily for us, that was going to give Hazelle a chance to contact us.

Mind you, I still didn't have a clue how we could extract Innata from my father's clutches. I believed it was the right thing to do, but an acid devil of guilt was sitting on my shoulder the whole while, whispering: *traitor, traitor, traitor! And you a kingsman's son!'*

The next morning, Pa sent Cyrrin and Gappy into the town with the cart to replenish our supplies. Petch took his turn on duty, patrolling the wall to keep an eye on the wayfarer lads. Folman led his mount down to the river for a swim while the caretaker chopped some kindling for us, so only Pa, Innata and I were in the common room. Innata's grim expression brooded like a coming sandstorm. Pa had locked her overnight in one of the rooms, and from the glower on her face, that unaccustomed privacy had not made her cheerful.

It wasn't long before she turned her ire on Pa, in a boiling rage.

'What right have you to treat me this way?' she demanded. 'I've been wearing the same filthy clothes since we left Breakedge. They don't even fit properly — they were given to me by the temple physicians because mine were so bloody. Yesterday I was soaked through to the skin, shivering with cold, and all I had to wrap around me last night were blankets thick with filth and fleas and bed bugs! What did I ever do to deserve this, Captain Hervan? Isn't it enough that I'm going to lose my life?'

Pa jumped to his feet snapping, 'Not another word!' His consternation was interesting, since I was only other person there. He was afraid she would blurt out something he didn't want me to hear. Even more intriguing, what was she up to?

I looked blank, pretending I wasn't much interested.

She took no notice and continued to berate him. He started to speak over the top of her, addressing me. 'Go take the other mounts down to the stream. You should have watered them by now.'

'I already have,' I replied mildly.

'Get out of here!' He pushed me hard towards the door as Innata continued her tirade.

'Oh, *I* know,' she said, words seeping sarcasm. '*I'm* to blame for what happened to you, aren't I? That night eighteen years ago when you were supposed to ... the night...' The words stuck in her throat, presumably blocked by the baffle.

Hervan shoved hard and I was tumbled out of the door, which he then slammed shut.

Innata, not to be outdone, raised her voice, only to have her next words immediately stifled, by a hand placed over her mouth at a guess. After that I didn't hear anything more.

I didn't know what had precipitated her temper, but I was certain of one thing. It didn't have much to do with her wet clothes, dirty blankets or lice. She wanted to ensure that my father kept me away from her. Yet she had previously worked hard to give me information.

At a guess, she'd decided the less I knew, the safer I'd be. Or perhaps this was her way of indicating to Pa that she was incapable of telling me her secrets.

*

I was in the tackle room repairing a torn trace when Pa came to find me. Innata was nowhere to be seen, so I suppose he must have locked her in again. Before he could say a word, I started in. 'What the hell is going on? And don't tell me she's some delusional madwoman that the King sent one of his captains to find!'

'That's the truth,' he said.

'Eighteen *years*? She can hardly have been more than a child eighteen years ago.'

'The King's business is not your business!'

'You treat Innata with a lot of courtesy for someone you've been hunting. Who is she?'

'Still your tongue, you fool!'

'The Griffin Carcanet. It was always given to the queen at the birth of a son. Was Innata one of the queen's ladies back then? Someone who took advantage of the queen's death to steal her jewellery? Is she the person who brought the carcanet to Breakedge?'

A servant of Queen Thalia's — that would explain such a lot. Or perhaps one of the King's lovers, someone who knew too much?

He took a deep breath, scowling. 'Taygen, best not repeat a word of what you just gabbed, or anything you heard, or you'll be heading for the gibbet yerself. Is that plain enough for yer?'

'To understand that, I need to know what all this is about.'

'No. You don't.'

'Pa, if you want me to keep quiet, you have to give me a reason.'

He considered that in silence. In that moment, something shrank, as if he'd sagged, become smaller. But no, perhaps it was more something within me that changed: a realisation that he was just a man, like any other, rather than that fear-inducing golden warrior of my childhood.

'All right,' he said with a sigh. 'You've the right of it. The Queen gave birth. A son, an heir at last, and lordy, everyone was celebrating. King Edwild, pissing drunk, brought his latest mistress into his royal bed. Next day, though, the baby was sickly and the queen still bled. Talk was, Queen Thalia was losing her mind. Her private apartments were full of quacks 'n' physicians and noble ladies and gods know who. Edwild asked us to get his fancy woman, Innata, out of his apartments and out of the palace, without her being seen, to avoid a scandal. He escorted her down the King's Steps to where my squad waited. She was wearing one of his cloaks and underneath she carried the Queen's jewellery box. But how was we to know that? Not as if she was some street whore he picked up in one of his drunken forays into the city gutters! She was a fancy bit, had connections to a noble family.

'The King said take 'er where she wants. Goddess Jenat's temple. She disappeared inside and never came out. Meantime, neither the Queen nor the babe survived the night. King Edwild was in a right rage. Blamed us for the missing jewels. Told us not to return until we'd brought Innata back to face justice. Every time we reported back, he gave the same reply: forbidden to return 'til we got her.' His tone was larded with bitterness. 'Now we're taking her back, along with what's left of the Griffin Carcanet. That's the whole sorry tale.'

I stared at him, trying to take that in. *Eighteen years of his life.*

But that wasn't all. We both knew what he was admitting to: all the lies he'd told us, his family. Or rather, the lies he'd allowed us to believe, of Hervan rising through the ranks in the King's Guard, being trusted and honoured by the King, when the reality was that he'd spent much of his life unsuccessfully hunting a runaway woman as punishment for his own supposed dereliction of duty, on the whim of a monarch. Doubtless the only reason he'd carried the rank of captain from a relatively young age was to make it easier for him to fulfil his task.

'I s'pose Spake stole the Griffin Carcanet from her,' he said. 'I don't want to dig no deeper into that.'

Which was to my advantage. But I couldn't help thinking that she must have had the help of the temples over the whole of Talodiac, otherwise Pa would have found her long before this.

One goddess at least was on her side. *Why?*

'That's a very sad story,' I said finally. 'Not one the King wants bruited about.'

'No.' He gave me a hard stare. I was sure he'd left much unspoken.

I nodded. He knew I must be aware of how dangerous the knowledge was to my safety. Fortunately for me, he couldn't guess how little notice I was taking of that danger.

*

Later, when all my chores were done and I was anxious to go find Hazelle, I asked Pa if I could go into the town. He refused. Evidently I was still being punished, so I did the next best thing: I sat on the wall bordering the road and watched the people passing by, most of them from the wayfarers' camp, a motley group of tinkers, day labourers, beggars and the like. Close enough for Pa to keep an eye on me if he wanted, but far enough away so he wouldn't see much if anyone stopped to chat.

Idly I watched one such fellow lurching along, leaning on a crutch and dragging his game leg. Unkempt hair, dirty clothes and filthy bare feet gave the impression not just of poverty, but of scant attention to cleanliness. He gave me a wink as he approached and I realised it was the foul-mouthed beggar from the evening we'd arrived.

'Oi, pretty lad, got a rickling coin for the likes o' me?' he asked, holding out a grimy hand. He appeared to be missing a couple of front teeth.

I shook my head.

'Never took you for a skinflint, Taygen.'

I blinked in total shock, for there was no mistaking the voice when she dropped the thick argot. '*Haze?*'

'Indeed. Don't come too close. Even I don't like the way I smell.' A gap-toothed smile. No, not a gap, just blackened teeth. The cunning bitch. I curbed a grin of utter delight even as I struggled to get my head around the detailed perfection of her disguise.

'Pox 'n' rots,' I said, wrinkling my nose. 'What have you been wallowing in? A knacker's midden?'

'Horrid, isn't it? Smells like rotting cabbage and dog droppings. Fortunately the reality is less noxious. But quickly, how's Innata?'

'She's acting as though she's as weak as a kitten. She's told me she's fine and well enough to ride. We'll remain here two days.'

'Where is she now?'

'They're keeping her locked in the larder most of the time.'

'Do you think it would be possible for her to get out late tonight?'

'Hmm ... probably.' I had my lock-picks still.

'Without raising a ruckus?'

'I think so. But one of the men patrols the field and the buildings all night. It might be difficult to get her over this wall without being seen. The gate will be locked.'

'Only one man?'

'Yes. They take it in turns.'

She scratched idly at her filthy hair while she considered that.

'Have you got *lice*?'

'Fleas, I think.' She shrugged. 'Look, Taygen, there's no need for you to get into trouble for this. You just set it up so Innata can escape, and no one will involve you. Not even if she and I get caught.'

I could ride on to Templebridge, lead an ordinary life, be my own man, discover the adventure of life in the royal city ... It sounded too good to be true. It took a conscious effort not to roll my eyes, yet I heard the promise in her words. She'd opened up the way out for me, so I could get on with my life. Another act of treason to be committed, yet my father need never know. *If* we were clever. And Innata — that's why she had argued with Pa. She wanted him to keep us separated, so that if she escaped it would look as if I'd had nothing to do with it. But if Innata disappeared, my father's hopes for redemption would be dashed.

I asked, 'Have you any idea who you are?' I had no clue.

'None. Have you?'

I shook my head.

'Does it matter?'

She was right to ask, for it didn't matter. What mattered was to choose the path that was honest, that was true. She was choosing to throw her lot in with the woman who had raised her, the woman who represented her whole knowledge of family life.

I took a deep breath. 'There's a couple of things you should know. Innata was feverish and started rambling. I found out what a baffle is, I think.' I explained what had happened.

'And it was applied by a *gerentia*?' she asked, looking at me in horror.

'I think so. Goddess Jenat's, I imagine. With Innata's permission, probably.'

'No! I can't believe that! No one would submit to something so ... so *diabolical* by choice!' Her shock was riddled through with anger.

'They might if the alternative was to be handed over to the King's justice. Haze, you're not going to like this, but my father says Innata was a court lady who was the King's mistress. My father and his men were tasked with quietly escorting her out of the palace to avoid a scandal the night the Queen Thalia died. They didn't realise she'd take advantage of the turmoil in the royal apartments to steal the Queen's jewellery box and run away.'

'You think she's a *thief*?'

'Well, what else are we to think? The other jewellery you spoke of her having might have belonged to Innata, I suppose, but we *know* the carcanet belongs to the Crown, to be passed down only to a queen who produces an heir.'

She frowned unhappily and shook her head. 'I can't believe she'd do that!'

'Haze, for goodness' sake, *she had the carcanet*! What else would explain that?'

'A gift from a dying queen to a loyal servant?'

'Holy Saffrin's balls, how likely is that? It is the symbol of the legitimacy of a royal heir!'

I looked back over my shoulder, at the barracks at the far end of the field. My father, his back to me, was talking to the caretaker at the wood heap.

Hervan, a kingsman all his life. Loyal to his monarch and his country, prepared to serve his lord in whatever way he was asked. Suffering punishment because he had allowed the King's mistress to escape with the Queen's jewels. He had not been given an alternative. Turning my gaze back to Hazelle, or rather to this grubby, pathetic lad of her masquerade, I thought of the life she was now contemplating. Hunted down, constantly on the move and in danger, never sure who she could trust, and for what? For a thief who would never be able to tell her the truth?

She tilted her head, watching my face. 'No need to say it. I know. I don't blame you, Taygen, I really don't. I'm just grateful you haven't turned me in to Hervan. I know it has cost you.'

'Do you have money?'

She gave a bitter laugh. 'Oh yes. The carcanet was only part of the jewellery in the box. A queen's ransom to live on, and I have it.' She patted her waistline, where she presumably wore a money belt under her clothing. She sniffed and wiped a tear from her cheek with the flat of her hand before adding, 'Her embroidery: that was the way she explained her income. I realise that now.'

'Then you can walk away, buy yourself a country estate in the duchy of your choice.' To tell the truth, I was wondering if I was missing something yet again. Last time I'd talked to her about Innata's life, Hazelle had been burning with resentment and anger at the lies she had been told by Innata her entire life, so much so that I'd wondered if she would do just that — abandon Innata and make a life for herself. Now she was more subdued, more troubled. More intense. The anger was still there, but curled tight.

'I could,' she agreed. 'But I also have to live with myself. Oh, Taygen, think! I don't care what you say. I *know* her. And you've just told me why she never explained anything. She *couldn't!* And there's another thing: she had the help of Goddess Jenat and her temples. Why would they help her if she was just a common thief bedded by the King? There has to be something we don't know!'

Just then four minstrels carrying an assortment of instruments strolled past towards Crowbridge. One of them gave me a cheeky grin. 'Surely, sirrah, a sweet-looking fella like yourself can do better than pass the time with a guttersnipe?'

'Oi, you pig-gut strummer,' Haze shot back indignantly. 'I got a real sweet nature, I do!'

'Maybe true, lad, but surely not as sweet spoken!' he said, rattling his tambourine.

One of his friends wrinkled his nose and added, 'And surely not as sweetly perfumed!' The four of them laughed and walked on.

'Listen,' she said the moment they were out of earshot, 'I do have a rough plan. But it depends on you being able to get her out of the building undetected. Is that possible? Are you still prepared to help?'

Possible? Oh, yes. A locked door was no barrier to me when I had a lock-pick. But to do it without implicating myself to my father? That would be much more difficult. 'Sure,' I said, inserting as much confidence into my tone as I could muster. 'I'll do my best to get her away if you promise not to implicate me if you get caught.'

She gave a shrug. 'We have to trust each other.'

'Well,' I said, 'you did buy me with a necklace.'

'A rather expensive bauble, as I recall.'

We both laughed, acknowledging that our whole relationship was absurd, a criss-crossed tangle of trust and suspicion, and not much of the trust being either logical or sensible. If I had to distil our relationship down to an explanation that makes any sense at all, I'd say it was simply that we *liked* each other. I don't mean as a lad and a lass wanting a roll in the meadow grass, but more each of us recognising the other as the friend we'd been missing out on all our lives.

'Tell me what you have in mind,' I said. 'And remember, she was badly hurt and I'm not that sure she has fully recovered even now. But maybe she's just pretending to be so weak...'

We made our plans, and she pointed out a thick patch of trees and undergrowth on the other side of the road as a suitable place to hide the two taldeer she would have with her, come evening.

'I could get a third beast, if you want it,' she added.

I shook my head.

We made contingency plans then, just in case things went wrong, but I won't bore you with those, Sianta. None of them was ever used.

When we said goodbye, she limped slowly away towards the wayfarer camp, while I headed back to the quarters. Halfway up the field, I turned to watch her. Even though I knew who it was, I could have sworn it was some street lad plagued with a severe disability. I was still shocked that I'd only known her by her voice. What kind of life had she lived to be so skilled at deception? I didn't know, but I had an ache in the middle of my chest as I watched her go. Gods below, I was about to ruin my father's life because of Haze and Innata, and even then I wasn't absolutely sure why.

I'll admit I'm a bit of a cynic when it comes to the gods. I think they gain as much from people as we gain from them. It's not as though they promise us everlasting life, like the Dekadani Godhead does. But our gods are knowledgeable and wise and if we want to live a good life, then we ought to listen. And according to Hazelle, Innata was constantly helped by the hierarchy of Goddess Jenat's priestess-hood, not just the night she had fled, but ever since then. That had to mean something.

I still wish that I could have come to know Hazelle better. What might have been ... It's a grief to me, the possible depth of which I'll never know. She might have become a lover, or more likely a lifelong friend. We had so much more to say to one another, but it'll never be said, and I'll never know what might have been.

*

And that, Lady Sianta, is where I shall stop. That's all I'm going to give you. My father will doubtless have told the King all that he and his men saw of what happened that night we tried to save Innata. It was dark, misty, damp, I will say that much. We were all ... disoriented, frantic. The stakes were high. In the confusion, I don't think any of us quite knew what was happening, or the sequence of it. The only reality I know is that my father brought me back to Temple-bridge trussed up like a calf for the slaughter as an offering to the King.

And now you won't even tell me if Hervan is still alive. I'm guessing that kings don't like to be magnanimous to those who know too many secrets, and if my father lives still, he won't do so for much longer, not if Edwild has heard what happened that night.

At the end of my life, it would be good to believe that I achieved something. That I did something worthwhile, noble, even. Instead, there's any number of things I'm ashamed of: stealing from my fellow citizens, harming my brother, disappointing my mother, betraying my king, bringing shame to my father. Because I'm not certain what happened that night, I'm not sure I have anything to balance out the bad.

You tell me I die soon. The King has returned to Temple-bridge and he will be informed of my presence. I will be executed.

Well and good. I am ready. And this account of mine? Have I told you the truth? That's up to you to decide. There is more I could say, but I don't think I will. Next time I see you, I think I shall ask you why you lied to me, why you attempted to play me for a fool. I may have been a lackwit lad from time to time, but I'm not entirely stupid.

One thing you never quite convinced me of: that the King would ever knowingly have allowed a written record of all I know. You can put a baffle on a person, but not on a story written on parchment.

So, who is powerful enough to allow you daily access to the prison, and to me, in the middle of the night, *without the King knowing?* Who could persuade Alzop — who wears the king's griffin on his surcoat — to let you into the keep in the middle of the night? It's a dangerous game you two play. Are you more frightened of whoever asked you to do this than you are of the King?

And ... *why?* Why does someone want this account of mine? What possible reason can they have?

You know what I think? If King Edwild finds out what you've been doing, you'll die beside me.

Signed,
Taygen Hervan-Gariane
Second three moon-month,
Year 19 of the Reign of King Edwild

PART 3

UNRAVELLING
A
TANGLED PAST

17

Haze woke to the reality of a cold meadow on a damp and misty night. She bit back a groan. She'd dozed off, which was *insane*! Waking fully, she blinked away the remnant of a bad dream.

Had anything changed while she'd dozed? She took a deep breath, told herself to keep calm, to concentrate. The ground was chilly and hard, its unevenness furrowing discomfort into her back. The darkness was bitter. A ghostly feathering of hoarfrost tickled the top of the stone wall beside her and tipped each blade of grass next to her face. Nothing stirred nearby, although there was a sound: the temple bell in Crowbridge, slightly muffled by the damp air, ringing out the hour: two bells. Taygen had agreed to meet her around midnight.

Where the mucking mire was he?

Earlier in the night she'd climbed into the grounds of the barracks to hide and wait for him where they'd agreed, under the shelter of a drooping bitternut tree just inside the stonework of the wall separating road from meadow. She'd curled up between the trunk and the stones for warmth, and some time later, she must have dozed off. It wasn't often she was that stupid, but stress had wrecked normal sleep for days.

She stood up to see what was happening. Peeking over the coping, all appeared quiet along the public thoroughfare on the other side, although her view was blurred here and there by tendrils of drifting mist. She couldn't see her two taldeer. Already saddled and provisioned, they were tied up out of sight on the other side of the roadway. A risk that; they were too close to the wayfarer camp to be entirely safe. Still, it was unlikely anyone would be travelling in the dark, especially since the town gates closed at sunset.

Gods, it was cold. Overhead, the smallest moon, the one wayfarers call the Ice-child, appeared blue-rimed amidst the strewn scatter of stars. It would have been lovely to have one of the warm cloaks she'd left with the mounts, but a cloak might have hampered a hasty exit over the wall. The only thing she had with her, besides her quarterstaff, was the small cloth drawstring bag strapped around her waist, containing coins and the remainder of Innata's jewellery.

Time dragged. More mist drifted past, trailing up the slopes from the riverside. As she turned to look at the military buildings, she breathed deep, then clapped her hands over her face, hoping to trap her breath to warm up her nose.

At the top of the slope, the barracks were dark and silent. Somewhere out there in the field was one of Hervan's guards, mounted on his taldeer as he rode the perimeter. She couldn't see him. 'Cyrrin will be on duty,' Taygen had told her, in the tone he used every time he mentioned the man — a mixture of resentment, dislike and grudging respect. 'He's thorough. Be careful.'

Careful. Right. She'd dozed off... And where the ten hells was Taygen anyway? Perhaps he'd changed his mind about aiding Innata's escape.

At least she now knew why Innata had always been on the move. Friends would have been a complication to a runaway. She heaved a heartfelt sigh. Gods' hearts, she needed more than just the two of them always living on a blade's edge. Always well fed, decently clothed and safely sheltered, but never wholly secure, never totally unthreatened, and definitely never settled. She could change her accent at will from a highborn lady of Rothengar to a lowborn actress from Calbeck and use the twang of half a dozen duchies in between. A muddle of skills and accomplishments, a history of manipulation and compromise, a lifelong intimacy with danger and excitement, adventure and change; all that was her life.

She hadn't minded it. She hadn't even minded not being entirely sure if Innata was family, or no relation at all. The default was always to pose as Innata's younger sister. And that's the one that for most of her life she'd hoped was true.

Only one thing had bothered her over the years: she'd never known the reason for the secrecy.

Always on the move, always seeking a man with crippled fingers, always seeking to know where there were redweavers, always treated with compassion and deference at Goddess Jenat's temples — those mysteries had annoyed her for years, but she'd learned not to ask questions because there were never any answers.

Innata the seamstress, mother, sister, aunt, guide, companion. The only person Hazelle Wayfarer had ever trusted, until Taygen. And now it seemed that at eighteen Innata had been a King's mistress, not to mention a clever criminal. There had to be more, a lot more to that story, because the temples of Goddess Jenat had helped them flee her pursuers for years. Had she been an innocent young woman fleeing a vindictive, vicious monarch — rather than a wicked woman of loose morals, dishonesty and greed? Had her theft been more one of desperation?

The image she had of Innata collapsing onto the street, slashed across the neck, life draining, blood — so much of it — pooling on the paving, draining into the cracks... Suddenly life had been reframed as fleeting and fragile. Safety declared itself easily fractured. Only Taygen's quick action had prevented her own discovery by Hervan.

To trust Hervan's son was ridiculously dangerous. Quite apart from his parentage, he was a pickpocket; hardly an upright citizen, and yet still she trusted, all because he had risked being revealed as a thief in order to save a child he didn't even know. And yet here she was, hiding near the barracks building, trusting Taygen Hervan-Gariane yet again, believing he would risk everything to free Innata.

Someone opened a door in the barracks and it squeaked horribly. She hunkered down at the foot of the tree, holding her breath.

'Who goes?'

Not Taygen, and not coming from the barracks, but a man's voice from near the stables. A shape moved out into the open: Cyrrin on duty, still mounted on his taldeer. He'd evidently been sheltering from the cold alongside the outer wall.

Taygen answered from outside the barracks, 'Only me!'

'Cold weather making you dribble piss like an old codger, eh?' No mist lingered around the barracks at the top of the slope, and his sneer carried in the crisp cold air.

'My bowels are on the run, not my piss,' Taygen snapped back. 'You can laugh yourself silly on your rounds while I freeze m'balls on the pot. Not the first or the last time to-night, either!'

She peered into the gloom and saw his shape scuttle across to the privy, doubled up as if he was in pain. Cyrrin laughed and urged his mount towards the river, disappearing a moment later into the mist. For a while, nothing moved. Then Taygen once more, soundlessly hurrying back up into the barracks. She could barely see him against the darkness of the building, and all was quiet until he reappeared, this time with a cloaked figure.

She stayed where she was, watching as they came towards her. They were horribly conspicuous as they crossed the meadow, dark shadows on white-rimed grass, leaving foot-prints behind like arrows pointing the way. Moonlight flood-ed the open field, even as mist gathered across the flats near the river. And Innata — she seemed so slow, no confidence in her step. Taygen had her by the arm, as if he feared she'd fall.

175

Haze picked up her quarterstaff and stepped out of her hiding place.

'Sorry,' Taygen whispered as they came up. 'One of the guards is sound asleep, but the other two went to gamble at the wayfarers' camp. I wanted to wait for them to return, but they haven't come in. You might bump into them walking up the road any time. Let's get her over the wall.'

Innata raised a hand to touch Haze's face. 'I'm sorry,' she whispered.

She didn't reply. She put her staff on the top of the stone coping and hauled herself up, a leg on either side. 'Can't see anyone,' she said softly. Since she'd last looked, the mist had crept along the road in billows that now surged and waned in confusing tangles. It also tamped down sounds, muffling the sough of the wind in the pines and the distance trickle of stream water on its way to the river. Bending down she hooked a hand under Thalia's armpit to hoist her upwards while Taygen boosted her from below.

'Thank you,' Innata said to him. 'I'll not forget all y—'

And that was the moment that all hell broke loose.

18

'Captain!'

The bull-like bellow in the meadow came from Cyrrin. One moment he hadn't been there, the next his mount was galloping towards them out of the brume near the river, its lowered rack of antlers slicing through the mist.

'*Hervan!* To me, now!'

Haze's heart thundered under her ribs hard enough to hurt. She grabbed her quarterstaff, leapt down from the wall to the road surface and whipped around just in time to steady Innata as she landed. An instant later Taygen thudded down beside them.

Another enraged voice joined the first, yelling from the other side of the wall.

'My father,' Taygen said, in a grim-voiced whisper.

She grabbed Innata's hand and pulled her across the road. As they plunged into the darkness under the trees on the other side, Taygen was hard on their heels, not something they had planned for.

At least Cyrrin wasn't yet in evidence. There was no way a taldeer could leap the wall with someone on its back, so he'd apparently decided to gallop for the gate rather than dismount and climb over.

'Our mounts are this way,' she said, then stopped, wondering just where she was. 'Somewhere.'

'You've *lost* them?' Taygen asked, incredulous.

'In case it's escaped your notice, it's dark here, and there's a flipping mist!'

Under the trees away from the moonlight of the road, filmy veils of moist air mocked her senses as they wisped through the trees. Disoriented, hustling Innata along at her side, she wasted precious time trying to orientate herself. When she did stumble on the animals, they snorted in a friendly fashion, but she was in a frenzy of agitation. Worse, it was too dark amongst the trees to mount up and ride out. She gave the reins of one animal to Taygen and led the other to the road herself.

Two beasts, three of them. Thunderation ... what were they going to do?

Back on the road, she turned to Taygen. 'Go back. Sneak into the barracks before they realise you were involved!'

'Too late. I heard Cyrrin yell to Pa that he saw me with you on the wall. I'm coming with you. I've got no choice.'

She hadn't heard anything like that. Puzzled, she wanted to challenge him, but he snapped, 'I have excellent hearing!'

'Only two mounts,' she said. 'Sorry. Go hide in the woods.'

'You're safer without us,' Innata agreed, taking the reins from him as Haze, still holding her quarterstaff, mounted up. 'Hervan's really only interested in getting me back to the King. Go make a life for yourself, lad.'

He boosted her up into the saddle. 'I'll try,' he said.

'They'll never find you if you're clever. You're a rich man now,' Haze added, thinking of the carcanet.

He gave a low laugh, which she couldn't interpret.

'That way,' she said to Innata, pointing south. They might meet the two guards Taygen had mentioned, but that was better than the certainty of meeting Cyrrin in the other direction. 'Get going!'

Innata dug her heels into her mount's flanks. The beast began to move, then shuddered. Its great head lurched towards Taygen, the antlers missing him by the width of a finger. Air gurgled in its throat as it staggered one more step, then fell. Taygen seized Innata's arm and plucked her free as the animal crashed on its side, folding up like a stringless marionette. They both fell as well, ending up half across the animal's flank, half on the road.

A crossbow bolt deep into the taldeer's neck told the story.

Haze froze in shock, then looked towards the wall. Hervan stood there, balanced on the coping, moonlight glinting on the metal of his drawn weapon as he sighted along another loaded bolt. 'Don't move,' he rasped, 'none of you.'

She judged they only had a moment before Cyrrin was with them as well. She could already hear the sound of hooves.

'My father doesn't make threats he's not prepared to carry out,' Taygen said, then dropped his voice to an almost inaudible whisper. 'And I can hear Petch and Gappy. They're almost back from the wayfarer's camp. The only escape would be into the forest. But Pa'll kill you first, Haze, if you move. Innata might make it.'

She knew he was right.

'I'm not going anywhere,' Innata said loudly, sounding irritated as she sat up. 'Put that damn contraption away, Captain. There's no need for anyone to die here and you know full well you have to get me to Templebridge in one piece so the King can murder me there.'

'Keep your mouth shut, woman,' Hervan snapped, 'or I'll gag you every inch of the journey!'

'Tut, tut, Captain,' she said scrambling to her feet, deliberately standing in front of Taygen as she bent to dust her knees. 'Is that any way to address a lady?'

'Watch yourself!' The words grated through clenched teeth. He switched his attention to Haze, saying, 'Get off that beast, whoever you are. Very, very carefully.'

Eyes on Hervan, she whispered, 'Did you betray us, Tay?'

179

'No!' He spat the word out, more in frustration than rage, she thought. He was still on the ground, partially hidden by the corpse of the taldeer.

The moonlight caught his expression of grief, etched it into her memory. Her anger and frustration roiled under her skin, rang in her ears, spasmed her chest. Nausea swelled, then receded, leaving her reeling. *Gods, she felt ill.* To have come this far and be thwarted?

'*Now!*' Hervan shouted. She imagined his finger tightening on the trigger with her in his sights. He looked red with rage. And that was odd, because everything was moonlit. Definitely ought not be red. Milky blue, surely. But it wasn't. Moon and mist, and the ground and the moonbeams and the fogginess all undulated in waves, and it wasn't blue at all, but blood-streaked.

Her nightmare thoughts blundered on, ridiculous, stupid, everything around her drowning in blind crimson fury.

'For Goddess' sake, Haze,' Taygen hissed at her. 'Get down!'

Carefully, she withdrew her feet from the stirrups, her staff still clutched tight, and then leapt out of the saddle on the far side so that the animal was between her and Hervan. A crossbow bolt zinged past her head so close she felt the air move across her cheek. She ducked behind the taldeer. She had no plan, but she could not control the rage flooding her, drowning her from within. To come this close, and to lose...

Red, cherry, claret, blood, russet ... she was going mad. *What was the matter with her?*

Everything around dissolved into curtain-folds of scarlet that twisted and spiralled, warp and weft on a rose-coloured loom, a deep wine-red sky, rust and ruby earth, blood-stained mist, wine-red threads weaving power ... access ...

Her ire rippled outwards through the air, a ruddy-coloured wave of heat and fear and terror.

Hervan may not have seen what she did, but he felt it. His hands jerked upwards and his reloaded crossbow bolt shot upwards far over her head making ripples through the colour. Her mount panicked, ripped the reins from her hands, and bolted. Cyrrin reined in close by, completely taken by surprise when his own taldeer threw him just as he was beginning to dismount.

Taygen stood up beside Innata. Both of them were staring in her direction, apparently stunned.

Not making any sense at all, Taygen asked. 'Where is she? What just happened?'

'I don't know,' Innata replied, her voice wobbling.

'Redweaver sorcery!' Hervan jumped down from the wall and strode towards them. 'Atticun save us, what you got yourself mixed up in, Tay? Be there no end to your treachery?'

Hazelle wanted to run, but weakness threaded through her veins, trembling her limbs, quickening her breath. Hervan halted next to her, but didn't even look her way. Which was just as well, as she didn't seem to have control over anything, not her thoughts nor her body nor her voice.

He shook a finger at Innata, his disgust turning from his son to her, berating her where she stood. 'See what you've done with your actions? You brought our land to this! Consorting with the gods-forsaken Netherlost ... You be payin' for your sins, milady. You'll face the King's justice! Cyrrin, get her back to the barracks, and don't take your eyes off of her.'

Neither Taygen nor Innata appeared to be listening. 'Where did she go?' Tay asked in an awed whisper.

'I rather think she wove a gate and entered it.' Innata sounded amused and smiled slightly as if the idea was something wondrous rather than shocking.

Haze stood stock-still. *Are they talking about me?* No, surely not. She was right there.

Cyrrin picked himself up from the ground. Two guards-men ran up on foot from the direction of the wayfarer camp, wanting to know what was happening and why they were all standing in the middle of the road.

While Hervan answered, Haze looked over at Inna-ta. 'What do we do now?' she asked in an urgent whisper, grateful to see that much of the red colour was fading into a uniform ruddiness. 'And what in all the ten hells happened just then?'

Taygen interrupted her, cutting her question short with a query of his own to Innata, not caring if Hervan heard them or not. 'Pox 'n' rots, you mean she went to the redweaver lands?'

Haze blinked, puzzled. Nothing was making sense.

'Kanter. It's called Kanter,' Innata murmured, grabbing Taygen by the wrist and tugging him with her as she backed away.

Cyrrin scrambled up, limping. Haze glanced at Hervan, now only an arm's length from all of them, but he was still refusing to look at her.

'Hazzie, my dear,' Innata said using a childhood nickname and her most do-as-you-are-told-right-now voice, 'If you can hear me, take hold of my hand, will you?' She extended her free arm in Haze's general direction as though she was only guessing where she was. 'Quickly, dear.'

Haze did as she was told, only to have Innata immediately drive her backwards, dragging Tay behind her at the same time. Hervan lunged at his son and grabbed his free arm.

Haze staggered. She was dizzy, disoriented. A swirl-ing vortex of crimson swirled around her. Taygen yelped, Hervan shouted something, but his voice came from a long way off. Weird, as he was standing right there. Cyrrin cried out as well, but the words made no sense. She steadied herself, all while struggling to peer through a haze of blood-coloured mist.

Innata's grasp still clenched her arm as if her life depended on the hold. 'Don't let go, Haze,' she cried. 'Whatever you do, don't let go!'

'What's happened?' Taygen asked, his voice several notes higher than usual. 'This doesn't feel right! I can't see Pa...' Which was ridiculous, as the captain's large hand was clamped around his arm.

Innata answered, still infuriatingly calm. 'I can't either. I think you are halfway through a redweaver gateway that Hazelle just built. Look behind you, both of you.'

Haze glanced over her shoulder as her vision cleared, expecting to see the dark road to Crowbridge shrouded in mist. Instead she was gazing through a red tunnel not much higher than she was tall. Its sides were woven like a wicker basket, except this was not of willow, but of strands of colour that twisted and writhed in the weave like living creatures, like eels perhaps, all of them blood-coloured. Fifty paces away it ended in a glimpse of a rural landscape: a copse of trees lit — impossibly — by sunshine.

'Oh, merciful gods...' she whispered, her chest heaving in shock.

Taygen swore.

'Are you coming with us, lad?' Innata asked him. 'I think it's your only chance.'

'I'm not sure I can,' he said, gesturing behind with his head. 'Pa grabbed my arm.'

Hervan, his face contorted with fury, was leaning away from Taygen, using his considerable body weight in an attempt to separate his son from Innata — who was leaning in the opposite direction, anchored by Haze's grip.

It was not a contest Hervan would lose. Already one of his men was coming to his aid, grabbing him around the waist to pull him away from the tunnel of red. The other, oddly enough, did nothing except stare, his horrified expression not only lit by the red glow, but oddly familiar.

The guardsman who had slashed Innata's neck.

Appalled, Haze made a gesture of negation with her free hand, as if she could wipe the scene away. It was just all too much. Incredibly, as if in answer to her gesture, all of them disappeared.

No, not quite.

Hervan's hand remained clamped around Taygen's arm, and half of his forearm was still visible, but the rest of him had now disappeared behind a blank wall made of opaque red colour. The sounds disappeared too. All the shouting of the men was instantly silenced. The road was gone, the guards vanished, the field and the forest obliterated.

She didn't understand anything any more. She was shaking like a barley stalk in a gale. 'I didn't do that,' she wailed. 'I'm *not* a redweaver. I don't know how to weave a gateway. It wasn't me!'

'That's debatable,' Innata said firmly, with unruffled calm. 'But we'll settle the truth or otherwise of that later. Right now I think it best that we walk into the sunlight there ahead of us and leave Talodiac behind us. Because if we stay, we are dead. Either now or in Templebridge.' She turned back to Taygen. 'As for you, lad, you have to decide for yourself. Perhaps your father loves you enough not to punish you.'

He spoke between gritted teeth, still straining to pull himself away from Hervan. 'Not so far as I've noticed lately.'

'Certainly he does not appear to appreciate you. Haze, hand me your knife, and I'll stab Hervan's hand and force him to stop hanging on to the lad.'

'Right.' She fumbled for the knife at her belt with her free hand and held it out, but as soon as Innata let go of her to take it, she and Taygen were jerked back towards Talodiac. Innata lost her footing and fell, bringing him down with her. He started to slip away, dragged along the ground. Innata threw herself on his legs.

Hervan's hand disappeared into the red wall. Nothing of him was visible any more.

Haze flung herself flat on Innata, grabbing her around the waist.

Innata grimaced. 'Not sure this is going to work.'

'Let go of me,' Taygen said. 'There are five of them and only two of you. I don't particularly want to be torn in two … and if you hold on, they'll drag you out as well.'

Haze shuddered. 'No, no, Tay! We can do this—'

'I didn't betray you,' he said. 'Either of you. I really didn't. And it's not right, what they did to you, milady. I don't know why you stole the carcanet, but I reckon you must have had a good reason. Right now, you've got to let go. Both of you. You've got to escape. Somehow.'

Haze tried to dig her toes into the ground, but was dragged still further away from the sunlight. 'No, Tay, try—' She felt a huge emptiness opening up inside her at the thought of losing him. She longed to stop it happening, but he ignored her and spoke instead to Innata. 'Let go,' he said. 'Remember me.'

'We won't forget you,' Innata said. 'That I can promise.' And she released her hold on his arm. He slid away, through what appeared to be a solid door.

Only it wasn't. It was something she — Hazelle Wayfarer — had built out of red magic. Just before his head finally disappeared, she cried out to him. 'I'll find you! I swear — I'll come for you.'

And then he was gone and there was a strange, muffled silence around the two of them. Haze stared at the solidness of the woven gateway, biting her lip so she didn't cry.

'He's a very resourceful lad,' Innata said gently. 'And he may well be safer there than we will be in Kanter.'

'Kanter?'

She nodded towards the sunlight, 'I think that's Kanter up there. What we call the Netherworld.'

19

'Jenat's tits.' The words were a mere whisper and for once Innata refrained from scolding Haze for swearing. 'How could this happen?' She took a deep breath and continued more firmly, 'It can't have been me. It can't! I can't do that sort of thing!' But even as she spoke, she saw twirls of red-weaving tendrilled around her like threads of mist.

'Well, I don't think *I* can,' Innata replied. 'Or Taygen. I think you really must be a Kanterine, and a redweaver what's more, my dear. But don't let us worry about that at the moment. We have more important things on our mind. How to lock that gate, for instance.'

'What d'you mean Kanterine? *What* gate?'

Innata climbed to her feet, looking at the blank red end of the tunnel. 'That one. Door, if you prefer.'

'What about wall? It looks ... solid.'

'Well, Taygen went through it, didn't he? It looked shut then, but it must have still been open, and what goes out can come in if they realise it. And who knows, Hervan may just be angry enough and brave enough to try. Although I suspect he can't actually *see* any of it. Neither Taygen nor I could see you when we were on that side of it and you were on this side. We couldn't see this tunnel either, you know, although I can now. To us, you just vanished! You do need to close it in case they work that out. Or stumble through it accidentally.'

'I don't know how!' She scrambled to her feet and snatched up her staff, which sometime or other she had dropped. 'I don't even know how I made it.'

'With sheer panic, I imagine. And thank the gods you did.'

She couldn't think of a thing to say.

Innata shrugged. 'Thanks be, the door is at the side rather than in the middle of the road. If you can't lock it, let's try walking down the tunnel into the sunlight, into another world. Maybe the tunnel will then disappear. Or something. At least from the Talodiac side. Come on.' Without waiting to see if she would follow, Innata strode off towards the sunlit world.

Haze hurried after her, almost treading on her heels, horribly aware that her own skin was still wrapped in wispy red threads. They didn't hurt and she couldn't feel them, but when she tried to brush them away it was like trying to flick away a sunbeam. 'Shit, Innata, do we really *want* to go to Netherlost?'

'Kanter. They call it Kanter.'

'Where redweavers come from. With their red conjury.'

'That's right. Redweavers like you. With conjury like you.'

'I didn't do any pissing conjury!' The red ribbons mocked her words. She wanted to howl. She halted, clutching her midriff.

Innata stopped and laid a hand on her shoulder. 'How many times have I told you: if you must swear, be more creative.' When that didn't elicit a smile, she reached out to cup her face with a gentle hand. 'It'll be fine, Hazelle. If there is something I have learned over the years, it's that redweavers are not nearly as wicked as we think.'

She straightened, outraged. 'You — You knew? That I—' But she couldn't say the words. They were too absurd. *You knew I was a redweaver?*

'No. But I can't talk about it.'

'Taygen spoke of a baffle—'

'I'm glad he mentioned that to you. But I still can't talk about it. I think it might be safer for us to go to Kanter right

188

now.' She pointed to the sunlight at the other end of the woven tunnel. 'That way.'

'And if we go there, how do we get back?'

Innata released her and touched the redweaving of the side of the tunnel instead. Nothing happened. It was solid and inert. 'This reminds me of something...' She sighed. 'I don't know how we'll get back. But I know Kanterines come into Talodiac all the time. And go back too. What they can do, we can do.' She shrugged and strode on towards the sunlight, still talking. 'From here it doesn't look all that different from parts of Talodiac, does it?'

'Oh, mizzle it! This is *insane*.'

When they reached the far end, Innata halted just inside the tunnel opening to stare out at what was visible: a pleasantly bucolic scene — rolling hills scattered with trees, bushes, wild grasses. Butterflies among the pink and yellow meadow flowers. Birds flitting overhead against a background of a smoke-stained sky. No animals they could see. The smell of the place had an acrid, unpleasant bite to it, though.

They exchanged a glance, but before Haze could make up her mind what to say, Innata had stepped out on to the grass.

'Should you do that?' she squawked, panicked, annoyed with herself for not being able to emulate Innata's quiet calm.

A moment later, Innata turned to look at her, and the blood drained from her face so suddenly it appeared she would faint. '*Haze?*'

'What?'

'Haze?' Innata was looking straight through her, as if she wasn't there. Her face was now the colour of snowflower petals. 'Haze? I can't see you! *Are you there?*'

She stepped out of the tunnel, staff gripped tight.

Innata expelled a relieved breath. 'Lady Jenat below! The tunnel disappeared, and so did you.'

Haze blinked in surprise. When she turned around, the exit behind glowed a soft pink, the weave of the entrance moving with gently wavy lines, like threads in a breeze. 'It's still there. Sort of. And I can see into it too.' She thrust her head back inside and the tunnel opened up in front of her, all the way back to the distant entrance. No sign of Hervan or his men. Or Tay.

Innata grabbed her hand and yanked her back. 'Sweet goddess, don't do that again,' she said. 'Your head just vanished.'

'Oh. I—I don't know what to say.'

'I could only see the tunnel when I was inside it. We had better remember this place in case we need it to return home.'

Haze glanced around uneasily. 'Can't we wait here? We're safe enough if the other end in Talodiac is really closed. We could wait a day or so, until we're sure Captain Hervan has moved on. Then we can sneak back. Look, there's a stream just over there. We might not have food, but we won't go thirsty.'

Innata slipped an arm around her waist. 'Hazelle, I know you've had a very traumatic experience. Put it behind you and start thinking again.'

'I am! I'm being sensible and cautious. Even though I have a *huge* grievance to discuss with you. Everything you ever told me my whole life was a lie!'

Innata pulled an exasperated face, but said nothing.

'We have a lot to discuss.'

Innata raised an eyebrow.

'What does *that* mean? —Oh. Oh, the baffle. You still can't talk about any of it. Muckle-rot. Can you, um, nod or shake your head if I ask you questions?'

'I can't give you any kind of answer to a question about myself and my past unless you already know about it.'

'That's — awkward. I still don't know who you are. Were. Or how it is you had the royal carcanet.'

'Right now we need to talk about what we do,' Innata said. 'Here. In Kanter.'

Haze opened her mouth to ask a string of questions, only to realise immediately how useless that would be. After a moment's thought, she said, 'We probably stand out like orange pips in a bean pod! Our clothing, the way we speak ... They might well kill us on sight. After all, look what we do to them when they cross the border into Talodiac! But you know what's really bothering me? You've just told me I'm a redweaver. That I wove that tunnel. I'm one of *them*. You told me that much ... The baffle didn't stop you.'

'Because you did the weaving, you have to acknowledge it.'

'That I'm a redweaver?'

'Yes. Apparently. I still can't tell you how it came about. I didn't know it until now. I think very few Kanterines are actually weavers.'

'You're saying I'm *Kanterine?*'

'Well, I've never heard of a Talodian redweaver.'

'What *can* you tell me?'

'Nothing that you want to know. I want to go on, Hazelle. I have questions to ask the people here in this land. I have good reasons for those questions, which the baffle won't let me explain to you. I'm sorry.'

Haze threw up her hands, exasperated.

Innata pointed to the hill in front of them. 'There's smoke over there. Houses, perhaps?'

'Could be people willing to cut our throats first. Innata, I *am* Talodian. I *feel* Talodian. Where I was born is irrelevant.' She stared at the wisps of red flickering around her hands and over her clothing and felt sick.

'Come, I'm going to have a look at this place,' Innata said. 'At least if I die here, I will have tried.'

Tried to do what? She suppressed a sigh. Pointless to ask. And the woman was so damn *calm*. She could have been suggesting a pleasant stroll to the local dressmaker.

But then Innata added, voice faltering, 'I can't talk about my grief, Hazelle.'

The words cut to the bone. She had to swallow before she could speak and sound nonchalant. 'I'll come with you. Out of curiosity. Try not to get us killed, all right?'

'I'll do my best.'

'And when we meet someone, what then?'

'We'll play it by ear.'

'In other words, if they weave a conjury, we run like a taldeer that knocked over a wasp nest?'

'No. We talk our way out of it. We are very good at that, Haze, both of us, and their tongue and ours are somewhat similar, or so I have been told.' Innata walked away from the gateway in the direction of the top of the rise.

She hurried to catch up, glad to see Innata was showing no signs of having been badly injured, even though the scarring on her neck was obvious. 'How can the languages be alike?' she protested. 'Kanter is gods-know-where, and yet we can understand them?'

'Some people say they are from our world too, but just from the other side of it. That might explain why it's daylight here and night in Talodiac.' Innata looked around, curious.

Far more interested in whether she could keep both of them alive when all they had was her staff, Haze muttered, 'I hope it's as easy to get back.' She wanted time to think about conjury. *Her* conjury. As hard as it was to acknowledge, being scared witless had been enough to make her create a gateway to escape. Which was preposterous. In fact, she had a ghastly idea that it was more as if it had controlled her, not the other way around. If this was redweaving, she wanted no part of it. She gave her hands a baleful glare. She still couldn't *feel* anything, but the red threads winked across her wrists, then playfully wove themselves in and out of her fingers.

She shivered and looked around. No one in sight, but there was an awful lot of smoke on the other side of the hill. And that smell. No ordinary fire smelled like that.

Her grip on her quarterstaff tightened.

They were halted by a sound even before reaching the base of the slope. Somewhere between a groan and a hiss. Not the kind of sound anyone wanted to hear in a strange land they knew nothing about. A moment later they came across a patch of flattened grass, with an animal lying in the centre.

Animal ... or monster?

The first thing Haze noticed was the stench. Not so much the stink of rot, but more of an apothecary's medicinal concoction. The second thing was that the creature wasn't dead. Not yet. It had a bolt from a crossbow right through the breast, so at a guess it wasn't far away from expiring. The hissing sound was air being drawn into its chest through the hole the bolt had opened up. The wound was leaking some kind of ichor, rather than blood.

All of which didn't *begin* to describe the creature...

In no way was it human, or anything like a human. It had a vague resemblance to a maroon-coloured praying mantis.

Except that it was the size of an elongated, emaciated man. It was at least an arm's length longer than Haze was tall.

Once she had a closer look, she decided even the mantis resemblance was superficial. True, like an insect, the skeleton was on the outside, but it had only four limbs. The front ones were more like arms with hands that ended in claw-like fingers. The two legs at the back were elongated and skinny, with viciously clawed feet. Its mouth parts had the complexity of a beetle's. A *huge* beetle with shredding mandibles the size of carving knives. Something oozed from its tube mouth that was greenish and, where it had pooled on the grass, the leaves had *shrivelled*. Possibly that was the source of the smell.

It was lying on its back, on top of its two pairs of grass-hopper-like wings. Its eyes bulged open, orbs more like the eyes of an owl. And they watched, not as an insect watches, but with intelligence and owl-like intensity, its stare flicking from Innata to Haze and back again.

'Sweet hells,' she muttered, 'what *is* that thing?'

'I think it might be an esklet.' Innata, surprising her yet again.

'How the ten hells do you know that? And what's an esklet anyway?'

'I have heard it said that redweavers — Kanterines — whatever they call themselves, speak of fleeing their land because of an invasion of what they call "esklet hordes". Giant, insect-like creatures. As you might imagine, that's a theory that has been well and truly ridiculed in Talodiac.'

'Picklemuck! Really?' She stared back at the dying thing. 'I swear, that beast would rip us to bits if it didn't have a bolt through it.'

At that, it opened up all its mouth parts, four pairs of pincers with a variety of cutting edges: serrated, scalloped, knife-edged and vice-like. It glared malevolently, slammed

GLENDA LARKE

all those mandible bits back together in a crunching, snapping gesture that could only be anger or threat — and died.

She swallowed back her fear as its life faded.

'Maybe the Kanterines have a good reason to flee through the woven gateways to Talodiac,' Innata said, apparently unruffled. 'That stuff it dribbled ... it burned the grass.'

They exchanged a glance, but neither had anything to add.

A moment later, all thought of the dead esklet was driven out of their minds by a living one.

It swooped down from the sky towards them, legs extended like an eagle about to strike prey, wings retracted into a dive. At the same time, it let loose a cry of rage and shot a targeted spray of green liquid in their direction. Innata flung herself to the right at the same time as Haze dived to the left. The liquid spit hit the grass between them. Stalks and leaves sizzled. Haze rolled straight back to her feet.

The creature retracted its legs into a folded tuck under its belly. Four wings, leathery and greenish, beat the air to turn its dive into an upwards curve.

Innata scrambled upright. 'Not exactly a friendly introduction,' she said. 'Maybe it thinks we killed its friend.'

'I think we have to assume it's coming back.' Haze's hands were already sliding up and down her staff as she tried to decide how best to use it against an aerial attack. Not something that had ever occurred that she might need to consider.

Innata glanced at the nearest coppice of trees and raised an eyebrow.

Haze shook her head. Even that inadequate shelter was too far away. They watched the esklet circle around. 'Should have worn a hat,' she muttered. She was far more scared of the spit than the clawed feet.

'I don't think it would make much difference.'

195

She was probably right. The grass was *dead.*

'Different tactics?' Innata suggested. 'Your call!'

It came in lower this time, so judging its speed was harder. Its wings beat the air insect-fashion. Its clawed feet were still tucked up.

Haze guessed it was more interested in spitting at them than in seizing one of them. 'Start running. When I yell, leap hard right.'

Innata fled, screaming, giving every indication of panic. The esklet instinctively banked to follow. Haze had hoped to intercept, striking at it from the side, but as it banked it tilted out of the reach of the polearm. She did the only other thing left to her. With the full weight of her body behind the throw, she lanced the quarterstaff as if it were a spear. Not at its body but at the outermost joint of the wing, which she guessed was the most fragile of the wing bones.

'*Now!*'

Innata leapt sideways. The beast spewed forth its poison and the staff slammed home. It tried to bank, but its wingtip flopped and it couldn't gain height. It crash-landed clumsily on its side in a way that further crumpled its wing. It screamed, a horrible yowl of pain.

Haze dashed to grab her staff from the ground before the beast could sort itself out. For a moment she danced around it, dodging wings and feet and claws as it thrashed. The mouth parts snapped and scissored, its tongue flicked in and out, even as its gaze glared and its voice moaned and whimpered.

By the time she manoeuvred herself into a safe position from where she could deliver a killing blow, she realised it wasn't necessary. The beast's soft belly had split open when it hit the ground and its innards had spilled out. It spasmed, wings and limbs jerking. She leant on her quarterstaff and went cold all over. If she'd hit the wing in any other place, they'd both be dead and the esklet would have been snacking on them.

She glanced around for Innata, but she wasn't there. Her heart lurched sickeningly. Up on the ridge of the slope a man was standing looking down at her. He held a longbow already strung, but with no arrow notched. They stared at one another, neither of them moving.

Then he turned his head to look away. She followed the line of his sight to the stream near the gateway. At first she couldn't see what had caught his attention, then Innata's head emerged from the water.

Realisation hit. Some of that foul esklet rot must have spattered Innata.

She snatched up her quarterstaff and ran. By the time she reached the stream, Innata had crawled out of the water and was lying on her back on the grass. From the corner of her eye to her chin on the left side, a line of blisters furrowed her skin as if someone had run a red-hot poker down her cheek.

'Innata?' she whispered. 'Does that hurt?'

'Excruciating ... Washed it off. Something's wrong though ... I ... I feel so strange. I don't want to go ... but ... but ... I keep thinking ... I'm back...'

'Goddess help us! I'm sorry. I thought it missed you.'

'Just a drop or two ... Haze, I feel ... splintered. I can't think straight. I'm slipping through cracks ... Is ... is that Taygen?'

She spun around. The archer had come down the slope and was approaching across the meadow, his bow now slung over his shoulder. He had to walk past the redwoven gate to reach them, and he didn't give it a glance.

Haze swallowed back her fear. 'It's ... it's a friend. I hope.'

20

Fear chilled Innata into a marbled stillness. She had no awareness of breathing, no perception that her heart still beat, no sense that her mind was capable of rational thought.

Maybe this was death?

Try to remember, you ninny...

Esklet poison.

Those creatures coming at them, their spit...

Hazelle was there. Remember? Was that right?

She blinked, and a tear slipped its way down her cheek.

No, not dead, not yet. She groped for memory, for meaning, for hope. But her gaze, fixed a moment earlier on the blue of the sky, was now seeing billows of blue silk just above her head, telling her she lay safe in her canopied bed. She was safe. Rescued.

No, wait. She knew that blue, that bed. It had been her own once. In Talodiac. But she wasn't in Talodiac...

Her body was rigid, but her mind drowned in grief and guilt. Everything was so *muddled*. Sweet Jenat, she was frightened. So *alone*.

And she wasn't Innata any more.

Is this what death is?

She scrabbled for reality, but the more she tried to reclaim Innata as her own, the more the memory trickled away...

Edwild...

He had dismissed the servants and ordered the guard at the chamber door not to allow anyone to enter, under pain of death. For her, there had been no kindness, although the full force of his venom was directed not at her, but at those who had done this. His words snapped with icy rage.

'Redweavers,' he'd said, spitting the accursed name as if it seared his throat to say it. Ordering her not to speak of what she'd seen, he'd stormed from the room, his body taut with fury. Part of her had been glad. She'd wanted to be alone. But, she wasn't, not really. There was that baby boy; that vile replica now asleep in Denniel's cradle. She stayed still, weary, sore, unable to cry, wanting to scream, every inch of her already shrieking in silent, unending pain. Her baby was gone.

Her son...

Vanished. Stolen.

Prince Denniel, son of Edwild of Talodiac and Thalia of Temar. She hungered to cuddle him in the crook of her arm and whisper her love to him. She yearned for the wisp of his breath against her breast. When he woke, she wanted to be the first person he saw. She would have called him Dennie for short, at least while he was a baby. She would have whispered her love into the sweet curve of his ear.

Outside, the bell of the King's Keep tolled the mid-morn. Outside, the townsfolk would halt their tasks to offer a prayer to their god of choice as they broke bread for the first meal of the day. Outside, all was normal.

She was in purgatory, happiness now only a bitter dream, joy soured into uncomprehending horror.

No. She must not buckle. Not now, not ever.

A fever dream. It isn't true.

Esklet poison. On her face. Remember? Wake up! You are Innata. Thalia... Thalia doesn't exist any more. She died.

She needed to think, to remember everything that had happened. Perhaps somewhere in the horror of the night there was a sliver of memory that would help return her son to her.

THE TANGLED LANDS

Dreams are muddling...
Haze, where are you?

*

Edwild had been alight with love and pride when he'd visited her after the birth. He'd kissed her cheek, murmured words of love and praise, and fastened the priceless heirloom collar and pendant around her neck in recognition of her place as mother of the heir. The diamonds sparkled their fire from the heavy gold lace of the collar, while a brood of dark emeralds, formed into the shape of the royal griffin, hung in between the unaccustomed fullness of her breasts. The famous Griffin Carcanet, ostentatious, garish, and worth more than any common man could earn in several lifetimes. It had graced the Queen Mother's neck until now.

When the King, the Queen Mother, and the doctors and most of her own attendants had departed, leaving her to rest, she'd slipped the gift under her pillow before asking the one remaining servant, Vira the wet nurse, to bring the cradle to her bedside. She'd parted the bed curtains and slipped out a hand to cup the softness of her son's downy head, and that was the way she'd fallen asleep.

No clues to what would happen next, no premonition, no warning.

Until she woke sometime in the middle of the night, knowing something was wrong. Her hand no longer touched the softness of her son's head; her fingers were curled on her lace-edged pillow. Opening her eyes, she found herself looking through a narrow gap in the bed drapes. The cresset lamp on the wall was still alight, illuminating the room, and the fire in the grate still burned. A figure crossed her vision, blocking the flame, then moved on.

Yet she could hear Vira snoring.

Someone else was in the room. It could have been any-one: chambermaid, handmaiden, even Edwild, checking on his son. Why then did she feel something was wrong?

Something out of place.

The *smell.*

The odours of the taproom of a wayside inn. Of common folk who rarely bathed. Of cheap ale. Of grease dripped on hot coals. Of sweaty bodies. Things she had not smelled in combination since she'd travelled across Talodiac on the way to her wedding.

Alarmed, she tried to move, yet couldn't lift her head. A heavy weight kept her pinned where she was — yet only the bedding covered her. She struggled to call out, but no sound emerged. Breathing took all her strength. A wave of terror and panic crushed her, yet she was inexplicably slipping into sleep. She battled the desire, and for a while succeeded. The intruder brushed against the curtains around her bed opening up the gap by another finger-width, allowing her a vertical view of the room beyond, just in time to see the cradle sliding away from her bed guided by a hand on the headboard.

Terror tumbled her thoughts. She called on Goddess Jenat for help with silent, garbled prayers. Her fingers made claws, as if they could shred the desire to sleep. She edged her hand inch by tortured inch across her pillow towards the bed curtain until she hooked her little finger into one of the folds.

A single flick, all she could manage, but enough to widen the gap in the curtains to a handspan. Enough to see the back of a man walking away from the cradle, carrying a bundle towards the open oriel window. He was muttering, but the words were ill-spoken and made no sense. The scream in her head emerged   as a grunt as her horror struggled to break free. The man turned to look at her.

His stare locked with hers.

He took a step toward her.

She opened her mouth to demand ... something.

And sank back into sleep, her mind shrieking her protest, her body unable to resist the red strands of the web of the sleeping spell he'd inserted into her mind.

*

She struggled to remember.

Esklet poison. On her cheek.

Everything was so muddled. She had to remember...

'Redweaving conjury.' Edwild had grated the words at her in the morning when she'd told him what she'd seen. All she'd known up until then was vague: rumours of children stolen, tales of crimson spells woven, making nightmares real. She'd heard arch-clergy scoff at such tales, but she'd also heard them preach of protection and safety for those who worshipped the deities and paid their temple dues.

But by the time Edwild had uttered those words, hours had passed and the intruder was long gone — and so was Denniel.

When first she'd woken, she hadn't even realised anything was wrong. The baby was crying and Vira, yawning sleepily, was lifting him into her arms. The cresset lamp had guttered and the first light of dawn edged into the room from the open shutter of the oriel window. The cradle rocked gently in the middle of the room.

She blinked, bleary-eyed, relief flooding in. Such a terrible dream. A dreadful nightmare. Her son was safe, of course he was. Thank sweet Goddess Jenat.

Yet memories remained, niggling. Why was the cradle marooned halfway across the room? Why were the oriel shutters wide open? She struggled to sit up, asking Vira who had let in the cold and who had shifted the crib.

'Netta must have been in earlier,' the woman replied cheerfully. 'I'll close the window.'

She sat up on the edge of the bed. The soreness between her legs was wet with clotted blood. Her breasts ached and she wanted to snatch her son away and feed him herself. A tentative suggestion to that effect in the weeks leading up to his birth had been rejected by all who'd heard it. Apparently, her only job as queen was to serve the King and produce more heirs. The prince's wellbeing was to be left to those more experienced.

The sourness in her mouth was an unpleasant reminder of things she did not want to consider.

Then Netta arrived to help her to the garderobe so she could relieve herself and change the bloodied cloth between her legs. Afterwards she refused to return to her bed. 'I shall sit on the window seat,' she said. 'Was it you who opened the shutters this morning, Netta?'

'No, m'lady. They were open when I entered. Shall I fetch you a drink? The physician suggested a warmed posset—'

Memory came surging back then, along with that icy fear.

She didn't answer. Instead, she knelt on the window seat and leaned out, shivering, even as Netta uttered a shocked protest.

She was looking straight down into the garden below. The Queen Mother had created that walled area and planted it with her favourite flowers. Most had been cut back over winter, and the plants were just beginning to green again with leaf-buds. There was no one there, of course, and the wall was sheer. The idea that someone could climb either up or down to the bedroom window was ridiculous. She was about to pull her head inside, when she saw something that sent her mind spinning, restarting the terror clutching her heart.

On the neatly raked flower beds, deeply indented footprints had laid a trail. She stared, trying to make sense of them. One line walking up to the palace wall, deeper steps much further apart leading away, as if someone had left at a run.

She drew her head back inside. 'Latch the shutters, Netta,' she said. 'Vira, bring the child to me.'

The wet nurse stared at her, then looked down at the baby still latched to her breast. 'My lady—'

'*Now*, Vira!'

The woman lowered her gaze and obeyed.

Thalia took the child on to her lap and stared at his face. He squirmed and whimpered, upset at losing his feed. The tiny curl of his ears, the pinkness of his cheeks, the purse of his lips, the tilt of his baby nose, the downy brown hair — all of it was familiar. She had taken note of every inch of him the moment he had been placed in her arms after he was born.

She closed her eyes, smiling, and bent to kiss the top of his head. Rough tangles against her lips were shockingly unexpected. She jerked her head back to stare, wide-eyed. What she saw was the same as ever: silky wisps. When she touched his head with her fingers, she felt the same softness. For a moment of agony, she was stilled.

Then, with cold resolution, she closed her eyes once more. She bent to brush her cheek across his head. When she relied on touch, not sight, there was no doubt. This child had hair that was rougher, longer, more matted. Still not looking at him, she breathed in. His smell. He smelled of smoke, of mustiness, of unwashed bodies and, yes, ale.

Shafted with spears of cold horror, she thrust the child back into his cradle.

Changeling.

Drowning in terror, she summoned both the King and the Lawseer and dismissed her servants without explanation. The Lawseer, carrying the title of Gerent, the highest-ranking archpriest of Atticun, the God of Law, Justice and Governance...

Gerent Vann, he would know what to do.

Edwild arrived first. When the door swung noisily shut behind him, he winced as if pained. His hair was tousled, and she did not believe he had changed his clothes since she'd seen him at her side after the birth.

He bowed over her hand, and he smelled of wine and perfume. 'My lady, I do believe you are in better health than I, this morn! How does my son?' Not waiting for a reply, he walked to the cradle.

She was about to speak his name and put her arms out entreating a hug, but then recalled something her mother had said to her just before she'd left home to marry. 'Remember, my dear, there will be times when you can treat your husband as a friend, indeed, as a lover. But he's a monarch and there will be times when a wise wife will treat him as her liege lord. The trick will be to know which to use when.'

'With your leave, sire, that is a matter I wish to speak on,' she said, and waited for him to incline his head in acquiescence before she plunged into her story. 'Last night, a man entered this room unbidden. I saw him.'

With all the clarity she could muster, she told him all she remembered. When he started to dismiss her concerns as the megrims of a new mother, she cut him short and showed him the footprints.

The sudden twist of his lips signalled scorn. 'I see them. But of what significance are they? The gardeners...'

'The gardeners rake the beds and leave them neat. Ask them.'

There was a long silence before he nodded. 'Very well, I will. But ma'am, if you are trying to tell me someone climbed this outer wall to open a shutter that was surely barred on the inside, in order to enter this room—' He shrugged. 'Then I must say I find your tale fanciful. At best. No man could enter the palace unseen. There are several walls to be scaled. No man could climb to this window without rope and help from within. No one can unbar a shutter from without. And to what *purpose*?'

'No man, perhaps,' she whispered. 'But what if the intruder was one of the Netherfolk?' Her voice quavered. Articulating her fears had brought her within a teardrop of losing control. 'What if one such came to steal our son — and replace him with a changeling?'

He gaped at her, more in astonished contempt than in fear. Then, frowning, he looked down at the child in the cradle. 'This is the prince. Exactly as he was when I saw him last night. Identical. Do you think I did not take note of my own son?'

I must be calm. He must not think me just a hysterical girl... 'See how soft the hair is? Close your eyes and touch it. And breathe in the smell of him.'

He opened his mouth as if to chide her, but then gave an exasperated shrug and did as she asked. Her heart thundered in her chest. She counted the beats.

Five, before he straightened. 'A whiff of ale? Is that the basis for your fears? Perhaps you should smell the breath of your wet nurse!' But he clutched at the cradle to stop his hand from shaking.

'His hair! Don't you feel the difference between what your eyes see and what your fingers feel?' When he didn't reply she added, 'I have just sent word to Gerent Vann, asking him to come. He will have the ability to see conjury—'

'The Lawseer has better things to do with his time than worry over the fancies of a mother suffering the effects of her travail!'

She shrank back from him, doubt dissolving her certainty. Was she crazed? She clamped a hand over her mouth as if that could stay the panic rising in her gorge. Before she could gather her wits enough to say more, someone knocked at the door.

Edwild strode to answer it. Half expecting him to take the opportunity to leave, she struggled to her feet to stop him.

The Lawseer could not possibly have yet received her message, but it was he who stepped into the room, closely followed by the Lord Chamberlain, Lord Ashwendon, who abruptly closed the door again in the face of the servant who had escorted them. Gerent Vann's blue robe was muddied around the hem, and his purple pearl-shell trimmed cap sat askew on his fair hair. He barely inclined his head in Thalia's direction, and his next words made it doubly clear he had never received her message. It was Edwild he addressed, saying, 'Sire, redweaver trouble. I've brought Ashwendon with me because we need to contain this somehow.'

Edwild stiffened. 'Trouble? Where?'

'There's traces of a weaving on the outer Palace Precinct wall along Templegate Walk. I have confirmed it, though 'twas an archpriestess of Goddess Granna who first saw and warned me. Worse still, on my way through the palace I swear I felt the prickle of a freshly woven conjury—' He broke off. Even in the poorly lit room, Thalia saw him blanch. 'Lord Atticun,' he whispered, calling on his God in his shock. *'They've been here.* Netherfolk. Can you not see it?'

'Of course I can't!' Edwild snapped. 'Where do you see weaving here? Tell me!'

Gerent Vann glanced around the room. 'The window. The shutters. Across the floor ... Sweet gods. The *cradle.*'

Ashwendon, a man well into his forties and normally coldly supercilious no matter what the problem, gasped.

Two strides brought Gerent Vann to the crib, but Thalia was there before him. White-knuckled, she gripped the wooden end of the cradle, supporting herself. 'Tell me it's not true!'

Gerent Vann shook his head. 'This child is clothed in a crimson weave of deception.' He looked up at his king and confirmed her worst nightmare. 'I believe it covers the appearance of another babe beneath.'

She'd stood by the cradle, shaking, the words of all three men blending into a single string of incomprehensible decisions as they planned what to do next.

Secret? Tell no one? Were they serious? Why weren't they doing *something?*

She swallowed her bile and listened as Lord Ashwendon undertook to keep the abduction a secret from others in the palace, as King Edwild told her what to do, his orders concise and brutal, never to be forgotten. 'Speak to no one of any changeling. Look after that — that abomination. We may be able to make use of it. You say you felt a difference only when you closed your eyes?' He cast another glance at the child, scowling in disgust.

She nodded, afraid she'd weep if she spoke, and looked to Gerent Vann, wordlessly imploring him to give her hope. Listening to her account, he'd shifted uneasily from one foot to another as if he would rather have been anywhere else but there. Now he said gently, 'What the eyes see is the redweaving spell, and that sight overrides other senses. For some gifted people, shutting one's eyes is all it takes to break the spell. Your touch and your sense of smell perceived the truth.' He bowed to her. 'Your Grace, you must be a woman beloved by the gods, for you also saw through this abductor's weaving when you had your eyes open last night. Perhaps you could have become an archpriest. You are truly blessed.'

Blessed?

She gaped at him.

Edwild reacted to the man's unthinking stupidity with a glare before turning back to her. 'Make sure your servants touch the brat as little as possible. Feed it yourself. Speak to no one of redweaving, or what you saw, or changelings. Understand?'

The thought of ever touching the abomination again brought acid to her throat. She swallowed it back and nodded.

'I shall undo the weaving—' the Lawseer began, glancing at the child, but the King interrupted him.

'Don't be an idiot! I don't want anyone to know what has happened as yet. Right now, you and I will scour Temple-bridge from wall to wall for the Netherfolk redweaver. As will *all* other gerents and archpriests with the power to see weaving. But no word of the prince being taken. Just say there was an attempt to enter the palace, which was foiled.' He shook a finger at the Lord Chamberlain. 'Ashwendon, you are the man in charge of the affairs of this palace. If there is a single word of gossip among the servants, your head will be the one that rolls first. Literally. Understand?'

Ashwendon nodded, then bowed. 'Your Majesty. It shall be as you wish.'

With that, Edwild turned on his heel and left the room, striding like a man possessed. The archpriest, with one scant pitying glance in her direction, scurried after him.

She was shuddering in the grip of horror beyond imagining, but when Lord Ashwendon spoke, he shook a finger at her as if she was a recalcitrant child. 'Milady, you heard the King. Up until now you have been an ignorant girl from a fishing village, playing at being queen. This is where you become worthy of our royal line. A worthy wife to King Edwild. There will be no hysteria. You will do exactly as we say, as the King determines. Do you understand me?'

She nodded, shivering, barely comprehending his words, yet knowing that to him she was irrelevant.

He turned on his heel and left the room.

They had abandoned her.

Left her alone.

No, not quite alone. There was that horror in the cra-dle, masquerading as Denniel. She shuddered at the idea of touching him. It. Touching it. The idea of putting it to her breast—

21

The archer was a tall, gaunt fellow, his clothes hanging on a bony frame as if he borrowed them from a much larger man. He looked human, if underfed. His initial words sounded friendly enough, but Haze wasn't sure she understood any of it.

'Greetings,' she said neutrally and waited for him to speak again.

He asked a question, and she heard the words 'esklet' and 'killed.'

She jabbed a finger at her quarterstaff. 'Yes, I killed it. With that.'

The man rattled off something else, and only then did she realise he was actually speaking Talodian, but it was larded with words she didn't recognise and generally spoken with such a heavy accent as to be almost incomprehensible. He fumbled in his tie-purse, drew out a small tin and opened it. Holding it out towards her, he gestured towards Innata's wound. Innata herself appeared to have slipped into unconsciousness. Her breathing was shallow, and her skin was far too pale.

Haze hesitated only briefly. Surely these folk would know how to treat esklet poison. She smiled her thanks, took the tin and spread a thin layer of the ointment it contained over the blistered flesh. When she'd finished she gave the tin back.

The man regarded her with an expression somewhere between puzzlement and suspicion and rattled off a series of questions.

'Please,' she said. 'Speak ... very ... slowly ... so ... I ... can ... understand.'

He was appalled. *'Talodian!'*

'Yes.'

'How—?'

She turned to point at the gateway. 'Can you see that?'

He gave her a blank look.

Obviously not. She pointed at Innata instead. 'Will she live?'

He shrugged. 'Mayhap.'

'Is there a healer?' she asked, spacing the words. 'A healer? A town nearby?'

The look he gave her was laden with mistrust, and he rattled off a series of sharply worded questions which she guessed were about who she was and where they'd come from. She looked back at Innata, who was now paler than ever, and made up her mind.

She stood up and walked over to the redwoven gateway. 'Can you see this?' she asked.

He didn't react.

'Watch,' she said and placed her right leg and her right arm inside the tunnel.

His surprise was all she needed.

'Yes. It's a gateway. I'm a redweaver. We came from Talodiac.'

Visibly shocked, he remained speechless.

She returned to Innata's side. 'She needs help. *Now.* Medicine. Do you understand?' She pointed back at the hill and the smoke still in the sky. 'Town?'

'Yes. Town. Healers.' He followed up with a flood of words all spoken too quickly, but in the middle she caught something about going to get a cart.

'Yes! A cart! Good. Please?'

He nodded and muttered something else which sounded a little like, 'After all, you killed an esklet.'

'Yes,' she said. 'We did.'

He turned and walked away, heading up the hill.

*

'Innata! Wake up! You're dreaming.'

Haze was close to panic. She had no idea if the man would return or not, no idea if he would bring help, but Innata was definitely feverish now, tossing, trembling, muttering. The scar on her neck from her earlier injury looked angry and inflamed. Where the esklet spit had hit her face, the blistered skin was raw.

She dithered as the time passed, until she couldn't bear it any more and decided to run to the brow of the hill to see if there was any sign of the archer. She told Innata what she intended to do, but there was no reaction from her. Her muttering was spasmodic and didn't seem to make much sense. Most of it was about a child. And some fellow called Ashwendon.

'I'll be back within a quarter hour,' she promised, and set off.

All she had seen so far of Kanter was a rural landscape familiar enough to have been somewhere in the central duchies of Talodiac. Trees that looked like shiver-oaks, but-terflies could have been Talodian Yellow Flutters. Even some of the meadow blooms were familiar; she could have sworn the splashes of pink in the grass were sunbud-clover flowers. The only truly alien oddity was the existence of the redwo-ven gateway.

Once she was on top of the rise looking in the other direction, the view changed into a living, breathing panora-ma of humanity. A flat plain was divided haphazardly by the sinuous curves of a broad river. Several miles away, a city on its banks spilled over an ageing defensive wall into the landscape, wooden dwellings crowding up against the outer stonework as if begging entrance. Four bridges looped across the river to where the town had oozed still further from the walls onto the far bank. Roads and lanes meandered through fields and meadows to farmhouses and hamlets. Nothing out of the ordinary at first glance. Seen from this distance, it could indeed have been in Talodiac, though an inordinate number of carts, wagons and tumbrels trundled along the roads, while people walked and rode in all directions, some leaving the city, some returning.

She wondered if it was a market day, but decided that alone couldn't account for the scene. There was the smoke for a start, curling up from several parts of the city as if buildings had been burnt. Something must have recently gone wrong to create the scene below.

Fortunately, she did spot the archer. He was sitting next to the driver of a talyak cart and they were heading in her direction. Their progress was slow as there was no track over the hill. He spotted her on the crest and raised a hand. She waved back and quickly returned to Innata's side, who was now only semi-conscious. When she grabbed Haze's arm, she called her by another name.

Edwild.

*

Servants brought Thalia nuncheon, and then left her alone once more. She forced herself to eat a few mouthfuls. Not long afterwards the child she was trying to ignore began to whimper.

My son. Will anyone feed him *when he cries?*

The thought seared. She wound herself tight in her shawl, as if the crocheted wool would hold together all the pieces of her that threatened to rip asunder. She allowed herself silent

214

tears, an unending rill sliding down to the corners of her mouth. She prayed, but not to Atticun, the usual choice for a queen. Instead, she turned to the Goddess Jenat, deity of women and children.

Lady, from today on, I serve only you. Bring me back my child, I beg you. I shall keep him safe in my heart until I see him again...

The impostor babe whimpered.

She'd heard legends of changelings. Folk spoke of mischievous Netherfolk, not *quite* human, born in Lands of the Beyond, folk who entered the world of Talodiac through hidden, glowing gateways. Their men were said to entice beautiful maidens to follow them to that netherworld; if a child vanished, then it had to be the fault of redweavers. Her own mother, Duchess of Temar, had laughed at the tales of changelings, saying it was probably just the way some parents refused to accept that any babe of theirs could be less than perfect. A deformed child must therefore be a changeling.

The only certain truth was that some Netherfolk, the ones they called redweavers, slipped into Talodiac through redwoven gates. They could weave illusions, tricking the eye, and the only people who could see their conjuries were the numerous archpriests and archpriestesses of the ten deities of Talodiac's Decasian Pantheon.

Why the Netherfolk came, no one knew for sure.

She stared across at the child in the cot, into its uncomprehending eyes, at the mouth that made a moue when the blanket touched a pink cheek, and felt a stirring of pity amidst her raging anger. A newborn baby at the mercy of the adults around him, to suffer or thrive ... She crossed to sit in the nursing chair beside the crib, gripping the wooden arms tight as she rocked to and fro, refusing to allow more tears to fall, or the scream in her throat to escape.

Still weary from the birth, still bleeding from the labour, what could she do? Everything depended on Edwild. The

King. Her husband. For the first time since their meeting, she thought of him with a detached dispassion. Plain of face, and not overly tall, he strode through life as if his physical attributes were unimportant, as indeed they were when one was a monarch.

Did she love him?

The night before she would have said yes. Now, she was not so sure. Yes, he had always taken the time to coax her to passion in his bed, and he'd uttered words of affection for which she was grateful, but how well did she know him? He had never bothered to be generous with his time. Now it occurred to her that however much he enjoyed her body, perhaps he found her youth and her company boring and dull.

She'd smelled attar of roses on his clothing that very morning; was that not a woman's perfume?

The changeling's whimper rose to a demanding wail, setting her teeth on edge. She leaned over the cradle, rage building. It lay there, tiny arms struggling against the swaddling, utterly helpless. She could kill it so easily; smother it with no more than the palm of her hand across its face. Such a simple thing to do.

Gods, how could she ever *think* of doing such a thing?

It pulled a tiny fist free of the wrap and waved it, and her rage dribbled away. It was just a baby, like any other that wasn't hers. This wasn't its fault, for all that it was one of the wretched Netherfolk. Doubtless it would grow up to be a red-weaver, but one might as well blame the fox or the wolf for killing a hen. Right now, it was just a helpless babe.

She unwrapped the swaddling that had once been Denniel's. The child had wet the cloth of the napkin, so she unfolded that as well, taking care not to let her bare fingers touch its skin and certainly not closing her eyes. Maybe if she did, she would feel a deformity, some creature that was not human at all. She dabbed it dry, aware only that it felt larger and heavier than Dennie, as if it was an older and stronger babe. Once it was dry and wrapped tight again, she balked at comforting it with her breast. Instead she wet a cloth with her milk and let it suck on that until it slept once more.

An hour later it began to howl. Afraid servants would come, or worse, that the crying would bring the formidable Queen Mother to her door to see what was amiss, she picked it up. It quieted for a moment, turning its head towards her breast. Her heart lurched. Whatever it was, it had not asked for this, nor deserved it.

Rage melted into compassion. She undid her gown and allowed it to find her nipple.

*

'Innata, can you hear me? It's Haze. The archer has brought a cart. We're going to take you to the city to find a physician. He's going to help me pick you up...'

'I'm waiting for Edwild. He went to find Denniel...'

What? 'Put your arm around my neck. We'll carry you to the cart— Oh, rot it; she's not hearing a word I say.'

*

Edwild returned shortly after dark, but it was another hour before he came to her bedchamber, alone. He did not glance at the changeling, now sated and asleep in the cradle, but strode over to her bedside. Thalia did not need his words to know his search had been unsuccessful; his bleakness and scarcely suppressed fury said it all.

He sat beside her on the bed, enclosing her hand in his. 'The Lawseer and I followed the traces of redweaving. The intruder climbed into the Royal Precinct from Templegate.

217

Probably used his conjury to make sure he wasn't seen. From there, he scaled the wall into the Queen's Garden, then clambered up to your oriel window, all doubtless with the aid of his godforsaken redweaving.

'Gerent Vann sent archpriests out in all directions, to see what scarlet traces they could find, but he and I followed the main trail down Templegate Walk.'

She sat up, reaching for him. 'And?'

'The foul colour led straight to a wayfarers' dosshouse just inside Marble Gate, a place called *The Twill and the Rose*, owned by a fellow by the name of Jordir Banlock. My guards broke down the door. Vann found traces of the red magic inside.'

'Our son?' Her whisper was barely audible to her own ears.

He shook his head. 'No sign of him. The landlord was locked in the cellar. He said three people had come five days past: a young woman with a tiny suckling babe and an older man, who'd said he was the lass's father and the child's grandfather. They suddenly appeared in the taproom late one evening and asked for the best beds.'

He snorted. 'Banlock's tale was that, unbeknownst to him, the man hung a fever symbol on the outer door sometime during the night. When Banlock woke in the morning, the other travellers were leaving in a panic because the man had told them his daughter had the black-spot fever. It was a lie, of course. Banlock said she was healthy and so was the babe. He says they forced him to close the inn and the man kept him obedient and unprotesting for days, using some sort of conjury.'

She wanted to ask a hundred questions, but her tongue refused to frame them.

'The redweaver called himself Mongrave. The woman appeared to have no weaving ability. At first neither of them went anywhere. They didn't speak much either, according to

Banlock. Last night, when the bell rang for Denniel's birth, Mongrave left the inn with the nurseling, leaving the woman behind. When he returned before dawn-break, he was carrying a baby. Banlock assumed it was the same child as they arrived with, or so he says. Mongrave told Banlock he wanted his grandchild to live, which I assume was a message for us, then they locked the innkeeper in the cellar.'

Light-headed, she tried to make sense of his words. 'He's ... gone, this man Mongrave? With Denniel?'

'I — I don't think we'll ever see him again, Thalia. They must have had a woven portal somewhere in the building. Our arch-clergy have found such things before. This one doesn't exist any longer, although the dosshouse cellar was thick with traces of redweaving according to Vann. It's our belief that Prince Denniel is no longer in our world.'

She shook her head in violent denial. 'No! D-Don't say such a — such a *terrible* thing! There must be a way to find him. There *must* be. The whole city can search. Every citizen!'

'So far, only the Lawseer, Ashwendon and I know the prince is missing. I want to keep it that way. Of course, all guards and priests are on the alert for redweavers, without being told why. All archpriests and archpriestesses are searching for traces of redweaving.'

Her shock left her breathless. 'But surely— Isn't it—? I mean, if everyone knows Denniel is missing, they might find him!'

'Thalia, one thing we know for certain is that the redweaver who was in this room went from here to *The Twill and the Rose*. No deviations. Vann said he tried to clear the trail but did a poor job because he was in too much of a hurry. He left smears as bright as fresh-spilt blood. If he handed my son over to anyone, there would have been a trace, at least a red whisper branching off in another direction. There wasn't. Worse still, there was no trace leaving *The Twill and the Rose*.

The Lawseer's conclusion is that they must have left through a gateway inside the inn. And as far as we know, such a gateway goes only to their own land.'

'But this — this Banlock fellow? What if he's lying? You believe his story?' She had no idea how she could sound so calm, so coherent, when all she wanted to do was kick and scream and batter at her husband with her fists.

Edwild released her hand and moved to the window to look out, his back to her. 'Vann says he doesn't think Banlock could have performed any redweaver conjuries himself, otherwise he would have appeared more tainted than he was. He has kept a respectable house for years, an honest fellow who minds his own business, so the neighbours and the town watch tell us. Never been in trouble. He says he's from Caulstone Water, and he has their Riverland accent.'

'You believe him?'

'No particular reason to doubt him. Although ... there were strong traces of redweaving in the cellar, some of it on Banlock. The Lawseer thought it possible the redweaver portal might have been down there. If it was, then Banlock might have seen them disappear and is lying to us. He's now in the prison of God Atticun's temple, being further interrogated by archpriests, just in case he is hiding anything.'

'He was tainted with redweaving?'

'Not to be wondered at. He lived in that inn with those horrors for days. They apparently left the foul scum of it everywhere, although I couldn't see it.' He turned back to face her, running a hand through his hair in a gesture of frustration.

She shuddered and fought to swallow the sobs that threatened. 'Why, my lord? Why would anyone want to do this, steal a child and give away one of their own in return? They want something, don't they? From us. From *you*. That man, Mongrave, he mentioned his grandson to the innkeeper?'

She gestured at the cradle. 'Did he mean *that* child? Was that a message for us?'

He shrugged. 'Possibly.'

'He was telling us to look after this baby'—she jabbed an agitated finger at the cradle—'and he'd look after Denniel. But he wants something before he'll return our son.' She rose and crossed the room to clutch Edwild's arm, forcing him to meet her gaze. 'That's it, isn't it? We can give it to him, whatever it is, can't we? And then everything will be all right.'

Once again, he was silent.

She forced herself to think. 'You don't think this is his grandson.'

He touched her face in pity. 'Unlikely. Just a replacement, a throwaway babe, to fool us and give them time to get away safely. They're not *decent* folk! From all reports they're godless heathens. We might not have known for days if you hadn't somehow seen him take the prince. He would have had time to clean up behind him and there would have been no red taint for the archpriests to notice. Once he was well away and all the weaving had disappeared, the demand would have been delivered.'

She winced. The truth danced in her mind, but it took her a moment to acknowledge it. 'You know what they want, don't you,' she whispered, her horror growing. 'You already know.'

'They left behind a written demand. With Banlock. Told him to deliver it when he could. He was stacking firewood under the cellar's delivery hatch when we arrived, intending to escape that way. He was going to tell the Watch, or so he said.'

'And their demands?'

He didn't reply.

Groping for understanding, she made a guess. 'It— It's not the first time they've asked for something.'

'No. It isn't.'

'But surely, Denniel can be saved. All you have to do is give them what they want—'

He interrupted, voice harsh. 'I will never grant them what they demand. The cost is far too high.'

She stared at him, reluctant to believe she'd heard correctly. 'Th-th-the c-cost is far too high if you do not! Th-th-they have given us a hostage to show us that they would honour their—'

'*Honour*? They have no *honour*. Anyway, I don't suppose for a moment that the creature in that cradle is of any consequence to their rulers.'

She shook her head in denial.

'I will *not* be blackmailed,' he said. 'I will have this abomination killed.'

Her despair dug deeper, raking her emotions and scorching her hopes to ash. 'You can't…!'

'I can do whatever I like. What I *must*.'

'But it will mean the death of our son! *Edwild!*'

'Madam, I am a king and my duty is to my land and its people. I will not do the bidding of evildoers from another world to save one babe. Not even my own.' His voice wavered, then regained its resolution. 'I can have other sons. *We* will have other sons. You are young and proved yourself fecund within a bare two months of marriage.'

He had drowned hope. She shrank away from him, aghast. This was the man she'd married, this pillar of iron? Royal honour, bounden duty, all coming before family and compassion and love.

Oh, Denniel!

Her mind scrabbled through memories for the right words to say. 'You can't turn your back on your firstborn,' she whispered.

'They dare to control *me*, the King of Talodiac? They would bring this land to its knees if I were to agree! Yes, the prince will die. My firstborn son. But believe me, if I accede to these redweaver stipulations, the horror would be worse. I'm sorry, Thalia. I grieve too, more than you can possibly guess, but at least the Netherfolk will know there is no point in trying blackmail again with another child — because I will *never* give in.'

She pulled her hand free and backed away. 'I don't understand! What can they possibly want that is so terrible you won't grant it to save your son's life?'

'Madam, that is not a matter for discussion between us. In fact, it is not a matter in which I am taking any counsel. Just be comforted by the knowledge that this decision is best for us all, for every Talodian, from the fisherfolk of your father's duchy, to the frontier patrols.' He pointed to the cradle. 'I will smother that babe, and we will tell our people that our son failed to thrive and has died.' A strangled sound came from the back of his throat, half laugh, half anguish. 'The changeling will have a state funeral. Not bad for a cast-off brat of those barbarians.'

Her breathing had speeded up, yet she didn't seem to have enough air in her lungs. She gulped and her chest heaved in answer.

Think. There had to be a way out. *Be calm.*

'You must never speak of this changeling,' he continued. 'Ever. People have panicked every time they think redweavers find a way into our world. The Duke of Menderby nearly went to war with the Duchy of Rothengar once, all because he believed the Rothengar countess he was to marry was really a changeling! And it wasn't even the truth. It was all because the poor woman had unusually bright red hair and she blushed a lot.' He regarded her sadly. 'We keep this secret. Do you understand?'

She nodded to placate him, but barely listened. When she found the right words, she whispered, 'No, wait, please. While this child lives, surely there's a chance they will keep Denniel alive, even if you don't accede to their demand. This changeling, he — it's ... it's a guarantee. A way of ... of saying that they are prepared to keep their side of whatever bargain they offered you.'

'*Bargain?* What they want is abominable. Impossible. Don't be naive, Thalia. I'd wager my whole treasury that no redweaver would leave a beloved baby behind in the arms of an enemy.'

'If—'

'*Enough!* Child, there is nothing to discuss here. This is not a decision I am taking lightly, and you demean me by implying that it is. I am giving up my son! My *heir.*'

She corralled her despair, trapping it deep inside. A heartbeat of time, that was all she had to halt a horror. Wiping her damp hands down the side of her lace wrap, she forced herself to be coldly calm, to find a sliver of possibility.

'Forgive me, sire.' She bowed her head, as if contrite. 'I — I lack your knowledge. Your wisdom. Such terrible decisions as these have never intruded on my sheltered life. I will do your bidding, of course. It is my duty as queen, as your wife, and as a woman bound by her fealty to the Crown. But — but it is hard.' A sob rose into her throat, and she swallowed it back. *Calm. Be calm.* 'I will be worthy of you and of my position. But ... but I do ask one favour. Something that might assuage my pain. No, my *guilt.* Something that will enable me to live with this decision after it is no longer revocable.' She slid to her knees at his feet, then winced as he hauled her upright and pain rippled through the soreness of her body. Gods, a day ago she had still been in labour.

'What favour?'

'I would talk with this Jordir Banlock myself. A mother needs — *I* need to know that my child was not ill-used. I need to hear it from his lips. Some slight breath of hope. Foolish, perhaps, but it will be all I have. And — and I would seek absolution from Gerent Vann for what we must do.' She waved an agitated hand in the direction of the cradle. 'To wantonly kill a child is surely a sin.'

'It's not *human*! It's a Netherfolk changeling. We can't even be sure what such creatures look like in their own land, for no one has ever been there. Perhaps they have powers of conjury to permanently change their appearance into men and women like us when they come here.'

She opened her mouth to point out that all gerents and all archpriests could see redweaving, so surely they would know something about what lay below it … wouldn't they? But no, now was not the time to rile the King. She said instead, 'You ask much of me. Acceptance of the disappearance of our newborn son, brought into this world by my travail and blood. Is what I ask really too much, my liege?' The tear that trickled down her cheek wasn't planned, but she allowed its fall.

His long silence terrified her, but in the end he gave a brusque nod. 'Very well. But this must be done in secret. Tonight. I believe Banlock is being kept in God Atticun's temple. I will send word to the Lawseer to expect you at midnight's bell. You will be escorted, but you must hide who you are.' He waved a hand at the door on the other side of the room that led through to his own apartments. 'You will leave through my door. No one will be surprised if they see a cloaked woman leaving my apartments when my wife is in-disposed and unable to come to my bed. Nor would there be

225

any who would imagine that a woman newly off her birthing stool would be so foolish as to go out into the night, risking all kinds of malodorous humours.'

Shocked, she realised his brutality was deliberate; he expected her to change her mind. *You know me so little*, she thought. And then, in wounded surprise, *The court expects you to have lovers? What have I not seen?* And finally, in wonderment, *I don't believe you've ever bothered to know me.*

When she said nothing, he added, 'I will have a palanquin and my guards ready at Royalgate.'

'I shall want to speak to the Lawseer alone.'

He inclined his head. 'Matters of conscience and absolution are always private. Although I would rather you did not do this. It is foolishness. *You* have no guilt in this, Thalia. None.'

He'd surprised her again, and her affection stirred once more, a faint reminder of what had been. 'The gods are merciful,' she whispered.

He turned to leave, saw the cradle and turned back. 'The changeling. Bring it with you. The conjury will fade over time and if you leave him in the care of servants, it may become obvious that he's no royal baby.'

And with that he was gone. The irony made her catch her breath in thanksgiving; she'd had no idea how she was going to take the child with her when the time came, and he had just made it all so easy.

Deathly tired, she lay down on her bed once more, but did not dare sleep. She needed to think. To plan. To wonder how much she dared risk.

22

The owner of the cart was even more taciturn than the archer as he guided the conveyance down the slope, heading for the city. As the details of what had happened across the plains became all too clear, Haze was not inclined to ask too many questions. Dead esklet littered the fields. Other carts heading into the city carried dead bodies, faces eaten away, skin melted, eyes burned from the skull, blood drained through holes eaten into flesh.

Ten hells, she thought, *a couple of drops of esklet spit ravaged Innata's face; it's no wonder people die...*

Scattered throughout the countryside were diseased patches where the land appeared shrivelled. *Scorched.* Plants withered, trees stripped of leaves, farm animals dead in the fields.

Every so often, huge rope nets hung suspended on buttressed poles across a field, the netting still contaminated by the red taint of weaver magic. Most of these contained entangled esklet corpses already giving off that unpleasantly caustic apothecary stink. The bodies were riddled with arrows and crossbow bolts, telling her it hadn't been the nets that killed them, or the redweaving; it had been archers. And how the pickled pox had the esklet been tricked into flying directly into the nets in the first place? Some kind of weaving magic?

She watched, unsettled and sickened. The people along that road all had one thing in common. They were thin. Underfed, like the archer. Skinny wrists as slim as pick handles poked out of coats made for larger folk. Cheeks were sunken, stomachs dipped between hipbones. Yet the grass in the fields was lush. The water in the river was clear and plentiful. What she wasn't seeing were crops. The fruit trees had no fruit, the fields were tilled but no grain grew, there was plenty of grazing but few farm animals to eat it.

These people, the men and women helping the injured into the city and grieving for the deceased, those grim-faced armed men riding past on their   taldeer, these were the despised Netherlost? They were no different from Talodians! They wept over their dead, helped their injured and probably grieved when their cattle died. They saddled their taldeer and buckled their shoes. Differences were slight: more women wore trousers than you would ever have glimpsed in Talodiac, and their hair was shorter; more of the men wore beards, but any one of them could have been born in Talodiac. Yet Talodians hunted and killed them as if they were vermin.

She took Innata's hand in hers and asked, 'Can you hear me?'

*

Someone was calling her. *Hazelle.*
Innata heard, and tried to answer, but pain swamped her, swept away her reply, took her to another place. To another hell.

*

Walking downstairs *hurt.*
The palanquin was waiting at the foot of the King's private staircase. She winced at every step, annoyed at her weakness. Edwild had insisted she carry the babe herself. 'You wanted to do this; you keep that creature hidden and make sure it doesn't cry,' he'd said, the steel in his voice honed on sarcasm to an edge that cut painfully deep.

Useless to point out that it wasn't easy to stop an unhappy babe from howling. She had tried to forestall problems by changing its wet napkin and putting it to her breast late in the evening. And she managed, clutching the changeling to her chest under the heavy, voluminous hooded cloak he had brought along for her to wear. Fortunately, there had been plenty of room under her gown for her to hide her jewellery box as well.

'What explanation have you given for placing a guard on my chambers and forbidding my servants and the wet nurse entry?' she'd asked.

'I said you were adamant you would feed the prince yourself, and that you were exhausted and wished only to sleep in between.' So, she was to take the blame. Thalia, the silly hoyden from the fisher-coast duchy, where the court was obviously riddled with ill-bred folk possessing vulgar manners. Gods, the Queen Mother would make her life an utter misery after this, if she ever had the chance.

But she won't. I'll make sure of that. A brave thought, surely, when she was by no means certain she'd be able to see her plan through.

'I've arranged for my personal guards under the command of a sergeant-at-arms,' Edwild said as they descended the stairs. 'Hervan and his men know how to be discreet. Cover your face now. I don't want them to guess they escort the Queen.'

Rebuffed, she pulled her tippet up over her nose.

He continued, 'I will ask them to deliver you to the temple's royal entrance. The Lawseer's secretary will meet you there.'

When they stepped out of the doorway into the courtyard, she ducked her head so that her face was in shadow and wondered if her husband was in the habit of ushering muffled women out of the palace in the middle of the night into the care of his guard. Perhaps that's what kings did. She remembered advice her mother had given her shortly before she'd left for Templebridge: 'Kings and dukes and princes, they do what they want. Do not make the mistake of thinking all husbands are like your father. If you want Edwild to dance to your song, you have to offer music no one else can. The secret is to find the right tune.' She'd thought bearing him a son was that song. How wrong she had been! Her father's advice was perhaps more relevant. 'Remember, no king wants to wake up one morning and realise that his queen is smarter than he is.'

She'd laughed and said, 'Surely that will not be true!'

He'd tapped her nose in rebuke, smiled, and replied, 'I know my daughter.'

And now Edwild was bending to kiss her forehead. 'Seek the comfort you need, my sweet,' he whispered into her ear, 'and then look no more behind, only ahead.'

His sudden kindness was as confusing as his lack of understanding. She gave no reply, glad he'd no idea of the nebulous, half-formed plan she had conceived.

Just as she stepped up to the palanquin, she glanced up and caught the eye of the young sergeant-at-arms, a blond-headed giant of a man. By the light from the palanquin lamps, she thought she glimpsed condemnation in his stare. She ducked her head, a flush rising in her cheeks as he opened the door for her. Stepping up with her burden, she hid the pain the movement brought. Edwild was still there, watching. She inclined her head in acknowledgement as it crossed her mind she may never see him again. A hard lump of grief settled in her chest, but the task ahead would brook no weakness.

*

The Lawseer's secretary escorted her under the archway carved with God Atticun's motto, *For the Greater Good of Creation*, to the inner sanctum. She thought bitterly that even though the King had dedicated himself and his royal line of descendants to the Arch-God of the Decasian, God Atticun had not served them well. The god and his priests had failed to protect Denniel.

The Lawseer, Gerent Vann, was seated when they entered his private study. He was dressed in a clean blue robe, his beaded purple cap neatly atop his long hair. Her first thought was how shrunken he appeared, as if the events of the day had sucked his vitality from him, leaving behind a body that was little more than a husk. He did not speak, or move, until his secretary had left them alone, shutting the heavy door behind him.

The look he gave her was distressed as he rose to his feet and bowed. 'Your Grace, I beg your forgiveness that we were not in time to prevent the redweaver's escape from the city.' He came forward, gesturing an offer to take her cloak.

She shook her head and clutched it tighter.

His brow furrowed. 'The red taint is strong about you ... What is it you carry that contaminates so?'

'Not what. Who.' She opened the cloak enough to show him the child. 'Did the King inform you of my wish to speak to the prisoner?'

'Indeed. I have brought the fellow upstairs from the prison cells. But my lady, ah ... He has been questioned.'

'Of course. But I have other queries.'

He gave an embarrassed cough. 'He is not — not in good health.'

She stared at him hard, stomach churning. 'You mean he was tortured?' Naïve of her not to have thought of that. Where she was from, they did not torture. Her father be-

231

lieved prisoners would lie to escape the agony as often as they told the truth.

He paled. 'The urgency and seriousness of the matter—'

'The King informed me that there was no direct indication this Jordir Banlock was involved.'

'We had to make sure he had nothing further to tell us.'

'And did he?'

'Nothing new.' He shrugged. 'I am of the opinion that he is innocent, but I will be honest with you. It is my belief that Netherfolk look just like us. Their language is similar, more a difference in lilt and some words. Were they to live here for a year or two, they'd sound just like us if they cared to learn. Redweavers are probably just Netherfolk who stand out only because we arch-clergy can see the evidence of any recent weaving.'

'Oh!' She was shocked. Before she had come to Temple-bridge, she'd heard of redweavers but more as if they were the beings of folktales. And yet here was the Lawseer speaking of them as if they could be living among the common-folk. As if he'd *known* some. 'I—I was not aware of this.'

'There was never a need for you to know.'

She wanted to throw those words back at him, but reined in her anger. 'The King said Banlock was tainted.'

'I did see the mark of redweaving on him, but it was slight, so I have no certainty he was responsible. It could have been simply because he was living in a redweaver's company for several days.'

'I still wish to see him. Alone.' He did not reply immediately, so she added, 'The King acquiesced to my request.'

'The temple is the domain of God Atticun,' he said in gentle remonstration. 'Even kings cannot command any of the Decasian Godheads. However, I have spoken to God Atticun, and he has granted me the honour of a reply. He sanctioned your visit.' From his tone, she gathered that the god's decision had not made him happy. He continued, 'An officer of the temple guards will conduct you to one of our disciplinary cells, which Jordir Banlock now occupies. You will be able to address him in private, but I do insist that the officer be close by to ensure your safety.'

'The King would not want the conversation to be overheard.'

He pondered that before replying. 'I will inform the guard to stand back, if Your Grace will promise not to approach Banlock too closely.' He cleared his throat, embarrassed. 'At the King's request, no one other than myself knows who you are, so please do not be offended if you are not accorded the high respect due your rank.'

She was incredulous. Did he really think she cared a fish-feather for protocol after all that had happened that day?

'When you return, I shall check that you have not been contaminated by any conjury. And please,' he continued, 'keep your face obscured. Do you wish to the leave the child behind?'

She shook her head.

23

The man lying on the thin pallet of a solid wooden bed in a priest's cubbyhole was weak and injured. The officer hung a lantern on the bars of the door, directing the light away from her and into the cell. While she waited for him to retreat to the end of the passage out of earshot, Thalia studied the dosshouse owner through the iron bars.

Banlock was naked to the waist, clad only in short breeks below. Blood from a cut on his forehead matted his brown hair and his chest was criss-crossed with welts, but it was his hands that drew her gaze. They were a bloody mess of torn flesh, twisted fingers and missing nails. Worse still, one of his thumbs had been lopped, the raw flesh then burned black to stop the bleeding.

She winced, stomach churning.

He levered open puffy eyes.

She steeled herself to ignore the injuries. To not consider the brutality that had caused them. 'Can you sit up?' she asked.

He didn't reply immediately, but he did heave himself upright. Blood trickled down his face to his chin.

'Forgive me if I don't stand,' he said in a whisper.

Gods, he was younger than she'd thought he'd be. Younger than Edwild, she guessed. 'I — I am sorry you were treated this way.'

Incredibly, his lips twitched upwards in a lopsided smile. 'Are you? Can't think why. Who are you, madam? A vision of a fevered mind?'

'The grieving mother of a child stolen last night.'

Every part of him tensed, from the wounded hands to his bloodied feet on the cold stones of the floor. His gaze sharpened. 'The *Queen* comes to see me?'

She let her tippet drop so he could see her face. 'They think you aren't one of the Netherfolk,' she said. 'But they will kill you anyway.'

He did not react.

'I know you are one of them. I want my son back.'

He sat still, his broken hands resting on his knees. 'Show me your face in the light.'

Keeping her back to the guard, she moved the lantern a little, and lifted the hood of her cloak away from her head with one hand, while still concealing the baby under her voluminous cloak. He stared at her for a moment and nodded before he dropped his gaze. 'I know naught, Your Grace.'

She knew he lied. 'I want my son,' she said. 'What do I have to do to have him returned to me?'

She stood, silent, waiting, heart thudding.

'What makes you think I be one of them?' he asked at last, lifting his chin so his gaze met hers. His eyes were blue and they crinkled at the corners, as if more accustomed to laughter than pain. 'Magic folk who can cast spells and conjuries! Yet here Jordir Banlock sits in his cell, crippled and twisted, waiting for the torture to start again come morn. I've no red magic, lady, and they know it. If I did, I'd be long-gone from this stone-hard hell.'

She leaned closer until her face was pressed against the bars. 'Do not underestimate us! Archpriests followed the red stain that led straight to your establishment from the palace. Your neighbours have tongues. Temple devotees talk to their priests. You came to Templebridge years ago and bought a house. You changed it into a dosshouse, a place where strangers are expected to come and go. It must have been you who named it *The Twill and the Rose*. Twill — a type of weave. Used a lot where I come from, among the fisher folk. Rose — a shade of red. Subtle enough not to be too obvious, but when redweavers come to your inn, I will not believe the name a mere coincidence!'

Given his injuries, his stillness was uncanny.

'Know this, Banlock. I was born to a money-poor ducal family living on the axe-edge of intrigue from stronger, bolder, richer neighbours who coveted our one asset: a safe harbour for trade ships. I learned early to read subtleties, to recognise mockery when it was intended. The name you gave your hostelry was your way of laughing at Talodiac. You were arrogant, Jordir Banlock. And brazen.' She shook her head in disbelief. 'Clever then, not so much now.'

When he still didn't reply, she continued, 'They will torture you until you die. The only person who can save you is *me*. Tell me what I have to do to have my son returned and I will see you freed.'

He snorted in wordless disbelief, and yet she read something else in his eyes. Not hope, not that. No, it was appreciation. He was admiring her attempt to change what had happened.

'I can do it,' she said, raising her chin. *I can.*

'Your King already knows what must be done,' he said. 'Only he can grant what they ask. If he does their bidding, his little princeling will be returned. Leastwise, that be what that Mongrave fella told me.'

'That was the name of the man who took the prince?'

''Twas the name he gave me.'

'What do they want of King Edwild?'

'D'you think they'd tell me?'

'Yes.'

He started to shrug, but a spasm of pain brought a gasp to his lips instead.

236

'*If* you don't know, you could guess,' she said.

'Summat that your man has to give, that none else can grant. You tell me what that'd be.'

'I don't know. And if he doesn't give them what they want?'

'His son — your son — will die. So they said. But who am I to say if men of their power speak the truth? If I was more than a dosshouse keeper, I wouldn't be here.' He started to raise a bloodied hand to his face, then changed his mind. He dipped his chin instead, wiping the blood trickling there onto his bare shoulder.

'And this child?' She threw back her cloak and showed him the baby. 'What is this child to you?'

His gaze sharpened with surprise. Again, she had to wait for his reply.

'Naught,' he said finally. 'I know neither his kin nor his lineage. The boy is a — a gesture, a way to say, "Look, we trust you with a child from our world. We'll uphold our part of the bargain. Give us what we want and your son will be returned, unharmed." At least, that be my belief. In that much, I am sincere.'

She weighed his words and came to the conclusion that he was hinting to her that this statement was true, while the others were not. A straw of truth in a wind of deception. 'And if we don't do what they ask?'

'The threat is there, but I've no idea if they'll follow through on't. My guess is that y'boy is safe for the time being, but your only guarantee he remain so is to do what they asked.'

'Such knowledge for an innkeeper from Caulstone Water!' The words mocked, her small rebellion.

He made a slight gesture with a crippled hand as if to say he admitted nothing, but she caught the faint twitch of his lips that followed, as if he appreciated her nerve.

She said, 'The King is refusing to give in to any Netherworld demand.'

'Not much of a papa then, is he?'

She sucked in a sharp breath. 'He is a monarch, raised to put his duty to Talodiac before his own wishes.' And every word of that was a dagger point twisted in her heart.

'Very noble of him. Not so pleasant for his lady wife.'

'Don't you *dare* taunt me.'

'Take no notice, milady. I'm just a dead man, breathing yet, while measuring the hours left to me on the fingers of one hand.' He smiled faintly. 'And that hand so mangled, I can scarce count the digits.'

Gods, he could joke? 'King Edwild says he will kill this child tomorrow. He does not want people to know redweavers penetrated the walls of the palace to my bedchamber, so he intends to say our son did not thrive and died during the night. This child is to be buried as Prince Denniel.'

'Ah. A hard man, your king.'

'I will not allow that to happen. This babe should not be'—she held back the sob that rose into her throat—'not be wantonly murdered. I want you to take him and go free. I believe that to be within my power to grant.' *Please, let that be the truth...*

He pondered her assertion, then shook his head. 'Somehow, lady, I think you be the one taunting me with possibilities. Your priests will not listen to you. They'll do the King's bidding, methinks.'

'Leave the priests and the King to me. I want you to take this child back where he belongs.'

'Lady, that can't happen.' He raised a battered hand to show her the full extent of his injuries. 'Most of my fingers are broken. I have but one remaining thumb, and that hideously swollen. I've broken ribs. I can scarce walk, let alone hold a babe, or care for it. Even if you could persuade your templemen and their torturers to set me free in the face of the King's rage.'

'All one needs is the right argument, and I have that.' She frowned, though, as she acknowledged the truth of his observation that he could carry nothing. She reviewed her options, seeking ways to tweak her plan. 'I can still have you freed, if you promise to tell the redweavers responsible that I will spirit this child away to safety and guard him, just to keep my son alive and safe.'

Incredulous, he blurted, 'You'd do such, if you could? Free me with no guarantees? Knowing I might choose never to deliver the message, knowing I might not even know to what man I should take such a promise? And what about the anger of some, if they discover your role in my freedom, and the prince still missing? Mayhap you've a beautiful soul, m'lady queen, but I fear your wits have gone a-wandering.'

Her temper flared, bitter and potent. 'I'm a *mother*. No one murders a child in my care. *No one.* This boy will be cared for. Nor do I walk away from my own son without trying everything in my power to ensure his safety. Know this, I kneel to Goddess Jenat, and she will *never* allow a child to be wantonly slaughtered. Can you help, Jordir Banlock? *Will* you help?'

To her surprise, a tear runnelled down the fold of his cheek, catching the lamp light. He stood then, propping the backs of his legs against the frame of the bed. 'Get me out of here, and I will do my best to keep your son alive and cared for. I pledge my word that I will try. More than that is not within my power.'

'You are a redweaver?'

'I'm no conjurer, lady. I can't weave a portal in an instant, nor trick the eye with illusion.'

Truth, perhaps, perhaps not, but no admission of what he was — or wasn't.

'There has to be *something* you can do.'

'Well … there is a way to send a message. Who will act on it, and *how* they'll act, I can give no guess.'

An admission from him at last. She took a deep breath. 'You cannot go to this Netherfolk world?'

He started to shake his head, and winced. 'Kanter,' he said. 'They call their land Kanter and they are Kanterine. As well your husband knows. Netherland, Netherworld, Lands of the Beyond, all your words, not theirs. The portal in *The Twill and the Rose* was destroyed. If there are other portals, I've no idea where to find them.'

The latter was a lie, she was sure. *Learn to read a man's muscles, Thalia,* her father had once told her, *before you trust his words. Watch the way he tenses, observe the curling of a finger or the droop of a lip. There is language in a bead of sweat, in the flicker of an eyelid, or the widening of a pupil.* The trouble was, she couldn't tell if Banlock's lie was about the existence of portals, or if it just concerned his knowledge of them.

'Jordir,' she begged, 'save these children. Not for my sake. For them. They are babies. They deserve a chance at life. And when you leave this place, remember that no matter what you hear, this child I hold will be alive and cared for. I pledge it, in the name of my son.'

He looked down at his broken body and a smile ghosted at the corners of his lips. 'I might do it for myself. I don't believe in an afterlife. This moment of living is all I have, and an hour ago, I thought it close to over. Get me out of here, m'lady queen, then the rest of my wretched existence will be dedicated to keeping your son alive and well. *If* I can find a way.'

His gaze locked on hers, and it was unflinching. Nonetheless, the mocking twist of his bloodied lips told her he thought she would never persuade the templemen to release him — or indeed to keep him alive.

'The prince's name again?' he asked.

'Denniel,' she whispered. 'We were going to call him Denniel.'

He nodded, chin raised, his gaze locking onto hers with such intensity that she took a step back. 'I will make you a gift of my real name. Kaillan. Kaillan Riverdell.'

Her breath caught. A gift indeed if that was a Kanterine name.

As she turned away, he murmured words under his breath. She wasn't certain she was supposed to hear them, but she thought he said, 'Your king is not worthy of such a queen.'

24

When they drove up to the main city gateway, Haze realised that someone with her looks could fit in here easily. The realisation sneaked into her thoughts to mock any remaining belief that she was Talodian. Perhaps all she had ever been was a throwaway child. An unwanted brat, one of the Netherlost, lucky to be rescued by Innata.

Suddenly, she didn't like that name, Netherlost.

Kanterine. These people are Kanterine. From Kanter.

Just inside the city gateway, the cart driver drew up in front of a covered area where some of the less badly injured were being attended by people who were, she hoped, healers or nurses. As soon as they arrived, several attendants came forward to talk to the archer and move Innata on to one of the empty canvas cots, already stained with someone else's blood. Haze, having already thanked the carter, tried to stay at Innata's side, but was soon hustled out of the way when several elderly women came to attend to her wound.

The carter drove away, but the archer stayed to speak to the women, after which he disappeared into the guardhouse at the city gate. She didn't see him again after that, but a little later an elderly man armed with a truncheon came to stand next to her. He didn't speak, but he did rhythmically tap the truncheon into the palm of his hand.

She sighed. Some things didn't need the spoken word. He was there to keep an eye on her until they found someone with more authority to deal with a redweaver who didn't speak their language.

At least the women were attending to Innata, washing her wound with a brightly-coloured potion, then applying some kind of paste. When they were done, one of them smiled at

Haze and waved a hand at Innata, as if to say all would be well, before moving on to another new arrival.

She resigned herself to waiting, pondering how to build another woven gateway, one that would lead back to Talodiac. When she looked down at her hands, the red threads of light were still there, but their vibrancy was fading, and she had no idea of how to bring them back to life.

*

I nnata surfaced through the pain and the noise. People groaning, crying, a child screaming somewhere. Strange words. Someone prodding her ... Where in all the world was she? Desperate to escape the throbbing in her head, the stabbing pain in her face, she turned away from the sound and burrowed inwards instead.

Think of Denniel...

*

G erent Vann, slack-jawed, stared at her. 'You jest, surely, Your Grace.'

Thalia shifted the baby into a more comfortable position and although the child screwed up its face, it didn't wake. He continued, 'This is not a time for foolish dreaming. Can't you see that Banlock knows too much? My lady, the King wishes to keep the presence of redweavers in Templebridge a secret from the general populace. Imagine the panic if they knew a red portal had opened up in our strongest walled city, the palace itself penetrated, the heir stolen!' The sick look on his face said it all. '*It can't be allowed to happen*. Quite apart from anything else, I can't free Banlock because — if he's just an ordinary Talodian — he won't keep his mouth shut. And if he is one of *them*?' He flicked a finger at the baby, his face pinched with distaste, perhaps even with fear. 'That one most certainly is. That child bleeds scarlet through his pores.'

She stifled her annoyance at his patronising tone. 'Rubbish. That's the weaving the redweaver did to make him the image of the prince. It's a *baby*. He couldn't weave a conjury any more than he can talk!' A momentary doubt prompted a sick lurch in her stomach. How could she be sure? Perhaps the child had powers beyond her comprehension. She groped for coherence. 'What is certain to me is that either Banlock is in league with the redweavers, or they have some hold over him. Either way, he's not going to be talking about this to anyone if we free him. Why would he?' Of that, she was certain.

'It doesn't matter if that's true,' he said with a sigh — the kind that told her he thought her naïvely immature. 'I obey my king, and my orders are to question the landlord of *The Twill and the Rose* until he has no more to tell, after which he is to die.'

'And God Atticun allows the torture and killing of a man in his own temple building?'

'That is not your concern.'

His dismissal rankled; nonetheless, she embarked on another line of argument. 'Gerent Vann, Atticun is the God of Law, Governance and Justice, and we both know this matter does concern the future governance of Talodiac. You are the *Lawseer*!'

'My lady queen, I think it is time you return to the King, and leave these grave matters to those who—'

'Sir, stop right there. You mock a woman who has lost her newborn son! This "grave matter" happens to be of utmost concern to me. If you release Jordir Banlock, I will hold my tongue about all that happened last night. If you don't, then I will spread this truth throughout the palace: that God Atticun and his Lawseer failed to protect the city and the newborn prince from redweaver conjury and extortion. Word of such a failure will spread through the court like fire through a slum in the summer heat.'

Sweet Jenat, did I really say that?

He spluttered. 'You can't be serious! To spill such knowledge is treason!'

She could have reminded him that the populace was notoriously fickle in their allegiance to any particular deity, and it was popular support that filled a temple's coffers, but decided her words had already had the desired effect. He was staring at her, aghast.

'Really?' she asked. 'Perhaps. You know more about the law than I. But all that matters to me is that I give my son the best chance to live.'

When he found his tongue again, he lashed out. 'I can't imagine that the King would be pleased with his queen's ill-considered gossip. I do not bow to the demands of an immature girl from a coastal fishing backwater, the seventeen-year-old daughter of a duke with all the standing of a country squire!'

'Eighteen.' Her ire burned in her cheeks. 'May I remind you that I am your crowned queen.' *And I know what you think of me now.* Had she not been holding the child, she might have struck him. Instead, she swallowed back her rage. 'A god's task is to maintain the greater good, which takes precedence over aid to an individual. God Atticun's duty is to further justice and maintain the stability of good governance. I've heard you preach those very words. Think of what may happen if an heir is missing, perhaps being raised by the Netherfolk to reappear when King Edwild dies—'

'Do you think I didn't take this whole matter to God Atticun for his consideration? I personally went before my deity on my knees and begged for guidance.'

Dismayed, she almost stilled her tongue. 'And?' she whispered.

'He — well, he has not yet given me guidance. *Yet.* That is not unusual. I take it as a sign that he trusts my judgement.'

'When you asked if I was to be allowed to meet with Banlock, God Atticun acquiesced. Is that not so?'

Hope. A sliver of hope surely...

He nodded.

'I wish to speak to him.'

'To God Atticun?'

'Yes!'

'Such a request is not made lightly.'

'Believe me, I do not make it lightly! I suspect that it is *you* who chooses who gets to see the god.'

He didn't reply, which told her she was probably right. 'I suspect too, that supplicants who make offerings to the temple of considerable value are often thus rewarded. I assure you, a queen has resources to be generous.'

In the silence that followed, she matched his glare with one of her own until he stood abruptly, with an exaggerated sigh. 'The King requested that I do my best to assuage your fears, so if speaking to God Atticun now is what is needed, I will conduct Your Grace to the inner sanctum. However, be warned: he rarely answers even his senior templemen, the arch-clergy. Or me, even.'

He turned to the private door at the rear of the room, opened it and waved her through. Closing it firmly behind them a moment later, he marched off down a stone-walled corridor. Lit by living glow-flowers planted in sconces, the passage smelled of both their spicy aroma and the mustiness of the cave moth larvae that lived on the blossoms. She did her best to keep up, babe in her arms, but every muscle of her body screamed at her, telling her she needed rest, needed anything but this. Then she thought of Denniel, bit her lip, and followed the Lawseer into the expanse that opened under the dome at the end of the passage.

She'd never been in a sanctum before. Few people had. She knew that although anyone might *ask* to speak directly with their god of choice, requests were rarely granted. Only a god's gerent came and went freely into the sacred heart of a god's temple. She shivered, wondering if to approach a god without invitation was not insanity.

Nonplussed, she found herself in an unadorned chamber. The domed white roof, the grey marble walls and the floor of dark red porphyry tiles were all undecorated. There was no furniture. Her attention was drawn instead to the madder and carmine glow on — in? Under? — the floor, directly beneath the centre of the dome. Depthless, restless, dominating, the light was so intense she could not focus on it. It glowed, yes, but the incandescence burned not with heat, but with icy brittleness in cold, dark hues. She discerned no shape inside. Movement, but no life.

The Lawseer, regarding her, waved a hand at it. 'God Atticun,' he said.

She trembled then, her knees threatening to collapse under her. There was nothing of comfort here, surely. No living being that she could see. She focused, staring at its centre, and thought she saw a ruby heartbeat throbbing in the colour.

'Approach closer,' he said, 'as far as the line of darker tiles, but do not overstep them lest you anger him. Kneel there. Tell our gracious deity who you are and the circumstances of your appeal. Be concise. Do not lie, for he already knows the truth. It is your interpretation he needs to hear, your sincerity.'

He stayed where he was as she walked forward.

The sudden weight of her audacity overwhelmed her. She — barely even an adult — was challenging the wisdom of the land's highest priest, questioning his judgement. Surely Atticun would think her arrogant, lacking in both manners and wisdom.

Still weak, still clutching the child, she clumsily sank to her knees at the edge of the line of slightly darker porphyry. The babe opened its eyes as the red light fell across its face, but he did not cry. Her thoughts ran on, panicked.

How could she have been so — so *stupid* to think a god would answer her prayer? Leastwise a deity many said was the greatest of them all? What had she been thinking! This was a *god*. A being so far removed from her human frailty and concerns, a being whose whole reason for existence was to maintain the balance between the need for law and order on the one hand and the frivolous wishes and desires of the individual on the other.

The swirl of light: it was depthless, timeless, ancient, ageless, soaked in power ... a moving, twisting ambience beyond her understanding. She wanted to weep. The air was heavy with a perfume she had never encountered before. When she breathed, she felt light-headed, not in command of her own thoughts, as if she were on the edge of a dream.

Then she remembered the feel of her son in her arms, the softness of his cheek against hers. She raised her chin, sought courage from her memory of him and told her story.

Afterwards, she was unsure whether she had spoken the words of her appeal aloud, or whether the god had simply absorbed them from her mind. All she knew was that she'd begged Atticun's forbearance and asked him to have Banlock freed in order to save her son. Had she explained her reasoning? She thought so, but the memory was muddled.

And her request was met with silence.

She crumpled, folding protectively over the child in her arms, until her forehead was touching the floor. Terror gripped her.

And then her fear was gone. Banished.

A quiet certainty that the god had spoken and granted her wish calmed her— but not because she'd asked, and not to save Denniel. It was for some greater good, and she must accept that.

Trembling, she sat back on her heels and glanced over her shoulder at Gerent Vann.

Ashen-faced, he indicated she should rise. 'God Atticun has spoken,' he whispered. He turned abruptly and headed back the way they'd come.

Before following him, she glanced back into the light. She could see no form within, but sensed a presence, a power barely contained, something sentient and ancient beyond her understanding. Yet … something … something old and tired. Fear shuddered through her.

'Thank you, Lord God,' she whispered.

As she left the chamber, her overwhelming thought was: *That is the most powerful deity we have? That?* Panic welled up from her guts.

Stop it. Stop thinking.

She blanked her mind, and with it, her fear.

Gerent Vann did not speak until they were seated back in his study, when — numbed and drained of all her passion — she asked, 'What now?'

He did not look at her, but contemplated his hands as he rubbed one against the other. 'In the morning, Banlock will have his wounds attended to, his money will be returned to him, and he will be given a free pass to remain within Templebridge for ten days to recover his strength. If he is found here after that, he will be seized. You should return to

249

the King and tell him what passed here. I must add that God Atticun told me before we left his presence that King Edwild is not bound by this decision. He must examine his own conscience.'

The tinge of pity she read in his words told her that he did not believe she had saved either of the children.

'An added piece of advice, milady. It is not wise to confront a god so ... so blatantly. Least of all God Atticun. His compassion has just been demonstrated, but it is not boundless. Nor is mine. Tread carefully.'

*

When Innata opened her eyes and stirred, Haze came close to collapsing in relief. She had never been so scared of the unfamiliar, and so terrified at the thought of facing it alone. 'Are you all right?' she asked.

'My face is sore.' Innata frowned. 'I've been having ... nightmares, remembering past ... past horrors. No, *reliving* them. For a time, I was eighteen all over again! Where are we?'

'A city near where the esklet were. Do you remember the attack?'

Hesitantly Innata fingered the dried paste covering her cheek. She nodded. 'It's not so painful now. I thought I was dying.' She glanced around. 'How long have we been here?'

'About an hour. I think they've sent for someone in authority. There's a man keeping an eye on us. I did try to speak to him, but he wouldn't reply. Maybe he didn't understand. Would you like some water?'

Innata swung her legs over the edge of the cot and edged herself into a sitting position. Haze handed her the mug of water the attendants had left for her. 'Are you sure you are all right?'

'I think so.' Between the sips of water, she voiced their problems. 'The baffle is going to make things difficult. I can talk to you about it because you already know about it. They don't. You'll have to explain to them.'

'They might just kill us. That's what we do to them, isn't it?'

'Then you had better be quick to point out that you are one of them, a redweaver.'

'Am I? Really?'

'Talodians are never redweavers. You are.'

She pulled a face. 'How is that even possible?'

Innata shook her head, then winced when it hurt. 'I don't know.'

'I have no idea how I conjured up a gate the first time, let alone how to do it a second time … and that's about the only thing that will convince them.' Not quite true. The wisps of red she wore were fading, but they would have surely still been visible to a Talodian archpriest.

'Do you still have my jewellery?' Innata asked suddenly.

'Yes, all of it. Except for the carcanet. I gave that to Tay.'

Innata nodded. 'You knew what it was?'

'Taygen told me. A piece bestowed on a Queen when she birthed an heir.'

'That's right. Haze, I'm now going to say something I want you to remember.'

'What?'

'I've never been a thief.'

'You didn't have to tell me that!'

'It's important that you remember it.'

'All right. I'm hardly going to contradict you. Right now, I'm more worried about Taygen. I told him I would come for him.'

'I heard.'

'Hervan is going to hand him over to the King's justice, isn't he?'

'I think that's very likely. The captain was already very unhappy with him.'

'I promised him. I've got to get back. We have to get back to the tunnel I made — but the archer who helped us get here — I showed it to him.' She glanced over to the town gate where the number of guards had swelled to eight. The man who appeared to be in charge was now speaking to a woman who stood with folded arms, frowning as she stared at Innata. She was wearing a man's clothing and carried no arms.

'You want to be a lad or a lass?' Innata asked.

'Your call.'

'Then lad. I have my reasons.'

Haze shrugged. 'As always.' She continued to study the woman at the gate. At first glance the only notable thing about her was that she had red embroidery around the wrists and collar of her coat, but then she saw little runnels of red light dancing over the woman's skin. 'Can you see that?' she asked Innata.

'The embroidery? Yes. Excellent stitching. She has money, but more than that. You're looking at a woman with some kind of status. That's what that embroidery says, at a guess.'

Haze sighed. 'She's a redweaver.' This was going to be a tough day.

25

Blatantly confident of her status, the woman in the embroidered coat dismissed the soldiers with a wave of her hand and walked over to where Innata still sat on the cot. She was elegant, in her thirties perhaps, rake-thin. As she came closer, the red lines of light wavering and shimmering across her skin and clothing were more obvious. She'd been using the weaving recently.

The woman looked Innata up and down. 'Talodian,' she said, the word loaded with contempt. It wasn't a question.

'I am, certainly,' Innata said, eternally polite. 'I go by the name of Innata Wayfarer. This is Haze Wayfarer. Seeing as he can weave a gateway between your country and mine, I suspect that he is Kanterine. We have not long arrived in Kanter, though.'

The woman turned to Haze. 'You wove the gateway? Yet they said you don't understand our Kanter speech! Were you brought up in Talodiac? The archer told us you killed an esklet. How can that be?'

How the many hells was she going to answer that? Haze swallowed, uncomfortable, and was silent, wretchedly aware of the wavering of colour that rippled around her, a match to the woman's.

Innata answered for her. 'And *you* speak like a highborn Talodian, with not a trace of any Kanterine accent. I wonder how that can be? We have information we will give only to someone in authority. And you are—?'

'A lore councillor of this city. My name is Jalondine. Lady Jalondine to you.'

Innata's lips gave the faintest of amused twitches. 'Lady Jalondine,' she said, inclining her head politely. 'Perhaps we

253

can continue this conversation somewhere more ... salubrious? We have come a long way today and are in need of rest. As you must note, I was injured by an esklet. Some clean clothes would be nice, too.'

Haze concealed a smile. Innata at her cheekiest best, playing at being highborn, beautifully polite and utterly cutting at one and the same time. And all that, even though she had not long ago taken a dip in a stream fully clothed, been out of her mind with some kind of poison-fever, then bounced along a dusty road on a springless cart for several hours to arrive in this town. As Taygen would have said, with a roll of his eyes, '*Aristos!*'

Jalondine inclined her head, an exact mirroring of Innata's. 'Of course. Can you walk?'

'I'll do my best. Haze, hand me my staff. I need to lean on something.'

Clever, she's changing a potential weapon into a walking stick...

'Then follow me.' Jalondine shifted her scrutiny to Haze again, waiting for a reaction. When there was none, the woman strode off, leaving them to scramble in her wake. Doubtless she wanted to indicate how little she feared them, but Innata had to concentrate on putting one foot in front of the other, while Haze was so appalled by the destruction of the city that she barely noticed anything else.

Buildings and streets were scarred by the esklet spit. Wood was charred, slate had cracked, furrows were scored into stone, bricks had dissolved — as if the city had the fragility of a doll's house. Even worse, the rich stench of death leaked into every laneway. The blood of a city's people soaked the cobbles and splashed the walls on either side of the street. What the spit did to people was hideous enough, but what happened to them if an esklet caught them was far, far worse.

On every corner she saw the stark despair on the faces of the mourning. She saw the clawed hunks of flesh ripped from the dead. She saw the bodies of those who'd fought to save their city. The unscathed men and women were hollow-eyed and sunken-cheeked. No one had a pinch of fat anywhere. By all that was unholy, even the children, big-eyed and bony-faced, were so ill-fed that a good storm wind would have sent them bowling down the street.

Jalondine looked back over her shoulder when they passed a sobbing family carrying a pallet that held the body and the bow of a young archer — what was left of him. His face had been eaten to the bone. 'Remember this,' she said, her anger barely controlled. 'Never forget what you see here today.'

'Those children are starving. How could that have happened?' Innata asked. 'This doesn't look like a land that has a famine.'

Vitriol ripped out of Jalondine, not so much at Innata, but at their situation. 'The esklet happened, what else?' She stopped and studied Innata's face. 'You really don't know, do you?'

They both shook their head. She gave Haze a long, hard stare before switching her attention to Innata. 'This is our first major attack this season. But we've been sharing our food with other places, worse off, for a long time.'

When Innata looked blank, Jalondine scowled and plunged into an explanation of sorts. 'Esklet eat flesh. They tear the throats out of animals — or people — drink the blood and gnaw the flesh off the bones. Farmers who tend their animals or their fields or their fish traps work out in the open. That makes them prey. As are their cows and talyaks and taldeer. If the esklet can't find such food, they spray crops or the grass with their vile spit. Plants die. Anything living beneath is exposed — field mice, ground birds, lizards, it's all food to an esklet. The rains come and wash the spit into the streams and rivers. Fish die. And we are left with no food to eat. *Now* do you understand?'

Haze could think of nothing to say to that, but Innata could. 'Where did they come from? And when? They can't have always been here. This city was once prosperous and thriving.'

The woman's face softened, for just a moment. She turned away to start walking again, but slower this time. 'Indeed, it was,' she said. 'There's always been esklet. One or two would arrive every year, windblown, from over the sea. Usually they were already dead on our shores by the time they were found, or they died soon afterwards. They were just curiosities.

'Just over a hundred years back, we had a small invasion of them on our hands. Flocks. Skeins of them appearing in our skies.' She quickened her pace and they hastened after her. 'Fortunately for us, esklet are easily deceived by our weaving. Redweavers bore the brunt of the battles then and have done so ever since.' Her pride was obvious.

And ironic, as Innata pointed out. 'But you didn't win.'

'No!' Jalondine's face tightened. 'We have told your people our history. Again and again, begging for help.' Neither of them said a word, so she stopped dead and turned to look at Thalia. 'You really don't know?'

'No, we don't.'

'We?' Jalondine raised an eyebrow at Haze.

'I don't know either,' she said quietly. 'I've never lived here, at least not that I remember.'

The lore councillor's gaze locked on hers and gradually the woman's fury drained away. In the end she apparently decided not to pursue the puzzle of who Haze was and settled for a history lesson instead. 'Those early raids were repulsed, but gradually the beasts gained a foothold and started breeding colonies. They chose the deep caves of the forested terrain of our wet coastal mountains. Steep, rugged, inaccessible. The caustic poison they spray from their throats is toxic as well as corrosive.' She pointed to Innata's cheek. 'If you'd been hit full in the face, you would have died a painful death. You were lucky. And you—' Her gaze switched back to Haze. 'That archer told me you threw a stick at the beast! I don't know who you are, but surely you know how close you were to being crunched up by its mouthparts?'

'Well, yes, as a matter of fact,' she said truthfully. For a moment she thought Jalondine was going to snap off a sarcastic reply, but in the end the woman just gave a nod, followed by a head shake, as if in despair of Haze's amateur battle tactics.

'Who are you taking us to?' Innata asked as they walked on once more.

'The Lore Council. Isn't that what you wanted?'

'Yes, I suppose so. My thanks.' As she spoke, Innata gave a slight downturn of her right index finger, part of the unspoken language of wayfarers. *Say nothing yet.* Haze kept quiet while Innata did her well-mannered best to find out as much as she could about what they were seeing as they walked on.

Much of this city had once been an extravagant confection of delicately filigreed stone, soaring arches, exuberant embellishments, polished statues, coloured glass and painted portals. Now tattered or smashed stonework was a sad reminder of what had been, while wooden buildings, largely confined to narrower streets, had burned.

Folk rode taldeer and carts were pulled by talyaks, but they were thin, ill-fed beasts. The streets were unswept. Drains stank. People wore much-patched clothing. This was no longer a place of prosperity and wealth as it must have been once. Apart from the esklet damage and the nets strung high above the streets between flagpoles, steeples and towers, to Haze the most unusual aspect was that she saw nothing that looked like a temple or any structure that might have been associated with a deity.

'We look so well-fed,' she muttered to Thalia. 'It's embarrassing!'

If Jalondine heard, she did not react, but marched on, grim-faced. Innata, determined to extract as much information as she could, asked what the city was called.

'Arethelis,' came the reply.

'And how is it you speak our tongue so well?'

Jalondine's reply was breathtaking. 'What makes you think it's your tongue?' she snapped back. 'It's the same language. The accent is different, that's all. Our legends tell us we have a shared past. If your people had held on to your roots, instead of turning to god-worship, you would know that!'

'*You* may sound like a Talodian,' Innata said, and waved her hand at the people in the street. '*They* don't.'

'I'm a redweaver,' she replied, as if that explained everything.

'And redweavers learn to imitate us,' Innata said, nodding. 'So that you can go to Talodiac and be invisible.'

Jalondine gave a derisive snort. 'No longer,' she said. 'Not from here, anyway.' She shot a look at Haze, adding, 'And we would *never* send a redweaver child. Never!'

'Someone did,' Innata replied calmly, smiling at Haze. 'Tell me, why do we share a language? How could that happen?'

'Who knows? Some say we were once the same land until some kind of cataclysm split us. The sea flowed into the gap to separate us. Others say Talodiac was the place we came from in our long ships in the beginning, and that's why we are so alike. Others say our similarities are fostered by contact. Weaving connects us, you see, whether you like it or not. Our peoples can mix, and often have. We have lots of explanations for our similarities. The odd thing is that Talodiac doesn't have any.' She shrugged, as if she didn't care which legend was the truest, but then she added, 'Maybe you should ask your gods what explanation they have.'

'What about your gods?' Innata asked.

'We have no deities.'

'No gods?' Innata asked, shocked. *'None?'*

Jalondine was offhand. 'Well, some rural folk leave offerings to the spirits of the ocean or the mountains or the rivers, or some such. I suppose they find such beliefs helpful. The same way you Talodians do, I guess, with your feeble temple glowbubbles.' She snorted. 'Some folk seem to need to believe they can influence their luck.'

Glowbubbles? Haze had no idea what she meant, but the word had made Innata wince.

*

The Lore Council building was as large as a Talodian temple, but its façade was unadorned and the massive doors at the top of the steps from the pavement were unguarded.

'Not a place that puts much emphasis on impressing the public,' Innata muttered softly as their guide mounted the steps ahead of them.

'Or on scaring them, either,' Haze agreed.

'Maybe they don't need to. Maybe everyone is scared into blue mulligrubs at the very thought of being tossed through a gateway to Talodiac as punishment if they put a foot wrong.'

She hoped Innata was joking.

Jalondine pushed open the main door and they found themselves in an empty entrance hall. She headed straight into a corridor on the other side and they trailed behind her to a door at the end. By the time Jalondine rapped on it, Innata looked close to total exhaustion.

The door was opened by a young man dressed in grubby clothes, although his shirt had red embroidery. His face was begrimed, his stance weary and his expression worried.

'Lady Adept,' he said with a perfunctory bob of his head to Jalondine before his gaze switched to those with her, eyes widening. Haze guessed their clothing shouted their origins.

'Loremaster Arongate within, Rovan?' Jalondine asked, stepping inside.

'Just returned. He's exhausted—' he began, but she had already walked straight past him, heading for a door on the other side of the room.

'Of course he is. We all are. At least we're alive.' She knocked, and without waiting for an answer, pushed the doors open and marched in. Innata lingered just long enough to smile at Rovan in a friendly fashion before following her. Rovan gaped at the traces of redweaving creeping up Haze's arms and, she suspected, still tangled in her hair the way it was in Jalondine's.

Haze had expected a large audience room; instead they were in a study with shelving heaped with manuscripts and parchment books, and a desk piled with papers written in a foreign script. Her gaze didn't linger on those, though, or even on the person seated behind the desk. Her eyes went straight to the wall behind him, which was covered with maps, and the largest one in the middle was undoubtedly Talodiac. It took her longer to realise some of the others detailed Talodian duchies or cities and were even labelled in Talodian script. A skitter of fear ran down her back. Right then, the security of her land felt as fragile as a winter spider-web in a snowstorm.

And then, another thought, even worse, bludgeoned any equilibrium she had left. *Not* my *land.* She was apparently Kanterine.

Goddess's tits 'n' bits, who am I?

The old, bald man behind the desk rose to greet them. He too appeared as if he had not long since come inside from the day's battle outside. Tired, dirty, grieving. Flung over the back of the chair was a gown of some kind, scarlet in colour. A tall scarlet mitre trimmed with gold was perched on the edge of the desk. He might have had more stature had he been wearing them both, but she was more impressed by the way an obviously tired old man gathered himself together when they entered, to clothe himself in the dignity of his position. He remained standing as Rovan introduced him as Lor'Adept Valli Arongate, loremaster and senior redweaver of the Arethelis Lore Council.

Jalondine, speaking in Kanterine, then sketched what Haze guessed was whatever the archer had reported to her, ending by saying in Talodian, 'And as you can see, the lad's a redweaver. The woman, Innata Wayfarer, is definitely not one of us.'

The Lor'Adept sat down with surprising abruptness, paler than ever. He said something, but it was in their mangled tongue.

'Sorry, I don't understand,' Innata said. 'And, please, forgive me. I really have to sit down.' With that, she made a show of lowering herself carefully, even as she surrendered the staff to Haze, who wrapped her hand around it, relieved to have it returned to her grip.

The Lor'Adept, addressing Haze this time, asked a question.

'Sorry,' she said. 'I really find it hard to understand your accent too.'

The look on his face would have been comical, if it hadn't been also horrified. 'But aren't you Kanterine?'

'I don't really know.'

'But—' He pointed at Innata. 'How did she get here?'

'I built a gateway in Talodiac. By accident. I don't actually know how I did that.'

They all stared at her blankly, as if she'd said the sky was made of cheese.

Innata said nothing, but glanced sideways at her and made a tiny Wayfarer gesture with her finger that meant "speak" and followed it with another that meant "large" or "everything". 'Remember, Haze,' she added, '*I am not a thief.* I stole nothing.'

Understanding hit Haze then, snatching her breath away like a physical blow. When she could breathe again, she whispered, 'Sweet Jenat, no. You *can't* be serious...'

'I can. I *am.*'

'She died in childbirth!'

'Well, quite obviously, *I* didn't. Think, Haze.'

She did.

But the first question that came to mind was, *Then who the ten hells am I?*

26

Jalondine frowned, exasperated. 'For pity's sake, just tell us what all this is about. We are not monsters, for all that you might believe and we don't have time for this. We have work to do, people to help, buildings to repair before the esklet return.'

Haze barely heard her. 'Innata?'

'I'm sorry, Haze. Say what you know. Everything.'

The three Kanterines were staring at them with increasing irritation. Haze could hardly blame them. And the tale was about to become even more preposterous.

She turned from Innata to the Loremaster. 'This woman,' she said, 'was chased from one side of Talodiac to the other for as long as I can remember, always moving, always on watch for the King's Guard. I travelled with her, not knowing who she was, or why we were always on the run. Or indeed, who *I* was. To me, she was just Innata. Innata Wayfarer.

'The only people who knew her real identity, I suppose, were Goddess Jenat's gerentia and archpriestesses. They always helped us. I found out only recently that Innata was unable to explain who she was because a baffle had been placed on her, forbidding her to tell anyone about her past. Even me.'

'A *baffle*?' Jalondine's tone was dismissive.

'I've heard of such,' Loremaster Valli Arongate said slowly. 'It's a weaving. It prevents someone mentioning a prohibited subject. In the past, we used to impose one on our people going into Talodiac so they couldn't be tortured into betrayal. We haven't done that for at least fifty years or more.'

Innata was shocked. 'A *weaving*?' She tried to say something further, but the words would not come.

263

Haze, her rage building, laid a hand on her shoulder. 'She cannot speak about any of this. She ... oh, codswiggles! She had *a son*!' She stared at Innata, appalled. 'You — and you can't even mention him?' She turned her fury back to the Kanterines. 'A weaving? Was it Kanterines that did this to her, then?'

'I assure you it was not!' the loremaster snapped. 'We don't even know who she is.'

'She — I think she just told me that she is Queen Thalia.' Haze almost choked on the words.

'The Queen died,' Jalondine said in protest.

Haze ploughed on. 'Supposedly, along with her son, Prince Denniel. But if she didn't die ... then I don't suppose her son did either.'

No one moved. They were all staring at her, so she shifted her gaze to Innata. '*That's* who you've been looking for all those years... That's why Goddess Jenat's temples always helped us.'

Jalondine snorted. 'And she couldn't say anything because of a — a baffle? Sounds all very convenient! What is this: another wretched Talodian trick?'

'Hush, Jalondine,' the loremaster said. 'We know the truth here, or part of it. If this is truly Queen Thalia, then it is we who should be apologising for the crime we committed.'

'*We* didn't commit a crime,' the woman protested. 'It was that wretch, Mongrave! He swapped the babies.'

Innata gripped the arms of her chair tighter.

'Is he dead, the prince?' Haze asked.

'No! No, of course not,' the Loremaster said. 'He's alive and well as far as I know. Mongrave brought him to Kanter immediately after stealing him from his cradle.'

Innata dragged in a deep calming breath before reaching out to Haze's hand. 'I'm sorry, Haze. I couldn't ever tell you.'

'How could they? That's — that's *despicable*.' Fury boiled inside her. 'So that's why we were always treated with kindness at Goddess Jenat's temples! All the archpriestesses knew exactly who you really were.' She swallowed, groping for the right words to say to the loremaster. 'I know Innata — oh, aaah. I suppose I mean Queen Thalia. She can speak of the past if the listener already knows those matters. Tell her what your people did, and why, and then she can ask her questions. For the sake of kindness, sir, tell her the truth!'

Beside her, Rovan stood wide-eyed, somewhere between disbelieving and utterly appalled. Next to him, Lady Jalondine frowned in a puzzled fashion, as though she wondered if she'd misunderstood. Their silence shrieked at Haze, but she couldn't decide whether it was screaming a warning, or just reflecting their shock.

Behind his desk, the loremaster had paled. He stared at Innata even as he reached out to pick up the ridiculous headgear of his office in order to jam it on his bare pate, perhaps in an attempt to appear more in command of the situation. 'The baffle was not placed by a Kanterine,' he said finally. 'But there *was* another crime. Committed by one of us, a loremaster, acting alone.'

Jalondine held up her hand. 'Wait. Admit nothing, Master! Why believe this lad's tale is true? It would mean there was a fake funeral for the Queen and the boy left by Mongrave? That's absurd.' She glared at Haze. 'Next this fellow will be telling us he's Mongrave's changeling!'

The silence that followed was strangely suffocating. The youthful Rovan shifted a wide-eyed stare from one person to the next, as if he didn't dare to blink because he might miss something.

The loremaster stared at Haze and licked his thin lips thoughtfully before finally remarking, 'Well, it might explain the existence of a redweaver who doesn't comprehend our

Kanterine accent. Although ... Mongrave could never have envisioned the babe would grow up to be a redweaver!'

She was a changeling? A Kanterine changeling, left in a prince's cradle? But she was a girl! She collapsed into the empty chair next to Innata as nausea swamped her. Innata reached out to clutch her hand even as the baffle placed on her began to crumble. 'Where is my son?' she asked. 'What did you do to him?'

It was the loremaster who replied. 'Right now he's in Tal-odiac.'

An even longer silence followed. Everyone was stilled, as if a sound or a movement would do some irrevocable damage. In the end it was Innata — Thalia — who took command of the room. She stood up, placed both hands on the desk and lent in towards the loremaster. 'I cannot ask the right questions. It is up to you to tell this story. To right a wrong. *Now!*'

Ten hells. She's a queen. Get used to it, Hazelle...

Arongate nodded. 'Very well. The name of the man who stole the prince was Lor'Adept Mongrave.' His voice quavered. 'Taking him was not authorised. Mongrave was punished for that and he has since died. He was posted to the nursery watch.'

They both looked at him blankly.

'The esklet nursery.'

'We met our first esklet today,' Haze snapped. 'We don't know what you're talking about. We've only just arrived in Kanter, remember. By accident.'

'Esklet females lay eggs, hundreds of them at a time, in inaccessible mountain cliffs and caves and crevices. We can't get near them. When they hatch, they are voraciously hungry, so the adults go searching for food in huge swarms. Mongrave spent the last years of his life on duty watch for those swarm irruptions. Eventually, he was killed and eaten.'

Thalia drew a sharp intake of breath.

'We are losing the battle over there on that side of Kanter, you know,' he continued. 'The city of Elbrock — that's where Mongrave was from — is a ruin now, with esklet living in the roofless attics and crumbling towers. That's where the changeling's mother came from. The gateway in *The Twill and the Rose* led straight to Elbrock, so that's where the prince was first taken by Mongrave.

'Kaillan Riverdell, also known as Jordir Banlock, was in charge of the gateway in Templebridge at the time. He un-wove the gate after Mongrave brought the prince to Kanter. Kaillan was arrested by Talodian priests, then released at your instigation, Your Grace. Because he's not skilled enough to weave a gateway of his own, he had to go to another Talo-dian city to find another gateway home.'

'Another gateway?' Haze asked. 'How many are there ever?'

Jalondine gave a twisted smile. 'More than you know. Our weavings tangle our lands together and you know nothing—'

'That's enough, Jalondine,' Arongate said. 'I was an adept at the Lore Council in Veritelis, our capital city, at the time when Kaillan Riverdell arrived there, about fifty days or so after your priests had crippled him. Tortured him. He told us what Mongrave had done, and what the Queen, ah, you, had promised. Until then, we knew *nothing* about *any* of this. When your king refused to negotiate, Mongrave was in-formed by one of his accomplices and they kept silent about the whole sorry plot. In the meantime, your King announced the death of Queen Thalia and her child. Kaillan always doubted the truth of that. It's a long time ago, but I seem to remember he said, "The Queen is a woman of courage and wit. She is not killed so easily." ' He smiled faintly. 'So it seems. As soon as Kaillan came to us, we removed the prince from Mongrave's care and placed him with a family of substance to raise in Veritelis. He was cared for well.'

'The mother of the changeling was not caring for him?' Haze asked.

'No. As far as I know, Mongrave deemed her unsuitable. I know nothing about her, or what happened to her. Before we took Denniel, he was being looked after by Mongrave's sister and a wet nurse. I might add that when the matter became public knowledge much, much later, Mongrave had many supporters among redweavers. People who felt that his desperate action to influence King Edwild was justified. We all wanted help. We wanted food. Arms to fight the esklet. Was that too much to ask?'

'And the changeling didn't matter in the larger scheme of things?' Haze asked.

He ignored that. 'We begged Edwild — and his father before him — for years. Aid was always denied. So Mongrave and a few friends concocted their plan. The kidnapping was an act of desperation.'

Anger — buried so deep Hazelle hadn't even known it was there — bubbled up to control her tongue. Sweet gods, she was being an empty-headed nick-ninny, and she didn't care. 'This plot was never in the interests of the Kanterine child left in Denniel's cradle, nor that of the prince!'

'The changeling boy was carried across the border from Kanter into Talodiac by his mother, who doubtless felt her son had a better chance of life there than in Elbrock. Possibly that was a feeling shared by all the mothers who volunteered their newborns. Back then, no one expected Edwild to be ruthless enough to kill a baby when the life of his own son would be jeopardised!'

Hazelle felt sick. 'All the mothers? There were *more*?'

'Mongrave couldn't be sure exactly when Queen Thalia would give birth, or whether a gravid mother waiting at the

Elbrock gateway to *The Twill and the Rose* would have a boy or a girl. Easier, you see, to disguise a child who is both male and newborn. As it turned out, the first child born was a boy and he was used. As I understand the plot, they only intended to proceed with the swap if there *was* a prince. They didn't think Edwild would care enough about a princess; Talodiac has never had a queen who ruled.'

Through all of this, Thalia sat bolt upright, apparently still restricted by the effects of the baffle.

Haze sucked in a deep breath. 'They wouldn't have substituted a girl for the prince?'

'No.'

The changeling could never have been her, then. So who the sweet hells was she?

'Haze, please—'

'Have compassion for the Queen, loremaster. For pity's sake, give her the answer: where is Prince Denniel now?'

He paled still further and switched his attention to Thalia. 'He returned to the land of his birth of his own free will on his eighteenth birthday, half a year past. When he left, he was in good health. I have no knowledge of what happened thereafter. Such crossings are inherently dangerous, thanks to the policies of your husband. We keep travel there to the barest minimum these days.'

Thalia struggled to speak, but no words came.

'You knew the prince?' Haze asked.

'Not well, no. But we did meet once or twice when he was a lad. He was well raised at the Magnate's court. Educated and trained as we do to our own. He speaks your language and is familiar with your customs. He knows who he was.'

'Magnate?' Haze asked.

'Our elected ruler. A redweaver, of course.'

Jalondine spoke then, for the first time in a while, addressing Thalia with a gentleness and an understanding Haze had not expected from her. 'I met him several times. He's tall and slim, fair-haired, good-looking in a watchful way … Not—not so outgoing in personality. Quiet, you know? No fool. I've heard he is one of our finest archers. Bookish, studious, intelligent, but not talkative. Some call him difficult. I think it's just more that he despises injustice and can be quietly stubborn and rebellious, as many lads of his age are.'

A single tear ran down Thalia's cheek.

Haze struggled to think of what to ask, but there were too many questions, too much that Innata — no, Thalia — needed to be told. She didn't know where to begin. And in the end, it was not her words, but the tragedy of Thalia's imploring gaze fixed on the loremaster that changed everything.

He stood and walked around the desk to her side and took her hand. 'The baffle. Who applied it?'

It was Haze who replied. 'Probably Goddess Jenat's gerentia.'

He nodded. 'Your Grace, allow us get rid of this the baffle altogether. Then you can ask your own questions.'

27

'I don't like this,' Haze said. 'Are you sure you should let him try?'

'I'd take *any* risk to get rid of this wretched baffle!' Thalia replied crossly.

For the first time since they'd arrived in Arethelis, they were alone. They had been given a guest apartment, which included two small separate bedrooms, and this was followed up by a supply of hot water, several clean but much-patched outfits, and a little food — much of which looked familiar enough to have originated in Talodiac. Perhaps it had.

Loremaster Arongate had promised to lift the baffle, but he had told them he would need the help of a third lore adept and so it would have to wait till morning. 'We're all exhausted,' he said, just before they left his office. 'We've spent two days fighting the esklet.'

'Fighting? You, loremaster?' Innata had asked. He must have been seventy at least, and his frailty was obvious.

'We are all redweavers to the day we die,' he said with open pride. 'We trick the esklet with our weaving, by baiting traps with the imaginary, by sending them flying headlong into things that they can't see because of our weaving.'

The nets, Haze thought. 'And yet you are not winning?'

He avoided answering by addressing Innata instead. 'My lady, rest now, sleep the night, and in the morning we will rid you of your baffle. Then you can tell us your story, and we'll send you back to Talodiac to find your son. And your companion here, can decide what he wishes to do. I know you have avoided thus far explaining who he is, but I am assuming he was the Kanterine baby taken to Templebridge to be swapped for a prince... How he happened to be a redweaver, I cannot explain.'

Innata, tired, had agreed to rest. Haze, nauseated, was silent, but her thoughts churned on. *But I was a girl ... and they didn't intend to use a girl baby. They had a baby boy to swap anyway, so I couldn't I possibly be Prince Denniel's replacement.*

Now, an hour later, clean and fed, with the outer door locked, Innata lay on her bed amidst a plethora of threadbare pink pillows and lavender-stuffed bolsters that had seen much better days, while Haze tried to instil more caution in her. 'You are going to allow them to practice their conjury on you? You don't know what they might do, even unintentionally!'

'No, but then I couldn't stop them anyway, if they wanted to do that without my consent. This is my chance, Hazelle. Come and sit on the floor beside me.'

She did as she was asked, leaning her back against the bed with her head close to Thalia's pillow. Thalia rolled onto her side so that her lips were close to Haze's ear, dropping her voice to a whisper. 'Walls sometimes have peepholes and listening cracks.'

She whispered back. 'You don't trust them?'

'Trust? No. I think right now they are discussing how they can use me. In exchange for meeting Denniel.'

'This has been one of your aims all along, hasn't it? Find Kaillan-Jordir, then come to Kanter if you could find a way, because that was where the fellow who stole the prince went. Mongrave.'

She paused and then, 'Innata, am ... am I the child they swapped even though I was a girl?'

'I can't answer that. Yet. I need the baffle lifted before I can explain everything.'

'If it's true — well, if you think I am looking forward to making the acquaintance of my fellow countrymen, think again. The mother of the changeling as good as tossed her baby away. She must have known someone would soon find out it wasn't a boy, and therefore wasn't the prince and probably not Talodian. The chances of a boy changeling surviving was as slim as a starving flat worm. If it was a girl — me — the chances were even less. I am certainly not interested in looking for that woman if she's my mother.'

'Tomorrow, you'll know.'

'*If* they can rid you of the baffle. Taygen told me that in your fever dream you said Gerentia Iria imposed the baffle on you. I'm guessing they helped you on condition they imposed a baffle so you couldn't talk about it. How the fiery perdition do these people here even know what a baffle is? They don't worship at our temples. I doubt they know any of our archpriests! I don't like this one little bit.'

Thalia shrugged, still unable to speak with full freedom, and perhaps too exhausted to try.

Hazelle lay her head back on the coverlet and stared at the cobwebbed ceiling. 'Sometimes I feel like I must be dreaming. People in the street — their language sounded like weirdly accented Talodian. But these redweavers, they speak like us. Those maps of Talodiac on the wall ... so *detailed*. Using *our* writing script. Totally different from the writing on the papers on Arongate's desk. The food they gave us, so familiar it might have been smuggled in from Talodiac. Innata, they are more like us than the desert Dekadani or our white-bearded whalers with their pale eyes. Gods, they must have been in and out of Talodiac for decades. Maybe even centuries, and we had no idea. They've been imitating us, pretending they are us, travelling back and forth through the woven gates. So that means that most of the time *we didn't notice*.'

'Jalondine said it: we are connected by their redweaving. We are tangled in their plight. This goes back even further than they acknowledge. Think of all our legends about changelings. Maybe the Kanterines are the origin of the magic folk in so many of the stories we tell children. The russet riders. The storm-dreamers. The scarlet firedrakes.'

Haze thought about that. 'Oh, frothing pickles. You could be right.'

'Interesting though that our stories always seem to make them into the villains.' Thalia shrugged again. 'Not important anyway. I'm staying here until I can relate my own history in my own voice. I have tried so hard to tell you the truth over the years, but the baffle muffled every attempt.'

She nodded. 'I can see the remains of their weaving on them, even on Rovan. I doubt any redweaver can hide from another redweaver that they've used a conjury lately. After all, that's how our archpriests recognise them, isn't it? That's why Lady Jalondine brought us here.' She fiddled with the tassels on the bed cover as she mulled over all they had learned. 'When the prince was stolen, did you know what they wanted in exchange for his safe return?'

'No. Edwild refused to explain. He treated me like a child.'

'And now we know. They wanted help to fight the esklet. And food. Arms, soldiers too, perhaps? What was so terrible about that?'

'Think about it. Was it possible that a King of Talodiac would order his armies to cross — through magic gateways we know nothing about — to another place in order to fight an enemy that is not endangering Talodiac in any way? An enemy that I doubt any Talodian ever encountered.'

'Oh. I suppose it does sound ... unlikely.'

'Edwild would have discussed it with some of the gerents. And listened to their advice. Oh, one more thought: we've left an unguarded gate open. What if the esklet find it and fly through into Talodiac?'

Her stomach lurched at the thought. 'Oh, muckit! I never thought of that. No wait, esklet can't see actual redweaving, can they? They see only the images woven to deceive non-redweavers. That's different. The gateway should be safe enough. Should we tell the loremaster where it is?'

'No. No, we might want to use it to go back. In the meantime, it might be an idea to find out how you made one to start with... Although I don't think it's wise for you to let them know that you want to go back to Talodiac.'

'Why not?'

'Come now, Haze, you aren't stupid.'

She sighed, not in resignation, but in intense irritation. In fact, she seemed to be doing a lot of sighing lately. Innata was right, of course. Allowing a redweaver who had no loyalty to Kanter access to Talodiac with all the information they were discovering? Absurd. 'Do you think they will kill me?'

'It's certainly possible. King Edwild would do that in a heartbeat if the position was reversed. You've got to be canny about this, m'dear. Worse comes to the worst, hint that you intend to stay.'

'Right. That's hardly likely to make much difference though. Oh, one thing I wanted to ask you. You'd heard of esklets before, hadn't you? When we saw that one on the battlefield, you weren't surprised by it.'

'I heard mention of them when I was ... younger than you. When I was ... Lady Thalia, daughter of the Duke of Temar.' She sniffed and wiped away a tear. 'Have you any idea how it feels to be able to *say* that? I also overheard a vicious flying animal described once, when the King was talking to Lord Ashwendon, the Lord Chamberlain. Stuck in my memory because of the seriousness of the conversation.'

'You do know that you may be a queen and all that, but you'll always be Innata to me. Just thought I'd mention that.'

'Right. No airs and graces.'

'No pomaded wigs at court balls.'

'Nor scented lapdogs carried by my footman, I promise.'

'And by no shade of a god's shadow am I going to address you as "your majesty". Or "my queen" or whatever the royal protocol is for the king's consort.'

'"Your Grace" is customary.'

'Not that either, sister.'

Thalia, Queen of Talodiac, laughed.

*

Seated in a shabby leather chair at the long table in the council chambers, Haze squirmed uncomfortably beside Innata. Thalia. Lor'Adept Valli Arongate introduced the grey-haired, dumpy woman sitting next to Lady Jalondine as Lor'Adept Betrill, and everything about her appearance told them she was the antithesis of Jalondine. Older, dowdy, less spry and definitely not interested in clothes. She murmured pleasantries of welcome, which sounded more dutiful than heartfelt. If she'd learned their tongue in Talodiac, then she'd lived with artisans in the backstreets of one of the towns of the Duchy of Personata.

Haze's first thought when entering the room was how shabby everything appeared. The table hadn't been polished in years by the look of it, and there were cobwebs thick in the corners of the high ceiling. Then the clothing of the red-weavers: well-worn, patched. Nothing new.

'That's what war does,' Thalia murmured as they walked across the room to the table and something gritty crunched under their feet. 'There's only time and money and energy for war and staying alive, nothing else. My grandfather told me that. He fought in the Western Island wars.'

After the introductions were over and they'd seated themselves at the table, Betrill said, 'None of us ever seed a baffle afore, though we've heared of it. We think we can deal with it. Won't be easy. Y'Grace must speak o' things the baffle don't allow you to say. Concentrate to get words out. Till it hurts.'

Thalia nodded, her demeanour outwardly calm, as ever.

Betrill then turned to Haze. 'Questions about her past. We can't see the baffle at the moment, 'cause the redweaving that made it is pickled old. Old weaving fades in colour, though not necessarily in efficacy if done by a master. We need to see it to unweave it. Once she struggles against it, it'll flare. You'll see. When it begins to fade, ask another question. Understand?'

Weaving? They were not only calling the baffle redweaving again, but speaking of its maker as a master of it... Shocked, her heart pounded in her chest. 'No, I'm not sure I do. I've never seen any signs of redweaving on her.'

'You might've done, if she'd tried real hard to tell you what was forbidden.'

'Let's begin,' Arongate said and waved a hand in Haze's direction. 'First question.'

She turned to look at Thalia. 'What — what was the first thing you saw, or heard, that told you a redweaver had come to steal Prince Denniel?'

Innata raised her chin and took a deep breath as if to speak, but no words came. She stiffened perceptibly. Her fingers shook. She tried again and again until she was white around the lips. A chain of bright carmine wisped around her like a breath on cold air. Haze watched it until Thalia gave up her attempt at an answer and the colour slowly faded.

Betrill gave a nod and Haze asked another question.

'How did you find out the baby in the cradle was not the prince?'

No success there either. Just another tendril of redweaving. *Redweaving.* Haze felt ill. Another question...

'Who was the first person you told?' And still more...

'What did you do with the child they left behind?'

'What did the King say about the kidnapping?'

'When did you leave the palace with the changeling?'

'How did you meet the man called Jordir Banlock?'

With each question, the three loremasters tensed and stared at Innata with fierce concentration. When she doubled up in pain, and the scarlet pulsed, Haze wanted to scream at them to leave her alone, but then each time she saw that the intricate weave of red vapour around Thalia had become a little fainter, a little less dense, and so she tried again. And again. And again.

'What advice did you get at Goddess Jenat's temple?'

Innata gasped. 'The Goddess told me ... to take the changeling, leave Templebridge and never return...' She flung up her hands to cover her face. Bits of weaving swept past in the air and were pulled apart into nothingness as fast as they appeared.

Haze gulped in shock. '*The Goddess* told you? The Goddess herself?'

'The Mulierseer, Gerentia Iria, wouldn't make the decision herself, so I asked to see the Goddess. I told her that no baby deserves death because of where it was born. She agreed.'

'And you asked for sanctuary for yourself as well?'

'I — I thought to care for the babe. To keep him safe. In hiding. Until I could exchange him for my son! Who else would ever want him to live?'

'Where did you go when you left the temple?'

'They sent me, disguised, to another of Jenat's temples. I stayed there a month. That was where I heard that Denniel and I had supposedly died ... After that I became a wayfarer...'

Haze took a deep breath and whispered, 'Am I the changeling?'

Thalia reached out to her and laid a hand over hers, 'Yes,' she whispered. 'You are. I'm free now. I can talk about it! I can tell you everything. I can tell everyone...' And for the first time in Haze's memory, Innata — no, Thalia — began to weep. Really weep. Shuddering sobs wracked her body until she bent double in her chair, shoulders shaking. Haze scrambled to kneel at her side and envelop her in her arms.

Gradually Thalia's sobs ceased and she accepted a kerchief from Betrill to dab her face dry and blow her nose. 'Enough tears,' she said finally. She stood, placed her hands palm-down on the table and leaned towards the three loremasters. 'Thank you. Very sincerely, thank you all for removing the baffle. But now I have questions to ask, and I want answers. *Why?* Why did Mongrave do it? What did he want from us?'

Wisps of red slipped through the air around the three loremasters; the remnants of the unweaving. Unsettled by Thalia's directness, they weren't nearly so assured now. The glances they exchanged were uneasy.

'Your son was well cared for,' Arongate said, sounding as if he was desperate to lessen the horror of the crime they had perpetuated. 'There was never any intention to harm the prince. Certainly not by those who cared for him. In fact, not even by Mongrave. When Denniel was twelve, he was told who he was, and he has been called Denniel ever since.'

Thalia stared at him, nonplussed, before asking, 'Why? Why tell him?'

Loremaster Arongate frowned. 'I — there's no need to talk about that now. You need to rest.'

'Rubbish! I need no such thing. I need to find my son. And before you start to worry that we will do you any harm, let me say that all I want is my son. And Haze needs to know how he can control his redweaving. Neither of us have any interest in fuelling Talodiac hatred of Kanter.'

'We have no knowledge of the changeling's lineage,' Jalondine said with a shrug. 'Kaillan did try to find the mother, but she left no trace. The name she gave Mongrave was false. She took his money, gave him her baby when Denniel was born, and afterwards slipped away into the streets of Elbrock unremarked. The whole area was under esklet attack and Mongrave himself only escaped because of his redweaving skills.'

'Indeed,' the loremaster agreed. 'In fact, the midwife and several more pregnant women who were still waiting in Elbrock all died. It was a shameful business that Mongrave was ultimately punished for and died for.'

'Mongrave might've been a great redweaver, but he always were a silly gudgeon.' Betrill shot a shrewd look at Haze. 'What if all the mothers had birthed a lass? If they'd lacked a wee boy? Did he no think?'

'Couldn't Mongrave have used weaving to make a girl baby look like a boy?' Thalia asked.

'Yes, of course. But eventually someone handling such a babe would have felt the difference and possibly raised the alarm too soon.'

Thalia gave Haze a faint smile that said much, then turned to Arongate. 'And you, sir, have still not answered my question! Why? What it is you wanted from my husband, and why would he not grant it? Oh, and there's another question. I need to know what you want from me. Because I am sure there is something you want in return for removing the baffle!'

He nodded. 'How did you get here?'

Thalia stared at him in silence, obviously debating whether to let him get away with his lack of a reply. Only when a flush reddened his cheeks did she answer. 'We were in a dire, dangerous situation, threatened by the King's men. In his panic, Haze, not even knowing what he was doing or what he could do, wove a gateway. Until that moment, I did not know for certain that Haze was Kanterine, let alone that he had any access to redweaving.'

'Happens that way some,' Betrill said, addressing Arongate. 'I was 'bout his age when it happened to me. However, I did come from a long line of redweavers. Haze must surely *not* have had any known redweavers in the family line. If he had, he'd have been too precious to have been taken to Talodiac as a babe. A redweaver born to an ordinary family is rare, but it does happen.'

Thalia sat down again, tapping her fingers on the wooden tabletop. 'An answer, please. What did you want from Edwild?'

Another silence.

'Oh, for pity's sake!' She threw her hands up into the air. All the Kanterines flinched. 'I am utterly fed up with being silent and compliant! I've had too many years of it. We will — *must* — be honest with each other if there is to be any cooperation. Let me make one thing quite clear: the King did nothing to save our son. He has been hunting me down as if I am a rabid dog ever since I ran away. I have been treated as a criminal in my own country, always hiding, always moving on.' She pulled at the scarf she wore around her neck. 'See this?' she asked, pointing to the scar. The King's own men did that to me. I owe Edwild *nothing* and am therefore disposed to aid you with whatever it was you wanted from him in the first place — if your cause has any merit whatsoever. And

Haze has a right to understand what it means to be a red-weaver!'

'Forgive me, Your Grace,' Arongate said, 'but I doubt if you are in any position to help us.'

'Oh? Haze has told me what he saw on his way into the city. You're losing this esklet war. I am still a queen. My son is still the heir. Not in a position to help you? *I'll* be the judge of that. Your problem will be whether I have any interest whatsoever in doing so.'

With that, she stood, hands on hips, every inch the royal queen awaiting their answer.

28

H aze held her breath.

After a long pause, Arongate nodded in Betrill's direction.

The elderly lady reached out a hand to cover Thalia's. 'Please, sit. You need to hear what we got to tell.' She waited until Thalia complied before continuing. 'When you first turned up yesterday, we'd no idea y'were Queen Thalia. Lady Jalondine was after wondering if y'were an envoy from the King, or some such. Someone with authority to deal with us, sent by some of the more high-nosed Talodians. We been trying to open up a chat, a discussion, for years. At first, we thought maybe Haze was a youngster redweaver, tasked with bringing y'here through a woven gateway. We don't personally know all our redweavers in Kanter, particularly not youngsters.'

Jalondine muttered something, in their Kanterine dialect. Haze didn't recognise the words, but the sentiment was clear. *They were too busy fighting a war, dammit!*

Thalia glanced from one to another of them, tilting her head with a thoughtful intensity, a look all too familiar to Haze, before she answered. 'You know,' she said, dropping her gaze to stare at her fingernails with a studied casualness, 'I think you had better begin even earlier. Go back to when redweavers first arrived in Talodiac. How did that happen. *Why* did that happen?'

'Oh. Right.' Betrill looked flustered and waited for a nod from the loremaster before she continued. 'There's allus been redweavers. Despised here in Kanter, even burned at the stake, 'cause people feared our powers. Rulers ran scared of us. People hated us 'cause we can deceive them so easy. True, some redweavers used their skills for crime and became bloated rich uptowner buzzards. Laws were made that discriminated against us. Best times, we could be performers, entertainers — appreciated for our so-called magic tricks, yet despised as folk. Eventually, redweavers got to set up lore councils in every city, with permission, to control ourselves and punish those who misused redweaving.

'Things changed most, though, when the esklet arrived.' She snorted. 'We were suddenly saviours and warriors.'

'And Talodiac?' Thalia prompted.

'Well, there was allus legends of people vanishing in a flash of red and never being seen again. Folk tales, y'know. Or maybe not. Maybe just redweavers who didn't know how to come back. But as far as we know for certain, the first real gateway was woven, quite by accident, 'bout a hundred plus or so years back. A redweaver built one in a panic during an esklet attack, without knowing what he was doing. Rather like Haze did maybe. Ended up in Talodiac. That man, eventually a loremaster, stayed there a while before returning through the same tunnel. Lady Jalondine's great-great-grandpa he was. Or was there another great in there, m'dear?'

Arongate intervened, impatient. 'His adventures are a whole other story for another time. Suffice it to say, he brought back one of your crossbows, much superior to anything we had, believing it an ideal killing weapon for disposing of esklet. And so, gateway weaving became part of adept training. If we start one in Kanter, it ends up in Talodiac, and vice versa. We can choose where to start one, but we can't choose where it ends. We only keep those that link cities.'

That's right,' Betrill said brightly. '"Build a gate and go to Talodiac, Adept! Stay there awhiles without betraying yerself. Learn their gabbing and customs and skills. Bring back anything that can be used to fight the esklet." Them making the trip were forbidden to disclose themselves to Talodians. Scared pissless we was that we'd again be feared and hated 'cause of our deception skills. Might have remained that way, if the esklet invasions hadn't got more frequent, more ferocious. People started wanting to escape to Talodiac and then stay there. Ordinary folk. Some started to pay redweavers to build escape routes. Can't blame them, y'know. Was real horror along our coast.'

'You can't build gateways to other places?' I asked. 'Like to the Kingdom of the Dekadani?'

She shrugged. 'We did try. But then, there have been weavers who disappeared completely, never came back, so who knows? As far as we are concerned, from anywhere in Kanter you'll end up somewhere in Talodiac. And the reverse is true, too. And y'can never tell *where* exactly — unless you use the same gateway. That'll always go back to the same place. But if you weave a new'un, you could pop out anywhere in t'other land.'

'Once the esklet war here worsened, we decided to keep open the gateways we had in Talodiac,' the loremaster added. 'The only way to do that is to have someone continually renew them on that side, as well as on this.'

'And Kaillan Riverdell was sent to keep a dosshouse inn in Templebridge?' Thalia asked.

'Ay. Not a particularly skilled fella, but good enough to keep the gateway open. Kanterines trained here first, then entered the cellar unseen and stayed in his dosshouse, undetected, while they learned 'bout life in the city. It was a disaster when we lost *The Twill and the Rose*, because by then it wasn't just about finding new weaponry or skills or learning what we could discover in Talodiac. It was a matter of life and death.'

As usual, Thalia was there before Haze. 'Because by then people were starving here in Kanter.'

'Yes.' The old man rubbed a hand over his bald head. 'Kaillan Riverdell was one of the most successful gatekeepers.'

Thalia nodded, understanding. 'You've been bringing food from Talodiac through the gateways?'

'We *buy* it,' Betrill said defensively. 'Grain, dried fruit, that sort of thing. We had gold, copper, tin, our crafts like jewellery, pottery and such. Here in Arethelis we managed. No one here dies of starvation. But smaller towns and hamlets don't have redweavers to access gateways. Not enough of us. We're spread too thin. With their flocks and crops ruined, the poor, the frightened, the homeless folk flock to cities. The strong can go to battle, but what happens to the mums and their kiddies? Or the sick'uns? The old? The blind? The crippled? How do we feed folk? So we started to send some of those folk to Talodiac. That was when King Edwild's father was king.'

Thalia nodded. 'People one way, food and ideas the other.'

'Ay, that's it. Exact.'

'Of course, this people trade became obvious.'

'Eventually,' Betrill admitted.

Arongate took up the tale again. 'It was supposed to be a short-term solution, just until we eradicated the esklet. But that never happened. After Edwild was made king, we sought to negotiate. That was not only unsuccessful, but inadvertently worsened the situation. It drew attention to the numbers of our people entering the land secretly. Your kingsmen — and many of the armed templemen from certain of the temples of the Decasian Pantheon — actively sought and killed all Kanterines they found in Talodiac. We call them refuge-seekers. Your King calls them invaders, thieves, enemies. Some temples call them infidels.

'We didn't ask for help against the esklet. We didn't threaten Talodiac with an esklet invasion via the gateways. All we wanted was to buy food and weaponry with our gold, and a place of refuge for our most vulnerable from time to time during seasonal esklet attacks.'

'And Edwild's reaction?'

Arongate heaved a bitter sigh. 'You know what that was. He *slaughtered* our most innocent. Those we sent to safety because they were very old or very young or incapable of fighting. His reason for perpetrating such a crime? We would flood your land with our people. Our gold would cheapen yours. We would pose as Talodians and steal your jobs by working for less. We would introduce disease. More gateways would mean more possibilities we'd bring in soldiers and seize your lands. We were less than human because we didn't worship your gods. We redweavers would have magic in our fingertips and we'd deceive and trick and rob your citizens. None of that was true. We were — are — just desperate. Terrified. We want to save our children.'

When Thalia said nothing, he added, 'I don't know exactly what Mongrave asked in exchange for Denniel's return, but it would surely have been food, weapons, occasional sanctuary for some, perhaps. All of which we would have paid for.'

That statement was followed by a long silence while the three redweavers waited for Thalia to say something. She sat very still but her gaze fixed each of them in turn with a wide-eyed stare, until each looked away uncomfortably.

When the silence became overpowering, Arongate had to speak. 'Now you've told us who you are, that changes everything.'

'How?' she asked, her expression stony. 'All I want to do is find my son. There's nothing new for me there. I've been looking for eighteen long years of grief and disappointment.'

She knew how to pile on the guilt, but Haze wondered if she would be successful with these people. They'd had to carry their own heavy weight of despair and were hardly going to worry about Talodians. She wondered, her terror growing, if in the end they might solve the problem of what to do with two interlopers by killing them both. Perhaps that would panic her sufficiently into weaving an escape gateway.

Arongate gamely ploughed on. 'We have heard that there is a lack of sympathy for King Edwild among ordinary Talodians because he has refused to remarry. Your being here has confirmed what Kaillan Riverdell told us: the King can't marry because you're still alive, and your gods know it.'

'A simplified version of the truth,' Thalia said. 'Goddess Jenat's Mulierseer — that's the temple's highest archpriestess — told the King that if he does go ahead and marry again, she will tell Talodiac that he lied about the death of Denniel and me. Edwild is afraid that will be regarded as treason. He has a very restless heir in his cousin, the Duke of Personata, who would love to take the throne, and that would present the fellow with a reason to overthrow him. Edwild would rather stay unmarried and in power. I represent the greatest danger to his seat on the throne.' She tilted her head at Arongate before adding, 'Just what is it you are trying to say, loremaster?'

Haze knew then that Thalia already knew the answer to that. She just had to get him to admit it.

Arongate swallowed. He didn't look at her, but fiddled with a quill on his desk. 'Mongrave kidnapped the prince hoping to force Edwild into sending us food and arms. Instead, Edwild told his land that the Queen and Denniel had died. Who was going to believe us if we suddenly said we had the prince? Now, however, we have *you*.' He shrugged apologetically.

Unexpectedly, Thalia laughed. 'You're wondering if it might be possible to depose or murder the King now, to put a lad who is Kanterine-raised on the throne of Talodiac? And you have me alive and well to prove that the King lied about our deaths. All the time I was looking for Denniel, that was a twist I never expected!' She leaned forward. 'But I suspect that you don't know exactly where Denniel is, do you?'

'Not … not precisely, no.'

'Do you know why he left? What his intentions were?'

'No.'

Haze snorted at that, and interrupted. 'I can tell you. It's obvious. He's looking for his mother!'

Thalia ignored the interjection. She had them where she wanted them: off balance, ashamed and uncomfortable. Her stare was iron-hard, her resolve undented. She grilled them as if she were a royal inquisitor. 'You've all been to Talodiac, haven't you?'

'There aren't many redweavers who haven't,' Arongate admitted. He was looking more and more exhausted as the conversation continued. 'It's part of our training. To perfect the accent, to learn to pass as a Talodian, to seek anything there that can help us survive here.'

She tilted her head. 'Is that all?'

'Aiding our refuge-seekers to go there and stay. That's more problematical. We have no official policy on that. But many individual redweavers…' Arongate shrugged. 'They want to help their families, their friends. They think they might be safer there.'

Betrill leaned forward and placed a hand across Thalia's. 'I always said Edwild's refusal was understandable, although not compassionate. Redweaving tricks the senses. Can be used to create illusions of normality while crimes are committed under its cover. Open too many gates, and mayhap the esklet find a way into y'land. Your King had much to consider.'

'Perhaps understandable,' Arongate said, 'but in the meantime, our children *die*. Our cities crumble. And our young redweavers sometimes weave gates without the consent of our lore councils, and lead people through. Mostly from our east coast, where the esklet are winning. We manage, here. Our people in this city are not desperate enough. Yet.'

'I don't blame the redweavers for what they do,' Lady Jalondine said, nodding. 'They've saved thousands. We should help these young rebels who manage these escape paths into Talodiac.'

There was a long silence then, as if everyone in the room was enfolded tight within their own thoughts. It was Thalia who finally roused herself enough to speak. 'You don't intend to let me go unless I help you with this plot to put Denniel on the throne, do you?'

No one answered.

'Why not?' Haze asked. 'Why not let you return?' She was beginning to feel she was a step behind everyone else. *Politics*, she thought. *I don't get it.*

'Because the moment we came here through a gateway, we knew too much,' Thalia said. 'What do you surmise prompted Denniel to leave, loremaster?'

'He didn't explain his intentions, or ask permission. I suspect he's an angry young man — used as a pawn by Mongrave, ripped from his mother's care, cast off his father. Who wouldn't be angry?'

Haze's fierce grip on her staff tightened. *Angry? Enraged more like!*

'And you don't even know if he's alive?' Thalia asked.

'No,' said Arongate. 'We don't. But he is also a clever young man. He knows as much as any of us do about surviving in Talodiac.'

'And he has been raised to believe himself the rightful heir to the Talodian throne,' Thalia said, her expression outwardly thoughtful. 'Were you always investigating the possibility of him overthrowing his father to have a sympathetic monarch on the throne of Talodiac?'

'No. Of course not. How could we possibly prove who he was?' Betrill answered. 'He does bear a similarity to his pa, but we got naught to prove his identity. Not even a baby blanket! Your whole country believes him dead. We looked after him 'cause it was our duty, given that it was one of our loremasters who stole him away. We couldn't return him because Edwild would have murdered him straight away, to cover his lie!'

'But now you have me,' Thalia said softly. 'And I can *prove* who I am. I can prove that Denniel did not die in the way the King said. And I have walked right into your hands and you have just rid me of the baffle. I can tell the truth. How very convenient...'

They all stared at her in silence, until Betrill gave a humourless chuckle. 'It certainly presents possibilities.' She sounded as if she didn't believe her own words.

'My reappearance would have repercussions.'

'Doubtless,' Betrill agreed.

'It would not guarantee you could put Denniel on the throne. Or even have him declared heir. He was raised a Kanterine! He knows his father's policies have resulted in the murder of people whose only crime was to fight the esklet war. He may wish to right his father's wrongs and that will hardly endear him to any Talodian. As much as I might rejoice to see it!'

Haze listened with increasing horror, the lump of fear inside her chest growing larger every minute. She'd believed so many *lies*. Thalia's whole life had been a fabrication from the time she'd left the palace. And for what? To find a prince who had apparently been whisked away to the Netherworld within an hour of being taken! What was the *point*? Innata — Queen Thalia — wasting her whole life for something so codswiggling unattainable. Maybe she ought to have stayed with the King. Had other children. Mourned Prince Denniel and moved on...

Innata's skill at extracting information from the unsuspecting had always been part of Haze's life, but now she saw that ability in a new light. This was not a wayfarer woman called Innata; this was a noblewoman who had grown up in a ducal court, graduating at seventeen to a royal cesspit of gossip and backstabbing, who'd had to live amidst intrigue, who'd had to watch the jostling of the nobles wanting to improve their status at the King's court. A woman who'd found herself at eighteen hurled into a life on the run with a babe in arms, a babe who wasn't hers. Haze understood so much more about her now. Thalia was an expert.

So much to be admired. *Gods,* she thought, *compared to her, I am nothing...*

Pain griped her stomach then, and she bent over double. Who was she, this Hazelle? A nameless child that these people didn't even know was a *girl* and not a boy? Bitter rage roiled through her. Anger at ... what? Fate? Mostly what she felt for Innata was an appalled compassion, but for the man who was king? For him she reserved a burning fury. How *dared* he treat his young wife like that? How dared he care so little for his newborn child? Let alone for Hazelle, whoever she was.

Edwild. King. Rotten to the core. He would have happily murdered a wee mite planted in a cradle as soon as it suited him to do so ... Her rage swirled. A redweaver had done this to her! A man no better than the King.

'Stop it! Stop it, all of you! Listen to yourselves...' Red tendrils whirled in the room, emanating from her, and she couldn't control them or hide them as they stirred up turmoil from deep inside. She leapt to her feet, sending her chair toppling backwards.

She saw them all wavering as if she were viewing them through rippling reddish water. They danced and swayed and her dizziness spun. She turned to Arongate and shook a finger at him, and he dissolved and reformed in twenty shades of red, hot burning colour. 'You play with people,' she said. 'One of your lore weavers *bought* me from my mother like I was a — a *thing*, and drew me through the gate into another world and abandoned me there as if I didn't matter. Only the Queen's decency saved me.' She turned, waving a hand at Thalia. 'But now you are doing the same thing, Inna— Thalia! Are you talking revenge and using your son, whom you've never met, to wreak revenge on his father? What if it led to civil war between the duchies? What does *he* — Denniel — want? You have to ask him before you do anything! And why did he go to Talodiac without telling the loremasters, anyway?'

No one answered, so she added, partially deflated, 'And all this time people are dying out there from horrible, horrible creatures who eat them for dinner while we argue.'

Betrill stood up and touched her hand. 'My dear,' she said gently. 'You are right. We must talk about all these things and do what is kind and decent. But right now you must be careful. You have woven another gateway and I don't know where it will take you if you fall into it. Take a deep breath and, very slowly, look back over your shoulder.'

Terror drowned her. She turned and glanced behind. She should have been seeing the door to the room. Instead, a couple of paces away, there was a woven gateway made of writhing red threads and behind it a short tunnel of red-weaving. At the other end she glimpsed an esklet in the sun-light, antennae waving. *Esklet?* There was something wrong about that. Something very, very wrong.

And then she was falling into blackness.

29

Haze woke up on her bed in the apartment with a massive headache. Innata ... no, *Thalia,* was there sitting beside her on the bed, while Betrill perched awkwardly on a nearby wooden chair.

'You're fine,' Thalia said, 'but you gave us a fright. Betrill says you have to learn how to manage your redweaving. She's going to teach you.'

She lay there for a moment, trying to herd her thoughts — which were galloping all over the place like undisciplined talfawns — into some kind of sensible order. She levered herself up on one elbow to look at Betrill.

'Just like that, huh? I — I become a redweaver? I spent eighteen years thinking you were the evil tricksters out to confuse and cheat us, and now I'm to be one of you?' She swung her legs over the side of the bed and sat upright, wondering belatedly if being so tactless was wise. Her head ached abominably. Long strands of non-existent scarlet ribbon slipped and slid from her into the air and over the bed covers. 'That's ... strange.'

Understatement. She felt sick.

'It's either learn to control it, or die when it rips you apart,' Betrill said. She shifted uncomfortably. 'You never have to use it if you don't want to, but you must learn how to keep it parcelled up safely.'

'Why wouldn't I use it?' she asked. 'I can help kill those horrible creatures, after all.'

'We need all the help we can get,' Betrill agreed, but her words sounded oddly hollow.

'I never asked to be a redweaver. It feels like a burden, not an asset. Why in all stupidities am *I* burdened with this if I didn't come from a redweaving family?'

'There is one possibility we are considering.'

'What's that?'

'You were taken through a gateway when you were a day or two old. As far as we know, nobody has ever done that with a newborn before. That might have affected you. Changed you.'

Thalia blanched. She said, 'My son—'

Betrill nodded. 'He might have been affected too. He has no Kanterine blood. He's ended up as someone who can see redweaving, but who cannot weave himself.'

Thalia winced. That was news to her. 'Like our arch-clergy,' she said.

'Yes, exactly. We call such people weave-sensitive.'

Betrill sighed. 'We've no idea if allowing children through a woven gate increases the chances of them being redweavers, but we did consider the possibility that it might not be healthy, and the High Lore Council has always banned children under one year old from being taken to Talodiac. Now that we know both you and Denniel have some talent, it looks as if it might be an advantage rather than a danger.'

Haze snorted. 'Advantage. Who says it's a good thing? And are you saying there might be something else?'

'An illness?' Thalia asked.

'Madness?' she suggested drily. 'The way I feel at the moment, that feels likely.'

'Far as we know, you and Denniel are the only ones. Mongrave had other babes waiting, but they were never used.'

'Let's return to what happens now, shall we?' Haze asked. 'How long is all this training going to take?'

'Varies,' Betrill mumbled, looked down at the floor. 'Few days to keep it contained. Years to fully master the intricacies. I'll be right honest though: there's no way redweaver folk will help you to achieve that kind of expertise.'

Haze glanced at Thalia wordlessly.

'I'll wait to make sure you're all right before I leave for Templebridge,' Thalia promised.

'They'll let you go back?' she asked.

'If they want my help, they'll have to,' Thalia snapped. 'And who best to persuade Edwild to help Kanter than me — and Denniel?'

Betrill looked uneasy, but she did nod. 'From here the connection is to Copperstone Crossways, not Templebridge. To Kaillan Riverdell's present safe house, oddly enough.'

'Kaillan was sent back to Talodiac?' Thalia asked.

'Yes. No use here, not after the injuries to his hands.'

'You must know which gateway Denniel used.'

'Of course. But he didn't stay in contact with the gatekeeper at the other end. He vanished.'

Haze frowned, remembering the glimpse she'd had through her latest gateway. An esklet feasting on something. She shuddered. 'The gate I built from here, where did it connect to?'

'Don't know. Unstable thing that, writhing all over the place.' Betrill shook her head as if in reproof. 'We unwove it as quick as we could.'

And they hadn't noticed the esklet? Maybe they weren't able to see down the woven passageway from where they'd been standing. She rubbed her forehead, as if that would help make sense of what she'd seen.

Betrill stood. 'I have things to do. We have to prepare for the next esklet attack.' She headed for the door.

Thalia waited until she had her hand on the doorknob before asking, oh, so casually, 'They aren't very intelligent, esklet, are they? I mean, you mentioned being able to deceive them with redweaving illusions, sending them hurtling into nets where they can easily be killed, or sending them towards banks of archers disguised as something harmless.'

'That's right.'

'You could easily disguise gateways as something attractive to them … a place filled with nice fat cattle, for example.'

Betrill flushed as bright as fresh redweaving. 'As I said, gateways from here lead only to Talodiac. That would be utterly, utterly unconscionable!' With that, she stalked from the room, visibly outraged.

When the door closed behind her, Haze remarked, 'Did you just get the impression that there has been some discussion, at one time or another, of doing just that?'

'I did indeed. Oh, possibly not her idea, but I rather think it's been discussed.'

Sickened, Haze went cold at the thought. Gods below, how was this horror ever going to be resolved?

'Copperstone Crossways,' Thalia said softly, a moment later. 'That's close to the Temar border.'

'You want to go home? Why didn't you anyway, years ago? I mean, if you'd gone back to Temar, you would have been recognised! Your parents would have known you. They could have exposed the whole lie!'

'Do you think Edwild didn't think of that? He told the Mulierseer — Gerentia Iria it was back then — that he was planting spies all over Temar. The moment I turned up there, if I did, Edwild would know and that would be the end of our family. Iria passed on that threat to me. So I never went back.'

'And now?'

'No. Not yet. Soon, perhaps. But not yet. I'm hoping they know I'm alive.'

Haze snorted. 'That's hardly likely, is it?'

Thalia smiled and headed for the door to her own room. 'Sometimes words are not necessary. You need to rest.'

With that she was gone.

Damn the woman. Yet another secret ... Goddess-holy muckles, but Queen Thalia of Talodiac was even more irritating than plain Innata Wayfarer.

*

Haze's education in basic redweaving started the next morning. Thalia was excluded from attending. The sessions were given by either Lady Jalondine or Betrill, theory rather than practical lessons; morning and afternoon and into the evening. They aimed only to show her how to keep her weaving skills under control, but in order to do that much, she had to know the theory of how it was done. Through it all, Haze felt a sense of unreality, as though this were all a mad nightmare. She hated it.

No one should have this power. No one. The power to trick the eye, to deceive, to make people believe something that was all a lie ... Oh, they taught the ethics of it and explained the punishments for transgressions, which could be death, but that didn't alter her distaste. They said there were checks and balances and all loremasters and adepts were closely watched, but they had not watched Mongrave closely enough to stop him from stealing someone's child and kidnapping a prince, had they? Mostly they wanted her to be able to control the free-flowing weaving that was emanating from her, unasked-for, unwanted and unpredictable. However, in order for her to understand how to halt and control her rogue weaving, she had to be shown the correct way to weave. In order to dismantle it, she had to know how it was constructed.

No one showed her how to weave a ladder that could be climbed, the way Mongrave had in order to access the palace to steal the prince, or how to disguise a person as someone else, as Mongrave must have done with her as a baby so that she could replace Denniel. It was abundantly clear they didn't trust her. She was never left alone, they discouraged her from practising, she never was allowed to complete a tunnel, and more often than not questions were dismissed with an airy, 'Oh, you'll learn that later on!'

She didn't mind.

Truth was, the whole redweaving thing terrified her. Betrill admitted that one of her own early attempts at building a tunnel had opened into the bottom of a lake, and another foray ended up in the middle of a fish market in Temar Duchy. As for the one Haze had constructed to escape Hervan, the loremaster asked her very politely to take Lady Jalondine to where it had opened in Kanter. When she did, she was shown how to dismantle it. That was easy enough, but she was astonished how awful it felt to close it down, like drilling a hole in her own boat in the middle of the ocean, leaving no way of reaching a shore. One thing she decided for sure: there was no way she would tell them that she was not a lad.

'Where's the gateway in Arethelis?' she asked Jalondine casually, after they left the site and were on their way back to the city.

'Not in town,' she said. 'It was woven from Copperstone Crossways in Talodiac to Kanter, not t'other way around, so we accepted the exit we got. The passage just missed being in the river here!'

'Oh.' Obvious when she thought about it. It was better to choose a nicely hidden beginning in Talodiac, such as the cellar of *The Twill and the Rose*, whereas it didn't matter all that much where it exited in Kanter.

She looked across at Haze curiously. 'Why do you keep on looking around? Surely our countryside is not that different to what you are used to!'

'Esklet,' she said bluntly.

'Oh, we have warning system for them! Look behind you.'

She gazed back to the higher hills edging the valley a league or more away and spotted something she hadn't noticed before resembling the trunk of a tall pine tree. 'That pole?'

'We call them the sentinels. There are hundreds of them, all around the country, one within sight of several others in different directions, all manned. Each has four arms. An extended arm means esklet are flying in from that direction. No arms, no esklet. All arms, we're in real trouble.' She sighed. 'It becomes second nature to watch the sentinels...'

'Esklet don't fly at night?'

'No.'

'How often do they come?'

'At the moment, every few days. Usually about two hours past dawn.'

Which meant there could soon be another attack.

*

After her fourth day of training, Haze told Thalia she thought she *might* have the skills to build a stable tunnel, but couldn't be sure because her training was more to prevent her power from escaping her control, than how to wield it. Nor could she unobtrusively practice because using redweaving always left its stain behind.

In the meantime, the Kanterines hinted to Thalia that she would only be allowed to leave Kanter peacefully if she agreed to help replace King Edwild with Denniel, or if she agreed to help Kanter blackmail the King into aiding their land. Haze's safety in Kanter would be guaranteed if Thalia agreed to either of those proposals. As far as Thalia could discover, the apparent loose thread in the weaving of either of these scenarios — one that remained unmentioned — was that no one had yet located Denniel in Talodiac.

More days crawled past. Lady Jalondine was as polite as ever, Arongate was watchful but considerate. Sixteen-year-old Adept Rovan was friendly and obliging, but new to red-weaving, and not well-informed.

It was what she read in Betrill's eyes that worried Haze most: pity, grief even, coupled with her constant watchful presence. That night, as she and Thalia curled up together in bed, she whispered, 'The woman pretends she's teaching me, but she'd more of a guard. They fear me because they can't be sure of my loyalties, or intentions. If I put a foot wrong, I'm dead. No one can imprison a redweaver, after all.'

'Haze, if you can, tell me what do you *want* to do, deep down.'

'Go back to Talodiac with you, of course. I'm angry, Innata.' Her use of the name was a quite deliberate attempt to remind Thalia of their past. 'What was done to you. What the King would have done to me, had you not fled. It needs to made right. And I need to be part of righting the wrong. Denniel — I may not know him, but I know how he *feels*. I know what sent him back to Talodiac. He and I, we are the reverse sides of the same coin...' Ruefully, she added, 'I don't feel angry with Kanter. The man who stole Denniel and left me there instead is already dead. I even feel sorry for the Kanterines — but I want to go home.' *I will come for you, Taygen, I promise...*

'Right. Then that's just what we'll do. Today a housekeeper brought clean clothes for us. She said if they didn't fit, to ask a servant to take us down to the laundry to find something better. So I did. There's a whole room full of old clothes down there, for men and woman, all shapes and sizes. I told the servant to leave me there to look for something to fit.'

'And—?'

'There's a selection of clothing under my bed now. What I need to know is how we can best leave Kanter without being caught.'

'But — if you stay and accept their help, you have a chance to return home a queen! And they are trying to find Denniel. Your best chance is to accept their help and—'

'No. I will *not* risk leaving you here. It's too dangerous. They don't trust you, and therefore they fear what you may do. I don't think they are evil people, but you could so easily be a danger to them, building your own tunnels between Kanter and Talodiac, for instance—'

'I think I could, but they haven't actually let me try. I have no idea where it would go. We could end up a long, long way from Templebridge, weeks of travel.' Better Thalia didn't know that the only gateway she'd woven on her own had led to a place that had esklet.

'You're worrying about Taygen,' Thalia said.

'Yes.'

'So am I. We both owe that young man. Is he your—?'

'No, he's not,' she said firmly. 'He's special, but not like that.'

Thalia gave a little snort of disbelief, so she felt compelled to explain, to put into words the muddle of her own tangled emotions. 'All those years on the road, there was never time for a friend. I learned to never even *try* to find a friend. Someone ... to feel I could *rely* on. Because if ever I got close to anyone, we'd move on and the friendship was lost.' Thalia looked stricken, so Haze added, 'It was just the way it was. At least now I know why. When I was little, it didn't matter. I had you. After that, I needed to decide who I was before I made a close friend.'

Thalia nodded. 'You care for him?'

'Yes, but not the way you're thinking. Taygen's … in a special place. He'll always be there. He's more like an exasperating brother. I think he senses that already, and I'm hoping he's fine with it.'

'But — you scarcely know him. In fact, *I* probably know him better than you!'

'Maybe, but he saw me through the worst time in my life and he was … steadfast. He could have betrayed me, but he didn't. Then when I -- I thought Hervan's men had cut your throat? I was *there. I saw it!* There was so much blood... I was frantic. If Taygen hadn't been there too, I would have done something appallingly stupid. He gave me his word he'd help, and he kept it.' A lump in her throat suddenly made it difficult to talk, but she stumbled on. 'And then on the road outside Crowbridge, he sacrificed himself for us. He went against everything he had been brought up to believe in. He's a friend I'm *not* prepared to lose. Ever.' She brushed away an irritating tear. She would *not* cry.

A short silence, then Thalia said, 'I am truly sorry. I dragged you all over the country and I couldn't even explain why. It wasn't fair.'

'No. But then you never had a choice. I don't know who's made me the most furious: Mongrave? Banlock-Riverdell? King Edwild? The archpriestess who imposed the baffle on you? What they did was — was utterly despicable!'

'Not all decisions are easy. Not all decisions are between good and evil.' Thalia frowned in thought. 'Can you make a gateway and we take it wherever it goes?'

'Horribly risky. If I try and fail, it will be obvious to every redweaver. Make a mess of it, and we'd never have another chance.' *And there could be esklet at the other end.*

'Better to use their local gateway then. I know where it is. I asked Rovan at breakfast.'

She laughed. 'Just like that? That lad is just too innocent to be left on his own.'

Thalia grinned. 'Two leagues upriver on this side of the river. Large white building. An esklet raid,' she added. 'That's our chance. When everyone is busy defending the place, we leave.'

Energised, Haze sat up on the edge of the bed. 'How?'

Thalia continued to whisper. 'The laundry room is key. It's part of a whole complex of attached buildings belonging to the Lore Council. Storehouses. Armoury. Forge. Work-rooms with tailors and dressmakers and cobblers. Ordinary folk from the city come in through a back gate to help whenever there's a lull in esklet attacks.'

'And how do you know that?'

'I chatted to the folk down there this afternoon, of course.'

'And they were happy to speak to a Talodian?'

'Oh, they didn't know who I was. I told them I was practising my Talodian accent because I would be going there soon. I also said I was a bit deaf. If I didn't understand them, I said I didn't hear what they said.'

Thalia ignored Haze's exaggerated sigh at her gall and added, 'One of the things they do is alter Kanterine clothes into Talodian fashions for future refuge-seekers.'

'And yet they told us they don't encourage people escaping to Talodiac, that rogue people smugglers are to blame?'

'That could be true. I don't think it is happening much — yet. But they are preparing. They're losing this fight, Hazelle. Once they can't handle the numbers of people coming into the city, they will send them through to Talodiac. Which is not a good solution for anyone.'

'You think they've resigned themselves to losing the city to the esklet?'

'I don't know. Not something they'll ever admit to us. Anyway, I have Kanterine outfits now. A man's for me, and a woman's for you.' She bent down to pull a lace-edged mobcap from a bundle under the bed and whirled it on her finger. 'When the next esklet attack occurs, we leave through this back gate. We head out to their woven gateway. If we can't use that, then we just find a nice quiet spot where you can weave your own gate.'

'In the middle of an esklet raid. Right.' She took the mobcap from Thalia, pulling a face, unconvinced that linen and lace would do anything at all to protect her head from esklet spit. 'This is hideous. And it's for old ladies.'

Thalia shrugged. 'Maybe you can work out how to use redweaving to disguise us as fence posts or something?'

Haze sighed. Again. 'I'll see what I can pry out of Rovan the Innocent.'

As it turned out, she wasn't granted that chance.

*

The glorious reverberation of bells in the city, a sound that ought to have heralded a festival or some other happy occasion, was the signal that the closest sentinels were signalling that esklet were on their way. The council building erupted in answer with shouted orders and scurrying feet.

Haze and Thalia dressed in the newly borrowed clothing, Haze cursing the idiocy of long skirts at a time like this. 'I am not wearing the petticoat—' she began.

'Yes, you will,' Thalia replied tartly. 'It's another layer of protection against esklet spit.'

'Oh.' At least the skirt was separate from the bodice, which meant if she wore her trousers underneath, she could abandon the skirt later. She sighed and finished dressing. A moment later someone knocked at the door. 'Should we answer that?'

Thalia frowned, and the knock turned into an urgent hammering. 'I'll answer it,' she said. She cracked the passage door open to find Rovan was there, a large key dangling from his fingers.

'Esklet,' he said. 'The bells, that's the sign they've been sighted. Another half hour and they'll be here. I — um — was sent to lock you in your room. Er, to keep you safe. Lor'Adept Arongate wanted to make sure you won't come to harm...'

She smiled pleasantly and plucked the key from his hand. 'Oh, thank you! We were so scared!' Shutting the door in his face, she noisily locked it. It was a moment before she heard his footsteps retreat up the passage. 'Not the brightest candlewick in the candelabrum, is he?'

They exchanged a smile and prepared to leave as soon as they were sure he was gone.

*

It was probably the easiest quick escape from a building they'd ever made from anywhere, and there'd been a few over the years. They waited a short while until they could hear nothing stirring on their floor, then made their way down to the laundry. That whole area was a bustling muddle of the Council Chamber's servants and outside townsfolk crisscrossing the back courtyard between the storerooms, apparently with previously allotted tasks that involved preparing and carrying away stretchers, buckets of water, wet cloths, bandages and weaponry.

There were no redweavers in sight and no one paid either of them any mind at all. As they brushed past the serving maid who had been waiting on them at the Lord Adept's table, she didn't react and clearly did not recognise them. Not to be wondered at, perhaps, as Haze was skirted, with her hair tucked up under a mob cap, while trouser-clad Thalia was leaning on Haze's quarterstaff like a man twice her age, with her own hair concealed under a workman's hat with a floppy brim. She carried Haze's pack hoisted on her shoulder as well, prepared to use it to shade her face if necessary.

The back exit of the laundry opened onto the towpath that led through the river gate. Along the top of the wall, archers were erecting and arming their ballistae and the heavy crossbows that were called arbalests in Talodiac. One archer, catching sight of them as they scurried out of the city, yelled after them. Haze thought he called them "piddle-brained ninnies" but no one made a move to stop them. A quarter of an hour later they had left the city behind, and shortly afterwards spotted the first esklet fighting over the carcass of a talyak still hitched to a cart that had not made it to the shelter of the city in time. Fortunately, this was on the main road, not on the towpath they were using, and they were spared the sight of whatever happened to the cart driver. They hurried on.

'We have a choice if any of them come towards us,' Thalia said, as coldly calm as ever. 'Either a dive into the river, or you create a gateway. I'll follow your lead.'

'Oh, thanks. Just what I need right now, more stress.'

'Well, you always did say I didn't give you enough independence...'

Gods, the woman could be annoying. 'That's not independence. It's a choice between me drowning under the weight of sodden petticoats, or weaving a gateway to ... oh, I don't know, Captain Hervan's bedroom in the Templebridge barracks, maybe?'

'That'd be fine. He won't have reached Templebridge yet. And you're a strong swimmer.'

'Not in these ridiculous frilly petticoats. Decasine dammit, I *hate* skirts!'

'Save your breath, my dear, and run.'

*

They almost made it. The first phalanxes of esklet passed them further inland, intent on catching stragglers along the main road. The white, marble, one-storied building that housed the woven gateway to Copperstone Crossways was in sight ahead, a surprisingly small structure at the end of a coach driveway that branched off from the towpath they were following. Panting and close to exhaustion, they ran towards the doors.

A hundred paces away three esklet peeled off from a flock and homed in on them as they scudded at full pelt up the driveway, gravel scattering under their shoes. Thalia still managed to sound unperturbed as she remarked that the door might be locked.

Hampered by her skirts, Haze stumbled. She tore at the waist ties and pulled it up over her head, running blind. When she emerged from under the skirt and looked back, the nearest esklet was barely two lengths behind. Its mouth parts opened outwards like a waterlily unfolding its petals in the sun. She *heard* it hawk up its spit.

Overwhelming horror avalanched through her senses. She flung the skirt into the air and threw herself forward in a flying leap, sending Thalia crashing to the gravel with herself on top. Just in front of them the gravel bubbled and spat as esklet spit hit the ground.

She rolled off Thalia and glanced up. The first esklet was wheeling around for another attempt. The second beast had flown into the windblown skirt and was blinded by its copious folds. All its gyrations to free itself mid-flight failed, and it crashed head-first into the solid trunk of a nearby tree. The sound was glorious, and it tumbled, broken, to the ground. The third esklet was a bare thirty paces away, angling in on them like a pin to a magnet.

They had seconds to live.

That's when the weaving came, borne on Haze's terrified, gut-wrenching panic, twisting its scarlet and crimson around her limbs, throbbing in her throat, welling bloodied tears into her eyes. She breathed in the choking, acrid, burning smell of the spilled pool of esklet saliva. She clutched at Thalia, hugging her.

The last thing she saw of Kanter was the building doorway ahead. A huge metal padlock locked the outside bar in place, sealing that sanctuary out of their reach. And then the crimson swallowed them, turning their skin to a pink fever flush. She saw nothing else of that world, nor heard its sounds. Now the red ribbons in the air tangled and twirled against a dense background of a deepening cherry-coloured mist.

The silence all around them — apart from their panting — was deafening.

PART 4

REWEAVING
THE THREADS

30

'Get off me, please.'

Gods! Still the polite noblewoman. Haze looked up. She was shaking uncontrollably. She was not looking at sky. There was no sky. Happily, there were no esklet either. She rolled off Thalia onto her back and stared upwards at a wriggling network of glowing red threads.

Thalia sat up, dabbing at her face with her kerchief. 'You gabe me a bloodied dose,' she mumbled.

'I saved your life.'

She sniffed and wiped away blood and snot. 'Did you have to leebe it dill the las' moment?'

'You weren't running fast enough.'

'Who was the slow one? You were *behind* me!' She wiped away the last of the blood, sniffed hard and looked around. 'Another tunnel of yours?'

She gave a noncommittal grunt in reply.

The mist gradually cleared until she was gazing at the writhing red curve of tunnel walls. She stood up and looked back the way they had come. Red skeins intertwined in an intricate wavering wall that was slowly stabilising. She concentrated and made sure it was utterly blocked. Looking the other way, the tunnel continued around a corner out of sight.

'No esklet,' Thalia said. 'Nice throw, by the way. Told you that you should wear that skirt. Came in handy, didn't it?'

'It flipping near killed me! Gods' light, who can run properly in half an acre of frills?'

'You did just fine. Shall we find out where this goes?' Without waiting for an answer, Thalia started down the tunnel.

Haze picked up her quarterstaff and set off in her wake. About a hundred paces further along, the woven wall bent sharply to the right, and no sooner had they turned the corner than it ended in a junction to a larger tunnel of a subtly different weave. 'That one's not mine,' she said.

'Whadda you bean?' Thalia looked at her bloody kerchief in annoyance and blew her nose again.

'Just like you'd recognise your own embroidery, I recognise my own weaving.'

'Looks like embroidery threads after a kitten has got into the sewing basket.'

'Exactly. I don't know what I'm doing.' Jabbing a finger at the wider, neater tunnel ahead, she added, 'That's not mine. That's like an intricate willow-basket weave.'

'Good,' Thalia said cheerfully, stowing the handkerchief away. 'It can only be the tunnel between Copperstone Crossways and the Arethelis gateway, right?'

Haze shrugged in answer.

'You go first. You're the one with the staff. You can deal with all the dragons.'

'Don't joke,' she said bleakly. 'I've no idea where we are now, but I can tell you one thing. Last time I created a gateway by myself, it went straight back into Kanter, to a place where there were esklet, *a lot* of esklet.'

Thalia stared. 'You mean when you were in the council chambers? Are you sure?'

She didn't bother to answer, trusting her expression said it all.

'None of the others noticed,' Thalia pointed out. 'Are you saying that you saw real esklet, which means you built a portal that led somewhere into *Kanter*? That's not supposed to be possible.'

'Either that, or there are now esklet in Talodiac.'

'Oh. Right. Well, my guess is the Arethelis gateway is to the left, so let's go the opposite direction. And bear in mind that you've just created another tunnel —one that evidently ended right here, entering a Kanterine tunnel. Still, I assume, inside Kanter.'

'In other words, I've done it again. My tunnels don't go to Talodiac.'

'Well, not so far. Might be well to remember that.'

It was a long and boring walk. The tunnel twisted and turned every which way, lit only by the glow from the weaving itself until they neared the end. There the glow dimmed and the tunnel terminated in a woven gateway. Haze paused, but Thalia didn't hesitate. She gave it a push and it swung open. The room beyond was pitch-black. Luckily, the light from the gateway was enough to see a lamp on a bench just inside, with the wherewithal to light it.

When the wick caught and they were able to look around, Thalia said, 'I'm impressed.'

The room was filled with varied food items: pumpkins, sacks of grain and flour, apples, dried fruit, onions, root vegetables, casks of vinegar, pickles, salted meat and smoked fish. 'All to be delivered to Kanter, I suppose,' Haze said.

Thalia gave a low laugh and Haze turned to see what had prompted her amusement. She was looking at the label attached to the cord binding a sack of grain, and held it up for Haze to read:

Bloodied Braid Lodging House, Trove Lane, Copperstone Crossways.

'So?' I asked. 'What's so funny?'

'Jordir Banlock. Or should I say, Kaillan Riverdell. He named this place. He wanted me to find him.'

Haze had no idea what she meant.

'Blood: red. To braid: to weave.' Thalia shook her head, amused. '*The Twill and the Rose* all over again.'

'The lob-cock!'

'A message for me. But I never found the place, or heard of it.' Thalia gave a rueful shake of her head.

'He *wanted* you to find him?' Her head reeled. 'Why in all the frippery frets would he want to do that? He *stole your son*!'

'I don't believe that lay easy with his conscience. Besides, it was ... our unspoken agreement. I saved his life and secured his freedom from God Atticun's temple. In exchange, he undertook to do whatever he could to keep Denniel safe. I believe he did just that while he could. Sent back to Talodiac, he hoped I would find him so he could tell me that much.'

Confounded, she stared at Thalia, studying her face in the candlelight. 'You met him and *liked* him?' She felt as though she'd been punched in the midriff.

'Yes, I did. He was a brave man. I think he was deeply troubled by what he was asked to do by the man who gave him the orders. That Lor'Adept Mongrave, damn his soul.'

'And you would *forgive* this Banlock-Riverdell?'

'I forgave him long ago. Perhaps he was a better man than my husband. Sometimes ... sometimes there are no easy paths.'

Haze sat down on a stuffed grain sack, speechless.

'He suffered horribly for what he did,' Thalia pointed out. 'God Atticun's clergy tortured him. Probably on Edwild's orders. Certainly with Gerent Vann's knowledge and agreement. If Kaillan Riverdell is on the other side of that door over there, you will see the evidence. He was a tormented, courageous man, one who deprecated his own situation with wry humour even as he suffered the agony of torture and faced death.' She was silent for a moment, then added so softly that Haze almost didn't catch the words, 'The night I grew up.'

Haze stayed silent, trying to get her head around what Thalia was telling her.

'We didn't have that long a conversation,' Thalia continued, 'but I believe we understood each other. Liked each other, even. Perhaps. We certainly understood the other's suffering. I was eighteen and I thought him old, but in truth he was probably not yet thirty. Part of me always believed he would do his best for Denniel.'

Haze threw up her hands in a gesture of incomprehension. 'I'm beginning to believe I don't understand *anything*. The *clergy* tortured him?'

'Oh yes. They were going to continue the torture until he died. The worst part was they didn't even really believe he was Kanterine. They thought he was most likely just the keeper of a dosshouse, an innocent caught up in a Kanterine plot. But they didn't want to risk making a mistake, so they started to cut him to pieces hoping to find out.'

'That's ... horrible. And God Atticun *approved* of that?'

'I imagine so.'

'What the —? Gods below! I *really* have trouble with that.'

'I think a lot of people would. Unfortunately, it was not something I could ever say.'

'That is ... beyond my comprehension. And now you're telling me that Atticun, the god above all gods, advocates torturing an innocent? What kind of beings are they?' The very words sounded insane, as if she were questioning whether the sun rose every day.

The smile Thalia gave Haze then was grimly enigmatic. 'That baffle muddles my tongue yet, especially when it comes to talking about the gods. Let me ask you a question instead, about the redweaving of a tunnel — the passage —

whatever you want to call it. When I am inside, I can see the weaving of the walls.'

Haze nodded.

Thalia continued, choosing her words with care. 'It's the most astonishing shade of red. Crimson. Scarlet. Flaming carmine. Not quite sure how to describe such a shade of living colour; I have no such hues in my sewing box. And the weave is not static; it moves like — like threads of mist in a breeze, except rather less ethereal. It's almost alive, at least at first. Is that how it appears to you?'

Haze nodded again.

'Well, that's the closest description I can give you of a god. A deity of living red hues, hues that can blaze the colour of a setting summer sun, much brighter than your weave. Or, as in Atticun's case, the deepest red of damson plums or blood cherries. They both spoke to me: Atticun and Jenat. Not with words voiced, but inside my head. From that, and from what was relayed to me through the Mulierseer, Gerentia Iria, I came to see that there is a rivalry between God Atticun and Goddess Jenat.

'Ordinary folk might divorce, but never a king, not if a queen has shown herself fertile. When the King declared his Queen and his son had died, he thought he could marry again. But Goddess Jenat, knowing I was still alive, wouldn't allow it. Which is why I have to be dragged back to Temple-bridge and killed. Then, even the Goddess has to allow his remarriage.'

'And you kept me alive, all those years...'

'I hated you for a brief day, but in the end you were just a babe with a babe's needs and a babe's charm, then a stubborn, inquisitive tot, and finally a tomboy who was the daughter I never had, with a spunk I admired; the adventurous child I never birthed, who was willing to wield a staff for our protection. Your origins no longer mattered. I loved you.

316

I loved you more than the boy I knew less than a day. I love you still and always will.

'I did take you every year into the presence of a Jenat archpriestess, as I had sworn to do before they would let me take you out into the world. None ever saw anything amiss. No hint of redweaving.' The expression on her face was more wry than comforting. 'Shall we go and see if we can find Riverdell?'

They climbed the stairs up from the cellar to the door at the top. It wasn't locked and they stepped out into a deserted, darkened room. Haze thought she heard a faint sound of music, but it was gone before she was sure. Thalia held up the lantern and they looked around. A long trestle table and a number of stools indicated that the room was probably a refectory, designed to seat as many as twenty for a meal or a drink of ale. A stale smell of sizzled fat from a spitted roast lingered in the air.

Quarterstaff firmly gripped in her hand, Haze walked over to the single window and glanced through the distortion of bottle glass to see the blur of a moonlit pump yard beyond.

'Well, we know its Talodiac,' Thalia said, 'because in Kanter it's still daytime.'

A door opened somewhere on the floor above and a shaft of light shot across the landing at the top of the stairs that led upwards from the refectory. A man's voice cut through the darkness from above. 'Coming!'

A moment later the speaker padded in stocking feet to the top of the stairs, a lighted candlestick in one hand. He stood there for a moment before saying, 'Only two of you? I was expecting porters for the cargo!'

When Thalia said nothing, Haze replied. 'I imagine they are held up by the esklet attacks. Are you Jordir Banlock?'

'Sweet weaving, Not heard that name in years! But aye, that's who I was, once.' He started down the stairs.

'How did you know we'd arrived?' Haze asked.

'You tripped a bell-pull when you opened the door from the cellar,' he said cheerfully as he descended to our level. 'It tinkles in my bedroom. What's news from Kanter, Adept?'

'Nothing good,' she said, carefully neutral. Red threads lingering on her skin and clothing had obviously pegged her as a Kanterine redweaver. She didn't disabuse him, but she was trying hard to tamp down the anger she felt. This was the man who had so casually allowed her to be left in a foreign land to an uncertain future, and it was difficult to feel anything but burning rage.

He walked to the central table and lit the oil lamp there to give them more light. Even though one of his thumbs was missing, he didn't fumble. 'I use my real name among friends. Kaillan Riverdell.' His accent was that of a townsman in any one of the central duchies.

'Hazelle Wayfarer,' she said, watching him. Broad of shoulder, all muscle and sinew without any hint of a paunch, he was not quite what she'd expected in a dosshouse keeper. He carried the scars of a tempestuous past: misshapen fingers, that missing thumb, the odd way one of his wrists was twisted, an indent on his cheek that spoke of a bone once broken, an old esklet acid burn along his forearm. Some might have thought all that made him ugly, but had she not known his history, she would have thought it enhanced him, made him more interesting.

'Hazelle?' he asked, absorbing the femininity of the name even as his glance, devoid of expression, took in the mixed message of her quarterstaff, the frills of her bodice, a woman's mobcap still jammed over her hair and a man's breeches.

As the lamp wick brightened, he turned towards Thalia and waited for her to give her name, but she was silent. Instead, she reached up and removed the artisan's cap she had worn as part of her outfit. Her hair tumbled out, cascading to her shoulders. His gaze locked on hers and, as Haze watched, both of them ceased to breathe. Their mutual silence lengthened, until the suspense of it was almost painful.

In the end, it was Jordir who moved first. Kaillan. Several awkward strides took him across the room to her. Tentatively he reached out and when she didn't step away, he took her hand and raised it to kiss the back of her fingers with gentle reverence.

'My lady,' he whispered. Her hand lingered on his deformed one as he added, 'A day I longed for. Dreaded would never arrive. 'Til this moment, I could never be entirely certain you had survived...'

When she didn't answer, he added, 'But then, the King never remarried. So I hoped.'

Thalia gave a faint smile that neither repelled nor encouraged and dropped her hand. 'I am not the girl you once met. I've encrusted the silk of that innocence with tempered steel. It has served me well.'

'You—' His tone abruptly changed to one of wonder. 'You've come from *Kanter*!'

'We weren't there long. You could say we fell through a gateway accidentally.'

'Denniel? Did you meet him? Have you seen your son?'

She shook her head, disconcerted, dismayed. 'Alas, no. You have not heard? Denniel has been several months here, in Talodiac. I came so close, but now — are you saying I have to start all over again? You don't know where he is?'

The truth and the grief etched into those words broke Haze's heart.

'Sweet weaving!' Kaillan whispered.

It was hard to tell in the lamplight, but Haze thought he'd paled. She leaned her staff against the table and folded her arms. Neither of them took any notice. She wasn't even sure either of them remembered she was there.

Thalia continued, 'Apparently he came through a gate without permission. No one knows where he is now. I have not met him since the day he was stolen from me. I lied just now,' she added with a sigh as she crossed to the table and sat down. 'I am not made of steel. I am broken.'

'No,' he said in protest, pulling up a stool beside her for himself. 'No. Not you. We'll find him. I swear it. D'you know what he was seeking?'

'How can I say?' she cried. 'I do not know him!'

He blanched. 'Forgive me. Nitwitted question.'

'You tell me where he would go,' she said, and the words were steeped with bitterness. 'They said in Arethelis that you helped raise him. I believed — I believed just now that at last my luck had turned. Of all the gatekeepers...' She swallowed. 'I thought I'd got lucky. You, here. I thought you would be able to help...'

He licked his lips as if his mouth was dry. 'I came to know him well. Made it my job to do so, 'cause of what I did to you both. Thought it my duty to watch over him. Guilt, you know. Plus ... the woman who gave up her baby to replace the prince, I didn't trust her. As it turned out, she'd disappeared by the time I arrived back in Kanter. Denniel was forty days old by the time I saw him again, and he had another wet nurse. I was glad of that. *She* was a fine lass.'

Haze swallowed the bitter taste in her mouth and waited, stilled, for him to go on.

He looked at his hands, lacing and unlacing what was left of his crippled fingers as he spoke. 'They wouldn't let me come back to Talodiac, not then. I tried to send a message to you, through a gatekeeper, to one of Goddess Jenat's temples. Did you get it?'

She shook her head. 'No. Though an archpriestess did tell me the Goddess knew Denniel was alive and well, but didn't know where.'

He snorted. 'They knew. I sent the same message once a year.'

She lowered herself into a chair as if her legs could no longer hold her upright.

'I'm so sorry,' he whispered.

'Tell me,' she said. 'Everything.'

'I asked to become part of Denniel's household. They gave me that much. I never moved out. Not for twelve years. At first, I thought of it as a just torment fuelling my remorse, a constant reminder of my guilt, but...' He hesitated, embarrassed. 'But it became a labour of love, even before he was out of his swaddling. Such a serious, thoughtful lad, even as a nipper. He — he's the nearest I'll ever have to a son.' He glanced at her again and must have seen the tears on her cheeks. 'Threads and tangles, my lady, I do not wish to grieve you. I would grovel at your feet rather than say words that hurt.'

'If you speak of caring for my son, how can those words hurt? I must rejoice that there was someone, who had once known me, who cared enough to watch over him. I thank you, Kaillan Riverdell.' Words genuinely felt, but Haze knew her well enough to know that they cut deep nonetheless. He had loved her son and watched him grow, when Thalia had been denied the chance. It must have left a bitter taste. Gods, how this Mongrave had made a ruin of her life, of all their lives! Had he lived still, she would cheerfully have cut his heart out.

'Go on,' Thalia said, scarcely more than a whisper. 'What happened when he was twelve?'

'I insisted he be told who he was and how he ended up in Kanter. I — I felt he was old enough to know. It was a dreadful shock to him. He was angry with me for keeping that secret so long. I told him what I could about you. Described what you'd done to keep him alive. Told him I believed you were far too canny to have died as the King said. He demanded to be taken to Talodiac, even though I'd made it clear that King Edwild would rather see him dead than resurrected.

'A few days later, while still absorbing the shock of all that, he started to see redweaving, just like Talodiac arch-clergy. He was taken away to attend the Redweaver College in Verison. That's when I came here. But I suppose you know all this now seeing as you've been in Arethelis?'

She nodded. 'Wasn't it dangerous for you to return?'

'I needed to find you, and I'm not much good at fighting esklet. True, I'm not much of a redweaver, but I can repair a weaving, or unweave another's.' He gave a wry smile. 'Gatekeeper is all I'm good for. Hoped enough time had passed for my life at *The Twill and the Rose* to be forgot. And I was sent here, not Templebridge.'

'A day or two's ride from where I was born. Tell me, what do you hear of my parents across the border?'

'Both well, as far as I know. I'd have heard if Temar had lost its duke or duchess.'

'And Denniel?'

'Not seen him for years. I send a letter back home every time someone passes through to Kanter. For several years he never replied. Think he was angry with everyone, struggling to find himself, neither Kanterine nor Talodian, neither full redweaver, nor yet ordinary either. But he finally got over that and replied to my letters. Became a good archer, fighting esklet. Learned all about Talodiac at college, as well as redweaver theory. Wasn't easy. He was bullied, mocked for his lack of weaving ability. He hinted several times that he wanted to come and see me here, but I told him he should wait till he graduated. I answered all his questions about Mongrave, about you, about what you did, about his father. Everything I knew.'

'How did he feel about being the rightful heir to Edwild's throne?'

'Furious at his pa. He wanted to know his mother, not the King. And he hated Talodiac for its crimes against our people. He's wiser now, but still has a Kanterine point of view. I reckon he wonders if sitting on the throne of Talodiac might help Kanter. We could be trading freely through the woven gates, sending out wounded to your Goddess Hetha's temples for healing, that sort of thing. I tried to be honest with him in my letters. You and I both know that a king may set his arse on the throne because of his birth, but he only gets to keep it there if the nobility and the duchies respect him. Denniel would first have to prove more than his birth to inherit. Folk would still say his loyalties were elsewhere. They would be right.'

Thalia swallowed and looked away.

'He's a fine, upstanding young man,' Kaillan said, gently. 'Thoughtful. Angered by injustice. By the time he finished with college, he was desperate to come here. To find out things for himself. Asked for permission to visit Talodiac and was turned down. He wrote me 'bout that, an angry bitter letter of a young man thwarted. I begged him to be patient, and I sent a request to the Redweaver Council in Arethelis to reconsider their decision. I guess he didn't wait to hear back.'

Thalia stood then, in full command of her equilibrium once more. 'Tomorrow I will write a very long letter to my parents in Temar, to let them know I am alive, and what I'd like them to do.'

Haze blinked, puzzled. 'But they wouldn't believe that such a letter came from you, surely. They think you're dead!'

'I doubt it.'

Kaillan caught on before Haze did and gave a bark of laughter. 'What did you do?'

'For years I've been sending unsigned letters to my old nursemaid, Oprinna. She was given a grace-and-favour apartment in the palace after I left to marry Edwild. I knew she'd pass on the letters. I'd never write anything in words, but just draw a picture, always something that only my mother, my father or Oprinna would recognise. Like the time I cried over the death of a kitten. Or got into trouble because I drew in a book. That sort of thing. And I'd sign the pictures with a drawing of a little girl wearing a dress, but with a kitten head, and a finger raised to cover her lips. When I was a child, only in private, my father used to call me "kitten". I was careful. I'd ask a roadside scribe to address the envelope so that the writing would be unrecognised and always different.

'Perhaps Oprinna has died by now, but if so, the letters would have been given to my mother.' She sighed. 'Tomorrow, I will begin the hunt for my son again, but right now I am tired. Have you a truckle I can sleep on?'

He scrambled to his feet. 'Of course. There's better than that. If you will come upstairs—'

She looked past him to Haze. 'Wait here, Hazelle. Jordir — no, Kaillan, you need to have a long conversation with her. In truth, she deserves much more than that from you, but I will leave her to explain.' With that, she swept past him to start up the stairs and, after a puzzled glance at Haze, he hurried after her.

Haze sat down with a thump on a chair at the table. Thalia had left clues for her family all these years? When was she going to learn never to underestimate that woman!

31

Haze took off the silly mobcap, laid it on the table and looked around. There were mugs, a carafe of wine and a jug of water on a shelf, so she poured herself some wine, watered it down and quenched her thirst while she waited.

When Riverdell came downstairs again, he said, 'She tells me that you and I have much to discuss.' He eyed her empty goblet. 'Would you like some more wine?'

'Yes, please. Watered, if you don't mind.'

He obliged and poured himself a goblet of wine as well. 'I'm at a loss. I don't know who you are. Should I? I can't say I know if you're lad or lass, either. Sorry.'

'I pride myself on my ability not to be memorable as one or the other. It's saved my life on occasion. Innata — or rather, Thalia, and me — we've been wayfarers since I was born. I might not have known it, but I've spent my entire life running from kingsmen. Blurring the lines of who I was has been useful.' She shrugged. 'I play a part, and when I do, that's who I am. A lad or a lass, I don't much care what people think.'

'Queen Thalia says I must ask you who you are.'

'I was born a girl. I *am* a girl.' She sipped the wine, watching his face over the rim of the goblet. 'Don't know my parentage. I was taken from my mother by a man who cared nothing for me. She tells me we met then, you and I, in *The Twill and the Rose*. Mongrave left me in a prince's cradle, eighteen years ago.'

He lowered himself on to a stool opposite on the other side of the table, as if his knees had given way. 'The — no. If you are a girl, not possible. That child was a boy!'

'Was it?'

He stared at me in shock.

'Did you actually see the babe unwrapped?' she asked.

He thought about that and after a moment, shook his head slowly. 'No. No, I didn't.'

She waited, watching him. He had expressive eyes, and she saw them change as he recalled the past, progressing from denial and disbelief through doubt, then shock, to resigned acceptance. 'Sweet weaving!' he whispered, stricken. She held his gaze, as he murmured, 'What can I say?'

'I don't ask for apology. I just want to know who I am.'

'I—I don't know.'

The words hollowed her, excavating a big gaping chasm where once there had only been an ache.

He added, the words halting, apologetic, 'I can give you your mother's name, or at least the one she gave me: Arien, a washerwoman. Daughter of a drudge and a besom-maker, so she said, from Brickletown.'

'You believed at the time that she was my mother?'

'She was certainly someone's mother — she had milk in her breasts.'

'Tell me, from the beginning.'

'I was in Templebridge. I hadn't seen Mongrave since I left Kanter. Then one day he arrived unheralded at *The Twill and the Rose*. He'd come with this mad plan of his, to kidnap the prince. He was my superior, so I had no choice but to obey. I helped him with the details: plans of the palace, for example. The actual kidnapping was simple enough for a redweaver with his skills, but he needed time to escape with Denniel afterwards. That was why a substitute baby was necessary. He'd wanted to exchange babies and disappear, with no one the wiser for at least a day. That way I'd not have been involved, the inn could have remained as a Kanterine safe house and the ransom note would have been delivered in secret later.'

'What mother wants to surrender a newborn?' she asked, the words bitter on her tongue.

He looked away, unable to meet her stare. 'Let me tell you what was happening then. The esklet were winning the war. Brickletown, where your ma said she came from, didn't exist anymore. It was gutted in repeated attacks. Folk fled or they died. Eaten. Surviving townsfolk fled to the nearest city, El-brock, but it was clear that'd have to be abandoned too. The wealthy had already fled. Those remaining had no way to move. If they set off walking, they'd be meat for esklet dining. The closest city was better defended, but the poor would have no place to live even if they made the journey safely.

'Mongrave told me he appealed to expectant mothers still in Elbrock. He was prepared to give a small fortune to any woman who'd be delivering a babe round a certain time, but only one would have to give up their babe — and then only if she had a boy around the same time as the Queen had a boy.

'Arien brought you to *The Twill and the Rose*. Those others, still pregnant, remained at the Kanter end of the tunnel. Mongrave believed your mother had a boy, I'm certain about that. How he was fooled, I don't know.' He shrugged. 'Maybe Arien promised the midwife some of the money Mongrave was giving her.'

Haze must have looked sick, because he added gently, 'All those women thought they and their babies were soon going to die in the esklet war if they couldn't pay for an armed escort. And all but one would leave with their own child anyway. The one whose boy really was left behind was promised a fortune; treble what was offered the others.'

Haze's stomach spasmed. Her mother had made a hideous choice. A chance to save her child and a certainty to save herself. Maybe she'd believed the baby would be better off in Talodiac, that no one would kill the changeling. Maybe she had other children to save, and Haze was the price. Maybe she didn't care whether her baby lived or died. Maybe it broke her heart.

He continued. 'Arien was a rough woman, hardened by a tough life of poverty. I reckon she gambled, and she won.' He gave a bark of laughter, but it contained no amusement. 'Can you imagine? Mongrave had this complicated plan all plotted out, yet in his overweening arrogance he never personally checked the most basic element to enhance the possibility of success: to make sure the baby was a boy! He took somebody else's word for it.'

'But he had to exchange my clothing with those of the prince. Surely he would have seen I was a girl.'

'Arien told him you would bawl and wake the palace if you felt chilled. She suggested he weave the prince's likeness into you *before* he unwrapped you. That way you'd stay asleep through the lengthy weaving process. I remember her telling him that; now I can see why. Mongrave didn't need to know what you looked like, he just had to know Denniel's appearance. I'm guessing he stripped the royal babe, imprinted that image into his redweaving and created the illusion of him on to your skin while you slept, clothed. Only when that was done did he quickly undress you, check that the weaving appeared correct, then replace your swaddling with whatever the prince had been wrapped in. Swiftly done, all in a dimly lit room.'

'A baby boy might not have much of a pecker, but surely when the swaddling is being changed, it's enough be felt by a nurse! Or a mother.'

'Something did indeed go wrong, didn't it? Queen Thalia realised you weren't her child and raised the alarm.'

'And you don't know what happened to this Arien?'

'No. Perhaps that wasn't even her real name. If it was, she would have changed it later. She'd got money to go anywhere and be anyone. Mongrave's dead, and he's the only person who might possibly have known more.'

'The midwife?'

'Never met her, never heard her name. I don't know who the other mothers involved were, either. I'm sorry.'

In wrenching disappointment, Haze's stomach heaved queasily. 'You believe I'll never know.'

He gazed at her, studying her face in silence. Then he said quietly, 'On the contrary. I think you already know who you are. You're the person moulded by your experiences and raised by one of this country's finest, bravest women. None of this ought to have happened. I'm sorry if this sounds brutal, but I think you were lucky it did. I spent a week with Arien. In all this mess, you're the only one better off at the end of it. You had Thalia instead. That's my honest opinion.'

He took her mug and refilled it with wine. 'Here, drink this and I'll show you where to sleep.'

'I'm not tired. Over in Kanter it's still daylight!'

His lips quirked up and she reluctantly conceded that his lopsided smile was oddly charming. 'We have an expression for that,' he said. 'We call it "time-hobbled". It's when you're either tired or wide awake at the wrong time because you've travelled through a gateway.'

'Where do you think Denniel is now?'

'Templebridge. That's where he will have gone looking for the truth.'

'How can we get there from here?'

'Best way? By water. We're upstream on the Candabeam River; a barge takes about twenty days. Drawn along tow-paths.'

She counted up the days since they'd parted from Hervan and Taygen. A flash of memory burned in her mind's eye: Hervan's fury-twisted face as he grabbed his son's wrist, the desire to hurt blazing within him. *More than twenty, sweet hells.*

'Denniel is no fool,' he said, noting her expression and thinking to comfort her.

'It's not Denniel that concerns me! I don't know *him*. I'm worried about my friend. Captain Hervan's son. He helped us and they caught him. I'm hoping I can find him in Templebridge.'

'Ah. Queen Thalia mentioned that. Said he saved you both.' He hesitated, then added gently, 'You glow with redweaving, did y'know that? Out on the road you'd easily be spotted by one of the arch-clergy.'

'You want me to wait here until it disappears?' she asked, horrified at the idea of yet another delay.

He gave her a long stare and must have seen the tears welling up in her eyes. 'Not necessary. On the river you can travel safely. No barge folk'll have the skill to see your redweaver glow.'

She tried to swallow the lump in her throat.

'A slow, safe journey can have other advantages,' he said. 'Queen Thalia tells me you haven't been taught all the ways to use your power. I could go with you both. I'd have an opportunity to teach you on a barge. I'm a poor weaver, possessing little talent, but I do know how to develop a student's weaving skills.' When she looked dubious, he added, 'I got an apprentice here who knows enough to look after the gateway in my absence.'

She stared at him, not hiding her puzzlement. 'Why would you want to help me?'

'Because Queen Thalia has asked it of me. Because ... I was involved in what happened to you both in the past. I can't undo that, but I can help you now.'

'I don't want to be a redweaver.'

'Naught evil in it. Though an oaf with a rotting heart might use it for evil, I s'pose.'

'You don't know the first thing about me.'

He raised his eyebrows in question.

'I'm a redweaver with a foot in two worlds,' she said. 'Who knows which side I'll come down on? I don't know myself what I'll do with that kind of power.'

'I don't know either,' he agreed, with another of those wry smiles. 'But I'm willing to trust the Queen. She raised you. Travels with you still. Reckon your choices'll be good ones.' He fiddled a moment with his wine goblet, no longer looking at her. 'We share the same pickle, you and me. Where do we hang our loyalty? It *is* possible not to choose one side or t'other. Instead, we can decide to do what's right each time a need arises. I made a mistake with Mongrave, simply 'cos I thought I owed allegiance to my loremaster, no matter what the consequences. I know better now.'

She said nothing, but she felt the stirrings of appreciation for the man. Trust, of course, was quite another thing.

*

They moved at the pace of the flow, tying up to the bank at night. The bargee and his wife did all the work, so it was up to the passengers to entertain themselves.

Kaillan's own lack of ability with redweaving might have been a lifelong frustration, but he was a skilled teacher and Haze spent much of the journey learning the finer details of weaving a gateway from a man who poked fun at his own difficulties doing just that. He tutored her in how to build illusions too, which she found more interesting. She practised assiduously, creating small, visible objects that had no physical dimension, all while sitting on the barge deck, her back to the bargee, hidden by the cargo. Gods only knew what the bargeman and his wife thought they were doing, but they'd been paid enough not to care.

Haze even tried, and failed, to learn "solid weaving", where an illusion had form as well as appearance. The rope-ladder Mongrave used to climb to Thalia's palace bedroom window was one such, but it was a weaving skill mastered by very few. As for her gateways ending up in Kanter even when they'd started in Kanter — Kaillan said that was unheard of, but did suggest it might have been another effect of her being carried through a gateway so young.

On that barge journey, he spent just as much time with Thalia as he did with Haze. The two of them would sit on the deck at the prow, deep in conversation, with their bare feet dangling over the water the way children do. Haze guessed that Thalia wanted to learn all she could about Denniel, so she tried not to feel these conversations as a stab to her heart. Through no fault of his own, the prince had not been in Thalia's life, and wanting to know all about him was so understandable she found it hard to justify the annoyance she felt. Still, it was hard not to feel jealous. Harder still not to be puzzled by the way Thalia looked at Kaillan. Jenat's tits, Kaillan had done nothing as Mongrave stole her child, yet Thalia could smile up at him now and laugh at his banter?

One night when they were tied up to the bank, Haze woke because it was so hot below. She padded up to the deck, bedded herself down with her blanket on the wooden decking and was soon asleep again. Much later she was awoken by a soft laugh. She opened her eyes and saw the outline of a couple ambling slowly arm-in-arm along the tow path towards the barge. A man and a woman; her head leaning against his shoulder. They halted nearby for several minutes, melding into a single silhouette against a pre-dawn sky. A murmured conversation followed, punctuated with soft laughter before they broke apart.

Only when the woman stepped lightly down on to the deck and continued on below did Haze realise, deeply shocked, that it was Thalia. The second figure stayed on the towpath watching the sky beginning to colour. About a quarter hour later, he too stepped down onto the barge. Haze stared at him, and in the gentle glow of dawn, he glimpsed her glower.

His breath expelled in a sigh and he came to crouch on his heels beside her. 'Sorry you saw that.'

She sat up, outraged. 'How dare you. How *dare* you!'

'How can I not?' He gave a sort of rueful, half-embarrassed laugh. 'I think I loved her from the moment I met her in Atticun's Temple, all those years ago.'

'You expect me to believe that?'

He shrugged. 'No. But I saw compassion in her eyes when she saw how I had been tortured. *Compassion!* After what we'd done to her?'

'You ruined her life! Have you no … no decency?'

'Decency is the only thing I have now. That, and my love for her.'

Haze sat there, speechless, aghast.

'Imagine,' he said, 'If y'can. I was one of them who caused her the greatest grief a woman can have, and in return I raised and loved her son. For eleven years, I possessed everything I'd stolen from her. Every moment of joy was also my punishment, for it was ill-got. Worse, I didn't know how to find her again to make amends.'

'Did you even *try*?'

'Oh, yes. I tried. But the temples of Goddess Jenat hold their secrets tight.'

As daybreak seeped light into the sky, she saw tears on his cheek. 'Hazelle, if it would make her happier, I'd plunge my dagger into m'heart. But she's not that kind of woman.'

He bowed his head, stood up and went below.

After that, Haze refused to notice when Thalia's bunk was empty, but she knew she and Thalia would not travel the roads together again, no matter what happened. Part of her recognised that had been unlikely anyway. She needed a friend, not a mother or a sister. She needed her own life. And she was beginning to understand she didn't need to hunt down her history. Her past was gone; what she needed was a future. She was jealous, of course she was, but she could also be wise enough to recognise that.

She began to see the wisp of an idea of how to build a life.

The trouble was she had no idea where to start looking for Taygen. Kaillan had a better idea of where Denniel would have started looking for his mother: Goddess Jenat's temple, because Kaillan had once told him he thought the Queen would have asked for sanctuary there.

'I also told the lad that as long as the King didn't marry again, he could be sure Queen Thalia still lived,' he added.

Kaillan was understandably reluctant to go anywhere near a temple, even Jenat's. In fact, he left the barge the night before they reached Templebridge, saying he would walk the rest of the way to the city. He would lodge in the Kanterine hideaway that had replaced *The Twill and the Rose*. 'It's also possible Denniel will have gone there,' he added. 'He knows it would be a good place to start.'

'And my friend Taygen?' Haze asked before he left. 'If Hervan brought him back to be punished, where would he have been taken?'

'King's Keep. That's within the Palace Precinct. If he was brought back alive at all.'

'He'd break out of the keep,' she said, only half-believing her own words. 'And he'll leave a note at Jenat's Temple; that was our arrangement.'

'I doubt it,' he replied, after a short silence. The look he gave her was kindly, but his words were brutal. 'People don't escape from the keep.'

Thalia, who had been listening, looked away from her, deliberately avoiding her gaze.

'What?' Haze snapped at her.

'Nothing.'

'What do you know that I don't?' she asked, folding her arms and pursing her lips, her favourite way of signalling that she wasn't going to let this go.

'Well, I think Captain Hervan wouldn't want to be the one doing anything that would ensure the *death* of his own son. Punish, yes. However, Cyrrin worries me. Hervan's lover.' She took a deep breath. 'Viciously nasty man, jealous through and through. He hates Taygen. I saw it, again and again.'

'Taygen'll escape somehow,' Haze repeated. 'Probably done so already.' He'd made mistakes, yes, but he was smart. And she was darn sure that he had the means to bribe a guard. The carcanet had passed through his hands, and he was light-fingered...

By all the fiddling gods, Tay, you had better have found a way. Because, if you haven't, you're either dead — or I'll have to use my redweaving to break into the King's Keep.

32

Taygen lay unmoving on the floor of his prison cell.

If he opened an eye, he could see where the blood had seeped out from the wound he'd made on his head, a thin trickle that widened outwards as it pooled in the dips of the stone floor.

High above his head, daylight entering through the slit window in the outer wall of the keep was fading to twilight. His cell gathered the gloom, hoarding it in the corners, from where it oozed as a dark wash across the flagstones to slip under his prison door and join the deeper gloom of the narrow access corridor.

He felt oddly tired and wondered idly if that was the impact of his blood-loss. He couldn't afford to fall asleep, yet he didn't want to move either. How much longer before she came? Half an hour at the most. He eased a crick in his neck, but that brought the back of his head against the sharp edges of the stone flakes filling one of his discarded stockings. Shifting slightly, he tucked the offending item out of sight under the tangles of his long, dirty hair. He winced, took a deep breath hoping to halt the onset of drowsiness, and thought back over his incarceration.

When they'd first arrived at Templebridge it was already dark, so they'd slept the night in the barracks next to God Saffrin's temple. The next day, before Hervan left to make his report to his superiors, he ordered Cyrrin to deliver Taygen to the King's Keep. 'The keep,' he said, grinding out the words to his son, 'is the traditional prison for enemies of the King. For traitors.' He watched as Cyrrin first tied Taygen's hands behind his back brutally tight, then dropped a noose over his head. Taking hold of the other end of the rope and smiling all the while, Cyrrin mounted his taldeer and rode out of the barracks into the city streets with Taygen stumbling as best he could alongside. His father watched them go, the burning anger in his eyes banishing any hope of forgiveness. Taygen had not harboured much hope of that anyway.

He hadn't deserved forgiveness either, if it came to that.

Jav ... blind. Because of me.

After a stop at Saffrin's Temple, where a watchful soldier was tasked with keeping a trussed Taygen silent and safely tied for a further uncomfortable hour while Cyrrin vanished into the temple. To pray, he said. When they finally arrived at the keep, the captain of the guard in charge told Cyrrin that the King was visiting the northern duchies and was not expected to return until just before the midsummer festival.

'You're in luck,' Cyrrin told Taygen as he handed over Hervan's written orders to the captain. 'You'll live a little longer.'

'A sequestered prisoner?' the captain had asked with a frown, after reading the parchment.

Cyrrin nodded. 'Them's the orders.'

'A request direct from the Battleseer is certainly good enough for us,' the captain replied. 'We don't get too many of those! Does the lad have a name?'

'None other that matters. Call him traitor.'

The captain laughed. 'Very well, though he looks a tad young to have achieved much treason.'

Cyrrin snorted. 'Size has nothing to do with the blackness of a treasonous heart.' He spat on Taygen's feet and departed.

The captain called for one of the Watch and went to sit behind his desk. 'Hands tied *and* a noose? Just how dangerous are you, lad?'

'Not at all. I'm Taygen Hervan-Gariane. Captain Hervan's my father. I didn't live up to his expectations, is all. He thinks humiliation is good for the soul.'

The captain blinked in wide-eyed surprise, re-read the orders with a frown, then pursed his lips, apparently deciding it was better not to know the details. He ordered the duty guard to take the prisoner to a nearby cell, adding, 'No one is to speak to him, unless they want to feel a whip on their backs. Spread the word.'

As he was escorted away, Taygen brought his acute hearing into play, more out of habit than hoping to hear anything valuable. He was rewarded though when he heard the captain say, 'Send a message to the Lady Sianta. This new prisoner's a bastard of a problem, way out of our league.'

Left alone in the pitch dark of the cell, Taygen was forced to guess — from the intervals that food and water arrived and his slop bucket was removed — that he was there over two days.

No one spoke to him during that time.

On what he guessed to be the night of the third day, a woman came bearing a lantern with a guard he'd not seen before, wearing an unfamiliar uniform, to escort him to quite another part of the keep. To his utter astonishment, she introduced herself as the King's Historian.

'Historian?' he asked. 'Really?'

'You may address me as Lady Sianta.'

During a long, hurried walk through the labyrinth of the darkened keep, she'd refused to answer his questions. They'd climbed several sets of spiral staircases to arrive at his new cell, so he assumed he was somewhere near the top of the tower. The guard, a fellow of forty or so, was built like a bull; all shoulders and neck and muscled torso perched on thick haunches and wiry legs.

'Alzop has been deaf all his life,' Sianta said, 'so he never learned to talk. If you want anything, you will have to ask me.'

'He's my only guard?' he'd asked, baffled, trying to sound indifferent. This was all wrong. King's Historian? What in all ten hells was that: an apologist for regal crimes?

'That's right,' she answered. 'I can only assume King Edwild does not want you telling secrets to anyone other than me.'

'I'm told the King's not here.'

'He's not,' she admitted cheerfully. 'The order came from Lord Ashwendon, the Lord Chamberlain. But take no comfort from that, lad. Ashwendon generally knows what the King desires. I fear there's to be no reprieve for you. If you want your story to live on after you die, I offer you that choice: tell me your tale. There's no compulsion, but I will give you pen and ink and parchment. I'm told you're the son of a captain of the King's Guard, so I assume you can read and write.'

Now, as he lay there on the floor bleeding, Taygen wondered — not for the first time — just who had signed the orders that had brought him to this cell.

It was sparsely furnished. Coarse, straw-filled sacking and a single threadbare blanket was all the bedding provided. It would not have served him well in cold weather, but then he was unlikely to need it any more come winter. A small but solid writing desk and stool sat in the opposite corner, to aid the writing of his story. The high window in the outer stone wall was barred and inaccessible, and probably not large enough to squeeze through even had he been able to reach it.

His latrine was a narrow hole in one corner. When he listened carefully, he thought he heard the sound of water at the bottom of that stench-filled darkness, but it was so faint he couldn't be certain.

The door to the cell was wooden, reinforced with iron. It had a barred window cut through at eye level, the bars too closely placed for him to squeeze an arm through. The key-hole was out of reach below and did not penetrate the door to the inside. Not that he had his lock-picks anyway; Cyrrin had found and confiscated those.

Alzop came once daily bringing food and water, which he pushed through an iron hatch at the base of the door. Each time he left, the hatch was tightly bolted. Sianta came every couple of days to take away what he'd written and bring him fresh paper and quills and ink. Neither she nor Alzop ever entered his cell.

The quietness of the place was puzzling. On his way in, Taygen had seen only closed doors nearby, and as time passed he'd heard nothing from behind them, even with his sharp hearing. Nor had he heard anyone other than Sianta and Alzop use the corridor.

The first thing he'd done was to check the desk and chair carefully, to find they were held together by wooden pegs. The paper, the goose quills, the wooden inkwell: none of it was of any use other than to write. He did have two iron nails that he'd eased out of Innata's talyak cart one night, one from either side of the tailgate. He'd brought them into the prison tucked underneath his toes. The Keep guards had stolen his shoes, but they hadn't been interested in his filthy stockings, or the soles of his feet. In the seam of his tunic he still had two diamonds, in the collar he had a small sapphire, and in the hem was a roll of gold leaf, all from the carcanet, but he suspected using any of those as a bribe might not be successful. Not with Sianta or Alzop.

As the days dragged by, Sianta's visits were the highlight of his imprisonment. She always came alone, at night, bearing a bright lantern and something additional she thought he might like to eat or drink; a stick of caraway seed bread, perhaps, or an apple or a lidded mug of beer.

Once he was sure he could predict the time of her visits as well as Alzop's, he used a nail to ease out the wooden pegs that held one of the table legs. He jammed both nails into the peg hole on the leg to make a makeshift hammer which he then used to chip away at the stone floor. The table was easily reassembled before either Sianta or Alzop was due to visit. The chips of stone he accumulated under his mattress, eventually packing them tightly into the toe of one of his stockings to make an amateurish substitute for a blackjack.

It nestled at the back of his neck now, out of sight.

The room dropped into darkness as the last lingering of summer twilight vanished. He could no longer see his blood on the flagstones.

Earlier, he'd nicked a vein in his arm and then, just to make sure there was sufficient blood to look as if his injury was severe and knowing that head wounds always bled a lot, he'd scored what was left of the nail across the back of his skull. The blood loss had indeed been impressive. In fact, he was wondering if he'd been too enthusiastic, but he'd wanted to set a scene: a foolish lad trying to climb the wall to that barred window using the line of excavated niches he'd made up the wall as far as he could reach while standing on the desk.

He waited, blind in the darkness, thoughts awry with doubts, heart thundering with tension and fear. One chance. The only one he'd get. And gods only knew if he had the right of it. He was hanging his hope of success on two obser-vations: every night that Sianta came to see him, she'd come from the direction opposite to the one used to bring them there in the first place, and every night that she'd come he'd heard the metallic tinkle of the bunch of keys at her waist, the same keys — or so he hoped — that she'd used to open his cell door on the day he'd been imprisoned here. He was gambling that her ring of keys would not only unlock his prison, but also any other doors between him and freedom.

341

He saw the shine from her lamp under the door before he heard her footsteps. He lowered his lids until he could barely see through his lashes. Sweat beaded on his forehead, trickled into his ear.

She called his name through the open bars in the door. He neither moved nor answered.

Time dragged. No sound of a key turning in the lock. He dared not look or move.

'Taygen! Taygen! What happened? Taygen! Can you hear me?'

He stilled his breathing as much as possible. Shallow breaths, the movement of his chest barely discernible.

Then, at last, the click of a key. The swish of her gown as she strode to the table, put her lamp down.

Wait. Wait. Not yet.

Two strides across to his side, her shadow falling on his face. And finally the sound of her kneeling beside him.

He plunged upwards, eyes snapping wide, blackjack grabbed up, his arm swinging. Her reaction was instantaneous, flinging herself sideways. Fast. She must have suspected he was playacting. The stone-laden stocking hit her across the neck instead of behind the ear. She rolled away, but her skirts hampered her as she strove to rise. He hurled himself against her legs, toppling her backwards.

The blackjack was useless in a close-fought brawl. He dropped it and grabbed her by the upper arms. He was the stronger, but she was tall and heavy boned. His distaste for wrestling a woman, and a middle-aged one at that, hampered his actions. Mannerly madness, yet difficult to discard even when his safety depended on it.

She had no such qualms. She grabbed the discarded stocking in her fist and — in spite of his clawing grip on her arm — rammed the stone-chip loaded end into his nose. He bled again, profusely. She jammed her knee into his genitals, but lacked the leverage to do too much damage.

He rolled her over onto her back with him on top, wrenching the loaded stocking from her hand. She lunged upwards and clamped her teeth, hard, around his nose. Pain rocketed upwards through his sinuses. He crushed the sharp edges of the stones in the stocking into her throat. She gasped and he jerked his head away from her. Another attempt to knee him in the groin failed because he was kneeling on her skirts. She squirmed and struggled, but his strength prevailed. All the fight drained out of her when he rammed the sock hard into her open mouth. The knit tore and the rock chips spilled.

While she choked, coughing and helpless, he rolled her over on to her stomach. Wrenching her hands behind her back, he used his other stocking to tie her wrists together. To make doubly sure she was not going anywhere, he bunched up the long skirt of her gown and tied it into a knot at the back, effectively hobbling her.

After that he hauled her unceremoniously over to the wall and propped her up in a sitting position. She spat out the last of the stone pieces and glared at him. 'What the ten hells do you think you're doing? You *attacked* me! I'm an old woman! I was your *friend*. I've done everything to make your imprisonment as comfortable as possible. You could have been in a vermin-infested cell with twenty flea-ridden reprobates on a starvation diet. What did I do to deserve this? I'm a *historian*, trying to validate your life and preserve your story—'

'Oh, please,' he said, scrambling to his feet and dabbing at his bleeding nose with the back of his hand. Gods, it hurt a ridiculous amount. 'There you go again, taking me for a gullible clodpoll. Whatever you are, it's not a historian. And the King would never allow me to talk to anyone, let alone write down all that I know. How could y'believe I was so ... so lackbrained? Just 'cause I'm young, I'm a dimwitted bonehead?

Or is it 'cause I'm from Breakedge and y'think all southern-
ers are dolts with skulls stuffed with desert sand?'

She swallowed. He could almost see her thinking, waking
up to the fact that she had underestimated him.

'Historian, my skinny arse,' he added.

Her eyes widened in an expression that was supposed to
be innocent shock. 'What? What are you talking about?' A
trickle of blood dribbled from the side of her mouth and he
looked away, repressing his ripple of guilt. He could almost
hear his mother telling him men who hit women were like
the scum of mould in the jam jar, worthy only of the midden
heap.

'Oh,' he said, walking to the table where she had placed
her sling bag and the lamp, 'I s'pose at first I half believed
your twaddle-tale, before I had time to consider the idiocy of
it. Guess I needed to believe in *something* that'd give me hope.
But y'know what? Even then, there was this little voice in my
head whispering the truth: for a start, King Edwild is far too
clever to countenance the existence of a written truth of his
perfidy to reside in some library.' He turned her bag upside
down and rifled through the tumbled contents. 'Eighteen
years ago, some of the kingsmen started to hunt a woman
down. She was a thief, apparently. In possession of the royal
Griffin Carcanet. A woman who could not explain who she
was because of something called a baffle, placed on her by
one of the arch-clergy. The King was terrified that one day
she might be able to say who she is and why she had in her
possession a piece of jewellery gifted to the Queen. When
his men found that woman, the logical thing to do would be
to kill her on the spot and return the jewellery to the King.
Right? Problem solved!'

He cocked his head at Sianta. She didn't reply.

'But no. Even when she was badly injured, the King's
Guards did their best to bring her back to Templebridge

alive! You know what I'm thinking? She wasn't the King's mistress who stole the Queen's carcanet, after all. Maybe she was the Queen herself. The gods won't let Edwild marry again until they are sure he doesn't have a living wife. They — or perhaps their gerents — need to see her corpse.'

'That's a ridiculous story!'

'I agree. A king erecting a statue to his son and wife and doubtless weeping at their "graveside" even as he hunted her down as if she was rabid wolf-bitch. Ridiculous.'

He frowned at the scatter of her belongings. A comb, a coif, a drawstring purse. He opened that and spilled the coins on to the tabletop.

'Thief!' she spat at him. She had tensed as taut as a bow string.

He smiled and shook his head, dismissing the silliness of her feigned indignation. 'Would such a king allow anyone to record the real story of his queen? Trusting t'would only be read by an historian? Would he even want such a story writ on paper for future generations? He'd lose in posterity whatever stature he'd earned in life! Would such a king ever trust anyone to keep such a secret?'

He glared at her, his contempt bitter in his throat. 'I may be young, I may be from the back sands of the kingdom, but I had a fine ten-year education at an army school, in a city that benefited from its contact with peoples from other lands. You needed a better story.' He scooped up the coins, replaced them in the purse and shoved it inside his tunic.

'It's a sacred duty of historians to keep secrets,' she said with righteous indignation. 'Our guild has served kings for generations—'

'Never heard of your guild.'

'As you just admitted, you're a desert dweller from the back borders, hobnobbing with sand-flea barbarians. I'll admit I was surprised to find you could read and write.'

'Tut-tut. Pettiness and name calling. I expected better. Though p'haps you're right. I do lack the polish of the honest townsman, for I am stealing y'money. Sorry, milady. I am indeed a rapscallion.' He turned his attention to the rest of her belongings. No quills, no extra ink, no treats. She had intended this to be her last visit. Unfortunately, there was nothing to tell him who she really was. He filched her comb, her nail file, her small knife, the polished metal mirror she carried, the vial of whitening cosmetic powder. He almost discarded the tiny bottle of perfume, then decided that just because he had long since ceased to smell his own stink, it didn't mean other folk would be as oblivious to it. He hadn't washed properly since Crowbridge.

'You won't get away with this,' she said.

'Perhaps not. But dying in an escape is an improvement on execution, don't y'think? And perhaps to your advantage. After all, I wouldn't have a chance to tell anyone about the woman who comes as a spy into the King's Keep with her own set of keys and her own pet jailor who can't tattle what he knows. I don't think King Edwild'd be at all pleased to find out the sneakiness you've been up to in his name. Don't think he'd be pleased with your employer, either, whoever that is. I can guess, of course. Got to be someone powerful with a lot of resources...'

He picked up the last of his written story on the table, rolled it up and stuffed it down the front of his tunic. 'You'll never know, will you, what happened next? I never really intended you to read this part. Though you could chat to my pa, I s'pose.'

'Your pa? He's been sent to the borders. Stuck on the edge of the desert in the Punishment Brigade. And as for you, you can't escape! This is the King's Keep, under God Saffrin and God Atticun's protection, by all that's godhead holy!'

Pa: another consequence to lay at his door. Relief. Dismay. Guilt. Shame. He felt them all. But then, maybe she was lying.

'Hmm. Hasn't done you much good, has it?' He took up her knife and bent over her. She tried to shrink away, but he ignored her movement and cut a large square of cloth from the bottom edge of her over-gown. He poured water over it from his water jar and used it to wipe the blood from his face and neck. 'Sorry about that,' he said cheerfully unfazed. 'There's a little bit of water left. I suggest you drink it now, 'cause I'm going to use your coif to gag you. I don't think there's anyone nearby who can hear you scream from here, but I'm not going to take any chances.'

He brought the jar over to her and tilted it to her lips. She drank what was left, and said, 'There's no need for a gag.'

He could almost admire her aplomb. Almost. 'Perhaps not, but I won't take that risk. Don't worry. Alzop always drops by just after dawn. You'll be freed in another eight hours or so.'

She started to protest, so he whipped a wad of her coif between her teeth, drew it tight behind her head and knotted it there. It wouldn't stop her from making a noise, but it would stop her from shouting anything intelligible.

He doubted it mattered anyway.

After all, he'd tried shouting for help and no one had ever come.

33

Before Kaillan left the barge, there was one last conversation the three of them had that left Haze unsettled. Like a dish of overly rich food, it sat uncomfortably in her guts, and no amount of cogitating made her feel any better about it. Kaillan's gentle probing had helped Thalia to cast off the final tendrils of the thrall of her baffle and once it had faded into memory, she told them both more about her meetings with the two deities, God Atticun and Goddess Jenat, immediately after her escape from the palace.

'Those two are beyond human comprehension,' she said. 'Too powerful for a normal person to even contemplate.'

Kaillan glanced behind to where the bargeman was leaning on the tiller at the back of the vessel. The fellow had a plug of soper weed firmly stuck between his teeth, and a dreamy blankness to his face. Even if the bargee had been entirely sober, it was unlikely he could hear. His wife, in the tiny galley below decks, was out of earshot. 'Truly?' Kaillan asked. 'I mean … what is their power? What do the gods *do*?'

'Well,' Haze said, butting in, 'we know Goddess Hetha heals, don't we?'

'Healing is not illusory,' Kaillan conceded. 'But then, in Kanter we heal wounds and injuries too, without gods. We use solid weaving.'

'Really?' Thalia asked.

'To repair cuts, patch torn vessels, mend broken bones and such, yes. The weaving fades away eventually, but by that time the body has repaired itself. Doesn't help with illnesses, of course.'

'Goddess Hetha can cure diseases,' Thalia said. 'Well ... some. At least in Hetha's temple in Templebridge. I've heard stories.'

'Her archpriestesses know a lot about medicines and setting bones, I'll give you that. And the Goddess herself has power, I believe. But I also know about people who went to her and still died. And what about t'other gods? How powerful are they, really? Far as I can see, all Atticun and his priests do is advise and pontificate about the law. People obey because they fear their god.'

'What are you getting at?' Haze asked.

'If God Atticun is all-powerful,' he said softly, 'why didn't he go inside my head and discover what he wanted to know? I was a prisoner in his temple. The King's son was missing. And yet he apparently just let the priests torture and mutilate me to find out if I really was from Kanter. And they failed. How powerful is this Atticun of yours? Maybe he has the knowledge of ages in his head, but no actual *supernatural* power.'

Haze was shocked. People didn't say that kind of thing about the gods. They just didn't. 'That's got to be blasphemy!'

'Sure, it is,' he agreed calmly. 'Doesn't make what I said any less valid. Atticun exists, but I think maybe his power comes to him through his archpriests and acolytes. People's *belief* in him grants the priests their power over the populace.' While she was still trying to digest the blasphemy of that, he continued, 'And the other gods? Take God Saffrin. He has power because the army worships in his temples and because the King consults God Saffrin's archpriest, the Battleseer, on peace-keeping matters. In effect, maybe he's the one who directs the army and law enforcement, rather than the King or God Atticun!

'Then there's Goddess Granna, the guardian of crops and cultivators. She has power because the farmers worship her and bring a tithe of their harvest to her temples. Her well-fed, well-dressed priestesses listen to the farmers and learn. Over centuries they gathered information on plant diseases, how to treat them, where and when to plant crops — it's *knowledge* they dispense, not magic. Same with God Logar, the god of forests, whose priests listen to foresters and woodcutters. Zanaz, Goddess of Wanderers, has power because travellers bring her knowledge of the byways when they talk to her priestesses. And so on. You, the people of Talodiac, give the gods power with your information. Gods have been alive for centuries. They have very long memories to call upon!'

Haze stared at him in shock. Thalia, though, nodded. 'Maybe. Goddess Jenat certainly has all women on her side, even if their main allegiance might be elsewhere.'

'Hetha can heal,' Haze said, adamant. 'I've seen that happen. Thalia, remember when you had that horrible fever?'

'Might have been the medicine they gave me,' she pointed out.

'I suppose so.' Her admission was grudging. 'Though I think the healing power they have is something more ... more magical. God empowered? And you both are forgetting one power *all* the arch-clergy have. They can see redweaving!'

'Is that even a power?' Kaillan asked. 'Or is it just like being born with acute hearing or good eyesight? Do they become arch-clergy *because* they can see weaving, or do they get that power to see weaving after being raised to arch-clergy status?'

'I'm not sure,' Thalia replied. 'They don't talk about it, ever, as far as I know.'

'We don't worship any of your Decasine in Kanter,' Kaillan said. 'Here in Talodiac, though, I find the whole Decasine Pantheon is an invaluable source of help and advice.'

'What do the Kanterines believe in?' she persisted. 'Who are your gods?'

'We don't have them. Well, only in myths and legends. Some say they granted us the power of redweaving. It's all a bit vague on details. Some say our original gods had a huge bust-up. Threw redwoven storms and thunderbolts at one another in devastating wars. One tale says that the magic expended during that war was what split the country into two. Kanter and Talodiac.'

'Can any of that be true?' Haze asked.

'People couldn't read and write back then, so all we ever had was oral legends. Morality tales if you like. Lots of contradictory variations too. In none of them do the gods seem particularly nice! Ever since, we've believed we're better off with them all dead.' He turned to Thalia. 'Most people here, except for the clergy, never see a god face to face, right?'

'From what I've heard, gerents and gerentias report to their god personally. And perhaps a few top arch-clergy too. I know sometimes Goddess Jenat meets with ordinary folk.'

'A gerent or a gerentia is only found in a temple where their god resides,' he said, 'so there's only twelve of them in the whole of Talodiac?'

She nodded. 'Most in Templebridge, though Goddess Granna is over in the in the market town of Pelle Crossways while God Logar is in a timber town in Rothengar. And God Sheshan is in the capital of my Duchy, Temar, on the coast where I was born. It's a fishing port and the place where eight rivers finally flow into the sea, an appropriate residence for the God of Waters.'

'And you may well be the only person living who has met two gods of the Decasine,' Kaillan said.

She shrugged. 'I'm not sure whether to be honoured or scared out of my wits.'

'Tell us what they are like, those two gods,' Haze said.

Thalia glanced towards the stern to make doubly sure the bargeman could not hear. 'They didn't speak. More like …

communing? Goddess Jenat ... All I saw was blinding scarlet light. The colour of blood with light shining through it. Too bright to look at for long. I could feel power throbbing inside, roiling, burning, yet without heat.' She gave a little laugh. 'That's the best I can do. You need new words to describe a god.'

'Both gods the same?' Haze asked.

'God Atticun was a much darker colour. Grimmer. More like a storm at dusk on a thundery day. I could feel kindness in the glow that was Jenat. None from Atticun, just grumbling power. Which is also rather odd.' She struggled to express herself. 'Perhaps the best description would be to say there was frustration there in him.'

'Why would a god feel frustration?' Haze asked. 'They are surely omnipotent! They can do whatever they like!'

'Are they? Can they?' Kaillan asked. 'What if you had a mind, with all the knowledge of the world, yet no body?'

When he dropped those words into the conversation, it stopped Haze dead. She felt he'd just uttered something very profound, but she couldn't quite absorb the full extent of its meaning.

A long silence engulfed all three of them until Thalia spoke again. 'I think it was Goddess Jenat who implanted the baffle in my mind, although Gerentia Iria, who was the Mulierseer then, was there too. I felt the Goddess's compassion. Atticun, on the other hand? There was no feeling there for me. Whatever he granted was for him, for his reasons, not mine.'

'God Atticun wanted Denniel to live,' Haze said, slowly, 'right? What other reason could he have had for releasing Jordir Banlock to take a message back to Kanter?'

Thalia was pensive, tapping her fingers on the barge railings. 'Perhaps all he wanted to do,' she said finally, 'was to get me to take you back to the palace, where Edwild would have had you murdered. God Atticun told Gerent Vann, in front of me, that Jordir Banlock the innkeeper was to be released and given safe passage in the morning. But apparently he also told the Lawseer, privately, that Edwild could do what he wanted with regard to the changeling. Gerent Vann told me that. Perhaps he wasn't meant to, but he did. Carelessly or deliberately, I don't know, but it was enough to warn me that the changeling — you — was still in danger. That was when I asked to go to Goddess Jenat's temple.

'I believe God Atticun's main aim was for me to return to Edwild to have more children. He thought that if I was persuaded that Denniel was safe, then I would do that. He sensed things, Haze. God Atticun. He *knew* that if I thought Edwild was responsible for Denniel being killed, I wouldn't willingly go back to his bed. Letting Banlock go free was a small price to pay. I doubt he knew or cared if Jordir Banlock was just an innkeeper or a redweaver.'

'The God *could* have lied to you if he wanted,' Haze pointed out. 'Said he'd save Kaillan, but then killed him as soon as your back was turned.'

Kaillan shook his head. 'God of Governance,' he said. 'Bound by his own rules. Plus, Gerent Vann thought I was going to die anyway. He said as much when he pushed me out the door.'

A flock of marsh stilts flew past, and Thalia's gaze followed their flight to where they landed gracefully in unison on a sandbank. 'You're right. God Atticun is not merciful or caring. He was happy enough to have Jordir Banlock tortured to death. He didn't care. I don't think he cares about people, just … issues. Issues of rule. If he breaks rules, then ordinary folk will break them too.' She touched Kaillan's crippled hands as she spoke and her voice wavered. 'The Law, and the law alone, matters to Atticun.'

He said, '*I* wonder if what he wanted was to make sure King Edwild *didn't* make any kind of agreement with us Kanterines.'

Haze's head was reeling. All her ideas of godly behaviour were being eroded.

'So God Atticun released me with my message for Kanter,' Kaillan continued, 'but at the same time he told Gerent Vann to tell the King to do whatever he wants, knowing — because the Lawseer would have already told him so — that Edwild wanted the changeling dead.'

Thalia blanched. 'And releasing you was just a sop to me, an eighteen-year-old mother still bleeding from the birth, in shock because her child had been stolen. When I left their temple, they thought I would go back to the palace. I might have done so if Gerent Vann hadn't let slip that Edwild was free to do what he pleased.'

Haze winced. 'And none of them cared for me any more than one cares for a ... a soap bubble!' She swallowed. That hurt. And worse still, she sounded like a spoiled child complaining about it.

Thalia turned her head and put her hand over hers. '*I* did,' she said. 'I made up my mind to leave you at Goddess Jenat's temple as soon as I realised Jordir — Kaillan — couldn't carry you. What I wasn't sure about at first was whether I should return to Edwild myself.' When Haze looked at her doubtfully, she smiled with more than a hint of mischievousness. 'Remember this, though: when I left the palace, I was not only carrying you, but I was wearing the carcanet and carrying all the jewellery that I could fit underneath my clothing!'

She turned to Kaillan. 'You believe God Atticun thought Kanter would blame Edwild for the changeling's death, once they heard about it. And that would stop them trying to come here for safety? That's not terribly logical. It was much more likely that the changeling was a nobody, which was in fact the case. Mongrave must have known that there was an excellent chance the changeling would die. He just didn't care.'

'A nobody. Right. Thanks,' Haze said.

'You weren't nobody to me,' she said.

'These gods of yours.' Kaillan frowned as if he had something profound to say. 'Powerful, yet also powerless, relying on their clergy to gather information, then to follow their gods' commands.'

Neither of them replied.

'What do frightened people do?' he continued. 'They make threats. They send messages to back up the threats. Atticun allowed me to go free. A tortured man, carrying a message: "Look at this fellow! If he is one of yours, this is what we do to Kanterines." And then, if the King killed the changeling and the Kanterines found out, that would be another message, "Look, we even kill your children. Keep away from us!" That's the same message they've been giving Kanter since the time of Edwild's grandfather: "We'll kill everyone who comes through a gateway, if we find them."'

None of that answered the question uppermost in Haze's mind, so she asked: 'Kaillan, why are the gods, and the clergy, all so scared of you? The refuge-seekers are so ... so insignificant. Half-starved runaways. Do they think Kanterines will bring the esklet through?'

'No, it's not *esklet* that worries them,' Thalia said. 'It's *red-weaving*!'

'That's it exactly,' Kaillan agreed. 'Hence the status given to the folk who can see weaving. Anyone who can do that ends up as one of the high clergy.' He grinned at me. 'You've got a job for life, Hazelle.'

She pulled a face. She couldn't think of anything worse.

He added, 'Your clergy don't know that redweavers are far too busy warding off the esklet attacks in Kanter to worry too much about Talodiac.'

Later, though, after Kaillan had left, Haze considered all he'd said. Were the gods and clergy terrified of redweaving, or in a panic about a limited number of skinny refugees and their children? All the high clergy could see illusions, the residue left by redweaving and, most importantly, woven gateways. She wondered why none of them had ever had the guts to use one of the latter to reach Kanter.

After a moment's consideration, she found a partial answer easily.

The gods forbade it.

The question was ... *why?*

*

The next day, after Kaillan had already left, the bargeman poled the barge across the widening shallows close to Templebridge. They watched from the deck as the city slowly revealed itself, the towering temple spires topped with the golden symbols of the godheads being the first structures visible, followed by the stolid squat towers of the King's Keep. Next came the verdigris palace rooftop, then the surrounding slates of the tall townhouses, and finally the crenellations of the city's grey outer walls.

'Eighteen years,' Thalia whispered. 'And I never found him.'

Haze couldn't think of a single thing to say.

Thalia changed the subject. 'That whole thing about you and Denniel having the ability to see redweaving, and you being able to weave...'

'Passing through a gateway as a newborn is as good an explanation as any.'

'Possibly. But then, why don't you both have exactly the same ability?'

'Maybe because I was born in Kanter?'

'Maybe. Or maybe because a few days later you were taken into the powerful presence of two gods. I wonder what that did to you?'

'I was there with you when you went to see *both* the gods?' she asked, astonished. 'In the gods' inner sanctum?'

Thalia nodded. 'I wasn't going to leave you alone.'

She sighed. Two gods, an unheard-of privilege, and she'd never remember a whit of it.

Later, as they walked from the riverside into the city and on to Jenat's Temple, strolling past the public buildings with their grey stone walls clasped between the overhang of the green copper roofs and the black-streaked jasper of the street cobbles, she thought it a city worthy of being the home of seven of the ten gods of the Decasine.

Impressive, solid, old, prosperous.

Ruled by a man who had once wanted her murdered.

She thought of people in another land melted and seared by esklets, people who dreamed of sanctuary within Talodian borders, and shuddered. Dismissed as evil, when the truth was they were just human.

They are us. I am them.

They knocked at the door of the temple and were admitted immediately. Nothing unusual in that; there wasn't a Jenat's Temple in the whole of Talodiac who didn't know that 'Innata of Temar' was to be admitted without question, even if they had no idea who she was. They were ushered into the presence of the Mulierseer, who had only been Sister Agrina when Thalia had last seen her. Now she was Gerentia Agrina,

357

and when she rose to her feet as they entered the room, the colour drained from her face.

'Milady,' she whispered, 'thanks be! The Battleseer informed me you'd vanished on the road to Crowbridge, taken by redweavers to Kanter...!'

34

Taygen gave a cheery wave to Sianta and locked the cell door behind him. As he started up the prison corridor with her keys tucked into his belt, her lamp in one hand and her small knife in the other, he was wryly aware that he'd enjoyed his ascendancy over her a little too much. Worse, though, he also acknowledged that he ought to have killed her. Sianta dead would probably have made his hold on life a little more secure.

Gods, he thought, *Pa was right about one thing. I would never have made a soldier.*

His bare feet made no sound on the flagstones as he headed away from the cell in the direction Sianta used. No doors opened on either side and the corridor soon came to an end at a descending iron spiral staircase. No openings, no landings, no windows, it continued into the darkness below to what must have been the deepest level of the keep.

At the bottom, the only way forward was a downward sloping tunnel, narrow and mean and dark, leading into a musty blackness. He pushed on, alert, knife gripped tight, trying to recall the evening he'd arrived in Templebridge with Hervan and his men. In Breakedge, respectable citizens would have been heading home at that hour, so he'd been astonished to see Templebridge still throbbed with life and commerce after dark. The warmth of a summer evening brought people out onto the streets. Oil lamps with odd, sleeve-shaped wicks and tall glass chimneys decorated the counters of shops and stalls, giving off haloes of light brighter than ever he'd seen before.

Cyrrin had needled him, unable to resist a scornful jeer. 'Country boy, eh, never seen the brightness of sleeve-lamps before this?' He hadn't, but he'd appreciate them now.

The tunnel ended in a set of steps and a trapdoor with a heavy iron bolt shot across it from underneath, presumably by Sianta after she'd entered the passageway. He listened until he was sure all was quiet on the other side before sliding it back. Still nothing. He cracked the trapdoor open. He was peering at floor level into a silent, darkened room, hardly larger than a cupboard. He climbed out and closed the trapdoor behind him. There was no bolt on the upper side, just a recessed handle. The room had a single door, and he thought he caught distant sounds from the other side.

Music. Voices.

Nothing close by.

Trying the door, he found it had a treble lock, recently oiled, that required three different keys. A quick rifle through Sianta's keyring found the correct ones to use. Inching the door open a moment later, he peeked out. The doorway was recessed, its alcove opening on to a narrow laneway squeezed between high walls of windowless buildings. He retreated, pulled the door closed and locked it again from the inside.

Breathing a little easier, he put the lamp down on the floor, sat down in front of it and propped Sianta's small mirror against the wall, angling the lamp so that it illuminated his face. Curse all gods, but he looked like a hog's arse, covered in dirt with his hair as tangled as brambles after a gale. His beard could have easily harboured a cockroach or two. And as for his nose, it was already swelling up where Sianta had bitten him. He sighed, picked up the knife and started to hack away at his locks. At least the bitch had kept the blade sharp.

Ten minutes later he had done all he could to shorten and comb his hair and beard. As a final touch, he lightened his skin with Sianta's powder, then dabbed his face and neck with her perfume. If she sent her minions out looking for a swarthy bearded man with long tangled locks and brown eyes, at least part of the description no longer applied. It wasn't enough, though, he knew that. On his way into Templebridge, he'd looked for folk with his southern dusky skin, and not even one in ten matched his description.

He burned all of his hair clippings in the lantern flame and swept the fine ash into the cracks of the flooring. After a final look around, he extinguished the lamp and, leaving it behind, unlocked the door and stepped outside. The lane was deserted, gloomily dim in the shadows cast by the walls of the buildings that hemmed it, until it slipped unobtrusively into another quiet street. Following that brought him into a busy square. He paused to orient himself by locating the dark silhouette of the palace roof against a starry sky, and not far away, the solid, ugly stone tower of the much older keep. Between him and those buildings was the encircling wall of the Royal Precinct. The tunnel had passed under it out into the city.

He grinned, turned his back to the wall and set off across a square thronged with people. After his days of prison solitude and quiet, the noise of a diverse crowd enjoying a warm summer's night was an assault on his already keen ears. A fiddler played and people sang with drunken abandon. The laughter and squeals of a crowd watching stage players mingled with the clatter of wooden barrow wheels over uneven cobbles. Tantalising aromas drifted his way: barbecued meat lathered with garlic, buttered grilled river fish, juice-laden fruit freshly cut, griddle cakes still hot and sweetly sugared. His mouth watered, but he needed to get out of there as quickly as possible.

He pushed his way through the crowd until he came to a stall selling grilled lamb on a stick.

'One rickling a piece,' the matronly stall holder said, lip curling with distaste as she took in his filth and breathed the ripeness of his body stink that even Sianta's perfume could not entirely hide. 'And I got no alms for unwashed pups.'

'Hey-o, be no call for snippiness, mistress,' he protested, dropping back into the street vernacular and accent of a Breakedge road mender. 'I be a fresh shoot in the big bustle and were shoved into a midden by some of your city sprigs who took exception to m'looks an' stole me shoes, the toads. But's proper true, I be short of coin, lest I hie me to a goldsmith.' He laid a rickling of Sianta's money on her outstretched hand. 'Give me a stick of yon wares, and tell me: where I can find me a goldsmith?'

Her eyebrows shot up in surprise. 'Oh, aye. That's a likely tale.'

''Tis not likely at all, lest some'un tells me where to find a goldsmith now, is it? Would y'have me starve for a lack of direction, mistress?'

'Money Street, o'course,' she said, taking his coin and handing over the grilled meat. 'On the right, four lanes down.' She pointed in the direction she meant. 'Open till ten strokes from the King's Keep bell.'

He thanked her and melted away into the crowd, savouring the greasy morsel of meat as he went.

The goldsmith shop was guarded by a giant of a man holding a halberd. As soon as the fellow saw him halt, his lips pursed and he ran his hand up and down the pole of his weapon in open threat. 'Whatcha want?' he asked. 'No begging here. Lest you want to lose a leg, or worse.' He reached up to tap the axe blade at the top of his weapon.

'Me business is with t'goldsmith, not tha'.'

'He don't deal with no thieves. Respectable business this, understand?'

'I've gold to sell.'

'Show me.'

He flashed his hand open to show what he gripped there: part of the gold setting he'd purloined from the carcanet.

Probably worth about ten silvers. He knew he'd be lucky to get half its value. Unlucky, he'd be arrested for theft.

The halberdier stood aside and jerked his head at the door. 'Watch yerself,' he warned. 'No sticky fingers!'

Inside, the broad counter that ran the width of the room was lit at either end by two of those bright oil lamps. A bald-headed, elderly man on the other side looked up from reading a broadsheet. His gaze flicked over Taygen from the rankness of his hair to the filth of his bare feet.

'Been filching something, lad?' he asked bluntly.

'Nah, though s'pose you'd doubt them words, right?' He laid the gold on the counter.

The goldsmith took up a pair of spectacles and perched them precariously halfway down his thin nose. He reached over to pick up the gold, then examined it carefully with a magnifying lens. 'Hmm. Once part of the setting for jewels?'

'Ay.'

'Gold, you say?'

'Gold, I knows.'

He watched fascinated as the old man tapped it with a piece of metal, possibly a magnet, then picked up a small file and rasped away at a tiny piece of the surface. Squinting through his magnifying glass at the groove he'd made, the goldsmith nodded to himself. He then fetched a bowl from a cupboard and opened a drawer at the back of the counter to take out a small stoppered bottle.

'So far so good,' he said, and pulled up his kerchief over his face. 'Stand back, m'boy. This stuff is noxious.'

Without taking his eyes off the goldsmith, he did as he was told.

The man dispensed a tiny drop from the bottle so that it fell into the groove in the gold, after which he washed it off with water. Once again, he studied the piece carefully, before removing his kerchief and saying, 'Gold all the way through, I'd say. I'll give you three silvers.'

'Be worth ten!'

'Possibly. But I have to make a profit.'

'Tha's no profit. Tha's theft!'

The old man laughed. 'Well, you have the right of that. 'Twas stolen, I've no doubt. But not by me.'

'Aye, not by me, neither. 'Twas gifted in exchange for service.' True enough. Sort of.

The old man snorted and took off his spectacles. 'Lad, don't go looking for a fortune when you're freely offered a bounty.'

'Seven silvers. Or I'll take it elsewhere.'

The jeweller looked past him to the open door where the halberdier stood on the stoop, his back to the doorjamb so he could keep watch on both the street and the shop interior. 'Really?' he asked.

Taygen glanced at the halberdier and let his face fall, as if he was resigning himself to the lesser amount. Out of the corner of his eye he saw the goldsmith relax, and used that moment of inattention to snatch his gold back. 'Five,' he said, poised to run.

The jeweller jumped, then unexpectedly laughed. 'A lad with gall. You've had it toilsome of late, I'm guessing. Tread carefully, m'boy, or one foot will trip the other and your nose will end in the mire.'

'Mayhap. But this was gifted me. An' I ask fair price.'

The goldsmith sighed, opened another drawer and counted out five silvers from his cashbox. 'Count yourself lucky that no one has registered a piece like this as missing lately. If that had been on the register, I'd have called for the guard. Take the coins, lad, and use them well.'

Damn the man, he'd made him feel he was ten years old again.

Out on the street once more, money in his pocket, he doubled back to the main square, this time avoiding the food stalls to find the barrows that sold used clothing. He handed over a whole rick in exchange for a set of clothes, laundered but obviously much worn, including drawers, darned stockings and a pair of scuffed used shoes. He even received some rickling coins in change.

With the clothes tied in a bundle and the stockings and shoes on his feet, he set off across the square once more. On the far side, wanting directions to a respectable bathhouse, he stopped to ask a young woman selling flowers on a corner. She wrinkled her nose, muttered a scathing remark about gutter-scum and turned her back. An old lady selling hot roasted calby nuts was more obliging, perhaps because he gave her a rickling in exchange for a cabbage leaf cornet of her wares.

The bathhouse was large and busy and only for men, soap supplied, hot water plentiful, but towels an extra. 'You want a shave and haircut, it's extra too,' the matron on the door said, her raised eyebrows signifying distaste for his hair and beard.

'How much?' he asked, wondering what she would have said if she'd seen him a couple of hours earlier.

She sniffed. 'An extra three ricklings.' It was a statement, not a suggestion. 'And for another rickling we'll cut and clean your nails. Unless y'think going about looking like a peat digger gives the girls joy.'

He paid up, and an hour later he emerged from the bathhouse feeling lighter, more cheerful and a great deal cleaner, dressed in his new clothes. The dirty ones he'd popped into the furnace that heated the water when no one was looking — after extracting the remaining jewels in the seams. Ten minutes later, doing his level best to imitate Hazelle when she was at her most uppity, he rented a box bed for the night in the dosshouse recommended by the barber who'd cut his hair. He went to bed hopeful that he hadn't left much of a trail behind him, and that no one looking for a long-haired barefoot escaped convict would think it possible he was such a lowborn rascal.

Although there was the matter of his swollen nose...

After an early breakfast, he headed out into the street again and walked for another half hour before asking for directions to a clothier. He was recommended a bespoke tailor with a workshop on the upper floor of a row of shops. Fortunately, there was no need to order clothing; the man had a good selection of items already sewn, including a coat with brass buttons. He left the establishment with a much-reduced purse and — as studying his appearance in the clothier's mirror confirmed — appearing considerably more prosperous than he had on entering it. It was a pity about the nose...

His next stop was at a barber-perfumer's, where he had yet another trim to his hair. This time, he asked for the latest style, which included the bleaching of a hank of hair over his forehead, a fashion he'd noted to be popular with young men of Templebridge. He emerged sometime later with a white streak. He didn't see that it served any purpose except that it told everyone he had money to spend on frivolities, but that was exactly the impression he was trying to convey. Better still, the redness of his swollen, battered nose had now been made less obvious by the application of a masking cosmetic.

He also now had the name and address of a jeweller, courtesy of the garrulous barber. He arrived at this establishment mid-morning after buying a new leather purse and strolled in as if he felt at home. In truth, he felt like a Breakedge toad in a birdcage of exotic parrots. Women with elaborate coifs and jewellery and extravagantly wide skirts giggled and fluttered elegant feather fans as they sat sipping tea brought by uniformed servants, all while viewing the latest geegaws displayed on black velvet trays.

It took a while to convince the man who came forward that he didn't want to buy anything, but rather sell a stone, but finally he was taken through into a back room. Apparently, such a sordid transaction had to take place out of sight of other customers.

'I've been a mucklehead,' he said to the jeweller with a heartfelt sigh, choosing this time to imitate the accent of the Templebridge-born teacher of his schooldays. 'Gambling, y'know. And now I need to pay off my debt without my father finding out, so my darling mama prised this stone out of one of her necklaces. Mind you, she gave me *such* a scold…' He opened up his palm to display the diamond. 'I am so ashamed of myself!'

His petty thieving days in Breakedge had given him no idea of how much such a diamond was worth, but he did know how to haggle. It took an hour, during which he made it out of the backroom twice, once almost to the front door, declaring it would be better to face up to his father than sell the gem for so little, and the second time stuttering that his mother would never forgive him if he couldn't cover the whole cost of his gambling debt. Both times the jeweller enticed him back and finally they agreed on a tidy sum.

When he did step back on to the street with a full purse, pride-filled at his own achievements, he came face to face with one of God Saffrin's temple soldiers wearing the uniform of the town guard. His smugness vanished faster than a drunkard's beer. He stepped to the right, the fellow stepped to the left and for a moment they performed a little dance in the street, his heart hammering loud enough to throb in his ears.

'Clear off, you frilly-fop of a prick,' the man snapped as he pushed Taygen out of the way.

He steadied himself and expelled the breath he had been holding. The guard disappeared around a corner without a backward look, but a glance up and down the thoroughfare was enough to send a shiver up his spine. Others wearing Saffrin's colours were fanning out to enter the shops and bang on doors.

A hunt was on, and he had a horrible idea they were looking for an escaped prisoner. He sucked in his cheeks, threw his shoulders back and lifted his chin, as if that was enough to show the world his innocence. Inside, his heart drummed his panic.

Was he really that important?

PART 5

A NEW
PATTERN

35

When the Mulierseer, Gerentia Agrina, entered her private sitting room on their third day in Jenat's Temple, she was as taut as a sail in a storm, rigid with anxiety. Thalia rose to greet her, hoping she exuded a regal calm even though she had an absurd desire to throw back her head and scream.

'Is something amiss, Most Reverend?' she asked.

'There's a young fellow in the public meeting room.'

Thalia schooled her face to give no indication of the way her heart leapt with fear and hope. 'And?'

'A southerner, by the look of him, swarthy fellow. He said he has a letter for Innata. The acolyte on duty asked him to wait there and came to fetch me.'

Hazelle leapt to her feet. 'It'll be Taygen!'

Gerentia Agrina's eyes widened. 'Captain Hervan's son? After what you've both told me, I think it's more likely that lad would have been sent off to a labour camp as punishment for helping you escape.'

Thalia bit back disappointment. Not Kaillan. Not Denniel. Why was it that the closer she came to Denniel, the worse the waiting was? She scolded herself. *At least we can be glad if Taygen has escaped.*

'This person, is there some way we can see who it is without him seeing us?'

Agrina nodded. 'Of course. We have to look after the safety of the women who take refuge here. Follow me, milady.'

She led them through the maze of rooms and corridors to a peephole into the waiting room. Thalia stood back to allow Hazelle to look first.

'I think it's him,' Haze said, sounding puzzled. 'He's wearing uppity clothes though. And what's he done to his hair? It's striped!'

Thalia took her turn at the spy hole. 'Uppity clothes' was the way Haze described the attire of the nobility, and sure enough Taygen was wearing a tailored outfit that included an embroidered waistcoat and a carefully arranged cravat. His straight black hair now sported a dashing white blaze over his forehead.

'Bless his boots,' she said, intrigued, 'he *has* altered somewhat since we last saw him, hasn't he? I think perhaps I know what happened to the missing pieces of the carcanet. Clever lad.'

Hazelle snorted. 'He's still just a Breakedge pickpocket, all brass and balls. Wait a moment: what missing pieces are you talking about?'

Thalia smiled at her serenely.

'Do you *want* to see this fellow?' Agrina asked.

'Oh, yes,' Thalia replied. 'We do indeed.'

The look the Mulierseer gave them both was troubled. 'Through that door over there. I will leave you to be private.' She turned and walked away, mumbling something about wishing her predecessor was still alive to deal with all this.

'The missing pieces?' Hazelle asked.

'Later.' Thalia pushed open the door to the reception room, where Taygen was leaning against the mantelpiece of the unlit fireplace, legs crossed at the ankles, a studied pose of someone with time on his hands and not a worry in the world.

Hazelle rolled her eyes but couldn't help chuckling. 'Who are you trying to bamboozle, you codswiggler?'

'And I'm glad to see you, too, Haze.' The pose dropped away and he came across the room and took her hands. 'Ac-

371

tually, you can't even *begin* to guess how much.' After which statement he gave her a hug, before he turned to Thalia and took a deep breath. 'Milady. I thought … maybe…' He swallowed and started again. 'I thought maybe you'd both just disappeared forever. Or died. Or something. It was *horrible*. Pa said it must be a redweaver gateway. Then I thought—' He gave a broad grin. 'I am *so* glad you are both still alive.'

'Well, you seem to have landed on your feet,' Haze said, looking him up and down. 'Is that *lace* on your cravat?'

'I believe so. Secondhand, but I wanted something that didn't remind anyone of me.'

'Believe me, you succeeded. And don't tell me. You're in trouble. Again.'

'Yes, for treason, I believe. No trial that I know of, very vague accusation, but I was told my execution was scheduled for some time during the Summer Festival, which I understand starts the day after tomorrow?'

'But your father, surely—' Haze began, her eyes widening in shock.

Thalia held up a hand to halt her words, saying instead, 'I'm delighted to see you in one piece.' She crossed to the peephole and stuffed her kerchief into the opening. 'And I'm grateful for your help and your courage. Haze said you'd escape. She has considerable faith in your abilities to wriggle out of trouble.' She pointed to the group of chairs furthest from the peephole. 'Best we sit over there.' As she settled, she gestured at Taygen's outfit. 'We need to hear the whole story. Do I take it that my jewellery was of use?'

He had the grace to look embarrassed. 'Immensely. I'm even staying at Templebridge's best hostelry, *The Duke's Arms*. Marvellous what you can do with a few diamonds and a little gold. My father almost ruptured his eyeballs when he found out you'd taken the carcanet with you when you escaped the camp. You have *no* idea! Tell me, are you *really* Queen Thalia?'

'Ah, you've been doing some thinking, it seems,' she replied.

'After all that confusion on the roadway outside Crowbridge, Cyrrin made some mention of a herring-fisher duke's mannerless daughter, or something similar, before Pa gave him a clip across the ear to shut him up. Did get me thinking...'

'I was only ever elevated to the image of a beautiful, much-loved queen *after* I died. All those flowers laid at the feet of the statues of me in numerous town squares? Remorse, not grief.'

Haze stared at them both. 'The carcanet?'

'I plundered a few pieces,' Taygen admitted.

'And I took what was left,' Thalia said. 'Seemed a good idea. It is, after all, something that can prove that I am who I say I am. I stole it the night I escaped from Hervan's clutches. Easy enough; he didn't think he had to protect anything from me. I was locked up, after all...' She grinned. 'It's been in the pocket in my petticoats ever since. Better you didn't know.'

'What happened to you both?' Taygen asked. 'Was it a redwoven tunnel, as my father reckoned? You just ... disappeared. Both of you!'

'It's a very long story,' Haze said.

'We have time to tell it,' Thalia added.

'Good,' he said. 'And I want to ask you if you know anything about a woman called Sianta Tory-Cress. Who says she's the King's Historian.'

'Is there such a post?' Thalia asked.

'I'm beginning to think there isn't.'

'The only Sianta I've come across was a priestess of ... God Saffrin, I think. She came to court once.'

He nodded. 'That's what I figured.'

'I can't imagine how you've come across her, or what she has to do with anything!' She heaved a sigh. 'I think we have much to tell one another, not all of it good. We none of us are the same people we were when last we were together. Now, who is going to start?'

*

When it came time for Taygen to tell his story, Thalia saw a new side to him, one he had never been able to display under the watchful eye of men like Hervan and Cyrrin, and she began to understand the earlier rapport that he had established with Haze. His cheeky boldness now emerged, made palatable by his brutal honesty concerning his own culpability. Hazelle, of course, accepted nothing at face value, but probed and questioned until Taygen had detailed at least some of the horror of his transport to Templebridge, bound and beaten, the object of his father's rage and Cyrrin's sadism.

The words emerged raw and ragged, his devastation at his father's rejection made all the more poignant because it was clear Taygen believed it justified. When Hazelle protested, he said quietly, 'It was my stupidity that blinded my brother. Whatever Pa did, or said to me, came from his pain. I'll never blame him for it. There was no better man alive than Jav.' He glanced at Thalia. 'Pa paid a heavy price. Sianta said he's been sent to a punishment regiment along the desert border, though I don't know whether she told the truth.'

None of them could think of anything to say to that.

One of the young acolytes brought them a meal as the sun sank low in the sky and reminded Taygen he would have to leave. 'In half an hour,' she said, smiling over her shoulder at him as she left the room.

'And this Sianta?' Hazelle asked when they were alone again. 'Who is she?'

'What she told me didn't ever smell right. I played along, even after I was certain much 'twas pickling nonsense. She knew who I was. She knew you were alive, milady. She said that you and a young man with a polearm had been spirited away by redweavers. She wanted me to write down everything, from the time I met you. Everything. And so I did. Didn't think it would make any difference to any of us, after all. The King was wanting to murder you anyway. My father reported to the King's Guards immediately we arrived in Templebridge. He asked Cyrrin to take me on to the Keep. But Cyrrin stopped off at Saffrin's Temple along the way, where he picked up another set of orders, this time apparently from the Battleseer, Gerent Ruthgar.'

'Who do you think Sianta is?' Thalia asked.

'High status. Possibly a saffrine archpriestess? She has a certain ... arrogance. Presumption of her own importance. Bit like an officer in the army.'

'She is saffrine,' Thalia said, 'if she's the person I'm thinking of. She had a lover in the court, a lady-in-waiting of the Queen Mother. When you arrived and Edwild wasn't in Templebridge, Cyrrin in effect delivered you to the Battleseer's men, right?'

'Well, it was the King's Guard in Keep's Keep to start with. But he also handed over whatever paper he received at God Saffrin's Temple to the officer on duty. For a couple of days, nothing happened, then I was spirited away by Sianta.' He sighed. 'My father and his men have a divided loyalty. They are kingsmen, but they worship God Saffrine. My father is more the King's than the God's. Cyrrin, though...'

Hazelle gave him a puzzled grimace. 'Why would this Sianta want a written account?'

'Blackmail,' Taygen said.

She gave a disbelieving laugh. 'Blackmailing who?'

'The King, of course!' he replied. 'Think about it. King Edwild told the world the Queen and his son died just after childbirth. There was a state funeral, he erected a statue commemorating them and he played the grieving husband. He knew the Lawseer and the Mulierseer were aware you were still alive, but I suspect he thought they would let him marry again in the interests of the nation. That didn't happen. And now? If you want to blackmail or control the King, what better way than to have a written account from an eye-witness of the Queen's survival and capture? Cyrrin told the Battleseer, who then had me squirrelled away in a remote cell. I doubt the King knows about any of this yet. I escaped the day he returned.'

A cold shiver skittered up Thalia's spine.

Hazelle clutched her head, then jumped up to pace the room. 'But why does a flipping gerent have to blackmail a king into doing something in the first place? Wouldn't a simple request work? If a gerent or gerentia asked me to do something, I'd assume the request came from the god and my bones would be clanking with fear until I obliged!'

Taygen nodded. 'Me too. It couldn't have anything to do with Kanter, redweaving and refuge-seekers, could it?'

Thalia leant back in her chair. Blackmail did make horrible sense. And Kaillan had said the gods were not as powerful as folk believed … Dread scratched at her thoughts as she delved deep into her past. 'We need to think carefully about all this. Why did God Atticun free Jordir Banlock/Kaillan Riverdell and give him leave to return to Kanter? At the time, I was naïve enough to think a god would care about Prince Denniel, but Atticun's not known for his compassion, nor for his concern for individuals. His cause is stability. Fanatically keeping things as they are. The rule of unbending law. He and his priests don't like change.'

Taygen nodded. 'What is it that destabilises Talodiac most, and has done for decades? What would Atticun hate most?'

Hazelle frowned. 'I assume you're not thinking of the Candabeam River flooding, or a duke squabbling with his neighbours, or border raids from the desert marauders. Those are the sort of things ordinary folk worry about. Red-weavers are not quite real to them. I know better now. Kan-terines crossing the border, that happens. Magical deception is real. Esklet exist.'

'Esklet? What are they?' Taygen asked.

'You don't want to know,' she said.

'Redweavers never seem to do anything too terrible to us,' he said. 'I saw some once. They were half-starved and un-armed.'

'Jenat's clergy,' said Thalia, 'they insisted I bring Hazelle to them once a year. I know why now: they were looking for signs that she was a redweaver, because that's what frightens them most.'

Taygen nodded. 'What I saw done to refuge-seekers by God Dargan's men; it was … brutal.'

'Considering what I could do with redweaving if I honed my skills,' Hazelle said, 'I can't blame Talodiac for worrying. The power to deceive … But what's this got to do with black-mailing the King? The King doesn't have to be blackmailed into keeping redweavers out. He'd want to do that anyway! He's always done it. And why doesn't Atticun just tell King Edwild what to do — or not do? He's a god! No one defies a god.'

'You're right,' Thalia admitted. 'We're not wholly on the right track with this. I wish Kaillan was here. We need his advice.' She looked across at Taygen. 'He sent a note earlier today, saying he was on Denniel's trail, but the prince had moved out of the Templebridge safehouse he was in, and none of the Kanter refugees hiding out there were sure where he'd gone.'

'It's hectic out in the city. Because of the Summer Festival preparations.' Taygen grinned. 'Plus, there are soldiers everywhere, looking for me. I even got stopped and asked if I'd seen a scruffy-looking fellow southerner.'

'What did you say?' Hazelle asked.

'I said I tended not to notice scruffy ruffians.'

She laughed.

Thalia dragged the conversation back to the topic. 'You're right, Haze. There was a time when Edwild did exactly what he was told by the arch-clergy. Atticun told him not to bargain with redweavers to secure the return of his baby son, so he didn't. Atticun told him he couldn't marry again, so he didn't.' She thought back. A god and a goddess. Similar, but also different. Atticun carmine-dark. Jenat so crimson-bright. Both just a glowing and opaque red light, seething with power. 'Something bothers me.'

Before either of them could ask what, the Mulierseer returned to the room to tell them it was time Taygen left.

'Will you be safe?' Hazelle asked. 'Surely they are still looking for you?'

'They're searching for a bearded fellow in dirty clothing who hasn't two ricklings to rub together. Don't worry, I'll be fine. I'll come back tomorrow. Early.' With that, he grinned and left.

'Wretched fellow,' Haze muttered. 'He's *enjoying* this.'

Thalia laid a hand on her arm. 'Let him,' she said. 'Believe me, since he left Breakedge, there's been very little enjoyable in his life.'

36

'Oddly enough, this is the same room you and I had when you were a babe,' Thalia said, looking around their bedroom in the temple that evening. *Gods, I was so young, so naïve...*

'Do you regret doing what you did?' Hazelle asked. 'Running away, I mean. Now that you know that Denniel would have been fine no matter what?'

'No. Of course not. If I'd stayed, you would have been killed! And besides, all respect I had for Edwild vanished with the decision he made. He should have negotiated.'

'But it would have meant going against his god.'

'He should have demanded answers from his god,' she said bitterly.

'That's ... that's an odd thing to say. We are supposed to worship gods. Offer them obedience. Honour them. Accept their demands. Not demand answers!'

'Indeed.' Thalia sighed. 'I'm not the same person I was then. I was hardly more than a child. A little younger than you are now, and much, much more naïve. Not to mention scared.'

'And you're not scared now?'

'No. I'm not. The gods don't impress me anymore. Their clergy, yes, often. Some of them are upstanding, brave and generous, worthy of admiration and respect. Some just scare me.'

'That's got to be blasphemous! And you've met two gods. How can you say that?'

'Maybe *because* I've met them. I think Kaillan was right. Gods are powerful, not because of some inherent magical ability, but because they have *knowledge*.'

'Because worshippers tell them stuff.'

'Exactly. I like Taygen, by the way. He has courage and a sharp mind.'

'He's changed a lot since I first met him. I didn't know about his brother.'

'That happened a day or two before we left Breakedge. I found out from Cyrrin, who was always happy to harm the lad in whatever way he could. Nasty piece of work, that man. He's the one who came galloping up the road when we were about to ride away.'

'Taygen could be an idiot, you know. Wanted his father's approval but could never earn it because he wasn't saffrine, so he played the fool.'

'He just needed to grow up, and I rather think he has. Stick by him, Hazelle, and he'll be your friend for life. You need friends. You need your own life, your own path.'

'I know. And I will.' Her lips twitched. 'He is a dolt sometimes, but we'll always be there for each other. But you: what are you planning, Innata?'

The choice to use her old name right then was deliberate, of course. She gave Hazelle a level glance. 'I don't want my old life back. It would be nice to remove the throne from under Edwild's backside, but I can't see that happening. What I want is the knowledge that Denniel, you and I can all live safely, without always having to worry about being hunted down as if we were rabid dogs. Right now, I think you ought to go to bed. I have a feeling that tomorrow is going to be a long day.'

'But—'

'Bed.' She turned to leave the room.

'Where are you going?'

'I think I need to indulge in a little blackmail myself.'

'What?'

'Well, let's call it ... negotiation.'

'With whom?'

'Always wise to go to the top, don't you think?'

'You can't mean the goddess? Just like that?'

Thalia smiled and swept from the room. Sometimes she enjoyed being a queen...

On her way to the Mulierseer's office, she met Agrina coming to look for her. 'That man you want to see,' she said, 'the Kanterine. He's here. Asking for Innata. At this hour!'

Her heart lurched. 'It must be something important. Where is he?'

'In the waiting room. A *redweaver* in our temple! It's not proper for *any* man to be here at this hour, let alone a red-weaver. Goddess Jenat will not allow such. But he's refusing to leave without seeing you!'

'No one is going to use redweaving here, I promise, Most Reverend.' Thalia headed towards the waiting room, leaving Agrina scurrying to catch up. She found Kaillan standing, arms folded, under the disapproving eye of two acolytes. He winked at her, which made one of the girls giggle. Agrina pursed her lips in remonstration.

Thalia patted her hand, saying, 'Never mind. I will step outside to talk to him. I'll ring at the women's gate when I wish to re-enter. Come, Kaillan.'

Once outside in the cool night air, she closed the temple visitors' door and leaned back against it with a sigh of relief. His eyes, lit by the lamp over the doorway, twinkled at her. 'Like being back in the schoolroom, is it?' he asked.

'A bit. It's good to see you. I've been so worried. Have you found Denniel?'

'I found out where he's been. Working for a city carpenter setting up the stalls and stages for the Summer Festival.'

She was incredulous. 'Inside the Palace Precinct?'

He nodded. 'He's been staying in the artisan quarter of the city with the other festival workmen, but tonight he didn't return with them to their lodgings.'

She'd forgotten to breathe and had to drag air into her lungs. 'You — you think he stayed in the Palace Precinct when the workers left.'

He nodded. 'Aye. I know the lad. I'm guessing he's intending to confront his pa.'

'In the *palace*?' Fear crawled through her, trailing icy cold in its wake. She groped for calm. 'Not so easy. He might have entered the Precinct today as a workman, but the *palace* has its own encircling wall, with guards at the gate. That's never open to the public.'

'My guess is he'll try. That he wants a private confrontation.'

'And you think he'll try that, *tonight*?'

'Yes. He won't succeed in getting hold of Edwild, though. I believe the King has a brand-new mistress in the city and sleeps at her house, coming back to the palace early morning.'

'Denniel's not going to know that, surely.'

'He'll know, believe me. Everyone's gossiping about it! My guess? Denniel plans to get into the palace tonight from the Precinct gardens, hide there and confront Edwild tomorrow.'

She clutched at him in the half-light from the gate lamp as several drunken revellers stumbled by. 'How can you be so certain you know what he'll do? You haven't seen him for years!'

'I raised him through the years that counted.'

The words were gentle, but they flayed her. She made a sound, a catch in her throat, and he winced. She said, 'We have to stop him.'

'I can try entering through the main gate with the workers tomorrow morning.'

'No. You'd never get into the palace. We'll all go right up to the front door with Gerentia Agrina, in her carriage in the morning.'

A group of young people, laughing and talking, ambled by. She smelled baked apple and hot candied nuts as they passed. 'You know,' she said, watching them. 'I've never been to the summer night market in Templebridge. Not something a queen was ever permitted to do.'

'Then allow me,' he said proffering an arm. 'I have coin in my pockets and it's still two hours to curfew.'

She hesitated.

'Tomorrow is another day,' he said.

His tone was one of warning, so she knew the words were no glib aphorism. This might be the only chance she'd ever have. She nodded and took his arm. Five minutes' walk brought them to the bustle and noise of the market square. The years fell away, and for a moment she was a child back in Temar out in the street with her cousins, where a duke's daughter could eat bread and pickled fish from a market, or run barefoot on the sand of the beach...

Kaillan bought her preserved plums on a stick and they watched the acrobats and the puppet show and laughed at the street mummers. She giggled when the plum juice dripped down her chin and he wiped it away.

A stolen interlude, she thought. *Enjoy the moment for it will not last...*

Even if she and Denniel were united, there was never any way she could scratch back the lost years, she'd never have the slivers of countless memories that should have been hers. She looked up at Kaillan. 'I want to see my statue here,' she said. 'Do you know where it is?'

His eyes widened. 'Yes, it's on the other side of the square, near the wall of the Precinct.' He hesitated. 'Are you sure?'

She nodded. 'I've seen others. But Templebridge's is the only one that Edwild personally ordered. I imagine that he was rather upset that other cities followed his example.'

Kaillan slipped an arm around her shoulders and steered her through the throng until they emerged into a quiet area on the other side. It was darker there in the shadow of the Treasury building, but the sculptured marble of the statue gleamed in the soft light of seven mourning candles at the base of its plinth. A carpet of flowers covered the marble feet of the seated figure bending over the babe in her arms.

Staring at the tenderness carved into the soft, sweet curves of this girl's face, Thalia was unable to find much resemblance to the eighteen-year-old she had been. She read the words on the plaque beneath: *Lady Thalia of Temar, Queen of Talodiac, Beloved wife of King Edwild, Duke of Templebridge and the Riverland.* 'Beloved?' She turned to look at Kaillan and snorted. 'As for remembrance lilies and mourning candles ... I'll guarantee Edwild is not responsible for those.'

'I doubt even he is that cynical. From what I've heard, here in Templebridge women regard you as some sort of symbol of womanhood. They talk of you as a sweet young girl, tragically dying to bring an heir into the world.'

'How Edwild must hate that! If he wants anything, it is for me to be forgotten. His first queen has a statue too, placed just outside the Precinct gate. Mine is tucked away in a shaded corner.' She shook her head in bemusement. 'Kaillan,

384

Haze's friend Taygen is staying in *The Duke's Arms*. Can you bring him with you tomorrow morning?'

'You have a plan?'

'I intend to bargain with Edwild. Find a solution that suits everyone. I have leverage. And I intend to go to Goddess Jenat tonight to enlist her help.'

'Just like that?'

'Just like that.'

He smiled, bemused, but she knew it was more in appreciation rather than scepticism. 'You will come with us tomorrow?' she asked. 'It's not actually necessary.'

'Oh, yes, it is. He is the son I never had. I would gladly die for his safety. And you know I lost my heart to you the day you faced me with such dignity and courage in a temple cell.'

'Nonsense!'

'How could I not? Oh, perhaps not with the heart of a lover, not then, but one filled with reverence at your courage. I could never forget. Never forgive myself. All those years...' He took a deep breath. 'Now? Never doubt this: it's more than guilt. More than atonement. More than reparation. More than an obligation to be at your side when you face t'other man who wronged you. It's everything I have. Everything.'

She swallowed. 'I would be glad if you were there,' she admitted. 'You give me courage.' She touched her fingertip to the scar on his cheek. 'Thank you for taking care of him. For loving him. For loving me.'

'We'll come as soon as curfew is lifted.' He enfolded her in his arms, and she felt the shiver he gave. Not desire, she knew. Not then. In that moment, it was guilt at what he had done, and she cried for him, for them both. 'Take me back to the temple,' she whispered. 'I need to see the Goddess.'

37

Thalia emerged from the bathroom feeling nauseous. She leant for a moment against the wall outside the door. Such a stupid time to be let down by her body, just when she needed all her wits about her. Not unexpected, though. What was it her mother had been wont to say?

Slack off and ease down ... A rope can only take so much tension before it snaps. Sailors' cant from Temar Duchy. Her mother had been a ship's captain's daughter at the time she'd married. Thalia slipped her hand into the pocket hidden in the copious skirt of her dress and fingered the letter there, sent post haste from her father, and delivered the evening before. Scant words, scribbled in a hurry, cautiously cryptic in case it fell into the wrong hands, but full of joy and promise. *On our way, kitten. Hand-in-hand with Persons who appreciate the promise of sea breezes.* The message had puzzled her until she realised the capital letter for "Persons" was not a mistake.

'You look awful,' said Hazelle from across the room.

'I feel awful too. Ate some rich food in the market last night. Silly me.'

'Kaillan and Taygen are here.'

'Already? The sun is hardly up!'

'The acolyte who came with the message indicated Gerentia Agrina is *not* happy to have male visitors this early. She apparently is entertaining them.'

Thalia answered with a calm she didn't feel. 'Oh dear. She was excluded from my meeting with the Goddess last night and she wasn't pleased with that either. We had better rescue her.'

By the time they arrived in the waiting room, Taygen and Kaillan had apparently cajoled away most of the Mulierseer's peevishness, as she was calmly chatting with them both. *Goddess preserve me from these two*, Thalia thought. *They could charm the nose-ring from a talyak.*

She raised an inquiring eyebrow at Taygen when she noted he was carrying a polearm. She'd seen him practising with Hervan's men, who had been merciless with him, but he had not carried it the day before.

'Bought it last night,' he explained. 'Thought it might come in handy.'

Agrina frowned. 'There's no place for weaponry in this temple! This is not the Battleseer's territory.'

Wordlessly, and with a suitably contrite expression, he laid it down on the floor.

'Most Reverend,' Thalia said, 'last night I was privileged to receive the Goddess's guidance on how to proceed.' Not quite the whole truth, but it would do. The Goddess had actually seemed impatient and disgruntled, if either of those emotions could be attributed to a deity who had neither an audible voice, nor a visible face. 'Goddess Jenat is of the opinion that King Edwild needs to ... adjust to changes.' Nicely vague.

'He's not my concern. Nor is Prince Denniel my concern any more, as he is no longer a child. He is of age.'

Thalia quashed a rush of anger, raised her chin and delivered a chilly, '*I* am, though. I am a woman and a mother. And I have the Goddess's tacit assent to what I intend. We want you to get us into the Palace Precinct. In fact, into the palace. No one would ever refuse a gerentia entry.'

Hazelle laid a hand on Thalia's arm. 'I could use my redweaving,' she said brightly. 'Disguise us as Gerentia Agrina and an attendant priestess. Easy enough.' She gazed at Mulierseer as if committing her face to memory.

Agrina, horrified, sucked in her cheeks. 'You're not a redweaver!' she cried when she finally gathered her wits enough to speak. 'There's no colour anywhere around you. We've been checking you your whole life!'

'I was the one who wove the gate on the Crowbridge Road. That was the first time, so it is all rather recent. I have practised since, but not for a few days and the colour has faded now. Really, you have no need to fear me, Gerentia. I know what we owe to Goddess Jenat's temples over the years.'

The Mulierseer paled, then glared at Thalia. 'You let me believe that the Crowbridge gateway was opened up from inside Kanter!'

Kaillan quickly intervened. 'Most Reverend, I am here to make sure that all this runs smoothly today. Archpriests from both Saffrin's and Atticun's Temples will be keeping an eye out for redweaving inside the Palace Precinct. King Edwild has surely been concerned about the possibility of a red-weaver incursion ever since Prince Denniel was stolen away.'

Thalia shot him a look. 'Can't blame him for that.'

'Never mind,' Haze said, dismissing their reservations with an airy wave of her hand. 'I can create enough mayhem to keep everybody busy. And if the worse comes to the worst, I can open up an escape gateway for all of us.' She put on her most contrite expression, one Thalia knew well, as she added for Gerentia Agrina's benefit, 'I don't *want* to hurt anyone. I'm *not* Kanterine, for all that I was born there, but I *am* a redweaver. If you won't help us save the prince, I will use my weaving skills to do so.'

By now, all the colour had drained from the Mulierseer's face and Thalia wondered if the woman was going to faint.

'I think, Most Reverend,' Kaillan added quickly, 'it would be better if you were to gain us entry to the King. The Queen wants her son kept safe. Surely Goddess Jenat is on her side. We would not propose this otherwise.' That was true enough.

Thalia just wished the Goddess had slotted into Agrina's mind the same information that had been slotted into her own: the Goddess was fed up with King Edwild generally and his continued persecution of his queen in particular. The last impression Thalia had of Goddess Jenat's thoughts — borne inside a turbulent storm of whirling red — had been an exasperated feeling that it was a great pity that women didn't rule the world.

And something else she had not yet had time to consider: the Goddess had been hiding something.

Agrina's hands fluttered in distress. 'No one from our temple is exactly welcome in the palace now, as I am sure you must realise! The King knows you survive only because of the help we have afforded you. He'd see us all banished to another city, Goddess and all, if he could enforce it.'

Thalia inclined her head in acknowledgement. 'Then think: a queen in the palace once more.' She smiled. 'One who owes your temple and your goddess a debt too large to ever be paid in full!'

'You would go back to him?' the Mulierseer asked, astonished.

She shrugged. 'Who knows what will happen today?'

Just when the silence began to become embarrassing, a pale-faced Agrina slumped in capitulation, sinking back into her chair. 'I'll order my carriage. It will take all five of us.' Then, with one last spark of rebellion she glowered at Thalia. 'You are my queen, but be careful, Your Grace. It is a dire thing to upset a god with folly.'

'Oh, I agree,' she said. 'Now call for your carriage. Then, as soon as the curfew lifts, we can leave.'

Their gazes locked for a moment, then Gerentia Agrina left the room.

Taygen grinned. 'Formidable!'

Thalia waggled a finger at him. 'You don't have to come, you know. You are free now...'

389

Taygen shrugged. 'I love taking a risk. Failing of mine.'

'You won't be at risk,' Hazelle replied, looking him up and down. 'No one is going to take you seriously with that hair. Let alone recognise you as Hervan's son. You look like a badger with a bad haircut. And what's with the nose? It's even bigger than it was yesterday!'

He touched it, and winced. 'All to the good. I don't look like myself.'

'Huh! You'd do better to use that stick of yours as a crutch rather than as a weapon. Don't forget I know what your polearm skills are.' She paused and then amended her final word. 'Aren't.'

'I practiced with my father's men on the way here. Until they tied me up after Crowbridge. Ask the Queen.'

'On your head be it!' She turned to Thalia, her humour fading. 'What are you doing? Are you going back to the King? To be his queen? *After what he did to us?*'

'Don't be butterfly-brained, Haze. Of course not. Who mentioned that?'

'You did!'

'No, I didn't. We are going to the palace, not going to pay homage to the King. Right now, let's think about what to wear for this meeting. A widow's veil is in order, I think. I don't want anyone to recognise me before I am ready for it.'

*

Thalia, squeezed between Hazelle on one side and Agrina on the other, sat bolt upright in the carriage as it jolted its way across the cobbles. Taygen and Kaillan sat opposite. Their quarterstaves lay under the seat on the carriage floor. Haze had refused to wear a dress and had tied her hair at the nape of her neck like a lad. 'Just in case I need to fight,' she'd said. 'Or run.'

Thalia herself had borrowed a widow's crepe veil and was finding it hot and beyond irritating. 'Appalling garb,' she growled. 'Gerentia, this indignity is an insult to women.'

'The veil? Is it really that bad?'

'Horrible. Can't you discourage its use? And why no widower's veil? Pity Edwild didn't have to wear one when he "killed" me.' Her thoughts were in chaos, but she knew she appeared calm. Easy enough. She'd had plenty of practice over the years at keeping her fears to herself.

In contrast, the Mulierseer was hunched miserably on the seat next to her, pale and ill at ease. She'd given instructions they were to proceed as fast as possible, so one of the coach-men was squeezing the bulb of the carriage horn to clear the street ahead while the four taldeer pulled the vehicle at a spanking canter. Agrina shifted uneasily against the cushions of the seat with every bump of the carriage.

Oh gods, Thalia thought. *I have been so mean to her.* She touched Agrina's arm and said, 'Most Reverend, thank you for your help. I'm sure the Goddess will reward your loyalty.' A lie. She wasn't sure of anything, let alone the mind of a deity. She was still puzzling over the very last thing Goddess Jenat had slotted into her mind: *God Atticun and God Saffrin seem to have forgotten that we are all equals ... and it is time that they are reminded of that.*

But Atticun wasn't an equal. He was the Arch-god!

'No good can come of this,' Agrina whispered, but her tone was more of resignation than of rebellion. 'The prince has been raised in the Netherworld. By redweavers! I don't necessarily believe Kanterines are wicked—' she added to Kaillan, although her tone was dubious. 'However, we have been taught that redweaving is an evil, evil magic.' Turning back to Thalia, she added urgently, 'We do not know the nature of this man. We should return to the temple—'

Kaillan leaned forward to lay one of his crippled hands over hers. She shuddered, but he was relentless. 'Do you mean me, Most Reverend? Or the prince? I am a redweaver. Not a very skilled one, it's true. I do not believe I am a bad man. I helped to raise the prince. We are all here to undo the evil that was done when he was stolen from his cradle as a babe, his mother was left bereft, and a king lost his way. Today that evil will be undone. The King must acknowledge his son.'

'Change is not always good,' she muttered. 'He could be toppled from the throne. We could have another civil war between dukedoms.'

'Have faith in me,' Thalia said, the remark sharp-edged.

Kaillan acknowledged that remark with the slightest of smiles. 'What do we do when we reach the palace?'

'We'll split up. The Mulierseer and I will ask to see the King.'

'Will he already be back in the palace though?' Taygen asked. 'If he's been sleeping with his mistress in her townhouse—'

'An unmarked carriage with uniformed guards leaves the lady's house every morning around dawn,' Kaillan said.

Thalia nodded. 'Taygen, I'll rely on your hearing to tell us what's happening.'

'Will they object to the staves?' Haze asked.

'If they do, we'll say the Mulierseer needs walking sticks for the stairs. Taygen and Kaillan, as servants, will probably be sent to the servants' quarters on the ground floor.' She nodded at them both. 'Use that opportunity to search the palace for Denniel if you can; otherwise just talk to the servants. Kaillan: Taygen has incredible hearing. If an interloper has been found in the palace, someone somewhere will be talking about it and he'll hear it. And if Denniel spots *you*, at least he will know he's amongst friends.'

'There's no archpriest living inside the palace?' Kaillan asked.

'No,' Agrina replied. 'The King has always refused that.'

'If he's still the same man he was,' Thalia said, 'on an ordinary day he'd be with the Lord Chamberlain at this hour in the Privy Chamber. It's tradition. I doubt things will have changed much.'

She had a flash of memory: the King's desk, an enormous table so heavy it would take ten men to shift it. And there, on the side furthest from the King's chair, the symbol of his power, the Sword of Governance. A much bejewelled weapon, although in the past it had been a war blade when his great-great-grandfather, then Duke of the Riverland, had united the duchies under a king. 'He'll be unarmed, but there is some sort of ceremonial sword on the desk.'

'There won't be any hiding what we are after today,' Haze said. 'Once we are safe inside the palace, I can use my weaving to escape if need be.'

'Only if absolutely necessary.' She looked across at Kaillan. 'The King was there when you were questioned in *The Twill and the Rose*, wasn't he? Would he recognise you?'

Kaillan smiled. 'He was. But believe me, I don't look at all like Jordir. He was young and handsome, no scar on his face, no crippled hands.'

'Hmm,' she said, unconvinced.

'And what do Taygen and I do if we do find Denniel?' Kaillan asked.

'Bring him to wherever we are. Rely on Taygen's hearing,' she said. 'The Privy Chamber is one flight up the main stairs, third door on the left. Unlikely there will be any servants on that level at this hour. Servant quarters are top floor. They use the back stairs and at this hour they'll be cleaning the main bedrooms next floor down.'

'If the prince has already been found...' Agrina began, then faltered to a halt.

Thalia stilled. There it was again, that oddity that told her that it wasn't fear of the King, or even of the Goddess that made the Mulierseer nervous, but something else entirely. Change, perhaps? Some people did find that frightening.

The woman was worried about things changing.

'At least Edwild is not likely to call in half the barracks when he sees me,' she said. 'He'll be trying to keep this quiet.' She smiled slightly. 'If the Most Reverend will stand at my shoulder as witness, then we have a chance to negotiate something for all of us.' She laid a comforting hand on top of Agrina's.

White-faced and pinched around the mouth, Agrina muttered, 'King Edwild will not sit calmly at any negotiating table.'

'I know. Once, I hid to keep Denniel safe. Then I thought to keep Hazelle safe. Now it's time I came out into the open.'

'The monarchy...' Agrina began.

'Right now, my only aim is to see that nothing happens to Denniel. I'm praying that we are not too late. And hoping that Edwild will think it a bad policy to kill me a second time in front of you, Most Reverend.' She patted the back of Agrina's hand. 'All will be well, you'll see. Ah, here we are.'

The coach slowed, then pulled up at the gated archway that led into the Palace Precinct. The palace, the keep and the barracks of the King's Guard all lay within, surrounded by the parade grounds, the extensive gardens and the ornamental lakes, which would soon be open to the public for the midsummer festival.

She breathed deep. How many times had she passed under this stone arch with its carving of the royal griffin coat of arms? Too many to count. She'd thought herself happy then, but in truth she'd never felt truly at home. She'd always been on edge, worried she'd offend the Queen Mother or the court ladies with their cutting tongues. Always afraid she wouldn't please the King. Gods, she'd been such a *child* then. The Queen Mother had died since, and the thought of the ladies no longer intimidated her in the least.

Why ever had she acquiesced in the first place when her father had told her of Edwild's proposal of marriage? The offer had been flattering, of course. He had visited their duchy once with his first wife and he'd taken the time to listen to her thirteen-year-old prattle. But those reasons alone would not have been enough when she was seventeen. No, it was when she was told the coffers of her father's duchy would benefit if she agreed to the marriage. It was the promise that the question of a dowry would never be broached. No one had forced her, in fact her parents had been more reluctant than glad, but she was a good daughter, doing the right thing for the kingdom's poorest duchy.

Once, she had been meek and obedient.

Well, never again. And now, if she'd read that note correctly, her father had hinted by the word 'Person' that Temar had formed an alliance with Personata Duchy, offering them access to the ocean through Temar, or even giving them a port of their own. Their duke had been wanting such forever … Temar had bought themselves a powerful friend.

The officer in charge of the guards at the gate noted Goddess Jenat's insignia on the carriage door, glanced inside to salute the Mulierseer and signalled his men to give the carriage access to the grounds. A little later, as the carriage passed the King's Keep at a walk, Taygen peered up at the tower in silence. On the other side of the carriageway, the grass between the formal gardens and ornamental ponds was littered with tents and the pavilions being erected for the coming celebrations. Everywhere the bright blue coats of the King's Guards were visible, scattered among the workers and gardeners and entertainers just arriving through the tradesmen's gate.

'I won't leave your side, Thalia,' Hazelle said. 'I'm the only person who can get you out of there in a hurry if things go belly-up. That is, if you don't mind ending up somewhere in Kanter again. I hope I can build a gateway fast, but you need to keep close to my side.'

Agrina spluttered, momentarily speechless before gasping, '*Kanter?* You would go *back* there, voluntarily?'

'Not if I can help it,' Thalia said.

Agrina frowned at her. 'If we both get out of this alive, you and I have to have a serious talk. There are ... things that have to be decided.'

'I agree,' she replied. 'I think you know that the world has to change.' Agrina looked away, but Thalia glimpsed the tears in her eyes anyway. *I'm right. I'm sure I'm right. There's something else wrong that I don't yet know about...*

When the carriage pulled up once more, it was at the gateway to the palace grounds. Four guards on duty, the gate closed. She lowered her veil. 'Pull yourself together, Most Reverend,' she said.

Agrina, her face still drained of colour, fixed a haughty gaze on the officer who approached the carriage window, and said, 'The Mulierseer to see the King, at royal request.'

The guardsman did not question that assertion, but murmured a suitably deferential acknowledgement and gave the signal for the gates to be opened. The coach drove through and the taldeer proceeded at a sedate walk around the curve of the drive towards the unguarded main doors of the palace.

Thalia leant forward and raised her veil to study the facade and refresh her memory. Up there, on the third floor:

that had been her bedroom overlooking the walled Queen's garden. And those windows further along on the corner, that was Edwild's apartment. Scanning higher, her gaze snagged on an anomaly, an asymmetry in the perfect patterning of windows, architraves, gables, cornices and mouldings.

She grabbed Kaillan's arm. 'Look up there! Top floor. Does that look like broken glass in the open window beneath the eaves?' Her heart was thundering under her ribs, but her voice never wavered.

Kaillan ducked his head to see through the carriage window better. 'Yes, I see it. A broken pane. That's a rope coming down from the roof. See that? It disappears inside that same window.'

'Denniel,' she whispered, trying to convince herself of its truth. 'Must be.'

'He was always climbing. Training to go after the nesting esklet on the cliffs.'

'What room is it?' Haze asked Thalia.

'Servant quarters. I never went up to that floor.' How odd. Almost two years living in the palace and there was a whole floor she'd never even seen. 'The room beneath is the King's bedchamber.' Thoughts jumbled, a mix of terror and despair and fear.

If he has been caught...

No, wait. If they'd caught him, wouldn't they have removed the rope? Straightened the shutter? Would the gardens not be teeming with armed guards? Her hands remained neatly folded in her lap, but she had to push away another wave of nausea.

So long. So much fear.

She must not lose courage now. Deep breath. Shoulders back. Chin lifted.

'Clever lad,' Haze murmured. 'Brave, too. I like him already.'

The carriage came to a halt. Taygen reached for the handle of the door, but Thalia shook her head. 'We wait for the footman. We arouse no suspicion. Most Reverend, everyone, compose yourselves. The Mulierseer descends first, then me, then the three of you. You will remain at least two paces behind us, Kaillan in the middle. Carry the polearms as if they are wayfarer staffs, not weapons. Look sleepy, bored, not alert.'

She watched as one of Agrina's coachmen mounted the steps to the main door. Protocol demanded the palace footmen within wait for the bell before opening the doors. She shuddered slightly, reminded of a life governed by the unwritten laws of tradition.

The bell was pulled and two footmen emerged, dressed in satin pantaloons and beribboned shoes, garb that was a fashion tradition from an era long gone. She watched as the coachman delivered their message: *The Mulierseer, Gerentia Agrina, has a crucially important matter to discuss with the King. The Mulierseer regrets the lack of appointment, but begs an urgent audience...*

'No sign of anything amiss,' she said quietly. Although neither of the footmen were old enough to have been around when she was queen, she wore her veil, hating the heavy, suffocating blackness of it. 'He's not been found yet, if he's here.'

Agrina's eyebrows snapped together in a frown, but she said nothing. The coachman returned to let down the carriage steps and open the door for her. He held out his hand to assist his mistress to dismount. 'Stay with the carriage,' she told him. 'Both of you. Be ready to leave.'

Thalia raised a hand to her neck, checking with her fingers that her fichu was still in place covering the carcanet at her throat, and followed. 'Remember, you are unimportant servants. Keep behind us,' she murmured to the others. As they mounted the steps up to the double entrance doors, now thrown fully open, her hands started to tremble. Chiding herself for being so stupidly timid, she clutched her skirts and followed the Mulierseer into the entrance hall.

This could be the day...

It was just as she remembered it: a large, cold space, built to impress, not to welcome. A few chairs placed against walls crowded with portraits of past kings and their families. Directly in front of her, the main staircase swept upwards. On the wall at the back of the landing, where the stairs parted to sweep around in matching curves to the next floor, her portrait still hung next to one of the King. Painted in her coronation gown when she was seventeen, she had the slightest of smiles hovering on her lips. The royal diamonds around her neck and the crystals and pearls glittering on her dress were all faithfully portrayed. Not so accurate was the calm tranquillity of her expression. Weighted down by the rich brocade and train of her coronation apparel, worried the oversized and weighty Crown would topple, all she'd felt was discomfort. Gods, but she had been so young.

Pickle you, Edwild! All these years and you've calmly kept my portrait looking at you, while your men hunted me like a trophy animal to be stuffed?

She tore her gaze away.

'We wish to speak to the King,' Gerentia Agrina said, addressing the footman now bowing formally to her. Her voice quavered, but fortunately it made her sound elderly rather than scared.

'His Majesty is closeted with the Lord Chamberlain in the Privy Chamber. If you will follow me, I will escort you to the reception room to await His Majesty's pleasure.' Having no idea who Thalia could be, he ignored her, but pointed to one of the side doors and politely suggested to Gerentia Agrina that perhaps her other attendants would prefer to wait in the servants' hall?

'Indeed,' the Mulierseer said, and waved Kaillan and Taygen away. 'I will keep my personal attendants, however,' she added, indicating Haze and Thalia.

The reception room was just to the side of the stairs, and the moment they were ushered in, Agrina seated herself on the nearest chair as if exhausted. Once the footman had left, shutting the door behind him, she muttered, 'He always does this.'

'Who?' Thalia asked.

'The King. Keeps me waiting in here. Just to show he considers the Goddess a lesser being than God Atticun. He'll send Ashwendon down to fetch me after I have waited a suitable time. Everything feels normal. Which means it's unlikely Denniel has been found here.'

'The more uninterrupted time Taygen and Kaillan have to look for Denniel, the better,' said Thalia. She sighed. 'I really never did like Ashwendon. It would be *much* better if he wasn't around when I meet up with Edwild.'

38

The last time Thalia had seen the Lord Chamberlain Ashwendon was the day Denniel had been stolen. Ashwendon had been cruelly rude. Now, when he entered the waiting room, she was confronted by a grey-haired, frail old man leaning heavily on a walking stick, but her dislike resurfaced in a flood of bitter memory.

'Most Reverend,' he said with a nod to the Mulierseer, 'this is most unexpected. You have not graced these halls in some time, I believe.'

'Indeed not,' Agrina snapped back as she stood. 'For reasons I believe you know full well. However, matters have come to a head and I need to see the King. Urgently.'

Thalia moved up to stand at her side, her lack of a curtsey an indication that she considered him an equal. He stared at her, frowning, unable to penetrate her veil, before turning his attention back to Agrina. 'In that case, please accompany me. Your servants may await you here—'

'I am no servant, sir,' Thalia said, 'and *my* attendant'—she indicated Haze with a languid wave of her hand—'comes with me. You, on the other hand, do not.' She pulled her veil away and dropped it on the floor, revealing not only her face, but the carcanet as well.

He stared at her, taken aback. 'Who are you?' he asked, but didn't wait for an answer, pointing instead at Hazelle. 'You! No one enters the King's presence with a weapon.'

Haze raised an eyebrow and smiled as she stepped up to Thalia's side and cheekily thumped her quarterstaff firmly down between them. 'Do you want me to knock him out, Your Grace?' she asked.

Incredulity rooted Ashwendon to the spot. Speechless, he stared at Haze, then back at Thalia, but this time his stare fixated on the carcanet.

Thalia smiled. 'Don't think of calling for assistance from anyone, Ashwendon. That would be *most* unwise, don't you think?' An incoherent splutter emerged from his mouth, so she continued, 'You once called me an ignorant girl from a fishing village. Do you remember? *I* do. Now, you will do as I say, in silence, or I will tell my servant here to use that polearm to jab you hard in the danglers. Oh, and consider this before you rouse the palace to our intrusion: there will still be those on the staff here who remember Thalia of Temar.' She smiled at him, mocking, enjoying his expression of utter shock, followed by increasing horror. 'Haze, my dear, do you think you could open a gateway? Because I rather like the idea of removing him from my sight.'

Haze grinned and nodded.

Mired in outrage, Ashwendon finally found his tongue again. '*You!* You *dare* to return here?' He switched his attention back to the Mulierseer and waggled a finger at her. 'And you: you're to blame for hiding her all these years!'

'You're the one who aided the King in committing the crime,' Agrina replied with a cold calm. 'Telling the land the Queen and her son had died, when both still lived. You should be grovelling at her feet, you miserable excuse for a courtier!'

But he was already turning away from her to Thalia. 'You traitorous Temar slut. Do you think you will get away with this? You are still under sentence of death. You're a fool!'

'I was never sentenced,' she said with a deliberately blithe wave of her hand. 'Sentencing implies a court case, a hearing of some kind. I was just hunted down. The only reason the King's men wanted me brought back was so Edwild could view my murdered corpse. A fool, sir? I've kept myself safe for eighteen years while the best of the King's men searched, but could not find me. We'll see who's the fool. I've eighteen years of anger burning inside me. Today is the day things change.'

'You think that old crone will help you?' he asked, nodding towards Agrina. 'The King has God *Atticun* on his side!'

'And Gerentia Agrina serves a goddess who represents *all* women, no matter where they worship. Think on that!'

'You won't leave this palace alive. One young man with a staff won't keep you safe!' Turning to the Gerentia, he continued, 'Where are your wits, woman? This is the King's palace! You threaten the peace of the nation bringing this ... this runaway harlot here?'

'I am merely a witness. To see the Goddess's justice done.' Agrina's words were strong, but she was ashen-faced.

Thalia raised a questioning eyebrow at Haze, who replied, 'I've finished. It opens in front of the red settee.'

'Put him inside.'

'With pleasure.' Haze stepped between them and poked at him with her pole, prodding him gently in the stomach until he was forced backwards towards the settee, spluttering incoherent, angry protests all the way. When he vanished from Thalia's sight, Haze said, grinning, 'He just thumped down on his arse in the passage. He looks rather shocked. He can see and hear us still, even though you can't hear or see him.'

'Can you see where it leads?'

'Looks to be some sort of meadow. Quite a short passage. If he's wise, he won't move.'

Thalia nodded. 'Ashwendon, listen carefully. You are now between Talodiac and Kanter. I assume you know what that means. Haze here is closing the gateway you just stepped through. Stay where you are and we will open the way back later, when I'm finished with the King.'

It didn't take Haze long. 'It's easier than I thought,' she remarked a little later. 'He's not at all happy.'

'I don't care. Don't look so appalled, Most Reverend. He deserved no consideration. We could have killed him. Let's go.' She threw back her shoulders and marched out of the door, heading for the stairs. One of the footmen was still on duty by the main doors, but all he did was spring to attention, staring straight ahead. Thalia hid a smile. A servant showing too much interest in a guest was considered inappropriate. Ridiculous protocol that now worked in her favour.

When she reached the landing, she paused to gaze up at the painting and give the Mulierseer time to catch up. 'That's a good likeness,' she remarked. 'Just add a few lines and a few grey hairs. I rather like the idea that I'm still there up on the wall, reminding Edwild every day that I'm still alive.' As she continued upwards, she added, 'I want no trouble, Agrina. I hope to avoid it.'

Haze pulled a disbelieving face at her, but it was the Mulierseer's gaze she felt boring into her back in troubled disbelief. Poor Agrina; she hadn't asked for any of this.

At the top of the stairs, Thalia set off along the passage, slowing down to allow Agrina to catch up once more so that they all arrived at the door to the Privy Chamber together.

There was no one around, no servants in evidence.

'Are you sure the King will be here?' Haze asked in a whisper.

'This was his usual routine. He never used to breakfast if he was out late at night.' Without knocking, she grasped the handle, pushed the door inward, only to wave the Mulierseer in first, deliberately tucking herself behind.

Denniel, she thought. *Where are you?*

39

As soon as they had passed through the door that closed off the servants' quarters from the rest of the house, Kaillan halted. He tapped his ear, asking Taygen to listen.

They were standing at the head of a long passage with doors along either side, some of them open. At the far end a set of stairs led upwards. Someone hurried out of a door on the right carrying a laden basket and disappeared through a door on the left. Taygen opened himself up to sound, gradually allowing everything audible to register in his hearing. Quickly he dismissed most of the background sounds — a crackling fire, pots bubbling on a stove, the sound of a scrubbing brush, water being poured — and homed in on the conversations.

Don't mix that in with the lard ... you're a pickle head for thinking to git under her skirts ... is Bridika from the bedrooms yet? ... ye'll no get to the mummery less you finish yer work today...

'Nothing that matters,' he whispered to Kaillan. 'Everyday stuff. But someone is following us from the front door.'

'Quick, up the servant stairs ahead. Walk as though we know exactly what we're doing.' With that, he set off, looking neither to right nor left. A girl came out of one of the rooms carrying a dish piled high with fruit and bustled past in the opposite direction without even acknowledging their presence.

Trailing behind, Taygen absorbed the sounds around him, horribly aware he was now an intruder in the Royal Palace, in the company of a redweaver, a crime that truly merited a sojourn in the King's Keep. How was it he always jumped from the bubbling pot into the flipping fire?

Shit. Tamp it down, Tay, you squawker; mind on the job.

They started up the servants' stairs. Once on the floor above, they paused again while he assessed the sounds. 'There's quite a few people on this floor,' he whispered. 'Some kind of housekeeper talking about supplies. Someone else talking payments. Nothing that could refer to Denniel.'

'Common rooms on this floor. Dining, reception, drawing rooms, salons, library. Plus the King's work rooms and Privy Chamber. Let's try next floor up first,' Kaillan murmured. They continued, passing a maid carrying a mop and bucket downstairs. She stared at them, but said nothing.

The upper floor was quieter, but he could still hear the chatter if he listened carefully. A maid and a woman discussed what m'lady should wear. A fellow complained about the smell of a pisspot.

'This is mostly the private apartments of courtiers and the royal family,' Kaillan said, looking around.

'How the sweet lickspits do you *know* all this stuff?'

He flashed a wry grin. 'Pox 'n' rot, Taygen, I was the pisser who had to plan the theft of Denniel, remember? Mongrave ordered it and I was left with working out how to pull it off, which meant finding out which were the Queen's rooms. I got hold of a plan.'

'Oh.' He swallowed back his shock.

'Aye, there's plenty of foul misery staining my hands, lad. That's one reason why I'm doing my best to make amends. Not that it's possible. How can you unweave the horror of what we did?' He sighed. 'Just can't.'

'Oh.' He was fairly certain the Kanterine now had a more personal reason to try. He'd seen how the fellow looked at the Queen, that odd mix of admiration, concern and, yes, something more if he wasn't mistaken. Reverence? Love? Both, perhaps. The man was younger than he'd expected, and it startled him to realise that Kaillan Riverdell could not have been out of his twenties when he was caught and tortured.

'Nothing here that could be about Denniel,' he said, after listening some more.

'Then let's see if we can find the room with the broken window. Upstairs one more stage.'

The rooms on the top floor were darker and smaller, the corridors narrower, the floorboards unpolished, the windows meaner. As far as Taygen could hear, there was no one on this floor at all. Servants didn't linger in their own bedrooms when there was work to do.

He had to admire how quickly Kaillan managed to orient himself. The fellow walked briskly down a narrow passage to his right, then opened a door. The room was an unused bedroom and the glass from the broken window still lay on the bed beneath. Kaillan looked around. 'He's good, isn't he, this prince of ours? Able to find an unused room in a palace of rooms.'

'How could he do that?' Taygen asked, impressed.

Kaillan bent to look under the bed. 'At a guess? No candle or lamp showing at the window late last night at a time when staff members would have been in their rooms. Figure he came into the precinct yesterday, spent the day working erecting a stage or something. Hid when everyone else was leaving. Once the moons set — last night that'd be about three bells — he used one of the ladders left lying around by the workers to climb on to the top of the wall surrounding the palace. From there he tossed the ladder away and jumped down into the palace garden.'

He crossed the room to look in the cupboards. 'Once there, he would have made his way up to the roof, using all the nooks and crannies of them pretty windowsills and frames 'n' such to haul himself up. Probably carried a coil of rope over his shoulder. Fine climber, that lad. Trained by our best. To go after the esklet nests. Beasts that attack us from the skies, you know. Anyway, sometime he swung down from the roof, broke the glass, and entered. Right above the King's set of rooms.'

'He couldn't possibly know that, could he?'

'Don't underestimate the lad. King's apartment has the biggest windows, plus it's a corner room.'

'Where d'you reckon he is now?'

'Not here, for sure, and no sign he ever was except for the rope and broken glass. Tell me, if you were him, where would you go if you wanted to talk to your pa the King, without anyone interfering?'

'Ah. His bedroom. If the King wasn't there, I'd hide out until he put in an appearance. Catch him alone so I could tell him what a bag of maggot-ridden worm-shit he is.'

'That's what I figure. Let's go. We just have to hope that he isn't found by some chambermaid or such in the meantime.'

They backtracked to the floor below, where Taygen was assailed by sounds from all sides the moment they started down the corridor. 'There's staff all over the place,' he warned in a whisper. 'Some fancy fellas as well, talking about what brooches to wear.'

Kaillan nodded. 'Tell me if you think anyone is likely to step out into the passage.'

Taygen walked beside him, enjoying the surge of excitement that always came with lawbreaking. It made him feel so damned *alive*.

'This must be it,' Kaillan whispered a short time later, indicating double doors with large ornate handles set within an elaborately carved door frame.

'Poxy pretentious,' Taygen said. There was even a small table outside the door, its sole purpose apparently to display a carved onyx ornament.

'Hear anything?'

He shook his head and picked up the carving to take a closer look. It was a mythical unicorn and given its small size, it had an impressive horn. It also had what appeared to be opals inserted for eyes.

'Then here we go. Be it we run into trouble, I'll rustle up some redweaving to confuse things, but I'm a lousy weaver, I warn you.'

He opened the door and they stepped inside. Taygen put the figurine back and followed. Kaillan closed the door behind them and held a finger to his lips. Carefully they looked around.

To Taygen's surprise, it wasn't one room; it was several. They were in an anteroom made comfortable with chairs, a table and an ornate fireplace. A door on the right led into a dressing room with wardrobe and padded bench; a second opened into the large main bedroom with two canopied beds. A cursory look indicated that there was no one there.

On the other side of the main bedroom, a mean, narrow door led into a servant's bedroom with a truckle bed and no window. Kaillan checked that out, but it too was empty and devoid of anywhere to hide. Yet another door led to the Queen's apartments.

Back in the main bedroom, Kaillan raised a questioning eyebrow. Taygen closed his eyes and listened. The faintest of rustles, so slight that normally he would not have heard it, tickled his hearing. 'In the wardrobe,' he whispered.

Kaillan grinned. 'Denniel, it's me, Kaillan. You can come out. You are among friends, though I'm as furious as a bee-bitten talyak, you chaff-stuffed grasshopper!'

The rustle in the wardrobe became more audible, the door creaked open and a tall, slim, fair-headed lad stepped out. His glance focused on Taygen's quarterstaff, then slid

409

across to where Kaillan stood. The astonishment on his face was comical. '*Kaillan?* How the blighted—?'

'Tush up! Got to get out of here, quick,' Kaillan said, grabbing his arm and dragging the utterly flabbergasted Denniel towards the passage door. Taygen cracked it open to poke his head out.

The prince opened his mouth to say something, but Kaillan made a chopping sign with his hand. 'Quiet. This is Taygen who's helping us. Your mother is looking for you and she's downstairs, probably with the King by now. I've no idea how any of this is going to end, but end it does, today. And there's no need to gape at me like a fish out of water!'

There was a short silence, then a raised eyebrow and a soft-spoken query. 'Can I roll my eyes quietly instead?'

Taygen smothered a laugh.

The corridor was empty, so Kaillan hustled the bemused prince in the direction of the main stairs. Taygen pulled the bedroom door shut behind him. He wanted to protest that it might have been safer to head back down the servants' stairway, but decided this wasn't the time for a discussion. Instead, he grabbed the onyx unicorn as he passed the table in the passage, hooking a leg of the carving into his belt in order to leave both hands free for his quarterstaff. Behind Kaillan's back he winked and grinned at Denniel and was rewarded with a genuine roll of the eyes.

'The Goddess Jenat's Mulierseer is with your mother,' Kaillan whispered, 'and there's also a relatively untried redweaver called Hazelle on our side. Young woman. Your changeling.'

'A *woman?*'

'Long story. Looks more like a lad, at the moment. Carries a quarterstaff too. By now they could all be in the Privy Chamber, next floor down. That's where we'll go first.'

'Good to see you again, too, sir,' Denniel said dryly. 'And glad to make your acquaintance, Taygen,' he added, inclining his head in polite acknowledgement with all the aplomb of someone at a town council function.

Taygen sucked in his cheeks. Pox 'n' rots, aristos were all bleeding insane. Still, he had a feeling he was going to like the prince. 'The pleasure's all mine,' he said. 'Possibly that is; if I can keep my head attached to my neck after today.'

'Muzzle it!' Kaillan was barely even whispering, but still managed to sound annoyed. Then his gaze locked with Denniel's and softened. 'It's good to see you too,' he murmured. 'Been too long, lad.' He reached out to place a hand on his shoulder. 'I've missed you. And y'mam's been waiting your whole lifetime.'

He turned away and continued into the main corridor at the far end. Taygen grinned. 'Welcome to our band of barmy budgers,' he whispered. When Denniel gave him a blank look, he added, 'Budgers. Housebreakers. Only the house just happens to be a pissing great palace.'

Kaillan glared at him over his shoulder, and he subsided, which was probably just as well, for when they reached the staircase three women were already ahead of them on their way down, laughing and chattering as they went. *Aristos,* Taygen thought. Real ones, if his glimpse of their embroidered jackets and feathered hats was anything to go by.

With a shrug, Kaillan started down after them, apparently confident they would not look back. When the women continued on their way down to the ground floor, they all relaxed a little. Kaillan halted and pointed along the first-floor corridor. 'Third door on the left.'

Taygen nodded and took the lead, relieved there was no one else around. He halted in front of the door to listen, but the solid heavy wood blocked all normal sounds except for a faint murmur of conversation.

He laid his ear to the centre panel.

His next words were a heartfelt, 'Oh, godsdamn!'

Clutching his quarterstaff tight, he leaned on the handle to throw the door open.

40

More than eighteen years had passed since Thalia had last put foot into the Privy Chambers. The moment she opened the door, she choked on memories. Newly married, she had made it her task to bring the King his nuncheon at noon if he had not already emerged from work at his desk. She had been young and pretty and sweet enough to receive a smile for the interruption, rather than censure.

How silly she had been. How naïve.

The public chamber was a long, narrow room with high windows running down one side. On the opposite wall a large fireplace was flanked by two life-sized portraits, one of Edwild's father, the previous king, and the other of his late mother, wearing a court dress and the Griffin Carcanet.

A few straight-backed chairs were scattered against the walls, but the centre of the room had always been clear of all furniture. Anyone entering had to walk twenty paces or more before they even reached the desk at the other end. The solid carved chair on the far side of this ornate piece of furniture was where the King sat to deal with the more mundane daily business of the kingdom and read the reports from the Treasury, the Chancellory and the duchies.

Where he sat now.

At the back of the room another door, now closed, led only into the King's retiring room with its attached garderobe. All was as she had remembered.

Edwild, dressed plainly in his morning clothes, quill in one hand, sat behind the desk. In his fifties now. Hairline receding. Face jowled. A sag to the shoulders, more weight where there had once been muscle.

He's aged poorly.

'Haze,' she whispered, 'Move away from me. Don't let him near the bell-pull on the wall behind him.'

Edwild had looked up when they entered, his expression changing to one of puzzled distaste when he saw the Mulierseer and surprise when he realised Ashwendon was missing. He rose, his eyebrows pulled together in a way that she'd once found intimidating. This time it was Agrina he fixed with his hard, disapproving stare.

'The reception room would have been more appropriate, Most Reverend,' he said. 'I expected Ashwendon to show you there.'

'I had no wish to be kept waiting,' the Mulierseer remarked with studied calm, 'so we elected to come along. I fear that Lord Ashwendon has been unavoidably detained ... elsewhere.'

Frostily dismissive, he said, 'Your visit is most unexpected. And who are these people? I had not scheduled time for a meeting. *Your* temple's unscheduled business is hardly of such import to the monarchy.'

Thalia stepped from behind the Mulierseer and began a deliberately slow advance down the middle of the room towards the desk, chin held high. 'Oh, really, Edwild?' she drawled, glad to hear her voice was steady. 'Considering the amount that Jenat's Temple and their arch-clergy know about *our* personal affairs, that's very condescending of you.'

He remained where he was, blank-faced, not recognising her and momentarily stupefied at being so bluntly addressed by a stranger.

'This is not a visit to exchange pleasantries,' she continued, fingering the carcanet. 'Gerentia Agrina is here merely to bear witness to the conversation you and I are to have, to ensure my safety and to attest, if necessary, to any agreement we may decide upon.'

She halted halfway down the room to tilt her head at him and raise an eyebrow. Nerves perhaps, but her amusement was real as she saw recognition dawn, then shatter into shock. She pursed her lips to prevent a laugh escaping and allowed herself a moment to enjoy his appalled disbelief and the way his face drained of colour, only to redden a moment later as his fury mounted. He had to take a deep breath, heaving the air into his chest because he had forgotten to inhale.

Fear nibbled at her calm, but she quelled it. He was just a man. A small man who had lacked the vision to deal with a tragedy, lacked it when he'd needed it most.

His untrammelled rage spilled over. 'How *dare* you come here! How dare you!'

'How dared you bury me before I was dead?' she asked calmly. 'How dared you raise a statue in my honour, even as you had your men scour the country to bring me back so you could murder me? How dared you keep my portrait on the stairs as if you wished to remember me?' She continued her approach, feeling more vulnerable now that she was alone in the centre of the room. 'How dared you not do everything in your power to have our son returned to us? How dared you not even tell me *why*?'

She paused briefly again before she reached the desk. A quick sideways glance told her Haze, while level with her, had drifted towards the fireplace with the Mulierseer dropping behind.

Good. She wanted Edwild's eyes on her.

Resuming her measured approach, she added, 'After all these years of searching high and low for me, I thought you'd be pleased when I came to you instead. I'm sick of running. I'm here, Edwild. Today we talk.'

'You fled your duty, madam. You disgraced your position. You rejected your obligations and debased your birth. You were never worthy of what was given you. I'm ordering your arrest! You were unfit—'

She stopped several paces in front of the desk and held up a hand in an attempt to halt his words, but had to talk over the top of his continued litany of complaints. 'Don't be ridiculous, Edwild. Just how would you explain my sudden appearance if you were to ask your men to imprison me?'

'I'll put a bloody sack over your head, woman!' he shouted. 'No one will ever know who you are! I'll have you hanged as an impostor...'

He lurched for the cloth bell-pull on the wall behind him, but by then Haze was already there. Her staff slammed upwards to crack against his wrist. He yelped in shock and pain, twisting away from her to clutch his arm to his chest in outraged disbelief.

For a sliver of time, his astonishment left him speechless. Then he turned on Haze in a fury. 'How *dare* you! Who are you? I'll see you dead for this—' The swish of the polearm under his nose brought his step forward to an abrupt halt.

Haze smiled at him. 'Oh, you've tried *that* once already. You didn't succeed then, and you won't now either.' She gently poked the end of her staff into his stomach as he reached for the bell-pull once more. 'Don't do that,' she said, pitching her voice into a lower register, knowing this was not the time to declare herself a woman. 'I go by the name of Haze Wayfarer, but I am the changeling child that you wanted to murder to keep another crime quiet.'

Her words rendered him speechless yet again.

'Calm down, Edwild, if you will,' Thalia said. She stepped forward, planted her hands on the desktop and leaned in towards him. 'And think. Will you ask Gerentia Agrina to un-remember me? Or will you have her murdered too? Along with her coachmen awaiting us outside and the sisters in Goddess Jenat's temple, all of whom know who I am and

416

where I am right now? And what about your own footmen who saw me arrive? Are you really so unwise as to tug on the bell-pull?'

'This is my palace, woman,' he said, nursing his sore wrist against his chest. 'I rule here. Not you. Not Goddess Jenat, either.'

'Best spend time considering how to keep my presence here ... unobserved, then. We can leave quietly when we're ready to do so. I can veil myself as I did when I arrived. But before that happens, you and I are going to have a considered discussion in front of the Mulierseer, in which you will undertake to leave me alone to live my life. Hunting me down has got to stop.'

He switched his glare to Agrina. 'I thought you hellions had tied her tongue with your baffle! You're to blame for this.' Leaning over the desk, he snatched the ceremonial sword out of its cradle. Haze stepped up to the side of the desk in warning, so he slammed the flat of the blade down on the table in front of her with sufficient force to send documents flying. 'Thalia, if this lackey of yours approaches me, he'll get this through his belly!'

Haze ignored the flying papers and maintained an expressionless stare, even as she held her staff at the ready.

Edwild swallowed, possibly realising that her polearm had a longer reach, took another deep breath and gathered his wits. 'Is he really the changeling?' he asked, his tone demanding an answer of Thalia. 'A *Kanterine*? You've brought someone from Kanter into the palace? Are you insane?'

He pointed the sword tip at Haze. 'Drop that polearm now if you expect to leave this room alive.'

This last was quietly said, but Thalia thought she caught a tinge of uncertainty in his tone. He feared redweaving. Good. She calmed her racing heart and contained her fear, reaching instead for courage honed sharp by years of flight and the certainty of all that was owed to her.

This confrontation, she thought, *is the culmination of half of my life. This is the one I will win.*

She smiled politely. 'We are here to redress a wrong. A wrong done to all of us, but especially to Haze Wayfarer and to our son.'

'You presume too much on my breeding, madam. No man of standing, let alone a king, could tolerate your past behaviour. You are beyond redemption!'

'*My* behaviour, sir? What about the conduct of a man who wanted to slaughter a child, all while believing that such an act would ensure the death of his only son and heir?'

'And me?' Haze asked. 'What makes you think I should die, sire? A Kanterine baby is no different from a Talodian infant. But then, I could have been stolen from anyone, even a citizen of Templebridge. You had no knowledge of my origins.'

'You came through a woven gate!'

'I believe you were never told that,' she said. 'It just suited you to think it. And why were you so eager *not* to bargain with the redweavers to save your son?'

Thalia sucked in her cheeks to halt a laugh. She might have known Haze would not be silenced by the presence of a monarch. *Gods,* she thought, *how much I love this daughter I have raised!*

Edwild blazed a furious look at the Mulierseer. 'Madam, you know the answer to that! You surely understand what I did.' He turned back to Thalia. 'You want to know what they wanted? They wanted free entry to our land with their magic. They wanted food. They wanted weapons. Why? They spoke of flying monsters as if we are children to believe in such things!'

'And they spoke the truth sir! See this scar on my cheek? The spittle of one those monsters did that. Speak not of things you do not know, Edwild.'

He spluttered speechless for a moment, then shouted, even as he waggled his finger at Agrina, 'They would have conquered us the moment there were enough of them inside our lands! Ask her. Ask any of the gerents. They will all tell you the danger of bargaining with redweavers. We *knew* what they were — we know now! They stole my son. They will flood our land with their warriors and their spells and their deceptions. I had no choice! I *still* have no choice. Even now we are finding a few who manage to slip through.'

'A few?' Thalia asked, puzzled, remembering all the information they had discovered in Kanter, and all that she now knew from Kaillan. 'A *few*?'

'Our soldiers keep our people safe,' he snapped. 'My Royal Guards and the squads and the battalions under the Battleseer's command in the service of God Saffrin. Men and women. That's their task and it's my duty to see they do it.'

Agrina stayed silent, so Thalia asked, 'You are ignorant of the thousands of Kanterines scattered throughout Talodiac, trading their wealth for our goods and food in order to feed and protect their people? There are woven gateways in cities all across our duchies! True, there are not many ordinary folk from the Netherworld now seeking refuge here, because they are so ill-used if found, but plenty of redweavers and Kanterine traders come and go. Many ordinary Kanterines have been here for years posing as merchants.'

The look the King gave her was blank, uncomprehending. *Sweet goddess, he really doesn't know.*

'Innata,' Agrina whispered in warning. 'Have a care.'

She heard the admonition and filed it away to think about later. It could have meant nothing, but it was another ember for the continued kindling of her understanding. 'Edwild, you really don't know, do you?'

'You've lost whatever few peasant wits you ever had!'

'No, it's just that I've learned so much in the past couple of months. And I think the gods and their gerents have kept so much from you. You think the army is yours to command, but I think they serve God Saffrin first. The arch-clergy don't serve you; they report to their gerents. The gerents don't always tell you what they discover. The man who stole our son? All he wanted from us was compassion for his people, but you wouldn't listen. Instead it was the Lawseer's advice you took.'

'You have lost your reason, lady.' His contempt was thick, but she saw fear in the flicker of his eyes. 'They took our son!'

She persisted, intrigued, sickened, still sorting through her own thoughts in search of the truth. 'Did your men not question Captain Hervan on his return to Templebridge recently? Did he not tell them that Haze and I mysteriously disappeared along the road to Crowbridge in a way that could have only been through a redwoven gate?'

'What lies are these, woman? Where is your truth?' Something about the way he tilted his head told her that his puzzlement was genuine. She was shocked. *Someone lied to him about that? Lied to their king?*

Her thoughts tumbled. Hervan might not have been able to see the weaving that night, but he surely knew exactly what had happened. He'd pulled Taygen back through a woven gateway on the Crowbridge Road. He must have known what he was doing, even though he couldn't see the weaving himself. Normally he would have reported immediately to the King on returning to Templebridge, but Edwild had not been in the city ...

Therefore ...

420

The Battleseer of God Saffrin had been informed first. And Cyrrin had taken Taygen to the Keep.

She said quietly, 'No lies at all, Edwild. I have been to the Netherworld. Kanter, as they call it. And I have returned, safely, to find that Gerentia Agrina was already aware of what happened to us — but *you* were not apprised of that? You weren't told that I disappeared through a gateway into Kanter? The gerents have been keeping secrets from the King?'

He gave her another uncomprehending stare. 'You truly have lost your mind, woman!'

Agrina winced. She approached Thalia, reaching out to grip her upper arm. 'Please, milady, I am not sure this is wise ... Goddess Jenat has not advised me of what to do. She is yet considering...'

Thalia, still shocked, glared at her. 'You knew. Goddess Jenat knew. *And the King didn't?*'

Agrina moaned in anguish. 'This is not your business, Milady. Please—'

'Do *not* underestimate me,' Thalia said, addressing both her and Edwild. 'Things change here, today. For all of us. For Denniel. For Haze. For me. And yes, for you too, Edwild.'

As if in answer, the door to the room burst open and Taygen and Kaillan entered side by side. Everyone turned to look, but the only person Thalia saw was the young man behind them.

The room — and everyone else in it — vanished from her consideration.

She knew him immediately. And etched him instantly into her memory, made him the image of the love she'd always had in her heart.

Tall and fair and lithe ... Her son.

She did not need to be told.

Denniel had come home.

41

Haze's first thought was one of relief.
They've found him.

He was a slimmer, taller, softer version of his father; his features less harsh, his stance less pugnacious. No one could doubt his paternity, though; it was sculpted into his features.

But he has Thalia's eyes, she thought, and was glad of that.

And even more glad to see Taygen unhurt and grinning at her.

She glanced at the King, now standing at the side of the desk. He'd paled so much she wondered if he might faint. Every nerve in her body was screaming at her to stay sharp, to hold herself in readiness. She moved closer to him, to where she was also in a better position to keep an eye on everyone. Kaillan jammed the door handle shut with the back of a chair.

King Edwild still held the ceremonial sword, weighing it in his hand in open threat. A king would surely know how to use a weapon, even one that might have been sitting un-sharpened on a desk for twenty years. Still, it had only half the reach of her quarterstaff. She could disarm him. But should she? She dithered. Fester it, a king had the power of life and death, no questions asked.

Rot it. Stay sharp, girl...

The Mulierseer, grey and pale and exasperated at the King's obtuseness, cried, 'Don't you understand even now? That's Prince Denniel! The heir to your throne.' She waggled a pointed finger from the King to where Denniel stood just inside the door. '*Your* heir. Your past is coming back to haunt you, Your Majesty. Wake up!'

'My *son*?' he asked, and the word was scathing. 'How do I know that? I did not raise him. *If* he lives still, he was taken to Kanter and raised as our enemy and he cannot inherit the throne! How do I know who this fellow is? Thalia's been roaming the country like a loose tinker woman. She could have had another child and be trying now to pass him off as mine. She was scum from a stinking fishing village of a duchy, not fit to be a monarch's—'

Agrina took Thalia's place leaning on the desk, to thrust her face closer to his. 'Oh, for Jenat's sake, grow up, Edwild! As a young man, you always were full of pomposity, but you're a king now, so show some leadership here.'

His pallor vanished under a flush of rage, but it was Thalia who was the target of his incandescent fury. He pointed the sword at her, the tip of it vibrating as if he could not contain his hatred.

Thalia didn't even notice. Hazelle moved closer to her. Better to be over-cautious. She wove a gateway, placing it facing the King, between him and Thalia. Agrina saw it and gave a hissed intake of breath in disapproval. Edwild and Thalia showed no signs of being aware of what she was doing. Neither did Denniel, whose gaze was fixed on Thalia. At the other end of the room, Kaillan saw, and gave her the slightest of nods as he and Denniel walked towards them. Taygen followed, taking it upon himself to be the prince's protector. From the expression on his face as he glanced around the Privy Chamber, Haze could almost read his thoughts: *What a pompous-muckle of a room!* A poor space to control if all ten hells broke loose.

She could feel the tension. Everyone taut, everyone barely daring to breathe.

With the framework of the gateway now completed, the weave became easier. Multiple threads shot away from the entrance, interlacing as they disappeared into the darkness of the lacuna joining Talodiac to Kanter. A shiver skittered down her spine.

I'll never get used to this.

Thalia, oblivious, remained transfixed, her world halted as she stared at Denniel. Love radiated from her, a wave of tenderness and concern and grief so strong Haze could see it in her face, read it in her stance, observe it in the way her lips curled up at the edges.

In answer, Denniel lit up from within. 'Mother,' he said. He quickened his step, walking straight down the centre of the room as though he owned it, ignoring his father and everyone else. If he noticed the glowing weave of the gateway, he gave no sign.

He stopped in front of Thalia. 'I always knew you'd be beautiful,' he said. His accent was a match to Kaillan's, all Talodiac, not Kanter. He reached out to take her hand.

'Let me look at you...' she whispered.

Haze wanted to weep. For Denniel. For Thalia. For herself. For the mother she would never know. She tried to pull herself together, but when she noticed a tear glistening on Kaillan's cheek and the joy shining in his eyes, she was undone all over again.

And then the King ripped the moment from them all.

Haze saw their mistake even as the disaster unfolded. They'd thought Thalia was the one in most danger. But then, how could they have known that when everyone else was transfixed by the meeting between Denniel and Thalia, the King would switch his attention from them, from his own son, to *Kaillan*? Who could have foretold that?

Kaillan, unarmed, had come to a halt near Gerentia Agrina in front of the desk. Unarmed, he had not considered he might be in danger. As far as he knew, the only time he and the King had crossed paths was when he was a young man without a scarred face or crippled hands.

But Edwild was staring at Kaillan's deformed fingers and missing thumb. 'You! It was *you!*'

Even then, Kaillan did not flinch. 'Sire?' he asked, with just the right amount of puzzlement.

Haze's heart turned over. To reach the King she had to dodge her own woven gateway. It took two strides more than it should have done. And that was the difference between success and disaster.

Even as she moved, Edwild leapt at Kaillan. 'I watched them crush your fingers!' he cried as he thrust his blade forward. 'You didn't know that, did you?'

Kaillan raised his hands palms outspread in an open gesture of conciliation. 'I—' he began.

It was all over as fast as the flick of a finger, but to Haze it unfolded in unbearable detail, as if time had slowed. Kaillan in shock, stepping away too late. The sword tip disappearing into his body, slick and silent and deadly. Her own leap towards the King as clumsy as wading through water. The look of surprise on Kaillan's face.

Edwild's grunt of satisfaction coming at the same time as Thalia's shout of denial and Denniel's agonised, '*No!*'

Kaillan collapsed to his knees, his body slipping away from the blade.

Edwild smirked.

Haze reached him, her staff smashing the sword from his hands with a savage blow to his arm. Kaillan slumped sideways against her lower leg, throwing her off balance. She came down on one knee still holding her polearm.

Edwild bent to snatch up the sword, only to find a foot planted firmly on the blade. He straightened and had to tilt his head upwards to meet the accusing blazing stare of his son.

The lad is taller than he is. Hazelle's stupid thought, weirdly satisfying. Anything to blur the horror.

'He's the only father I ever had,' Denniel said quietly into the hush of the room.

Then, with astonishing effortlessness, he picked up the man who had sired him and threw him into the woven gateway.

A collective gasp hung in the air as Edwild vanished from the room into the tunnel. He landed awkwardly with an audible thump, then slid along on his back between the woven walls.

Denniel turned to Haze and held out his hand to pull her to her feet. 'Close the gateway,' he said and dropped to his knees beside Kaillan. Thalia was already there, cradling him, her hand tearing at the cloth of his torn doublet. Taygen, having seen the King disappear apparently in midair, remained frozen.

Hazelle stared at Edwild still sprawled on the woven floor of the tunnel, clutching his arm and dazed with shock, face contorted in pain. Behind him the glow of her weaving barrelled away into Kanter. Kanter, surely, not Talodiac, because she caught a glimpse of a sky reddening with dawn, or dusk perhaps, in the distance. Without another thought, she wove a door to block the entrance. King Edwild could not return until a redweaver opened the gate.

That done, dreading what she would see, she turned to where Thalia knelt cradling Kaillan's head on her lap, bending to whisper into his ear. Denniel crouched beside her. His fingers were unlacing the ties on the man's doublet, pushing Thalia's hand away to see the wound. Blood seeped. Thalia handed him her fichu and he folded it, pressing it firmly over the wound to halt the flow, but there was no mistaking the paleness of Kaillan's face, or the dragging painful breaths.

Haze exchanged a glance with Taygen. He gave a tiny shake of his head, which she interpreted as his assessment that Kaillan might not survive. Gods' light, they needed one of Hetha's healers.

'Kaillan, Kaillan, please stay with us,' Thalia begged. 'We need you. *I* need you.' She looked up at the Gerentia. 'Agrina, pull the bell. When someone comes, tell them the King has ordered this injured man taken to the healers at Goddess Hetha's Temple.'

'Are — are you sure?' the Mulierseer asked.

'Do it!'

Agrina yanked the bell-pull, saying, 'There's a healers' tent at the fair. An arch-clergy healer in charge. Closer than the temple.' She headed down the room to remove the chair under the door handle.

'It's all right,' Kaillan whispered. 'Doesn't matter. Thalia, thank you. Sorry.'

'Not alone. Please, I can't do this alone. Stay, Kaillan. Please.'

'Denniel?' he whispered.

'I'm here.'

'For Kanter. Your mother knows. We spoke. Planned. Look after them.'

Ten hells, Hazelle thought, *what does he mean? I don't think I understand anything...*

'Don't you *dare* die on me!' Denniel cried. 'I've so much to say to you...'

'Oh, lad,' he said, still smiling. 'I know it all.' He turned his smile to Thalia. 'You made me the happiest man alive.'

*

427

Taygen could see life ebbing away as he watched. The Mulierseer had her lips pinched as tight as a talyak's arse, but Denniel and Thalia appeared devastated. Even Hazelle seemed bleak. He frowned. *Really?* The man had stolen Denniel from his mother!

'Haze,' Thalia said. She'd schooled her expression to a cool calm, but her face was as pale as the Cresta moon. 'Save him.'

'I don't know how!'

'Kaillan mentioned it. "Solid weaving" to heal wounds. The tunnels you weave are *real*. Others can weave an actual ladder that can be used ... *Real* things. Denniel?'

'Some can repair a wound.' He bit his lip. 'I've never seen it done, but I know wounds have to be done from the inside out.'

Kaillan might have been unconscious, but he dragged in air, a horrible rattling in his throat. Thalia swallowed a sob. 'He's scarcely breathing!'

'I don't know how to help,' Haze whispered. 'I don't know what to do.'

'Try,' Denniel said quietly. 'Please try. He is a good man. I know you may find that hard to understand, given what he did to you, but it is true.'

Haze made a sound that was half laugh, half sob. 'As it turns out, he gave me a better life.' She knelt down at Kaillan's side. 'I'll try weaving a — a tiny wall inside the wound. But you are going to have to move your hand. He ... he might bleed to death the moment you do.'

Denniel nodded. 'Tell me when you are ready.'

Taygen watched as she heaved in a breath to steady her nerves, then dug deep inside for the power he didn't understand and couldn't see.

A tiny smile flickered across her lips and he guessed she'd found what she needed. 'Now,' she whispered. Denniel

428

turned his face away, unable to watch as he removed his hand.

Someone knocked at the door and the Mulierseer stepped outside to speak to them. Taygen listened, hearing her give orders to fetch another three servants and a truckle as one of the King's visitors had been taken ill and needed to be carried to the healer's tent at the Summer fair. Taken ill? Not *quite* the truth. Even a gerentia could lie, it seemed. *At least this time I'm on the right side, surely? A gerentia, a queen ...*

Dreaming of being a kingsman was all very well, but fealty was apparently more a matter of complex politics than un-questioning loyalty. He sighed. Life was such a muddle. Why were choices never clear cut?

The Mulierseer returned and Hazelle finished whatever it was she'd done to mend Kaillan. The Kanterine still lay on the floor, unconscious and pale, his breathing laboured. The bleeding had stopped, but he was soaked in so much of his own blood it was hard for Taygen to believe he had enough left to keep him alive. Denniel knelt at his side, to place a hand on his forehead.

Haze came over to Taygen. 'I don't think he'll make it,' she murmured. 'I didn't really know what I was doing.'

He slipped a comforting arm around her shoulders, but couldn't think of anything he could say that would make her feel any better.

She turned to Thalia. 'Hetha's healers: most are arch-cler-gy. They will see the redweaving. I kept the weave threads very tiny, but...'

Thalia, who had been pacing the floor in silence, halted and said quietly, 'Yes, that's right; they would. Most Rever-end—?'

'It doesn't matter,' the Mulierseer snapped. 'The healers will do their job no matter what, and I think it highly unlikely they will notice such a tiny piece of redweaving in all that blood.'

Thalia nodded. 'We'd better move to the retiring room. Except for you, Most Reverend. Please stay here and deal with the servants. Ask them to request the healers to send a message here of Kaillan's progress after they have assessed his condition.'

'And you?' she asked.

'We'll keep out of sight, supposedly closeted with Edwild.'

Gerentia Agrina nodded, a quick jerk of her head in reluctant agreement.

Taygen picked up the two polearms and the sword, wiping the latter clean on Thalia's abandoned fichu. He returned Haze's quarterstaff to her and they both headed towards the door at the back of the Privy Chamber. 'I don't understand half of what's afoot,' he said. Why is Queen Thalia so beset over Kaillan? Wasn't he the redweaver who stole—?'

She cut him off. 'Yes. He helped, but apparently he didn't have much choice at the time. I like him. I'll tell you the whole story one day. Thalia will grieve.'

'And — all that about the King not knowing you went to Kanter? My father would *never* have hidden that from his king!'

'You said Cyrrin took you to the Keep, and he's more of a God Saffrin man.'

'Yes. And that was Sianta's allegiance too. It must have been her who had me moved. The King never knew about me. And never knew Thalia was captured!' He shook his head in disbelief. He was way out of his depth and he knew it. 'Sianta and her ilk — what a heap of rotting talyak-pats.'

As they entered the retiring room, he turned to look back to where Denniel and Thalia were standing side by side, still looking down at Kaillan's prone body. The Mulierseer had moved away to the main door.

Taygen had no trouble hearing Denniel's whisper to Thalia. 'I want to go with him.'

'So do I,' she said quietly.

'Someone should be holding his hand when — if — he dies.'

She was silent. They stared at one another, unmoving.

Denniel whispered again then, words full of astonishment and wonder. 'You *love* him.'

Still she didn't reply.

Taygen, shocked, was momentarily rooted to the spot, still holding the door open as mother and son remained caught up in the poignancy of the moment. Denniel stepped forward and hooked his arm into Thalia's and they both headed for the retiring room. Neither looked back to where Kaillan lay, about to be relinquished into the care of others, still in a pool of blood. Tears glistened on Thalia's cheeks.

Wishing he hadn't overheard the conversation, Taygen wrenched his gaze away and caught Haze's eye. She gave him the slightest shake of the head.

What do I know about anything, he thought. *I'm a just a lobcock sandworm from Breakedge.*

*

He longed to stay, but was drifting into a mist. So cold. He thought: *It would have been good to see Kanter skies again.*

So much to do. So much…

I wish I wasn't leaving her now.

Thalia. His heart ached. His fault. Now was the time to set things right, but he wasn't going to be there. *I was so lucky to have known her...*

His eyes were open, but the darkness was deepening and his thoughts drifted.

He couldn't see either now: the son he'd loved, yet not fathered. The woman who'd caught his heart with her courage in a prison cell, so long ago. Together at last. He'd helped Mongrave wreck their lives, the only two people he'd ever loved. Both here, together for the first time in eighteen years.

'Tangled threads,' he thought. *This is a good ending, Kaillan Riverdell. I hope they'll realise that.* But as he drifted away it was on a rising tide of rage, not acceptance.

Edwild must not win.

42

The retiring room was lined with bookcases and furnished with a settee, comfortable armchairs, and a small table with matching seats. Taygen glanced around and decided that, whereas the Privy Chamber exuded the language of power, grandeur and order, this was a cosier place, hinting at comfort and intimacy. Bottles of wine and goblets, a rug on the settee, imported southern dates in a jar, a foot warmer for cold weather in the corner, all indicated this was a place for relaxation.

While they waited for the Mulierseer, he turned his attention back to Thalia, who was asking Haze what had happened to Edwild inside the tunnel.

'I think he's fine,' Haze replied with a shrug. 'Bruised maybe. The tunnel's really short. I could see the sky, definitely in Kanter.'

'Whatever happens from now on, I'm relying on you if things go wrong. I want you to open up a tunnel and get yourself, and Denniel, to safety. You are both more important to me than anything or anyone else. Understand?'

Haze nodded. 'If I have to, that's what I'll do. Just remember that I'll come back. Somehow. What are you going to do now?'

Thalia moved to the window that overlooked the main gate. 'Talk to Edwild. Negotiate.' She wiped her tears away with the back of her hand. 'But right now, we wait.'

When someone finally tapped at the door, they all jumped. Thalia gave Taygen a nod, so he opened it a crack, saw that it was the Mulierseer, and let her in. The way she held herself reminded him of his mother at her most indignant.

'Your Grace,' she said, lips pinched, 'I told them to tell the healers he was one of the King's most valued servants and bade them take good care of him. I do *not* like lying.'

Thalia fixed her with a glare of her own. '*Oh?*'

Taygen bit back a laugh. The Queen had mastered the art of saying a lot with one word.

Agrina blanched. 'What do you intend, milady?'

'I've changed my mind. I thought it was possible to negotiate, to make private agreements with Edwild. I can't see that happening now, so I want the palace staff to know the Queen has returned with her son. That's the only way Denniel and I can keep ourselves safe. No more hiding for either of us. From now on, in public, everyone addresses me as "Your Grace" and Denniel as "Your Highness". She looked around at the four of them. 'Understood?'

'Are you *sure?*' This time it was worry that furrowed deep into Agrina's voice.

'I'm fed up with hiding. I'm fed up with the lies. I'm fed up with the running! I came to negotiate, but Edwild had other ideas. Now I'll do things my way.'

'You may lose.'

'I know.'

Taygen twitched his understanding to encompass the idea of Thalia being recognised as Edwild's queen. Fine. He could do that. But, bells and hells, what was going to happen right now?

'The King,' Haze remarked, carefully neutral, 'is going to be furious when I open that woven gate.'

'At least he doesn't have the sword any more,' Taygen said.

'Let's hope he doesn't meet an esklet in Kanter,' Haze replied.

'What's an esklet?' he asked.

'A flying creature. Unfortunately, their prey tends to be human.'

'You kidding?'

'I don't joke about things like that.'

'Quiet, both of you,' Thalia said, intent on her conversation with Agrina. 'There's only one decision we can make right now, and that's how to deal with Edwild. I don't care a fig for him, but if he wants to rule, then we have to feel safe. There will have to be changes. Unfortunately, I'm not sure he will change his mind about anything.'

'Mother—' Denniel began, then hesitated before adding, 'I think I should say this now. I haven't the faintest desire or intention to rule in Talodiac at some future time. I was not raised to rule anywhere. I was brought up to fight esklet and that's what I want to do. I only came here to find you. No other reason. I'm no Talodian prince!'

Taygen silently applauded Denniel's sense; if he knew anything at all, it was that being a king would be a picklemuck of a job.

A prolonged silence followed as Thalia weighed Denniel's declaration. Finally, she admitted, 'I thought you might say something like that. I don't blame you. I do have another solution, a better one, perhaps.' She turned to address the gerentia. 'I've walked and ridden the roads of Talodiac for the past eighteen years. I know its people. I know its temples and their clergy and their faithful. The only duchy I didn't go to was Temar, and I was brought up there.'

The Mulierseer gave a sharp intake of breath. 'You? You want to *rule*? Instead of King Edwild? We have no history of a queen.'

'We have no history of a queen being needed until now.'

A queen who ruled? Taygen adjusted his ideas. Why not? But ... *Thalia*? A woman he'd shared a cart with? Who'd had to pee behind trees on the journey? Now that was ... more than weird. 'Who is the male heir after Denniel?' he asked.

'There's no clear line,' she said. 'There are several second cousins of Edwild's from other duchies. They all hate one another. They already argue about who's the most senior. Is it governed by the wealth and size of their duchy? Or who's senior in age? Or who, other than Edwild, has the most direct line to the very first king? Actually, that's my father, oddly enough. A man who comes from the smallest and most humble of all duchies. We could return to the time of civil war if any one of them made a move on the throne.'

'Then why the frothing pickles wasn't the King allowed to marry again and get a passel of brats?' he asked.

Thalia sent him an appreciative glance. 'It was implied that God Atticun could not budge on the rules applying to the royal succession because he is the God of Governance and Law. I think there was another reason, which I'll explain some other time. The fact remains: the only way Edwild could marry again was for me to die.' She stared hard at Agrina. 'Most Reverend, it's time.'

'It's a dangerous game you play.'

Thalia shrugged. 'More dangerous to attempt to have me killed, believe me. Tell the gerents that, all of them. In fact, I will soon talk to the Lawseer and the Battleseer myself.'

Taygen raised an eyebrow in question at Haze, but she appeared just as mystified as he was.

Thalia turned back to Denniel. 'Do you trust me? I need Edwild to abdicate, thinking you will take his place. If you don't want the throne, no one is going to thrust you into it, I swear.'

He shrugged. 'I know what you did for me and I know what Kaillan believes about you, so yes, I trust you. But my *father* is not trustworthy, surely?'

She smiled. 'Oh, believe me, my plan might be scanty in detail, but I'm no longer a child running away with a babe in arms. Now I hold the sharpest blade and my knowledge is richer than any purse.' She nodded to Haze. 'Let's return to the Privy Chamber where you can re-open the gateway.'

Hazelle, expressionless, opened the door. Taygen glanced to where Kaillan had lain. Someone had attempted to wipe away the worst of the blood, but the floor was still smeared. He swallowed and looked away. 'Tell me where this tunnel is,' he said as Hazelle crossed to the front of the desk.

Thalia grimaced. 'Frustrating, isn't it? I can't see it either.'

'I've just opened it,' Hazelle said. 'I can see right through to the other end. The King's not there. He must have walked on into Kanter.'

'Is it daylight?' Thalia asked.

'Yes. Just after dawn, I'd say.'

'We'd better go after him.'

Agrina pursed her lips. 'I'm not going through any gateway. I'll stay and make sure no one enters the room. Don't be too long.'

'Can I trust you?' Thalia asked.

The Mulierseer glared. 'I would have thought I'd proved that more than once. I serve Goddess Jenat, not God Atticun! Where are your manners, Thalia!'

'I'm sorry. You're right. It's just that — I know how conflicted you must be. How difficult this must be for you, but I also believe you've been planning something like this for years.'

'This is *not* at all what the Goddess and I had in mind!' she snapped back, then sighed. 'But it is time. Which is why you shouldn't be going to Kanter. I'm relying on you, Thalia. You are essential—'

'No. I'm not! There are people like Denniel and Hazelle and Taygen and Kaillan on both sides of the weaving.' She turned to them. 'Let's go. Where's this gateway of yours, Haze? Oh, and you had better close it behind us. We don't want anyone blundering inside by accident. But for pity's sake, leave the tunnel extant. I don't feel like another barge journey through Talodiac afterwards in order to return to Templebridge.' With that, she took a step forward and disappeared.

Taygen turned to Denniel, holding out the ceremonial sword. 'Here, take this. Just in case.'

The prince weighed it in his hand. 'Not a weapon we use much in Kanter,' he said. 'Not much use against things that fly. I hope you're not thinking that I might need to use it on my father.'

'Curse me witless,' Taygen muttered as the prince headed off after the Queen and disappeared in turn.

'Sometimes you are such a lummox!' Hazelle grabbed his hand and pulled him after her.

One moment he was taking a step towards the desk, the next a tunnel of red surrounded him. It quivered slightly underfoot when he moved. *Saffrin's balls!* He could have been inside the woven stocking of a giant. A giant with a penchant for scarlet hose … Thalia and Denniel were already walking towards a faint light at the other end.

'And you sewed this thing, Haze? Embroidered it into being? Remind me not to upset you any time.'

She looked back over her shoulder, laughing. 'I haven't changed.'

'Like cock-eggs you haven't. You're a redweaver now! And that's the Netherworld ahead of us.' He brightened at the thought. 'Pickle me pink, this is something else. I don't suppose you can teach me how to build one of these?'

'Kanter. That's its proper name. And sorry, no. How to weave can be taught, but you have to be able to make the threads to start with. And that apparently has something to do with birth or inherited talent.'

'Might have known it.'

'It's not exactly something I wanted. Now, let me tell you more about esklet...' And in the five minutes it took them to walk to the end of the tunnel, she did just that.

Pickle it, he thought. *A polearm's going to be about as useful as a toothpick.*

At the end of the tunnel, they caught up with Thalia and Denniel standing just inside the opening, looking outwards in silence. Edwild was walking up and down inside Kanter, about twenty paces away, hands outstretched like a blind man trying to find his way.

A shiver of excitement ran down Taygen's back. *I'm here, in the Netherworld. Me, a sandgrubber from Breakedge!* He tamped down his surge of excitement to assess the scene for danger. The exit overlooked the downhill slope of a meadow, devoid of animals or people. He scanned the pale dawn sky: no birds, and nothing that could have been the dreaded esklet. Rooftops in the distance; a small town, at a guess, just a mile or two away. A cart track wended its way across the valley below. They'd know more when the day was brighter, but gods, it could have been Talodiac.

Thalia put a finger to her lips. 'We think he might have stepped out of the tunnel, not realising that he wouldn't be able to see it from outside,' she whispered. 'Now he can't find it again. He's hoping he'll bump into it.'

'What do we do?' Hazelle asked, whispering back.

Thalia pointed at the town and raised an eyebrow at Denniel.

'You don't have to whisper,' he said. 'No ordinary person outside a tunnel hears what happens within. I don't recognise the place. Good news, though. See that post on the horizon? That's part of the early warning system for esklet. No alert at the moment. But then, they only fly when there's warmth in the sun anyway. Is there any sign of Ashwendon?'

'No. Would he be nearby?'

'Not necessarily. That other tunnel could have ended anywhere.'

'I'm going to step out,' Thalia murmured. 'When he sees me, he'll come over. You all stay inside, out of sight. Just listen. Don't move unless he attacks. And I suspect he might. He'll be angry enough.'

Haze grabbed her arm, visibly perturbed. 'I'll go with you.'

Thalia shook her head. '*No.* I mean it. For now, this is between me and Edwild.' She waited until the King had his back to them, then stepped outside, deliberately walking away from the gateway so he wouldn't be able to guess its position.

Taygen held his breath as the King turned and saw her. The fellow limped unevenly across the meadow grass, his face a mix of relief and burning rage.

Must've hurt his leg when Denniel flung him into the tunnel, Taygen thought.

Thalia halted him with a hand held out at arm's length. 'Don't come too close. I don't trust you. We are in Kanter. The Netherworld. Remember this: I represent your single chance to return to Talodiac — because I know *how* to return, and you don't.'

He stopped abruptly several paces away, chest heaving as he reined in his anger. 'You can get us back?'

'I can.'

Confound it, she's gone too far away from us, Taygen thought.

'This is as good a place as any to have a discussion of just where our future takes us, you and me,' Thalia continued.

'*Discussion?* A discussion? That man threw me into this Gods-forsaken netherworld and you want to *talk?* Get me back to the palace!'

Thalia was unfazed. 'In a moment. Returning is easily done *if* I want. And "that man" was your son. If you doubt it, look in a mirror. But first, I want the answer to a simple question.'

He was taken aback, as if her lack of instant obedience surprised him.

'Lackwit,' Taygen murmured. 'He doesn't know her at all, does he?'

'He hasn't talked to her for eighteen years,' Haze pointed out.

'Edwild,' said Thalia, 'I want to know the reason you refused the demands the redweavers made that might have brought Denniel back to us.'

That, Taygen thought with sudden insight, *is for Denniel, not her. She already knows.*

Edwild stared at her, puzzled. 'Apart from the fact they are godless heathens with their sorcery? Our *enemies?* No sane person would ever even consider it! But I didn't have any choice anyway. God Atticun and God Saffrin made that abundantly clear through their gerents. Not surprising. They have always utterly forbidden the entry of the Netherlost, long before the prince was stolen, for good reason. These wretches have magic! Who built the gateway that brought me here? The lad you think is Denniel?'

'No. Haze. The person who was placed in his cot. Whom I raised. Who has the loyalties of a Talodian and the skills of a redweaver.'

'Do you mean to tell me you've protected someone who can betray us from within? Such a person has the power to bring us to our knees! You daft woman; if you'd stayed, we could have had other children, another heir. Everything would have been *fine.*'

'That could have happened anyway, if the gods had allowed a divorce and your remarriage,' she pointed out. 'Why wouldn't they change the law?'

He glowered at her. 'Blame your piss-brained goddess for that. God Atticun might just have bent the rules, but Goddess Jenat said royal marriages solemnised in a temple can never be undone, and she wouldn't budge. She's the one who kept you on the run! It's all her fault.'

Taygen raised an eyebrow at Hazelle.

She snorted and muttered, 'As if anything would have made one fly-speck of difference to Edwild anyway. He wanted us dead. He still does.'

'I've never understood why they couldn't change a stupid law,' the King continued. 'They are gods! But no. I had to produce your dead body. And now you want to come back and say this redweaver is my son and will one day sit on my throne? You're *insane!*'

'He's not a redweaver, and he's your *son.* All you have to do is look at him to know that much. When the whole of Talodiac discovers that you refused to even *talk* with the Kanterines about Denniel, when they discover that you have been trying to murder me ever since, do you think you'll keep your rear-end planted on the throne?'

'Who's going to tell them? You? Who's going to believe a delusional woman masquerading as a queen who had a royal funeral eighteen years ago? Who's going to believe you are who you say you are?'

'Oh, I think I'm quite recognisable. There's that portrait of me for a start, seen by anyone who ever comes to the palace, all because you wanted to play the grieving widower. I have the Griffin Carcanet around my neck. I have Goddess Jenat who will vouch for me. My parents are still alive and can identify me. They are on their way here, you know, with armed guards from both Temar and Personata. And of course, now that I've rid myself of the baffle, there's all kinds of things I can say. All kinds of ways I have of making my identity known, of proving who I am.'

His voice larded with contempt, he scoffed, 'Don't be ridiculous. Goddess Jenat will never go against God Atticun or God Saffrin.'

'No? She already has, hasn't she? She protected me when those gods wanted me dead. You underestimate the power of women, Edwild.'

He scowled, but Taygen watched the way he licked dry lips. *He's worried...*

'She sent a letter to the Duke of Temar from Copperstone Crossways,' Haze said in explanation. 'She asked them to come, I suppose.'

'I have a proposal,' said Thalia. 'Declare the miracle of the return of your queen and your son. Abdicate in favour of a regency. With me as regent for Denniel.'

He laughed. 'That's a ridiculous idea. Who ever heard of a woman regent? While the *real* king is still alive, what's more?'

'The truth will out if you don't abdicate quietly. God-dess Jenat's temples will spread the word of a king who sent soldiers to kill his queen, a king who did nothing to save his son—'

'So? You think that worries me? I have God Atticun on my side! I have my guards. I have money and power that you know *nothing* about. If I snap my fingers, my loyal men come running to do my bidding!'

'Like Captain Hervan? Did you know he came back to Templebridge to tell you I had escaped him through a gateway to Kanter?' She tilted her head in question, eyebrow raised.

443

He stared, then attempted to mock her with laughter.

'Who do you think rid me of the baffle?' she asked. 'Red-weavers!'

'You consorted with the Netherlost?' He could not conceal his shock. 'They are heathens, surely! You must be lying. How could they destroy the baffle a god decreed for you?'

'Quite easily, it seems.'

'You've just condemned yourself with your very words!'

'And you have been far too trusting, Edwild. Many of your own guards have been serving Gerent Ruthgar the Battleseer, putting his needs before yours. Putting God Saffrin before God Atticun. They betrayed Captain Hervan and his men. They fear a god more than they fear you. You know what I think? Those you surround yourself with now don't care if you lose your seat on the throne.'

He leapt at her, reaching out for her neck. She whirled away from him, but her heel caught in a tuft of grass. As she lost her balance, he grabbed her hand, jerking her backwards against his chest. His right arm encircled her neck.

'You always were a fool,' he said into her ear. 'Tell me how to get out of here, or we both die in this wretched land, and you'll be first.' He squeezed her throat cutting off her air, then relaxed slightly so she could drag in a breath. 'So very simple, milady.'

His other hand slipped into his doublet and emerged holding a palm-blade. For the briefest of moments, Taygen was back in the market the day he met Haze ... but this one was not the kind a pickpocket used. This was a killer's blade.

'Tell me,' Edwild said, showing her the instrument, 'or I'll cut your face to pieces.'

Denniel and Hazelle moved as one out of the tunnel and into the sunlight. The shock of their sudden appearance stayed Edwild's hand, but the dagger still rested on Thalia's cheek, the point pricking her skin as everyone froze.

Stalemate, Taygen thought, and stayed where he was. *He can't see me in the tunnel. I could kill him before he knows I am here.*

Regicide. You scat-brain, Taygen. Really?

43

She desperately wanted to speak. She had the words to halt her own murder. She was certain of it. But Edwild's arm was so excruciatingly tight around her neck she could hardly breathe, let alone talk.

Damn it, what a stupid way to die.

'Harm her and you're dead,' Denniel said.

My son. Gods, he is calm.

'Hurt her and you'll never get back to Talodiac,' said Hazelle.

My daughter. She couldn't breathe. Her vision danced with black spots.

'And if you don't lay down your polearms and step away from them, she's dead,' Edwild replied. 'Believe me, I'll cut her up piece by piece.'

She concentrated. No breath. No strength. She thought of fluttering her fingers, using the wayfarer's code Hazelle would recognise. Tell her to attack with her quarterstaff.

But Edwild might be quicker...

No, not Haze.

Not Denniel either. No son should have to kill his father.

Edwild moved the knife away from her face to prick her neck instead. His other arm now held her tight across the shoulders, easing the pressure on her breathing, but the threat was clear: *If you don't lay down your arms, I'll slit her throat.* She gasped, dragging air into tortured lungs.

The dagger tip jabbed close to her jugular, just breaking the skin. 'Show me how to get back to Templebridge, or she dies right here, right now. Your last chance.'

Taygen. Taygen, always throwing things. She forced out his name loud and clear in the cold morning air. 'Taygen!'

A mere heartbeat later, Edwild grunted and his head snapped backwards. Blood sprayed into her eyes. The arm around her fell away. Unbalanced, she toppled, sprawling across him as he collapsed. Then Denniel was there, kneeling beside her, hauling her up into a sitting position away from Edwild.

'Mother? Are you all right?'

Unable to speak, she drew in a whooping breath and flapped a hand at him.

'Jenat's tits,' Haze said, standing over Edwild with her staff end pressed into his neck. 'What the weeping heavens just happened—?'

Denniel used his sleeve to wipe away the blood on her face. 'The bastard cut her.'

'It's nothing,' she said.

He took a closer look at her cheek. 'Then where did all the blood come from?'

'Not me.' She winced and put a hand to her throat where the carcanet had dug into her skin. Damn the wretched man to oblivion, he had bruised her badly.

'Great gods,' Haze whispered. 'Look at this.' She was still bending over Edwild. Stuck into his eye was a sharpened piece of polished stone. 'I think he's *dead.*'

Thalia glanced back towards the gateway. 'Taygen?'

He stepped out of the tunnel. 'Ah. Yes, well.' He shrugged as if it didn't matter, but he was white-faced. 'It was all I could think of. If any one of us came close, he might have slit your throat. I kept out of sight, and chucked it at him. He's — he's not really *dead*, is he?'

Denniel bent to have a closer look. 'Yes, he is actually. There's something stuck in his eyeball.' He plucked a polished piece of onyx out of his father's eye and held it up for them all to see. 'I'll be beggared! I know what this is. You threw that ornament at him, didn't you? This is the horn from that carved unicorn you took from the table outside his bedroom!'

He scanned the area around and picked up the rest of the stone carving from the ground, holding it up to show Thalia and Hazelle. 'Here's the rest of it.'

'I had it stuck in my belt,' Taygen said.

'Yes, I noticed. That was no "chuck". That was skill. The horn went into his eye thumb-deep and snapped off.' Denniel glanced back at his father. 'He died on the spot.'

Taygen ran an agitated hand through his hair. 'I didn't mean to kill him, but he moved forward just as I threw.'

Denniel straightened up, shrugging. 'Don't let it worry you on my account.'

'Hells, Denniel. That was a *king*!' Taygen sat down on the ground suddenly as if his knees had given way. 'Regicide? What's the penalty for that? Burnt at the stake?'

'Not if I'm queen.' Thalia said, hoping she appeared more calm than she felt. 'But I don't think we'd better mention the *manner* of his passing. Do you?'

He took a deep breath. 'It seemed a better option than the sword or a polearm. I just thought to knock him out. The base was supposed to hit his forehead, but he moved...'

Hazelle leant on her quarterstaff looking down at Edwild's body. 'Can't say I'll shed any tears.'

'Me neither,' agreed Denniel, holding out his hand towards Thalia. 'He wanted us both dead.'

Thalia accepted his help and stood, brushing the dirt from her skirt.

'I just killed a king,' Taygen said. His face was a muddy colour. 'I thought being in the King's Keep under sentence of death was bad enough. Now...'

'You saved my life,' Thalia said briskly. 'No one here is going to accuse you of anything. I'll see to that.' Still, the implications of Edwild's death crowded her thoughts with a hundred different possible outcomes. 'I think we must get his body back into the palace, otherwise it'll be a disappearance that redweavers will be blamed for.'

'Take him back and you and I will be blamed,' Denniel said. 'We could just walk away right now, into Kanter.'

'No, son. That's not a life I would choose. Especially not ... not'—she took a deep breath—'not without Kaillan.' Gods, it hurt even to think about him. *He might be dead too.*

'Well, *someone's* got to be blamed for killing the King,' said Hazelle.

'What about an esklet?' Denniel suggested, handing the unicorn and its horn to Taygen. 'Keepsake.'

'I don't need to remember this, thank you!' He drew back his arm and threw both of things as far away as he could, watching them as they sailed through the air to finally thud into the meadow grass.

'I don't want Kanter involved in this in any way,' Thalia said. 'We take him through to Talodiac.' She bent over Edwild for a closer look at the damage done to his face. 'We can clean up the blood and cover the eye.'

Hazelle gave her a wide-eyed stare. 'What are you suggesting?'

'It's customary to put coins on the eyes of the dead because they sometimes fall open as the eyeballs shrink. We can hide the physical damage that way.'

'That's *not* what I was asking! I meant, how do we explain his death?'

'For Gerentia Agrina, I killed him accidentally. I pushed him, he fell on something that pierced his eye, and that's it. For public consumption, a different story. When I returned from the dead, he died of apoplexy brought on by guilt and the shock of seeing me and meeting his son for the first time.'

She looked around. Everyone was staring at her with varying degrees of doubt. 'As long as everyone realises Denniel is genuinely Edwild's son and believes he will one day rule, this will be considered the best way of avoiding the horror of an internecine ducal war. It will help that my father is a direct descendant of the first king. We will not tell everyone that he's spent most of his life in Kanter.' Their misgivings continued to be writ large in their expressions. She shrugged. 'The people in the street will love this. It's — it's sentimental. The dukes, well, the weakest among them, will give a sigh of relief. It avoids the possibility of a war between the contenders. Besides, the ones who really matter when it comes to who rules aren't the dukes. It's the gods. And I have what is needed to persuade them.'

An exchange of glances between the three of them told her their skepticism remained, but no one commented.

'Ashwendon?' Taygen asked finally.

Now that was a problem. Wretched man. 'I'll deal with him when and however necessary.'

She touched Denniel's arm, swallowing the lump in her throat, smothering the desire just to hug him and sob on his shoulder. 'I'm sorry about this, but you will have to put in an appearance occasionally in the future. Just so everyone knows you exist.' When he didn't answer, she added softly, 'Your sacrifice for Kanter. Your payment, from us: arms, sanctuary, food for your people, all gladly supplied. If you walk away, I'll have no legal claim to sit on the throne and nobody will care about Kanter. Believe me, we can do this.'

'I understand. I—I just don't like lying.'

'I didn't particularly like it either, but that's been my whole life. Deception is what kept me alive since I was your age.' Her grip on his arm tightened. 'One thing you can be sure of, though you may not have known it: I cared for you. Always.'

He bit his lip, staring at the ground. 'I — I did know that. When Kaillan told me all about you, about how you came to see him in prison, he told me you saved his life in order to save me. And that you'd run away from the King in order to be sure that I would be safe. I made up my mind then that as soon as I was old enough, I would come looking for you.'

There was an awkward silence, and he was close to tears, so Haze stepped up to tell him brightly, 'Once I knew about you, it seemed to me that we were two of a kind. Same age, not knowing who we really were. I *so* wanted to meet you.'

'Did you? I felt the same way about you! Once Kaillan had told me my history. Only — I thought you were a boy.' He sighed. 'But then, for much of my childhood I thought I was someone else. And then, once I did know who I was, I spent a couple of years in pointless anger, choosing to keep myself apart from Kaillan, the only person I knew who really cared for me. I was such an idiot.' He nodded to Thalia. 'All right. Let's do it. I'll play the heir-in-waiting, and you'll turn Talodiac into Kanter's ally even if they never realise it. But I won't ever be king.'

Hazelle walked over to stare down at Edwild. 'Four of us here,' she said, 'all connected to him one way or another, and yet not one of us cares even half a rickling piece that he's dead. I feel like just leaving him here, as a fitting ending. Sooner or later the esklet will find him.'

'A practical solution,' Thalia agreed without turning around, 'but no. My idea is better. Besides, there was a time when … he was an important part of my life. The father of my son. The day that Denniel was born, we were happy.'

Yet when she thought back, what she remembered was the smell of another woman's perfume on his clothing that day. 'He wasn't entirely a bad man, you know. Just a king before he was a husband, or a father, or a friend.' She sighed and bent to remove the chain he wore around his neck under his doublet.

'What's that?' Haze asked.

'The king's seal,' she said, showing her the oblong pendant. 'Passed from monarch to monarch, on their deathbed, usually. No promulgation becomes law unless it is stamped with this seal. No letter from the king has authenticity without this stamp on the page.' She snorted. 'The folly of symbols. As if power depends on what you hang around your neck.' When she turned again to glance at Denniel, she added, 'Kaillan has more compassion in a single tear than Edwild had in his whole heart.'

'There's a cart coming down the track,' Taygen said. 'Towards the town. We'd better vanish before the driver wonders who we are. Come, Denniel, let's carry him over to the gateway.'

I can do this, Thalia thought as she watched them pick up Edwild's corpse and bear it away. *I'm strong. The cause is worthy. Is that not enough?*

Perhaps it wasn't, but it was all she had. *Oh, Kaillan.*

She heaved in a breath of clean air, of meadow flowers and morning dew, and followed the others towards the tunnel.

44

They laid him down on the table in the King's retiring room. Denniel arranged the his hands neatly across his chest. Gerentia Agrina folded her arms, glared at them all and snapped, 'I need an explanation!'

Thalia nodded her agreement. 'It was an accident. Look.' She lifted the carcanet to reveal the circle of abrasions around her neck. 'He did that. He attacked me, tried to strangle me. There was a struggle and he fell. A pointed shard of stone entered his eye...' She shrugged. 'Hazelle, find the King's purse. We need a couple of silver ricks for his eyes.'

The Mulierseer's glower darkened still further. 'This — this was not what I envisaged.'

'It wasn't exactly my aim, either. But Edwild was not willing to discuss a compromise.'

'*You* can't rule; you *know* that. God Atticun decrees the succession must be in the male line.'

'Exactly. Denniel is the heir. I feel sure God Atticun will support my temporary regency until the rightful monarch is familiar with our ways and comes of age. A duke, as I recall, can take command of his duchy at twenty, but a king rules his kingdom only once he reaches twenty-five. Denniel won't be King for another seven years.'

Denniel contemplated the Mulierseer, his stare carefully neutral. 'Is it possible that could be the wish of the nation?'

'In such matters, only God Atticun's wish applies,' Agrina told him acidly. 'You've much to learn, lad. You're a Kanterine. That won't make you popular.'

'I'm a Talodian. Born in this very building, I'm told. Of Talodian parents.'

Taygen stifled a laugh.

Agrina looked back at Thalia. 'God Atticun will *never* allow someone from Kanter to rule here.'

'A conundrum,' Thalia said, allowing a trace of amusement to tinge her tone. 'Atticun is the God of Law, Justice and Governance. The law says that the first son of a king born to his legal wife is the heir. He has no choice and you know it, Agrina.'

The Mulierseer was silent.

Today, Thalia thought, *is going to be the day when I find what you've all been hiding.* 'I need to see the Lawseer. And the Battleseer as well, I assume.'

Agrina sighed. 'Yes, you do.'

'Are they the only two gerents, besides yourself, who know that Denniel and I didn't die after he was born?'

'Yes.'

'Why the Battleseer?' Taygen asked, obviously unsettled by the idea of God Saffrin's gerent being involved.

With another sigh, the Mulierseer sank down on the nearest chair. 'The Battleseer had to be told because Edwild was worried Hervan and his men might lack enthusiasm for the hunt of a legitimate queen unless they were sure God Saffrin approved.'

'I suggest,' Thalia said, 'that our story is that King Edwild died here suddenly, of apoplexy, as a result of his shock at seeing me and his son alive and well, and realising that his lie was uncovered. But for now, Agrina, tell only the Lawseer and the Battleseer of the King's death and of my presence here. No public announcement as yet. No mention of Denniel as yet.'

Agrina sighed unhappily and pulled herself to her feet. 'It's a dangerous thing you do, Innata. I cannot guarantee their reaction.'

'It's not them I'm worried about. It's their gods. And Innata doesn't exist anymore. Get used to it.' She laid a hand on the Mulierseer's back and deftly guided her to the door adding, 'I'll see you out to the Privy Chamber door. Don't mention my acting as regent yet. Say they have to discuss with me what story goes out to the citizens concerning my reappearance. Oh, and do tell them to come alone...'

*

Denniel watched them go, then slumped into the nearest chair in the retiring room. Outside, a hurdy-gurdy played a tinkling tune, the cheerful strains drifting in through the window from the summer fair grounds.

Grief washed through him, a wave of churning horror.

This was like fighting esklet. You killed one, but there was always another behind it. You didn't get time to breathe, to think, even to feel. *Kaillan's dead or dying and I don't even have time to think about it, to go to him...* He looked over at Hazelle. 'How dangerous is this?' he asked, forcing himself upright, striving to appear alert, trying to absorb the fact that the changeling he'd wondered about was actually a woman. 'I mean, would any of these people — gerents, nobles, servants, guards — try to kill me now, rather than have the possibility of me sitting on the throne in a few years' time? And what about my mother: is she safe?'

Haze thought about that. 'Goddess Jenat's clergy have always been wonderful to us, but ... I don't know anything about the others.'

'Technically,' Taygen said, 'for armsmen of any kind, God Saffrin comes first, before anything, even though armsmen are supposed to serve the Crown before the Battleseer. But after my experience with Sianta, I can't be sure of anything. If the Battleseer were to say he had direct orders from God

Saffrin, things would get murky anyway. And how in the name of all the gods is it that King Edwild didn't know my father had captured Queen Thalia and then lost her through a redwoven gateway? That's incomprehensible. I would have thought none of Hervan's band would have dreamed of deceiving their monarch. They lived and breathed loyalty. Except, it seems, his own partner. Cyrrin.' He sighed. 'This aristo stuff is as foreign to me as the ocean. Which I've never seen, by the way. And, Haze, what in all the shades of a god's shadow is Thalia up to now anyway?'

'"Her Majesty" to you, you Breakedge sand-beetle.'

'Oh, cobble it. This is the woman I've helped down from a cart so she could go take a leak behind a briar!'

Haze's smile was muted. 'All I know is that something has been stewing inside her ever since we accidentally ended up in Kanter. I think it is something about redweaving. But she hasn't confided in me.' She laid a hand on Denniel's shoulder. 'I'm so sorry. This should have been a wonderful day for you, meeting your mother for the first time. Instead, you might have lost the only man who was family to you in a real sense, and I don't mean the man who sired you.' He was silent, so she added, 'Kaillan, he taught me, you know. On the barge on the way here. About redweaving. He was patient and kind and intelligent and gentle. I— I didn't want to like him, at first. Then I realised he was wracked with guilt and, well, in the end I liked him a lot. I am so sorry. I hope he lives.'

'Thank you. I'll admit to feeling ... lost. Nothing's quite the way I thought it would be. Not that I know what I want anyway.'

'Yes, you do,' she said firmly. 'You want Kanter to be free of esklet. And while that battle is still being fought, you want Talodiac to help your countrymen. You want your people not to starve. And Thalia will help you achieve that. Don't under-estimate any of us. I can help fight esklet.'

'Oh, tickle my other foot,' Taygen said, unconvinced. 'And if the expression on Denniel's face is anything to go by, he agrees with me. If these esklet things are as bad as you say, you can hardly fight them off with a polearm! Me, on the other hand, I'm a dab hand at throwing stones. And knives. And any other—'

She arched an eyebrow. 'I have already killed one esklet.'

'You got lucky?'

'Luck has nothing to do with skill.'

He groaned. 'Don't remind me. I don't know whether to feel wretched 'cause I killed a man, horrified because he was a king, or proud-nosed 'cause I saved Queen Thalia's life and rid the world of a man who forced her to spend half her life fleeing in order to stay alive.' He ran a hand through his hair, messing up his white hank into the black. 'I think I feel terrible, mostly. Funny that, because for most of my life, all I wanted to do was join the rangers and do just that: kill people. Desert marauders, basically.'

She reached out to put a hand on his shoulder. 'I do have a plan.'

Taygen rolled his eyes at Denniel. 'When she says something like that, be wary. *Very* wary. Every time our paths have crossed, things go arse-end topmost.'

'I'll tell you later,' she promised as Thalia returned.

'That,' Thalia said, speaking of Agrina, 'is a deeply troubled woman.'

'Can we trust her?' Denniel asked, deciding he had to focus on one problem at a time.

'In this, I think so. She has a secret that has haunted her for some time, and I believe I know what it is. Anyway, right now she has promised to help. Tell me, Taygen, can you find the King's bedroom again?'

'Yes, of course. I don't know that I could do it without being seen though. We were lucky earlier.'

'Haze will go with you. Just act as if you both have every right to be there. I want you to go to the Queen's bedchamber, which adjoins the King's, to get me a gown. I need something to wear that looks more ... queenly.'

'You want me to get a *dress*?'

'Hazelle will pick something out. It will be one of my own.'

Hazelle gave her a look of disbelief. 'It's been eighteen years!'

'Believe me, a queen's best dresses do not get thrown away. They cost a small fortune. No one throws away something sewn with silk from across the Great Desolation, then embroidered with gold and silver threads. Formal dresses do not date. When I married Edwild, I wore the gowns of his first wife. And that whole pack of mistresses he's had would not have had access to the queen's clothing. Palace protocol is as archaic and as sacrosanct as the midsummer festival.'

She looked down at Denniel where he sat. 'Wise of you not to want to be king. Although fighting esklet must surely be more dangerous.'

'It's my duty. It's my country. I'm sorry. I don't want to leave you so soon. We don't know each other yet ... But every archer is needed. How long will you need me here to pose as the king-in-waiting?'

'Can you arrange to be in the city that's connected to Templebridge? That way you could come and go.'

'I could, yes. Of course. Haze could even build multiple tunnels to somewhere in Kanter from one of the palace rooms here.'

Thalia shook her head in disbelief. 'Edwild had no idea of what Kanterines could have done if they'd wanted...'

'We preferred to keep our resources occupied with the destruction of esklet.'

'I'm glad to hear it. That's the way we'll do it then: occasional appearances by you. Occasional chances to get to know each other.' She looked away to hide the way her eyes brimmed with tears, but he saw them anyway.

Unable to meet her gaze, he winced. Eighteen years of an ache in her gut for her missing son and now she was letting him go again, to please him. Why was nothing ever *easy*?

'If I rule here,' she continued, 'then Kanter will be supplied from our farms and our armouries and our fletchers and our ironworks. It will be fair trade, not charity. We could probably even work out a way eventually to provide temporary shelter for people in immediate danger during an esklet attack.'

'Any of that would make a huge difference to our suffering.'

'It was a promise I made to Kaillan too.' She gave a tired smile. 'Perhaps your best role might be as liaison between our two countries.'

Right then, that was a step too far to contemplate, so he didn't answer. He asked instead, 'When I'm twenty-five, what then?'

'When it comes to who rules, what God Atticun says goes.'

'Ah. But as I understand it, you tricked him when you allowed him to believe you were going back to my father with the changeling baby. Now you are planning to trick him again. Why would he allow you to sit on the throne?'

'I didn't deceive him! I spoke to God Atticun about you and Kaillan, not about my plans. In fact, I really didn't know for certain what I was going to do until I saw Goddess Jenat later that night.'

'There's something else that will help you,' Haze said. 'Women come to your statues all over Talodiac, asking you to intercede on their behalf... They leave flowers! They almost worship you.'

She pulled a face. 'I have grown in people's estimation since I died. You two go in search of some clothing more appropriate for a queen. Denniel, I know that you desperately want to go to Kaillan. So do I. But neither of us can do anything to help him and I do know that he will get the best care possible if he is still alive. Right now, we need to talk. We need to get to know each other...'

45

'Are we ready?' Thalia asked.

She'd been watching the main gate from the window of the King's retiring room and Mulierseer Agrina's carriage had just returned to the palace grounds, closely followed by two similar equipages. 'Gerent Vann and Gerent Ruthgar, the Lawseer and the Battleseer,' she said, 'and they really haven't brought a whole entourage with them either. It seems Agrina managed to persuade them to be discreet. Taygen, open the outer door to the Privy Chamber, then come back.'

She glanced around the room, thinking it resembled a stage set for a court mummery where they were the players awaiting the audience. And there she was in the lead role, the queen, clad in a green silk gown sewn with tiny crystals and velvet trim. Confound it; she had not thought to ask Hazelle to hunt down some silk slippers as well, but fortunately the skirt was long enough to cover the comfortable boots she wore. She didn't have a mirror to see herself, but Hazelle had assured her that the dress still fitted, while Taygen had cheerfully told her she looked exactly as he'd always thought a queen should look: over-dressed, over-adorned, uppity and damned uncomfortable. Wretched lad; he had a genius for homing in on fundamentals.

They'd moved the table, now doubling as a bier, to one end of the room. Edwild's body was covered with a dust sheet Hazelle had purloined from the Queen's bedroom. Thalia went to stand at the centre of the wall opposite the door, Denniel at her side. Hazelle was several paces away, while Taygen, having opened the Privy Chamber door to the corridor, came to stand on the other side of the retiring room. She'd forbidden them to hold their polearms, although both staves were within reach, propped up against the wall behind them.

'Hazelle,' she said, 'try not to say anything when they enter. No matter how irritated you are. And remember, they *will* be staring at you.'

'Yes, Your Grace,' Hazelle replied, her tone so bored and her expression so blank that Taygen couldn't help laughing, although he smothered his amusement when someone knocked at the door.

'Enter!' Thalia called out, with one last glare at Taygen. *Gods, what can one do with three full-grown half-brained sprouts?*

The door opened.

The last time Thalia had seen God Atticun's Lawseer, Gerent Vann, she'd thought him elderly, but he had only been in his fifties. Now in his seventies, his body was leaner and bonier, his grey hair more sparse, his face more deeply lined. He was followed by a broad, muscular man wearing the colours of God Saffrin, with Agrina behind them.

'Do come in,' Thalia said. She dipped her head slightly in homage to their rank and wondered what the Lawseer would make of her now. One thing was sure: she lacked the gentility and shyness of the eighteen-year-old girl she'd been when he'd last seen her. She narrowed her eyes in challenge. 'Gerent Vann, it is good to see you again, after all these years.'

Before he had time to reply, she switched her gaze to God Saffrin's Battleseer. 'And you must be the Gerent Ruthgar. May I introduce my son to you both? Prince Denniel, now king-in-waiting after the death of his father.'

The Lawseer switched his attention to Denniel, but his gaze immediately slid to Hazelle where she stood perfectly still, staring impassively at the far wall. The Battleseer was already gaping at her, appalled. She'd no way of ridding herself of the glowing ribbons of scarlet and pink that flowed over her skin and around her body, signalling her recent use of weaving to any archpriest.

'Your Grace!' Gerent Vann began. 'This — this *person* has—'

'Allow me to introduce her,' she interrupted, smiling pleasantly. 'Hazelle Wayfarer. She has travelled with me from the day she was placed as a changeling in my son's cot.' She paused a moment to give them time to swallow that unpalatable morsel, before adding, 'Remember, we have no idea who she is by birth. What *does* count is that she has certainly been brought up Talodian. I raised her myself. She is indeed a redweaver, as you can see. A redweaver who has allegiance to the Talodian Crown.'

There, stick that in your craw and let it stew there for a while...

Silence.

When the lack of response continued, she gave a deliberately audible sigh and said, 'Perhaps, Gerent Vann, Gerent Ruthgar, you would like to pay your last respects to King Edwild?' She waved a hand at the table. 'He lies there. We have not yet informed anyone but yourselves. Not even the Lord Chancellor. Denniel, perhaps you will be so good—?'

He stepped over to the table and drew back the cloth covering Edwild's upper body. The two gerents approached the makeshift bier, studied the King's face, and then, as one, genuflected in respect.

The Battleseer cleared his throat. 'How did he die?'

'Apoplexy, I would say. Being confronted by the two people he has been trying to catch and kill for eighteen years, Hazelle and myself, then being told that the young man with us was the son whom he wilfully abandoned to the Kanterines...' She sighed, shaking her head. 'It was all just too much. He collapsed flat on his face; hence the bruising. I believe he died immediately.'

Denniel, emotionless, pulled the cloth up over his father's face once more.

Still calm, she said, 'May I — once again — introduce King Edwild's only legitimate son, Prince Denniel of Talodiac? I am sure you can see his resemblance to his father.'

Her tone, she hoped, was pure steel. And no waver in her hard-eyed gaze, either.

It was the Lawseer who spoke first. 'What proof have you?' he asked. 'A family resemblance does not guarantee legitimacy.'

'Doubtless you will remember Jordir Banlock? He vouched that this person is the child he helped to raise.'

'What? *Recently?*'

'Indeed. Today, in fact. I have seen no reason to doubt his word. Mulierseer Agrina was present and can confirm that. King Edwild himself did not directly deny this young man was his son.'

The Lawseer arched an eyebrow in astonishment at the Mulierseer, who nodded and said softly, 'He neither outright denied him, nor did he confirm his parentage, although he did express some concern about his possible loyalties.'

Unflinching, Thalia added the lie. 'The King's final action was to place Denniel's hand on the royal seal.'

She gave Denniel a nod. He fished inside his tunic and pulled out the seal on its chain.

The Battleseer pursed his lips. Gerent Vann frowned. Agrina, unable to confirm or deny that last assertion, said nothing. All of them looked disbelieving.

Denniel inclined his head to the three of them and gave voice to the words Thalia had suggested as appropriate. 'Most Reverends, I acknowledge my inadequacy at this time to rule the country of my birth. My education about our institutions and laws is not sufficient. I need time and guidance.

I am eager to learn, but I have suggested to my Lady Mother that she be named as regent until such time as God Atticun agrees that I am sufficiently ... um, competent and schooled.'

The Lawseer and the Battleseer exchanged glances, neither willing to commit themselves.

'Oh, and one more small matter,' Thalia said pleasantly. 'Yesterday evening, I had word that the Duke of Temar will be arriving in Templebridge soon, with a contingent of armed men. My father is very fond of me and, at a guess, he is somewhat upset about how I've been treated. I suggest you might find it wise to mollify his ire. Perhaps you could see that they are all well accommodated while they are in the city? I understand that the Duchy of Personata now guarantees Temar's security. In return, they have been granted the use of a port on the Temar coast. I imagine that the Duke of Personata will send a token force of his men to accompany my father to Templebridge, along with a family representative. I am sure you will see to it that they are welcomed.'

Gerent Vann's eyes widened. 'I know nothing of this!'

'You do now,' she said, and turned to the Battleseer. 'Gerent Ruthgar, I wonder if I might have a private word with you?'

He bristled. 'I am sure that there is nothing you could say to me that warrants secrecy from my fellow gerents—'

She smiled as sweetly as she could. 'Perhaps it is I who require the privacy.' She stepped forward to take him firmly by the elbow, guiding him back into the Privy Chamber and shutting the door behind them.

He turned on her then, his anger flushing his face. '*Personata?* Your father brings an army?'

'Hardly. But Personata is proud of their fighting men, and they now have a reason to be supportive of Temar. If I were you, I'd think deeply about whose side you are on if there is any discussion of who should wear the Talodian Crown.' She smiled, fingered the carcanet around her neck, and added, 'Don't say anything unwise as yet, not until after I inform you of the identity of the other young man in that room.'

He looked at her blankly. 'I assumed he was some kind of superior servant of yours?'

'Not exactly, no. His name is Taygen Hervan-Gariane. He is the son of Captain Hervan of the King's Guard, and has been recently incarcerated in the King's Keep in a very odd fashion...'

He stilled, face draining of colour.

Guilt, she thought. *I was right.* 'You and I need to have a discussion about your loyalties and your intentions, Gerent Battleseer.'

'I do nothing without the permission of God Saffrin.'

'And you do not ever filter the information that reaches God Saffrin?'

'Never!' His appalled horror at the idea was transparent.

'Hm. I think I believe you. I rather think your heresy lies elsewhere. Yours. *And* your god's. And we need to have a talk about that.'

'Heresy?' The word was barely whispered.

She smiled. 'Wrong word, perhaps. Should I say ... Rebellion? Intended revolution? You see, I know perfectly well that Arch-clergywoman Sianta Tory-Cress reports to you. I just didn't want to mention this distasteful affair of kidnapping and treason in front of the Lawseer. I think Vann would take it very much amiss to know that you so blatantly interfered with Talodian law. You arranged the removal of a man captured by the kingsmen into a confinement under your personal staff. Why? You then compounded the crime by deliberately keeping information from the King. Worse still, that included the fact that the Queen had been seen disappearing into Kanter. How *dare* you withhold such information from the monarch, sir! Battleseer, what—in the name of Saffrin—were you *thinking?'*

He paled but did not answer.

'Could it possibly have something to do with your opinion of God Atticun's health?'

He grasped at the straw she offered. 'Certainly, his insistence that King Edwild not be granted permission to marry again was not rational. The King needed an heir! Anything less could have meant a ducal war! God—' He licked dry lips. 'God Saffrin is of that opinion.'

She kept her tone quietly reasonable. 'God Saffrin should not be interfering in matters outside his purview. I cannot know what was intended, but I suspect the account of events Taygen Hervan-Gariane wrote might have been useful to discredit the actions of the Lawseer and to cast doubt on the health and actions of God Atticun. I have a copy of part of it. I also have the two people intimately involved in all that happened. Plus, of course, I have my own account. You may relay that message back to God Saffrin. And you and your god will support my regency for my son. The existence of a healthy heir should gladden your heart, am I not correct?' She glowered at him. 'If you *don't* offer that support, then knowledge of this egregious, traitorous behaviour of yours will be disseminated to all the gerents and to the Lord Chancellor. Is that clear?'

Sweating, he said, 'Ah. Er, God Saffrin will be delighted to support your cause, of course. Contrary to what many believe, we do not welcome conflict. We lose supporters to death in times of war, and saffrine folk are too rare in the best of times.'

'Just to make sure we are in total agreement, may I mention that Taygen Hervan-Gariane has been most helpful in this matter. His written account will stay locked away as long as he and I and my son remain unthreatened.'

He opened his mouth as if to speak, but words apparently failed him.

She smiled pleasantly when he finally clamped his mouth shut. 'Shall we return to the others, confident of our future cooperation?'

He nodded, thin-lipped. 'Yes, Your Grace. Of course, I must refer this to God Saffrin and be guided by him.'

She gave a ghost of a smile. 'Of course.'

*

From the heavy silence and the frustration on Gerent Vann's face when she and a white-faced Battleseer re-entered the retiring room, Thalia guessed that the Lawseer's attempts to extract information from the others while she'd been gone had not met with success. She crossed to her original position in front of the fireplace, saying, 'Do be seated, Most Reverends, please. Everyone, in fact, for I have a story to tell.'

As they settled themselves, though, she remained on her feet. 'You must forgive me, but I have to go back in time to explain something of how I came to my present understanding. Before my father was the duke, he was Admiral of the Temar Fleet, protecting the trade routes and the merchant ships that sailed from Temar Port to the Western Islands.'

Lawseer nodded. 'I remember.'

'As a girl of eleven or twelve or so, I sailed with him several times. And one thing I remember from those voyages was how dissimilar those island countries were from Talodiac. The plants, the native animals and birds, even the weather. If ever you have been to Temar, you yourself would have seen the distinctiveness of the island sailors arriving to trade in our ports. Their appearance, their languages, their manner of dress, all different. Gerent Ruthgar, I imagine you have travelled to my home city and would know what I mean?'

'Yes. Yes, I do.'

'To change the subject: recently Hazelle and I were captured by kingsmen under Captain Hervan.' She waved a hand in Taygen's direction, adding, 'His father. Threatened, in panic, totally unaware until then of her powers, Hazelle opened up a woven gateway to Kanter. She and I escaped through it. Imagine our fear. As far as we knew, Kanterines were murderous folk.'

The Lawseer stared at her, appalled.

'However, we were welcomed in Kanter and looked after. Hazelle was taught how to manage her redweaving and she eventually returned us safely to Talodiac using her own weaving skills. In other words, all we'd heard about Kanterines and redweavers previously was a lie. As was the reason they were coming here to Talodiac.'

Lawseer glowered at her. 'They were lying to you, deceiving you with their magic—'

'You insult me, sir,' she snapped, pointing a finger in accusation. 'It is not they who have been lying! It is *you*.'

Shocked, he closed his mouth.

'Have you ever been there?' she asked.

'No.'

'Has anyone that you know of? Any of the arch-clergy?'

'No!'

'Do any of you know how to weave a gateway?'

'*No!*'

'Have any of you stepped inside a woven passageway?'

'No. It is forbidden. We unweave a gateway from this side and the tunnel then disappears.'

'Well, Hazelle *can* weave a gateway and a passage, and she and I have been to Kanter. *We've seen for ourselves.* So, please don't tell us what it is like. We *know*. You don't. We know that some Kanterines come here because they are under attack from monstrous creatures that invaded their land. We were attacked by those beasts, in fact.' She tapped the scar on her face. 'See this? I know the threat is very real. Do you want to dispute my veracity, Gerent Vann? Will you call me a liar to my face?'

After the shortest of pauses, he shook his head. 'No, Your Grace.'

'Good. Now let us consider another matter. One thing that struck me quite forcibly during the days we spent in Kanter was this: how alike our peoples are. How alike our two countries are. And how different we are from the Western Islands. Kanterine and Talodian are very similar languages. Our clothing, our architecture, our food, our customs — all similar. Even the meadow flowers, the taldeer, the songbirds. All recognisable.'

The two men exchanged glances and Thalia thought she read fear in that exchange. She continued, 'Kanter's night is mostly our daytime, yet we can still be within reach through the link of a redwoven tunnel. A strange magic ... links us. I have drawn my own conclusions. Yours may be different. Perhaps only the gods know the truth.'

The Lawseer glowered at the Battleseer, but neither spoke.

'Other peoples tell us their gods are immortal,' she continued. 'From the Western Islands and the Menkz marauders to the nomads of the Great Desolation. All those gods — as well as our own — are supposedly the creators of the world, to be worshipped and thanked. But you, Gerentia Agrina, and you, Gerent Vann, and perhaps you too, Gerent Ruthgar, know part of that is a lie, because you know what is happening.'

They stared at her in silence.

She said, 'Atticun, our Arch-God is ... well, not at all well, is he?'

46

The silence in the room was suffocating.

Thalia waited out their shock, her heart thudding as if she'd been running.

In the end it was Haze who broke the silence. 'Gods don't get sick or die, surely? Isn't that part of how we define a god?'

The three archpriests remained silent, so Thalia continued her theory. 'I would have thought so, yes. As far as I know, I am the only person who has ever spoken to *two* of our gods; to Jenat twice, in fact. I've also walked through a redwoven gateway into the woven tunnel behind it. Several times.'

Their stares bored into her, carrying a kaleidoscope of emotions. The Lawseer's sickly expression probably indicated an uneasy shame. The Battleseer glared. Agrina's distressed face spoke of grief. By comparison, Denniel's exuded intrigued neutrality, while Taygen and Hazelle just stared at her, fascinated.

She chose her words carefully. 'I had the privilege of speaking to two gods on the same night. They appeared to be made of light. One deep and dark and still, the other bright and vibrant and spirited. The first was God Atticun, who is our Arch-God by virtue of his greater age, the second Goddess Jenat. I did not give much importance to that difference. Not until after I had been inside a redwoven passageway to Kanter. There, I saw redweaving for the first time. I saw the weaving stream out of Hazelle as light, only to become solid walls. While inside the passage I could see its residue left behind on her, just as you archpriests can right now, even though I no longer can. It was vibrant and beautiful and alive, just as I remembered the glorious glow of Goddess Jenat within her temple.'

No one spoke. They were all so still it was as if they had forgotten to breathe.

She said softly, 'So *extraordinarily* similar.'

Still no reaction, although Agrina shifted uncomfortably in her chair.

'I've been told,' she continued, 'that with time the colour of a redweaving dies. Left unrepaired, it dulls and darkens, its vibrancy vanishes. It ceases to twist and move. I'm told it eventually disappears.

'On our way back from Kanter to Talodiac, we used two tunnels — one that was new, woven by Hazelle, and then one to Copperstone Crossways, which had not been used for some days or even weeks; its colour was dulled and sluggish. It reminded me of something. Later I remembered. Not something; some*one*. God Atticun, more than eighteen years ago. Like that tunnel, he was dark, tired. Compared to Goddess Jenat, it was as if … as if he was slowly fading away.'

Glancing from one archpriest to the other, she stopped, waiting again for anyone to speak. No one did. The Lawseer was refusing to meet her gaze now, while the Battleseer glowered. He held his hands steepled over his nose and mouth while he stared at her.

'Last night, Gerentia Agrina told me God Atticun no longer meets with anyone but you, Gerent Vann.'

He nodded, not looking up.

'You see where I am going with this, don't you?'

Still no one said a word.

'Tell me, is a god who is not immortal really a god?'

Hazelle gave a sharp intake of breath.

'Put another way,' Thalia continued, 'if they aren't gods, what are they?'

'You can't be saying they are redweavers!' Haze blurted out.

'No, for they do not weave, at least not in the sense that Kanterine redweavers do,' Thalia replied. 'But I rather think that any redweaver who spent time around any one of our gods would understand a lot more than we do. If they spread that knowledge, would our gods still be worshipped, revered, allowed so much power? Would people dedicate their lives to serving them?'

'I would!' Agrina glared at her. 'I do. I will. I will do so until I die. What the goddess has done is make the lives of women and children more valued. How could I ever turn my back on that?'

'Yes,' the Lawseer agreed. 'We believe in what we do.' He halted, grieving, dipping his head into his hands.

This was followed by another long silence, finally broken by Denniel, addressing the three arch-clerics. 'And *this* is why you are so adamant that Kanterines and Talodians have no contact? You are afraid that Kanterine redweavers would see too much. You were right to worry. If Queen Thalia could deduce all that from what she saw...' He shook his head, a look of utter disbelief on his face. 'And we in Kanter suffered because you were afraid that sooner or later one of us would discover your gods aren't eternal, all-powerful wondrous beings. They are just another type of redweaver? Ancient, yet still somehow doomed to one day *die*? I—I don't know what to say.'

'That our two lands were perhaps once ... one land? One people?' Haze added.

Ashen-faced, the Lawseer looked up at Thalia, 'Your Grace, what are you intending?'

Perhaps the others thought it was only fear they heard in his voice, but she knew better. She knew the fragility of their security, and he was warning her. For the moment, they were protected by Hazelle's ability to weave a gateway, an escape route. But that ability would also ever be a danger to all the gods...

To live safely, she had to allay that fear, not just for now, but forever.

She smiled at the Lawseer. 'Why, nothing! Why would I? Our people *need* our gods. What would we do without Goddess Hetha and her healing? What would I do as a queen without the advice of Goddess Jenat? Or of God Atticun, for as long as he lives? What would any of us do without the centuries of knowledge each of our deities possesses, which they use to serve and help us? *You* serve them, *we* bring our offerings to their temples and they *aid* us. I don't know how you will deal with the decline of God Atticun, but you will. You have powerful resources: your own priests and worshippers, not to mention all the other gods of the Decasian Pantheon. You just need to ask.'

She nodded to Denniel. 'I think we know *exactly* what to say: that this secret will never be revealed by any of us.' She waved a hand towards Hazelle. 'My adopted daughter can one day perhaps be a loremaster — that is, a redweaver of talent. Taygen is the son of a man and a woman who devoted their lives to their king and their country. Oh, and I think he would like to know just where his father is now. Denniel will one day *be* a king who understands two lands. And I — I will serve as regent as long as necessary. Not a word of the truth about our Decasian Pantheon will ever be leaked by any of us. In fact, I will go further. The less we know the better. We should not seek and will not seek to know your secrets.'

Gerent Vann still wasn't looking at her, and he was clasping his hands together to hide their tremor. 'In exchange for what?'

'Support my regency. Support my policies with regard to Kanter. We will trade with them. Help me to rid this land of its hatred of redweavers. Do that, and this royal house will support God Atticun's temple as it always has. All the temples, in fact.'

She could almost hear her mother's advice just before she'd left Temar: *Formal language, Thalia. Sound like you are the authority and people tend to take notice...* She let her glance move from one to another and back again, before adding softly, 'If you don't support us, if you dispose of us all in ways that I am sure are available to you, I cannot guarantee that your secrets will remain hidden. We have all left the proof of what we say in several different places...'

As the lie slipped from Thalia's tongue, Haze smiled sweetly at Gerentia Agrina and Taygen nodded to the Battleseer with an expression more smirk than smile.

The rascals, Thalia thought fondly.

The Lawseer was silent for so long, she began to wonder if he would reply. Just when she was about to give up, he raised his head to meet her gaze. 'God Atticun is much diminished. Yes, he grows darker year by year, yet he was the greatest of them all, once. Not even he knows how long he has. Perhaps he will be even be reborn.'

She stifled any appearance of doubt. 'And we would rejoice.' She turned to look at the others. 'Hazelle, Taygen, Denniel: would you be prepared to swear to keep silent about all you've heard here today, to swear now, or before God Atticun — or before any other of the gods, for that matter, if they demanded it?'

'Certainly,' Denniel said. 'If I am king here, why would I want to change anything so fundamental? Talodiac is prosperous as it is.'

Hazelle nodded. 'I'd so swear.'

'Sure,' Taygen added.

The Battleseer said nothing, but he did give an abrupt nod, before turning to Thalia. 'With Your Grace's permission, I shall withdraw,' he said, 'and leave the more mundane matters of state to the Lawseer and the Mulierseer. My skills lie elsewhere. And I need to consult God Saffrin. I do not speak for him.'

'Rubbish,' Thalia said, irritated. 'Of course you do. All the time.'

'I relay his words. Just as I will relay yours.'

She inclined her head and muffled her sigh. 'Of course.' She looked pointedly at Taygen, then back to the Battleseer.

Ruthgar bowed, still unnaturally pale, but she still did not give him leave to go.

'Another task for you, Gerent Ruthgar,' she said. 'Tell the King's Marshal that the King has died and the Queen and her son have returned. Suggest politely that he keep his mouth shut until he has spoken to me and the prince. You might suggest too, that he cooperate to the best of what I imagine are his many abilities.'

A smile of appreciation flickered around the edges of his lips. 'You, Queen Regent Thalia, are a very clever woman. Take care you don't overstep.'

'Oh, I think in time you and I will dance skilfully around one another without stepping on each other's toes, Gerent Ruthgar. We both know where our best interests lie.'

'And what about my father?' Taygen demanded.

'Ah.' The Battleseer raised an eyebrow at him. 'What about him? You might have been his son, but Captain Hervan was still going to hand you over to the King.'

'Pa had good reason. I don't much want to see him again, but he doesn't deserve to be killed for carrying out orders.'

'He's not dead, and he is no longer incarcerated. In the King's absence, I sent his whole squad to Breakedge to serve time on the borders. They know what happens if they talk.' With that, the Battleseer turned to Denniel saying, 'Your Highness, welcome back to Templebridge and to the palace.

We served your father and we will serve you when the time comes.'

Denniel inclined his head. This time Thalia had nothing to add, and the Battleseer left the room.

The Lawseer clambered to his feet. 'Your Grace, we have much to do. The Lord Chancellor and the Lord Chamberlain need to be informed the King is dead. Word should be sent to all the temples. Would you like me to attend to that last?'

'Once the Chancellor has been informed, I will have the Keep bell set to ring. Once you hear that you may spread the news of the King's sad demise. With regard to the Lord Chamberlain ... I've never liked Ashwendon. He will be replaced. Suggest someone else.'

He looked taken aback. 'I'll ... I'll give it some thought.'

'I think that is all I require of you for the moment, Gerent Vann. Thank you for your cooperation.'

They all breathed a sigh of relief after he bowed and left.

Agrina leaned back against her chair, hiding her eyes behind her hand. 'Why do I have the idea that I don't know half of what you've done?'

'Well—' Thalia began.

'No, don't tell me. I do not want to know!' She turned to Hazelle. 'You come downstairs with me, girl. I want you to get Lord Ashwendon back from wherever it is you put him!' She glanced back at Thalia. 'How you explain all this to him is up to you. He always was a silly, stubborn man. No loss to the monarchy. But he could be troublesome to you. He has a vindictive, nasty nature from what I've heard. Gerent Vann doesn't like him one little bit. However, he was useful to King Edwild.'

'The servants must be wondering what's going on by now—' Haze began.

Agrina did not let her finish. 'The servants do what they are told by people they recognise as their superiors. And at the moment, that is me. Come, girl!'

Sensing Haze was about to glare at being addressed as if she were a child, Thalia said quickly, 'Taygen, go with them and take your pole. Bring the fellow back here. And Agrina, will you order someone to go find out where Kaillan is, and how he is, and send back word to me as soon as possible.'

After the three of them had left, Denniel turned to Thalia, asking, 'Let me get all this straight. Did you just *blackmail* the arch-clergy and therefore the gods of the three most important temples of the Decasian Pantheon?'

'Hmm. Probably wisest not to mention the word blackmail.'

'All right. Let's say I thought I caught a decided whiff of something along the lines of: if you don't help me out, I'm going to tell the world that Talodian gods are really just a version of those dreadful redweaving Kanterines, sitting in our temples being both unjustly worshipped and gifted though our charity!'

She wagged a finger at him. 'Careful, Denniel. Say that too often and you might end up with a baffle on you for the rest of your life!'

He smiled and shook his head. 'Tell me, what do you think of us, really?'

'*Us?*'

'Ah. Us Kanterines is what I meant. Sorry. It's going to take a while before I remember that I am Talodian.'

She pursed her lips and gave him a look that she hoped would say more than any words of caution would, then answered the question. 'Perhaps we were all the same people once, until we were split apart by some great cataclysm long, long ago. We became two distinct nations, instead of one, yet always linked through the possibility of redwoven tunnels.

On the Kanterine side, some people were redweavers, whereas on our Talodian side, redweaving took a different form. Here, the more powerful were gods ... those with lesser power were the archclergy, people who can see redweaving.'

He stared at her, absorbing that. 'Neat!' he said finally. 'That makes me an archpriest?'

She laughed. 'I guess so, if you wanted. None of that past history matters now, not to me. We here in Talodiac will work with what we have.'

'I'm glad I came. I've missed having a mother all my life.'

'And I missed having a son.'

'I did have Kaillan.'

'And I had Haze.'

He walked over to where King Edwild lay and pulled down the sheet to look at his father's face once more. 'It's hard to imagine being this man's son,' he said. 'Kaillan was the best of fathers. But I was a fool, turning on him when I was twelve, blaming him for something that was never his choice. You were wiser. What made you trust him? You knew he'd helped Mongrave do what he did!'

She thought back. 'When I saw him, he'd been tortured, mutilated. He was in excruciating pain, believing he was going to die. Yet he could mock himself and pity *me* for my pain. I saw the shame he felt, I saw his compassion for me.' She sighed. 'I was a duke's only child. I knew all about duty to one's realm, especially to the smallest and poorest of realms. I never really wanted to leave Temar to marry your father, but I did my duty. And so did Kaillan when Mongrave told him he must. He did what he was told, but I saw his remorse. My heart told me that I could trust him to look after you. That belief has been my solace for eighteen years.'

Denniel nodded. 'He loved me without condition. I was the one who walked away, never him.'

'We came to Templebridge together, did he have time to tell you that today? On a slow barge! I came to know him well then, and yes, to care for him.' She rose and walked across to the window and looked out over the fairground. 'You must go to him, for I cannot. He may yet be in Hetha's tent in the precinct grounds.'

'You need me here,' he said flatly and pulled the sheet up over Edwild's face once more. 'You know that.'

'Yes, I do. Even though I know my father is on his way with a contingent of Temar guards and a supporting contingent of Personata soldiers.' *I hope.* 'I'm not sure when they'll arrive though. And right now I need to know if Kaillan lived...'

'I'll go when Haze and Taygen return.'

She nodded, and rested her forehead against the window. Outside the tinkling of the hurdy-gurdy wisped and faded on the wind.

*

When Taygen and Haze returned, they were alone. 'Gerentia Agrina sent someone to find out about Kaillan,' Haze said the moment she entered the room. 'We have news he's still alive, but not conscious yet. They halted the bleeding here in the healers' tent, then took him to the Hetha's temple.'

'Thank you. And Ashwendon?'

'We couldn't find him. When I saw he wasn't in the tunnel, I went in alone and walked through to the other end. I couldn't see him anywhere. I yelled. No reply. It was a deserted place, just scrubby hills and rocks. No sign of houses, or people. I dithered a bit, but then I saw three or four esklet in the distance, feeding on something, so I closed down the tunnel completely and unwove the gateway.'

'So even if he is alive somewhere, he can't get back into the palace.'

'Not through that gateway, no.' She shrugged.

'Did Agrina say anything?'

'She was more relieved than upset when I came back without him. She said to tell you she's gone to inform Goddess Jenat of all that's happened. Her exact words: Tell Queen Thalia I will act according to the advice of my goddess, as always.'

'Of course.' Thalia turned her attention to other matters. 'Taygen, I have written you a palace pass, stamped with the king's seal, so you can come and go as you please. I want you to go to Hetha's temple and follow up on how Kaillan is.' She held up a drawstring purse. 'Donate this to the temple, and let them know the palace has an interest in his good health.' She looked back at Denniel. 'Do you want to go with him?'

He hesitated, hearing her unspoken plea. She needed his presence. He dragged in a deep breath and touched Taygen's arm as he shook his head. 'Hold his hand for me, if that's what he needs. Be there when he dies, if that's what happens. Tell him we are safe, if he can hear.'

'Send word back if there is reason for you to stay. Use your judgement.'

'Your Grace.' He took the pass, then, his voice oddly husky, added, 'It's an honour to serve you.'

After he'd gone, Haze stood at the retiring room window that overlooked the palace entrance to watch. Once outside the gateway he turned to look back up and waved. 'Cheeky,' she said. 'He's never going to change.'

'I wouldn't want him to,' Thalia replied.

'What do we do now?' Denniel asked.

'We wait for people to come. The Lord Chancellor, for a start. Then a whole string of officials, the first of them any time soon.'

'Aren't you worried? What if the Chancellor and the others won't believe you are the Queen returned?'

'Some of them I've met before. I can remind them of that. Besides, no one will go against the Lawseer.'

Hazelle opened the window and the sounds from the fair swelled: hucksters, merriment and music. 'You really are going to be queen?' she asked. 'I mean, are you going to *rule*? You, Innata Wayfarer?'

'I am. Well, I'm going to give orders, anyway. Most of the work is done by the Chancellery. A wise monarch appoints people who know what they are doing, and listens to the advisers and the dukes before making decisions.'

'But *why*? I mean, we were happy, weren't we? On the road? Well, apart from the baffle and not knowing where Denniel was. But now your baffle's gone, and Denniel's here and he's said he doesn't want this!'

'Why? Because of Kanter, of course. Listen, both of you: I lost Denniel because a desperate man called Mongrave was trying to save his land from esklet and thought it could be done if Talodiac helped. What kind of people are we if we ignore those in dire need? Edwild had a chance to fix it, but he turned away. Now there's another a chance. And that is what I want to do. Fix it.'

Haze turned to Denniel. 'And is this what you want, as well?'

'Of course.'

'And when it's fixed?' she asked Thalia.

'Then I can walk away. If Denniel still doesn't want the throne, the next in line among the dukes can take over. Or better still, a Council of Ducal Representatives or some such thing.'

'Will you be safe?'

She gave what she hoped was a confident smile. 'The gods are on my side. How can I lose?'

Just then, someone knocked at the entrance to the Privy Chamber.

'Now it begins,' she said. 'Are you ready?'

Haze grabbed up her quarterstaff.

'You won't need that!'

'It's here, nonetheless,' she said. 'And so is my redweaving.'

From outside, a bugle call sounded in the distance and Thalia stiffened. 'Listen! Hear that? Tah-di-dum, tah-di-dum—' She started to laugh.

'What's funny?' Haze asked.

'That's the Temar anthem! "*Temar's marching, listen to the call*—"' She grinned and linked arms with Haze and Denniel, drawing them both with her as she left the retiring room for the Privy Chamber. 'First thing you must realise about your grandfather, Denniel: his timing is always impeccable ... And he does so love an entrance. Open the Privy Chamber door, Haze. At a guess, our first visitor will be the Lord Chancellor, and what better way to greet him than to the strains of Temar's anthem as my father's guard marches through the Palace Precinct up to the front door?'

47

The lamplight pooled on the desk, illuminating the report Thalia was reading on floods in the town of Basken in Rothengar Duchy, written by the mayor. She remembered the place; she'd been there once when summer rains had washed away the causeway and the town had been cut in two by the floodwaters for twenty days. The townsfolk had complained about being unable to reach their orchards because of the lack of a bridge, and there'd been a riot against Rothengar's duke, Lord Graddon, who had previously refused to fund one.

Now the Basken mayor was obviously wanting her to intervene. If she castigated the Duke for neglect, he would say it was none of her business. If she ignored the problem, the townsfolk would ask why they paid taxes to the Crown...

She laid the report aside for more consideration and picked up the next letter, this one from the office of the Lawseer. Doubtless yet another tedious matter that Gerent Vann thought she should know about. He was nothing if not assiduous in his desire to keep her informed of his opinions. She slipped the paper knife under the wax seal on the flap, but no sooner had she opened the sheet than someone knocked at her door.

Rising to unlock it, she wondered if she'd ever rid herself of the precaution of turning the key, or — as had been more common on her travels — somehow jamming a door shut.

Haze, Denniel and Taygen were all standing in the corridor.

Her heart turned over. Thirty days since the King had died, and she'd seen signs of their restlessness since day one, even though she'd kept them busy. Then, in the past ten days since Kaillan had left the ward in Hetha's Temple for the convalescence hospice outside the temple where visitors were welcome, she knew there had been plan afoot.

'Come on in,' she said. 'Given the hour, I'm guessing this is serious?'

'Important, yes,' Haze said. 'But not an emergency.'

'You're going to Kanter.' Thalia made it a statement, not a question.

Denniel nodded as they filed past and she shut the door behind them. 'Don't worry,' he said. 'I'll put in an appearance when needed, the obedient heir learning all the correct protocols.' He planted a kiss on her cheek. 'I spent four hours with the Chancellor of the Exchequer today. I had no idea that finance could be so...'

'Complex?' she suggested.

'Boring,' he said. 'Sorry.'

'It's just as well then that I am finding it fascinating, isn't it?' She waved at the seats in front of her desk. 'What have you decided?'

'We have a plan,' Hazelle said, refusing a chair and perching on the edge of the desktop instead. Denniel seated himself, and Taygen wandered over to settle on the window ledge. 'Denniel and I. We think we can make a difference, using my redweaving skills.' She looked around the anteroom. 'Did I ever tell you I like the fact that you moved into the King's royal rooms and not the Queen's? Nice statement.'

'Don't change the subject,' she said, sitting back down in her chair. 'Tell me what you intend.'

Haze grinned ruefully. 'You've been expecting this, haven't you? We've been experimenting with opening a gateway from that empty servant's room under the palace eaves, and I've finally managed to weave a tunnel that actually emerges near a major town in Kanter, instead of a bog or a mountain top.'

'Both of which did happen,' Taygen said, 'in early attempts. Knee-deep in black ooze was marginally better than dangling off a cliff face.'

'You've been to Kanter a number of times.'

'Yes. Night-time here, daytime there. We've been in contact with the Redweaver Council in that town.'

'I've noticed some unexplained absences.' Thalia swallowed her fear. *Denniel has a lot of experience.*

'I know,' Haze said. 'Kaillan and Denniel and I have been working out a way to exploit my aberrant ability to only weave tunnels that end up in Kanter, even if I start them there. We believe we can use them to kill esklet. If illusions of a tasty meal can be built inside a tunnel, visible through the gateway, we can entice esklet inside.'

'Trick them into a woven passage? And then what?'

'If we lock both ends, it becomes a cage. There's no access to Talodiac. We have yet to think of how best to kill them while they are trapped. Or we could starve them to death.'

'Has it never been tried before?'

'No, because Kanterines never wanted to risk esklet ending up in Talodiac. My tunnels don't have that problem. We need to spend time in Kanter, experimenting. Once we've sorted out how to kill them efficiently, I will have tunnels to build.'

'But esklet are everywhere all over the country!' She tried not to let horror creep into her tone as she stood up to pace. 'How many tunnel traps would it take to make a difference? Thousands!'

'It is going to be a long-term commitment,' Hazel agreed. 'Fortunately, I wouldn't have to close up or maintain and repair the tunnels. Just build them. Nor would I have to be the redweaver creating the bait illusions. Others can do all that. I can also build passages between towns in Kanter! Then archers could move quickly and safely to an esklet attack. Or townsfolk can escape from one.'

'Think, Mother!' Denniel said, his enthusiasm sparkling in his eyes. 'All these years, we've been losing ground. And people. And towns. Year by year. And now, with Hazelle, we have a way of reversing that. And with the arms and the food and the help from Talodiac, of course.'

We, she thought sadly. *We. He still thinks of himself as Kanterine. He always will.* 'That's good news. Please make sure the Kanterines know just how precious Hazelle is.'

Haze simpered theatrically, which elicited a guffaw from Taygen.

'I know, I know,' Denniel replied. 'She's the most precious thing we have.' He grinned at Hazelle and the way she smiled back made Thalia's heart turn over.

First love. I might have known it. Who else would understand where the other has come from? But her joy for them was tinged with fear. *Gods below,* she thought. *They came to say goodbye.* 'Remember, you should be at the next Dukes' Council,' she told Denniel. 'That's on the first Cresta Moon.'

He nodded. 'I'll be here, I promise. Even though it does sound like the annual acrimonious gathering of a feuding family. Don't worry, Mother, I'll look after the bairn.'

'Cheeky,' Haze said. 'May I remind you that you are actually *younger* than me?' She slipped off her perch to give Thalia a hug. 'We'll be fine. We'll come back as often as we can, I promise.'

'When do you leave?'

'Tonight. Just the two of us. Taygen's staying. If you need us urgently, he can come and get us. He has a key to that servant's room.'

'He can't even see a gateway!'

'I know where it starts, though,' he said cheerfully. 'I can blunder my way into it somehow, if necessary. And Kaillan told me to tell you that the hospice says they'll release him the day after tomorrow. He's not going to leave Temple-bridge, so he can always help. Oh, I gave him his pass to the palace, as you asked.'

She swallowed her fears and resisted the urge to smother them with instructions and warnings, confining herself instead to making sure they had all they needed.

'Innata,' Haze said, interrupting. 'Trust me. I've thought of everything. You taught me how, remember?'

She pulled them both into one last embrace. 'Off you go, then,' she murmured, 'before I'm tempted to cry.'

'They'll be fine,' Taygen told her when he closed the door behind them, 'even though I'm really the only mature one. Nothing like heaps of contemplation time in jail under sentence of death to melt stupidity from the bones.'

'Pah! You're all just as bad as one another.' She turned back to the desk, flicking a tear from her cheek. 'I've had some good news for you, by the way. I've got you some compensation.'

He was puzzled. 'For what?'

'Unjustified and illegal imprisonment. I have access to the very best of lawyers. God Saffrin's temple has awarded you a modest annuity for the rest of your life for...' She fiddled among the papers on her desk until she found the appropriate letter '...*"suffering, humiliation and unjustified deprivation of liberty."* There is a catch. You are not permitted to...*"publicly refer to the Temple of God Saffrin in ways which might diminish its standing."'*

He gaped at her. 'How in ten hells did you—? In fact, I've never understood how you got the Battleseer on your side at all. What did you say to him that day the King died?'

'I blackmailed him. I rather think God Saffrin envisioned becoming Arch-God if Atticun died, just as Goddess Jenat dreamed of the same thing... The Battleseer would have loved being the Grand Archpriest. Sianta was helping him. Gerent Ruthgar wanted all the gods to question the wisdom of Atticun's past decisions. He wanted to discredit a kingsman acting under the Lawseer's orders: your father. That's what your written account was going to support.' She gave a wry smile. 'Discredit that might have been justifiable from my point of view, but it wasn't in the long-term interest of anyone. I told the Battleseer I'd tell the other gerents and gerentias what he'd been up to.'

'And he caved? Well, bless his balls! I'm surprised...'

'It's easier to believe when you think of our Decasian Pantheon as being *very* old men and women ... rather than supernatural perfect deities.'

'Right. I'll bear that in mind.'

'Don't you want to know how much this annuity is?' she asked, and proceeded to tell him.

He gaped, slid from the window ledge to cross to the desk and kiss her hand. 'Bless *you*, Your Grace!'

'Now *you* are being cheeky.'

'Me? Never. The money will make such a difference. I— I want to help my brother and my mother.' He fiddled with the paper she'd given him, then raised his gaze to meet hers. 'I did think of going back to Breakedge to look after my brother, but my father's there now. He'll do his best for Jav and he wouldn't welcome my presence.' He was suddenly tongue-tied.

'Go on,' she said. 'You and I don't have many secrets worth keeping from one another.'

'Yes. I — I guess I have a lot to say.'

She had a flash of panic. 'Kaillan—?'

'No, no. He really is fine. I know you and he decided he should stay away from the palace until you felt more secure... Were you worried people will recognise him as Jordir Banlock the dosshouse keeper?'

'No. His appearance is greatly changed since then, but he feels my position is still precarious enough that gossip would be ... unfortunate.'

'He tells me he'll be heading the so-called Wayfarers' Trading Company.'

She nodded. 'Same sort of work he was doing before, buying items to send through to Kanter. Easier now, though, because the Company is not just a legitimate business: the Queen Regent and God Saffrin's temple own shares in it! If you want a position with them, just tell Kaillan.'

He shook his head. 'He offered one already, but ... no. Not for me.'

'What is, then? You don't need to treat me like a queen, you know. At heart, I'm still just Innata.'

He grinned. 'I know. I know all your secrets...' His smile faded. He hesitated, then blurted, 'I didn't mean to kill him.'

'I know. And I didn't intend him to die. Tay, if we here in Talodiac can make Kanter a safer place, then Edwild's death will mean something. Perhaps not something he'd have considered worthwhile, but it will be so.'

'What — what I'd like to do, in the long term, is serve you. You need someone right here, someone you can trust for the rest of your life. I've been listening, you know. To what goes on in the palace. And outside in the streets. I *hear* things I shouldn't all the time.'

'That weird hearing of yours.'

'The older I get, the sharper it gets. Dunno if it's a blessing or a horror. Right now, it tells me you have enemies. Old fogeys scared of petticoats, who don't like the idea of a woman having power. Doubters who wonder if King Edwild died the way we said he did. Nasties deliberately spreading scum about what you were doing for the past eighteen years. There's an elderly lady in the grace-and-favour apartments right here in the palace who calls you a whore. Gossip was tamped down while your Pa was still here backed by the Duke of Personata's men, and their soldiers patrolled the streets, but now that they've gone...'

'You believe I need to hear it all.'

'No. But you need to know who your enemies are. You do have your supporters too: people who didn't like Edwild for one reason or t'other. Women who look up to you as a symbol. I hear so much you need to know, all bubbling under the lid of the gossip pot. Better to skim off those rumourmongers right now, not wait till they spill poison over the stovetop. My mam used to say that, and she's as wise a person as I've ever met.'

'You're offering to be my ... what? Spymaster?'

'Spymaster? Is that a really a post?'

'I don't know. That's the whole thing about spies — no one knows they exist. Except the paymaster. Let's say yes, Queen Thalia has want of a spymaster. But, Tay, you do realise it carries a heavy burden with it, don't you? To deliberately seek out secrets and then decide what to do with them? That's not easy. That's a millstone you could wear around your neck for the rest of your days.'

He nodded without the hint of a smile. 'Your Grace, I already have to do that. I'd rather I did some good with it.'

'I know it would make my burden lighter. To be one step ahead of those who would bring me down? It would be a gift beyond price. Thank you. I'll arrange a salary and some innocuous title for you. Master of the Privy Chamber Portraits, or Equerry to the Queen's Library or something equally obscure and absurd.'

'Oh, I like that!' He grinned.

Her world felt suddenly lighter and she smiled back. 'Off you go. I have work to do!'

Once he'd left, she turned her thoughts back to the bridge in Rothengar Duchy. What if she promised the duke that the Crown would pay for a Queen Thalia Bridge. However, if he paid half the cost, she'd persuade the townsfolk to name it The Lord Graddon Bridge ... That might work. Lord Graddon, Duke of Rothengar, did so love to be admired.

She returned to her desk, only to remember the letter from the Lawseer that she had opened, but not yet read. Skipping the numerous salutations at the beginning, she perused the body of the missive.

Lord God Atticun, she read, *desires you to know that your gall and artfulness have given Him a new interest in life, with the result that He now hankers to observe the twists and turns of your future. Accordingly, He has asked me to write this note to say thank you, and wishes to tell you that He intends to make much more of an effort to live at least a little longer.*

Thalia blinked, astonished. She re-read the paragraph twice, then checked the imprint of the seal to make sure it was the Lawseer's and she wasn't being fooled by a trickster. It all appeared genuine, so she read on.

Being aware of your affection for that redweaver fellow who stole your son, inexplicable as such an emotion may be — even to the extent of bedding the fellow (according to Zanaz, Goddess of Travellers and Byways who has mentioned midnight trysts on one of her byways beside the river), Lord Atticun offers you the advice that queens should only ever have children by their wedded husband.

At this point she blushed, then started to laugh as she envisaged Vann being asked to write that down. Amused at her image of his discomfort, and impressed by what could only be the deity's teasing of his own pompous Grand Archpriest, she read on.

Lord Atticun has some concerns about the lack of interest Prince Denniel displays in actually ruling Talodiac one day. In addition, He feels that He personally owes Kaillan Riverdell something for the suffering he underwent within the walls of the temple. He has therefore requested Riverdell to present himself to me, so that I can bestow on him the status and respectability of a high priesthood, carrying the rank of archpriest. Riverdell will not be required to perform any duties of priesthood. Instead, I am to see to it that representatives of the Decasian Pantheon will all be invited to celebrate your marriage as soon as possible.

God Atticun also wishes to say that He finds both of you interesting, and it is hard to find anything interesting when one has lived for two thousand years or so. He begs your indulgence and requests that you humour him.

Salutations,

The Lawseer,

Grand Archpriest Gerent Vann.

By the time she finished reading, Thalia's chuckles at the thought of Vann having to write such a letter had morphed into untrammelled laughter. Some time later, still grinning, she walked over to the window to look out over the sleeping city. The dome of Atticun's Temple was a distinctive curve on the dark border of roofs and chimneys and towers, while beyond was a sky bright with stars.

What was she to think? That it was a good sign when an ancient mind, presumably born human in some far distant past, had a sense of humour and was now taking an interest in her happiness, even as he punctured the pomposity of his human representative? Or perhaps it was wiser to take all Atticun had said as a warning: a being made of light and anchored into the floor of a temple found it hard not to tangle himself in the lives of ordinary folk, so beware...

Or ... damn it all, surely it couldn't be that the god was telling her it was time her father, the Duke of Temar, who would have had his own claim of sorts to the Talodiac throne if he'd ever cared to make it, was presented with another grandson ... just in case the one he already had didn't want the job...?

She bit her lip, trying to be serious, but it was no use; she couldn't stop her chuckling.

It would be *so* good to see Kaillan again.

Acknowledgements

No book of mine has ever reached publication stage without help along the way, and this one is no exception. My beta readers —the friends who were brave enough to dive into those first drafts that included everything from missing words to plot holes — have once again been invaluable. Many thanks to Alena Sanusi (who has read the book multiple times from its very first iteration), Jane Routley, Barbara Holten and Mitenae. Gillian Polack and Darren Nash helped me subjugate a knotty structural fault into a vastly improved storyline. Thanks too to Abigail Nathan for a copy edit, although I hasten to add that if there are still errors, blame me. And to all those of you who have long been asking, "When's the next Glenda Larke novel?" — I hope you enjoy it!

About the Author

Glenda Larke now lives in Western Australia where she was born, but fifty years of her adult life were spent in Malaysia, Austria and Tunisia raising two daughters, writing thirteen novels, and teaching English to students ranging from pre-school to university. In Malaysia, she also worked in rainforest conservation and founded the country's first birdwatching body, producing its bi-monthly bulletin for ten years. As a writer she has been awarded four different Australian speculative fiction awards, including the coveted Sara Douglass Book Series Award for *The Watergivers* trilogy.

https://glendalarke.com/
@GlendaLarke

THE TANGLED LANDS